Richard Hooker, Ellen Martin

The feet of clay

A novel

Richard Hooker, Ellen Martin

The feet of clay
A novel

ISBN/EAN: 9783337046408

Printed in Europe, USA, Canada, Australia, Japan

Cover: Foto ©Andreas Hilbeck / pixelio.de

More available books at **www.hansebooks.com**

THE FEET OF CLAY:

A NOVEL.

BY

ELLEN MARTIN.

"Tell me the dream and I shall know that you can show me the interpretation thereof. Thou, O King, sawest and behold a great image. This image whose brightness was excellent stood before thee: and the form thereof was terrible. This image's head was of fine gold, his breast and arms of silver, his belly and his thighs of brass, his legs of iron, and his *feet* part of iron and part *of clay*."

NEW YORK:
BROWN & DERBY,
(21 PARK PLACE.)
1882.

SPRINGFIELD PRINTING CO.,
ELECTROTYPERS, PRINTERS AND BINDERS,
SPRINGFIELD, MASS.

TO

REV. A. A. LIPSCOMB, D. D., LL. D.,

EX-CHANCELLOR OF THE UNIVERSITY OF GEORGIA,
PROFESSOR EMERITUS OF VANDERBILT UNIVERSITY,

AS

A TOKEN OF GRATITUDE

For his past kindness; and of appreciation of his culture; his intellectual
greatness; and his goodness,

THIS VOLUME IS RESPECTFULLY DEDICATED.

CHAPTER I.

"You know, I suppose, that this hill took its name, Fort Hill, years ago from the Spanish fort, ruins of which can still be seen, and not from the Confederate fortifications," said Aliena Graeme to Major Baron, as on horseback they were ascending the steep road to the top of Fort Hill, one of the highest of the Walnut Hill range, upon which Vicksburg is situated.

"No, I was not aware of it, but it seems a pity that those old Spanish cavaliers should have been dispossessed by a more prosaic race," said Major Baron.

"Don't you think it may be the lapse of time that makes them seem more poetic than the present possessors? In a hundred years or so no doubt epics will be written about Confederate heroes, and some Homer may tune a lyre to this fearful fratricidal war."

"Time is a wonderful sorcerer, and no doubt throws a glamour over the past. There is no knowing what it may do or who may figure in romance or history. But to tell the truth, I regard the present too highly to worry myself about the future. I care little to figure in song or story. Give me the warm smile of beauty and the caress of the present and what do I care for the cold admiration of the unborn millions of ages to come?"

"There is a higher motive then than ambition, which leads you to peril your life in defense of your country," said Aliena, earnestly, looking into Major Baron's face.

"I lay claim to no higher motive. I don't profess, however, to be without ambition, but it is not the dead cold desire for fame which is usually meant by that term. How many men would, do you suppose, suffer the privations of this war, or take their chances of death for fame merely? Not many, I assure you. It is the coveted smile of beauty or fear of her frown that leads men on to the cannon's mouth. Give me my fame and reward now. *Vive le present*, that is my motto."

"There is, it seems to me, a want of breadth in that motto," said Aliena with a vague feeling of annoyance.

"It is my motto nevertheless. I desire nothing better than the present. If I could induce some lovely woman to make a hero of me, if only in imagination, I could be generous enough to sign a quit-claim, an everlasting deed to the cold admiration and dead hero worship of all the sirens of futurity. Do you think that such an ambition requires too great a strain upon the imagination?"

If manly beauty could have given a right to hero worship, Major Baron might well have laid claim to it as he sat his horse with that grace which constant habit alone can give, his closely fitting gray uniform buttoned to the throat over his deep chest, his broad straight shoulders and tall form combining manly strength and grace, while his clearly defined features, close cut hair, and carefully trained mustache added to his soldierly appearance. And Aliena looking at him earnestly said: "The commonest soldier in tattered uniform, with bare feet, may be a hero in enduring for the right."

"Your imagination is more vivid than mine then. To tell the truth, if I had the making of heroes of the flesh and blood humanity with which I am thrown in daily contact there would be very few heroes, I assure you."

"Hero worship may be inherent then in woman, and I would be sorry to give it up. It certainly affords me pleasure if my heroes should be but the coinage of my own imagination."

"It has been asserted that woman requires an embodiment for an abstract idea, and it may be that this innate tendency to hero worship gets her the credit of being more religious than man. Her heroes may be her stepping-stones from nature to nature's God. So after all it may be well to let you alone and not try to open your eyes, as did Puck the poor Titania's, if you choose to say,

> ' Come sit thee down upon this flowery bed
> While I thy amiable cheeks do coy,
> And stick musk roses in thy sleek, smooth head,
> And kiss thy fair, large ears, my gentle joy.' "

"You are laughing at me now, but according to your own authority we should have no heroes if we waited to find them without weaknesses. For Shakspeare says that even Cæsar, stemming the Tiber, cried, ' Help me Cassius or I sink,' and

> ' He that bade the Romans
> Mark him and write his speeches in their book
> Alas! he cried, give me some drink, Titinius,
> As a sick girl.' "

"Don't imagine I am trying to convert you from your heathendom. There is something far too fascinating in the possibility of being crowned a hero by some fair one myself, of being placed upon a pedestal, exhilarated by libations, and sweetly smothered in incense. I should make a most villainous missionary under these circumstances."

Aliena lapsed into silence for some reason as they rode on, and coming to the summit of Fort Hill they checked their horses and turning took a survey of the scene spread out before them.

Here the Mississippi river, sweeping around the peninsula, was for twenty miles in view. Beyond the bend the gunboats of the enemy lay in a great black, sinuous line, like some monstrous Python, waiting to devour its prey; while the masses of soldiers camping beside it seemed guarding the monster. Confederate earth works bristling with cannon and mortar faced the enemy and commanded the river, and for miles up and down the river-side the tents of Confederate soldiers dotted hillside and valley.

The town scattered picturesquely over the hills was beautiful with the delicate hues of the many-tinted spring foliage, of flowering, fruit, and forest trees; while back from the river the white columns rose above the evergreens of the cemetery. Between Fort Hill and the river the swamp was dismal with cane-brake, and with cypress of centuries' growth, from whose branches pended waving masses of long, gray, Spanish moss, making them impersonations of Ossian's heroes grown hoary with years: " Fergus with the feet of wind—Starmus, foe of strangers—Fillan, mist of the hill—as they bent to battle, their hair upon the wind."

As they gazed at the scene before them the clouds which had obscured the sun suddenly rolled away, and the pale shadows as though affrighted took their flight toward the dismal swamp beyond; the whole heavens flinging out triumphantly their flaming banners of purple and gold, tinging hillside, valley and river.

" What a gorgeous scene!" exclaimed Major Baron.

Aliena gazing in wrapt delight at the view before her made no response, and Major Baron continued, " I don't think I ever saw a more beautiful sunset even upon the Mediterranean."

" I am glad to hear you say that. I feared that love of home had biased my judgment. But a sunset across the Mississippi has a charm for me not to be found in one at sea. There is a sort of weariness to the imagination, of unrest in a sunset across a continuous, unbroken expanse of water, as of a bird that wings its flight it knows not whither."

Major Baron's eyes were resting upon Aliena's graceful form rather than upon the scene as she sat gazing with that wrapt, far away, dreamy absorption at the lovely view before them ; her dark, half-veiled, fathomless eyes glowing with a sort of lambent flame which an intense sense of the beautiful made sometimes play under the long dark lashes ; the sunlight bringing out the glory of her masses of golden brown hair, and giving a faint glow to the almost marble whiteness of her face.

" But the wings of your imagination may be stronger than mine," she continued, after a time glancing up at him, as though awakening from a dream.

" I am quite sure my wings would want to find rest where yours did," said Major Baron, his eyes still fixed upon her. Something in the tone and look rather than in the words made Aliena's color deepen as she caught his eye, and she proposed to resume their ride homeward.

Major Baron leaving Aliena at Castle Hill, as her home had been called, from its turreted construction and its elevated position, rode slowly down the winding graveled carriage drive, under over-arching trees to the foot of the hill. As he emerged through the great gateway into the road he exclaimed, " Confound those stupid fellows at camp. How can I go back to them after the poetry of this evening? " and taking a cigar from a beautifully chased gold case he lighted it, and giving reins to his horse, galloped down the lower river road, the beauty of which, with its open, moon-light water views, its lovely vistas, and its soft perfumed air, was not likely to bring him to a more matter-of-fact state of mind.

Colonel Sturdyvant called to him as he passed one of the fortifications. " Major, what is the matter? Are the Yankees about to storm our lines that you are in such a devil of a hurry ? "

" I don't care anything about the Yankees," Major Baron replied recklessly. " I only know that the outworks of the citadel are already carried, and all the fortifications in the world can't keep the enemy out; and what is more I don't care."

With which vague metaphorical rejoinder he rode rapidly on, leaving the bewildered officer to make the most of his information regardless of the traitorous impression his words might create.

CHAPTER II.

" Her mother is the lady of the house,
And a good lady, and a wise, and virtuous;
I nursed her daughter that you talked withal: "
        SHAKSPEARE : ROMEO AND JULIET.

" Here's a shawl for mistiss, honey, it might get cool and if it does don't forget to put it on her. Young folks don't always think of things, not but that you are always a thinking of mistiss too. But, mistiss, you know, you can't stand adzactly what you could onct," said Mauma, as Aliena always called her black nurse, who had followed Mrs. Graeme and her daughter to the carriage standing before the Castle door.

" Thank you, Mauma. I shall not forget it," said Aliena as she seated herself beside her mother, and the restive horses moved off. Mauma stood watching the carriage until it disappeared down the hillside, the sunlight bringing out the brilliant colors of her artistically arranged head-handkerchief, which surmounted her black face, her spreading features, and ample person.

She heaved a sigh as she turned to re-enter the house saying, " Just to think of the times and times I have seen marster help mistiss into that carridge, since she was n't no older than my chile a sittin there by her side—and him as proud of her as airy lord in the land." and shaking her head mournfully she continued as she entered the door, " But these times ain't what they used to be. Ah! if them good old times could only come back onct more, and I could see marster a steppin' in this door—Laws a marcy! Is that you, Dot?" exclaimed Mauma, throwing up her arms with a nervous start. " What on earth did you go and startle a body that way for?" she continued, addressing the black and tan terrier that had jumped fawningly upon her as she entered the hall.

Dot wagging his tail apologetically, Mauma continued, " You miss marster too, do you, Dot? Well, come along and I'll give you something to eat. Nobody shan't say I've neglected marster's pet if I do have to whip you off the parlor sofas sometimes, though I darsent to tell mistiss, for she'd let you stay there all day long if you wanted to, because marster loved you. And Miss Aliena! Lord! Lord! just to think of the times she'd a had if marster had n't been took?"

Mauma ceased talking at length, perhaps from lack of breath, as she ascended the winding stairway, lighted from above by the richly stained glass of the rotunda. And moving on she entered Mrs. Graeme's great purple-tinted room; which had a gloomy look in the dim light, with its dark, carved, old-fashioned furniture and its funereal, great, high post, square-testered bedstead draped like the windows with purple damask and lace.

Dot entertained himself while Mauma readjusted the room by making little runs at his own reflection in the cheval mirror, barking at intervals to attract the attention of the supposed canine intruder, or in making mystified reconnoissances in the rear of the glass. Mauma taking an artistic survey to assure herself that everything was as it should be, gladly left the room and the still, lonely house.

Descending by a back flight of steps she proceeded to the pantry to secure the promised *morceau* for Dot. Here, opening the door of the wire safe, she was proceeding to help herself to some cold meat when Susan, the black cook, a tall, thin woman of about forty, hearing footsteps in the pantry, came to see who was infringing upon her prerogatives.

Perceiving what she considered an unwarrantable encroachment, Susan exclaimed rather haughtily, " Malviny ? Malviny ? I say, what are you doin' in that there safe ? "

Mauma scorning to reply went on helping herself in silence to the meat, placing it upon a tin plate for Dot.

Susan, putting her arms akimbo and elevating her voice to a more emphatic pitch reiterated, "Malviny, I say, what are you doin' in that there safe ? Do you think," she continued, receiving no reply, " that I 'me gwine to let marster's dog starve to death—and he done gone where none of us can't go, lessen we walk the strait and narrer path to the shinin' shores of the New Jerusalim. I 've done give that dog more 'n seventeen dogs ought to eat, this blessed day," and wiping her face with the corner of her ample checked apron, after this prolonged burst of eloquence, she subsided for the time, possibly from want of fuel in a reply.

Mauma, having continued to help herself in silence until satisfied, now walked calmly out on the gallery in front of the kitchen, followed by Dot jumping at the plate in efforts to help himself.

"Is that all the manners you 've got ? " said Mauma addressing Dot.

Susan, glad of an excuse to commence again started with renewed vigor. " I 'll thank you ma'am I 've got as much manners as some other folks for all they take on so many white folk's airs. I don't go into other folkses things a meddlin' with what don't consarn me like some people that I know. And they need n't come a foolin' around me neither. I don't keer who they are nor what sort uv airs they put on. I think myself as good as them any day, and I 'll make them think so too ef they go to puttin' on airs around me."

Mauma, as though unconscious of Susan's existence,

quietly placed the plate upon the ground, and returned to the pantry for a chair, which she placed upon the kitchen gallery. Here she seated herself to see that Dot was undisturbed in his repast; which, truth to say, he seemed to relish wonderfully considering that he had already had "more'n seventeen dogs ought to eat."

Mauma, who apparently had been as tranquil under Susan's tirade as though it had been addressed to some imaginary being, at length unbent sufficiently to reply, as Susan appeared once more upon the gallery. "Look here, Susan, I don't want no foolishness from you—you know when I'm goin' to do a thing I'm goin' to do it—and I'm goin' to feed that dog whenever I get ready, and there ain't no use of you a talkin' to me. If it wasn't that you and me was raised most like sisters, and your mother and mine was the same before us, I wouldn't have took the sass from you that I have."

At this calm and philosophic speech, Susan thought it best to succumb, and assuming a less belligerent attitude, she dropped her arms to her sides and replied in a milder tone. "Well, sister Viny," a spiritual relationship which Susan occasionally assumed when she wished to be especially gracious, "you know we all has our ups and downs, and I didn't like your 'pearin' to think that I deglected marster's dog." And tempted to amiability by the opportunity for a social chat in the sunshine, she seated herself upon the step near Mauma for that purpose—leaning forward, resting her elbow on her knee, her chin supported in her hand.

Dot, having finished his refreshment, ran around to the front of the house, where nosing up and down the graveled carriage drive, he seemingly arrived at the conclusion that he might as well console himself for the time by a play with Hugi, a beautiful greyhound, who was lying on the smooth, green sward.

Hugi, apparently scorning any such undignified procedure, lay pretending to dose in quiet gravity, opening an eye now and then to make a reconnoissance; while Dot impudently disturbed his pretended slumbers by rushing at him with a quick bark, retreating and going over the same process again and again in hope of a response.

Tired at length of failure, Dot varied his efforts by rolling and tumbling over Hugi's head, and snipping at his ears, until utterly despairing of success in arousing him to social companionship he ran off upon another reconnoissance, nosing from side to side of the carriage drive down to the gate at the foot of the hill.

The little misunderstanding having come to an amicable ending between Mauma and Susan, they were in the meanwhile indulging in a social chat. "It 'pears like to me, Susan," said Mauma, "that everything is turned topsy turvy these times. They 'low that this war is goin' to do big things for us black folks, and the Lord knows I hope it will, for we ain't seen nothin' but trials and tribberlations sence it begun. I'd like powerful well to see the good old times onct more that we used to have. Since marster was took it 'pears like to me that everything is goin' wrong. Mistiss is grievin' herself to death—and my poor child! Lord! Lord!" and Mauma shook her head and heaved a sigh as though words failed her at this thought. "And just to think of the rejoicin' and goins on when she was born? And do you believe it mistiss forgot when her child's last birthday come? And she's goin' on now nigh on to nineteen her next birthday, that'll be about the fourth of July, and I do believe mistiss thinks she ain't nothin' but a chile yet, if she thinks about it at all; or about anything else but grievin' after marster. Susan, did n't you never take notice how much Miss Aliena's like marster's great aunt's picture in the dinin' room?"

"Yes, sister Viny, I has. I have seen jest that same pitiful look in her eyes sometimes that thar is in that picture, 'specially sence marster's dead."

" You may say that, Susan, you may say that, that picture has a pitiful look, about the pitifullest look I ever seen, and it wan't without no cause neither. I've heard my mother, that you know belonged to marster's grandfather in old Virginny, tell, time and time again, about marster's folks. They was all high quality people, way back to when they come from the old country, some lord or earl I believe it was that come to this country from England. You know old marster never owned your mother until just before he come out here from old Virginny," interposed Mauma, with an effort not to seem patronizing, continuing :

" Poor Miss Æmilia! that was her name, that you see painted in that picture—in her white satin weddin' dress, and fine lace, and pearls, and most no waist at all. My mother's told me time and time again, how, when Miss Æmilia married the President's brother, they turned the little pot into the big one, and such a bakin' of cakes and a roastin' of turkies, and a cookin' of good things never was seen. And how all the quality came to the weddin' drivin' up in their *coaches*, that's what they used to call carridges them times, and they never thought of drivin' less than four horses. And the ladies steppin' out dressed in silks, and satins, and velvets that could most stand alone, and shinin' in dimuns. How Mr. Jefferson was there, he was marster's grandmother's sister's son. He was walkin' round among the big quality folks lookin' grander than the President hisself, that was there, with his queue, and his dimun knee buckles, and his knee-breeches, and silk stockings, and dimun shoe-buckles. All the quality gentlemen dressed that way them times. And Miss Æmilia, the bride, was a lookin' prettier than any of 'em. And how Fido, that was old marster's big dog, got under the window that night and set up sech a howlin' that nothin' could n't stop him, and how old marster made my father, that was his coachman, take Fido and tie him. But ropes could n't hold him, and he got back and howled and howled worse than ever. Not that I believe in them sort of things neither, but the Lord has curus ways of makin' his will known. And it was n't no time before Miss Æmilia came back a drivin' in the same carridge she had gone away in, a lookin' so grand. But all the spirit had clean gone out of her now. She'd come back to die. And there was a shakin' of heads and a whisperin' round. And there was them that 'lowed she died of a broken heart."

"You believe my word, Susan, there's as many dies of broken hearts as of anything else. And it ain't always the qualitiest people that makes the best husbands neither. And my mother has told me often and often how," and Mauma's voice sank to a sepulchral whisper as she went on "that moonlight nights whenever Fido howled you could see Miss Æmilia, in her white satin weddin' dress and white veil, a walkin' slow-like up and down under the big oak where that smooth talkin' villun first asked her to marry him. And its the truth too, Susan, its the truth," said Mauma letting her voice fall to a still more mysterious tone, "for my mother seen her with her own eyes. And that was how old marster come to break up in old Virginny and come to this country, that was n't much more 'n a wilderness then."

"I always did 'low that that was the pitifullest pictur' I ever seen," said Susan in a suppressed tone, moving closer to Mauma, taking in a deep inspiration as she spoke.

"You tell the truth, Susan, you tell the truth when you say that—the pitifullest look possible, and how anybody could have it in their heart to treat a person mean with that look in their eyes is past my knowledge. I ain't got nothin' to say against nobody, but it does 'pear like to me that men can be the deceivinst creaturs sometimes that the Lord ever made."

"You 're right there, sister Viny, you 're right, they kin. I hope there won't be no dogs a howlin' about this place. I always heard tell it was a sure sign of death, to hear a dog howlin'."

."I don't 'low nothin'—but what I know I know—and what I've been a tellin' you is the truth," said Mauma.

"I heard a owl a hootin' last night and I got up to see whose window it was by, and it was in the big oak by the turret, right above Miss Aliena's room. I hope it don't mean no harm to nobody," said Susan.

"The Lord only knows. That's a mighty pretty spoken, handsome young man that's got to comin' around here—that Major Baron—but men are powerful deceivin', sometimes powerful deceivin'," said Mauma.

"That's the truth Viney, that's the truth," said Susan rising—continuing apologetically. "It's time I was gwine about my supper. It's nigh on to sundown."

Soon Susan's voice could be heard from the kitchen crooning one of those recitative, wailing chants in the way of a hymn so popular with negroes. Mauma's story had probably tinged her thoughts with superstitious fears which she was endeavoring to exercise.

CHAPTER III.

" Seat thee by me,
For there is a good spirit on thy lips
Which doth enchant the soul. Now such a voice
Will drive away from me the evil demon
That beats his black wings close above my head."
COLERIDGE : WALLENSTEIN.

Aliena entering the parlors one evening when Major Baron had been announced, found him standing so absorbed in looking at a picture as to be unconscious of her entrance until she spoke.

"I find a strange fascination in this picture," he said,

2

after responding to her salutation. "It grows upon me every time I see it. Can you tell me anything about it"

"Nothing more than what the picture suggests itself —not even its name or that of the artist. Father got it in Italy and always considered it one of his finest gems," said Aliena.

The picture represented an almost flat, desolate beach, without habitation of any kind. The sea, in low, drifting waves, stretched far in perspective. Near the water's edge lay a young girl, over whose form the waves apparently might yet wash. The drapery, clinging in close folds to the delicately rounded form, as well as the masses of dripping hair, seemed to indicate the fate that had befallen her. Over all was a dim, lurid, half-twilight; reflected in dun, dusky hues from the clouds covering most of the sky. These breaking apart left the moon shining in a white line across the girl, and lighting the wings of a solitary sea-gull flying in the distance. The whole picture was one of the dreariest, saddest imaginable.

"What do you think the picture suggests?" asked Major Baron, still standing gazing at it.

"There is no *débris*, nothing to indicate a shipwreck," said Aliena. "And in the drifting waves there seems to be no wrathful, sullen surge as though the sea were loth to give up its prey—as after a storm. It seems rather to lap her form with sad, caressing touch, like some wild, savage thing tamed to tenderness by helpless sorrow and beauty. The dreary look of land, and sky, and sea, seems to shut her up to hopelessness, and as a woman is supposed to have but one career, to disappointed love—and to suicide, perhaps."

"You have probably interpreted it aright, though it is hard to realize that such repose, sorrowful as it is, could ever have sprung from suicidal madness. Life seems to me too fruitful in happiness to imagine a condition so hopeless as to make suicide possible. Yet we know it does occur," said Major Baron with a sigh. And turning to Aliena he continued: "We have drifted into a strangely gloomy theme. Let us try some music and see if we cannot exorcise the demon."

Aliena had risen to comply with this request when Colonel Harvey was announced. She moved gracefully forward to greet him as he entered though she had met him only once before, but there was something about the quiet dignity of his manner and the determined look of his gray eyes which commanded respect and remembrance.

"Miss Graeme was about to favor me with some music, you will not object to hearing it, Colonel, I am sure," said Major Baron.

"Certainly not, that is a pleasure I rarely have an opportunity to enjoy of late," said Colonel Harvey gravely.

And Aliena walked on over the soft medallion carpet through the wide arch between the parlors to where, in an alcove in front of a lace draped bay window, stood her harp and piano. Seating herself at the piano she ran her fingers lightly over the keys, wandering into one of those vague, appealing German studies.

"That is very beautiful," said Major Baron as she paused, "but I thought you were going to sing."

"What would you like to hear?" she asked, addressing Colonel Harvey rather than Major Baron.

"Do you sing the Erl King?" he asked.

"We are haunted with horrors to-night," said Major Baron impetuously—but seeming to recall himself he continued in a tone which somehow jarred upon Colonel Harvey, "But sing it if the Colonel desires to hear it."

And Aliena, striking a few strange, rapid chords began to sing in a low, clear, flexible voice, which swelled to vibrant distinctness as she went on, her hands growing cold and her face white, while the terrors of the Black Forest, as depicted by the wild rush of weird music in the song, shivered through the child, the father and the strong, wild horse which bore them.

Colonel Harvey did not speak when the music ceased.

"That song is as gloomy as the picture. Do try something brighter," said Major Baron.

"Don't ask me, I can't sing now," said Aliena with a sort of shiver, rising from the piano.

"That song reminds me of Dwight Selden," said Major Baron when Aliena had again seated herself. "My college friend and traveling companion when we met you at Nice. You remember him of course. He learned that song while we were in Germany. I hear he is in command of a Massachusetts regiment. It is hard to think that after all our friendship we may meet as mortal foes, in deadly combat now—and yet it is by no means improbable." Major Baron paused, but as no one seemed disposed to speak he went on. "Did I ever tell you that I met Lieut. Massey, last summer, in Virginia; you know he was on the Susquehanna, at Nice that same winter. Judge Massey, his father, who was visiting him at the time, was one of the most elegant gentlemen I ever met, and his mother and sister were very pleasant. Lieut. Massey left the navy when Georgia seceded, and is major in one of their regiments."

"I am glad to hear that Lieut. Massey joined our army. I could scarcely imagine otherwise," said Aliena. And turning to Colonel Harvey she addressed herself to him. But the conversation seemed to flag, and Colonel Harvey soon rose and said rather abruptly, "It is time I was returning to camp." He had called upon business in reality. By request of the commanding officer of the post he had come to endeavor to induce Mrs. Graeme and Aliena to seek a place of greater safety, but had determined to await a more fitting opportunity.

Major Baron, however, also arose and saying good night they left together. Neither, for some reason, seemed in a very social state of mind, and for some moments not a word was spoken.

"Are you going to Major Watt's party to-night, Colonel?" Major Baron said at length.

"No, I care nothing for parties, especially now when

a bombardment is imminent. It may be expected any night. You know the enemy are intent upon passing with their gunboats."

" I am thinking of going any way. Anything to break the monotony of camp life. Will you have a cigar?" said Major Baron proffering one.

" Thank you, I never smoke," Colonel Harvey said rather curtly.

Lighting his cigar Major Baron smoked on in silence for a time, but impelled by a sense of propriety he said, " It is singular to see a soldier not addicted to tobacco in some form. I don't know what I should do without its calming influence."

" I generally manage to keep calm without extraneous assistance," said Colonel Harvey coldly.

" I wish I could say as much, but hot southern blood uncurbed in youth is not always the best possible investment."

" The value of the investment may depend upon the substratum of moral principle," said Colonel Harvey with a hardness in his voice which served to put an end to the conversation for the short time before they separated, the one for his fortification and the other for the ball to which he was going.

CHAPTER IV.

" But soon obscured with smoke all Heaven appear'd
From those deep-throated engines belch'd, whose roar
Embowel'd with outrageous noise the air.
Infernal thunder, and for lightning see
Black fire, and horror, shot with eager rage."
MILTON : PARADISE LOST.

Aliena Graeme the same night was suddenly awakened by the sound of cannon. Springing from bed she hurriedly dressed, while the firing from gunboats and garrison increased fearfully, and crossing the hall she entered her mother's room. Mrs. Graeme was already up and dressed, and descending the stairway together they intended to seek safety in the valley in the rear of Castle Hill, where they were accustomed to take refuge when the bombardment was unusually severe. Thither the servants, except Mauma, had already fled. As they reached the door the whizzing of shot and shell over-head, with the explosion of a shell with frightful con-cussion just before them drove them again into the house. Now, overcome by the desire to see what was going on, they ventured to the front of the Castle. There a spectacle never to be forgotten met their eyes.

At the firing of the first gun houses filled with in-flammable material prepared for this purpose at inter-vals along the river bank, had been set on fire. Fanned by the wind these now crackled and flamed, lighting the scene for miles with the lurid glare. Vicksburg, illumined by the burning houses, rose to view—tier upon tier—like a great amphitheater, in the curve of the river. Here cannon and mortar behind earth works were pour-ing a continuous fire upon the fleet of gunboats and barges that, piled for protection with cotton bales, were steaming around the narrow peninsula and on down the "inland sea;" their chimneys snorting fire and smoke which their rapid motion left in black clouds in their rear; while from the sides of the boats cannon and mor-tar poured a deadlier fire upon the devoted city.

The low hanging clouds, which had obscured the sky and favored the passage of the fleet, reflecting the lurid light, now trembled as with affright at the fearful con-cussion—as cannon-ball, grape and shell, whirring, whizzing, rattling and roaring, crossed and recrossed in meteoric splendor over head.

So fascinated were Aliena and Mrs. Graeme with the awful sublimity of the scene as almost to have lost consciousness of personal danger; but Mauma who had joined them in awe-stricken silence overcome by terror marked the nearer and more terrific crashes by the ejaculatory prayer, "Good Lord! have mercy on us. Good Lord! protect us."

Hugi and Dot whining, and trembling, came crouching to their feet; the two peacocks flew down with a hoarse discordant cry from their perch in the live oak; the mocking birds whirled, screaming around their nest in the magnolia tree.

The cotton bales taking fire at length upon one of the boats were thrown overboard; but continuing to burn, the waves, reflecting the glare, leaping up seemed to lap the boats in flame. The side of the boat, thus left unprotected, was struck again and again, and soon it became evident that the boat was sinking. And slowly settling it went down in the deep water, leaving hundreds of soldiers struggling and drowning in the surging waves.

Still the fearful firing went on. Another boat seemed about succumbing, adding horror to the scene. But the cruel drama was drawing to a close. The boats still firing broadside after broadside, steamed rapidly on down the river, and it became evident that the effort to pass Vicksburg was accomplished.

Mrs. Graeme, overcome by the horrors she had witnessed, accompanied by Mauma, re-entered the house. But Aliena held by a terrible fascination remained, eagerly watching the rescue of the soldiers from watery graves in the little boats that put out from either shore for that purpose. While from her woman's heart went up the prayer, "Lord, save or they perish." The light of the burning houses flickered out, gray dawn slowly merged into the roseate tints of morning, tinging earth and sky and warming to a more life-like hue Aliena's colorless face, as she still stood leaning with a wearied look of dejection against one of the columns of the colonnade, gazing at the now quiet scene before her.

The soft air laden with the perfume of early spring flowers was swaying the white banksia rose entwined about the column above her head, sprinkling her luminous brown hair and black dress with showers of the fragrant white petals as with snow-flakes.

The mocking-bird, rocking and swaying upon the topmost sun-lit tip of the live oak, was singing a rapturous love song to his mate safe upon her nest in the magnolia. The peacocks were calmly displaying their gorgeous iridescent plumage upon the lawn.

Everything was now so tranquil that it was hard to realize that a frightful drama, fraught with such dire disaster to the Confederate cause, had but just been enacted before their eyes.

CHAPTER V.

"Sighs, and slow smiles, and golden eloquence,
And amorous adulation."

Tennyson: Idyls of a King.

"It may be good-bye as well as good-night you are saying—as we have made up our minds to leave here," said Aliena Graeme to Major Baron the evening after the bombardment, as they stood upon the colonnade, having returned from a row upon the lake in the rear of Castle Hill, which had kept them until the full moon had risen.

"Leave here?" he exclaimed as though such a thought had never occurred to him, despite its obvious necessity, especially since the passage of the gunboats. "Why did n't you tell me before?"

"It pains me so to think of it that I have tried to banish the thought. I have felt all along that it was inevitable, that in mother's health the excitement was killing her, and we had been trying to make up our minds to leave, but Colonel Harvey came this morning to urge us to do so in the name of General Pendleton, and we have promised to go. It is hard to leave home with all its memories, its love, and its sorrow. But it must be, and what must be done had best be done quickly," she said, her voice quivering with emotion.

"It does seem hard that you must go, very hard," said Major Baron.

"Yes, it is indeed. Every spot, and sprig, and leaf seems instinct with love. And yet we must go, turn it all over to the cruel enemies of war, and set ourselves adrift."

"It is not to be wondered at that your beautiful home should have taken so firm a hold upon your heart," said Major Baron sadly.

"Any home with what I have had to make this dear would be loved by me, yet I cannot but feel that its beauty does make it dearer," said Aliena.

"Will you sing me one song before I go?" said Major Baron, and instead of leaving he walked slowly on with Aliena into the parlors to where her harp stood. Here she seated herself and her fingers wandered vaguely over the strings. "Won't you sing Savourneen Delish for me?" Major Baron asked, and without a word striking the chords preluding this pathetic old Irish ballad Aliena sang with tremulous tenderness, simplicity and pathos,

> "Oh! sad was the day when my love and I parted,
>   Savourneen delish, Eileen Ogg.
> Wan was her cheek as she wept on my shoulder,
> Damp was her hand, no marble was colder;
> I felt in my heart I ne'er more should behold her,
>   Savourneen delish, Eileen Ogg.
>
> Long I fought for my country, far, far from my true love,
>   Savourneen delish, Eileen Ogg.
> All my pay and my booty I hoarded for you love,
>   Savourneen delish, Eileen Ogg.
> Peace was proclaimed—escaped from danger,
> Landed at home, my sweet girl then I sought her,
> But sorrow alas! to the cold grave had brought her,
>   Savourneen delish, Eileen Ogg.

The song ceased, and Major Baron sat in silence beside Aliena until she rose and moved from the harp. They halted mechanically in front of a curiously carved ebony table, in the center of the arched way between the rooms, upon which stood an epergne of exquisite fresh flowers.

"You must have arranged these yourself.—It required an artist to do it," said Major Baron gazing at the flowers abstractedly.

"I did arrange them. If love for the beautiful could make me an artist I must be one. It seems to me they were never so sweet and beautiful as now that I must leave them."

"That is a very universal law I find," said Major Baron gazing at Aliena, whose humid eyes seemed intent upon the pelargoniums, tea-roses, jasmines and calla lilies; which, blended with delicate foliage and trailing vines, adorned the epergne, where a cupid, exquisitely carved in silver, poised above the head of a Flora, was crowning the goddess with flowers.

"I can't say good-bye to-night," he said after another silence, and taking a cigar from his case he asked permission to light it, and tearing an envelope in two, which he had produced for that purpose, he dropped half of it upon the table, lighting his cigar with the other, and glancing through the open window he said. "The moonlight is beautiful, we may never see it again together. Won't you come out upon the colonnade," and they walked on out.

Here they stood looking over the moonlight flooded lawn, the vases of flowering plants, the sloping hill-side with its trees, its shadows, and its soft rifts of moonlight, and beyond at the "inland sea" of silver, with the dusky sheen of the gunboats in the distance, against the black background of cane-brake and gloomy moss-draped cypress.

The evening breeze was sprinkling them with the petals of the roses above them. The soft April air was heavy with the perfume of roses, and jasmines. A mocking bird could be heard singing from one of the trees down the hill-side.

"It is beautiful indeed, more beautiful than I ever thought or than it can ever seem again," said Major Baron in a low voice. Aliena made no reply and he continued, "And you are really going?"

"Yes, we must go," she said with a tremor in her voice.

"I cannot say good-bye. I shall see you again," he said after another silence, and pressing her hand lingeringly he left.

Aliena remained standing upon the colonnade until the sound of Major Baron's horse's tread could no longer be heard, and then slowly turning re-entered the parlors. Here gazing sadly at the flowers she re-arranged one or two, touching them as tenderly as though they were truly things of life. As she did so her eyes fell upon the piece of torn envelope, and taking it up she found herself studying the superscription with curious interest. The post mark had-been torn away. It bore only the address Major Cecil Baron, Vicksburg, Mississippi, written in a cramped, feminine hand.

Hearing footsteps in the hall she put the piece of envelope into a book with a guilty feeling. It was only a servant and Aliena ascended to her room.

"Laws a marcy on us!" exclaimed Mauma as later she entered Aliena's unlit room.

"What is the matter, Mauma?" asked Aliena from her seat near the window.

"Bless the Lord! Honey, I thought you was a ghost," said Mauma, dropping into a chair near the door. "You look jest like one a settin' there with the moonlight a shinin' in acrost you. I wonder what possessed that triflin' piece, Nannette, not to light your light," and bustling up Mauma was about to light it herself.

"Never mind, Mauma, I don't want a light. Nannette is not to blame, I put it out myself to enjoy the moonlight. It seems to me it was never so beautiful as to-night. And after a few more days I shall not be able to see the moon set beyond the river for many a long, weary day, if ever," Aliena said sadly.

"You had better come away from that window, honey, and not be lettin' that night air blow in on you, or you mayn't live to see it set no more. When I come up this mornin' to see if Nannette had intended to everything, I heerd a woodpecker a peckin' right over this room, where the branches of the big oak come. It sounded for all the world like nailin' nails in a coffin, and I aint heerd that sound since the day marster was took. Not that I believe in them sort of things neither, but you know the Lord has curus ways of makin' his will known. Do you want anything, honey?" Mauma asked, seeing that Aliena was not disposed to talk.

"No, I thank you, Mauma, I don't need anything," said Aliena.

"Well. good-night, honey," said Mauma retiring with a formal courtesy, which she had doubtless learned from her mother, a relic of the quality manners of olden times.

The wind rose, and the clouds began to drift across the sky and to obscure the moon before Aliena retired for the night to restless dreaming.

In her dreams Aliena was again in the little boat upon the lake with Major Baron, floating in the soft moonlight. The odors of flowers and songs of birds were about her. There came over her a sweet feeling of rest. All the burden of life seemed rolled away, and humanity to have lost its materialism. The spiritualized essence, as though freed from "the muddy vesture of decay," etherialized, uncompressed, expanded, glorified, seemed to float no longer upon the lake, but on an ocean, into which boundless expanse the lake seemed merged; upon whose billows she rocked in happiness as illimitable as space.

Suddenly Major Baron seemed to disappear and in

the water was a horrible, black demon, showing his great teeth and rolling his frightful, lurid eyes. His hands, like fearful talons, clutched her now shrunken, humanized form, which seemed too small to endure the beating of her compressed heart, thumping and hammering against her side, as she writhed in his loathsome grasp. As he struggled to drag her down into the deep water, another form appeared, not Major Baron's, whose place it filled. He grasped the grim monster with an iron grip, and thrust him down under the water; and as he rose thrust him back again and again. Holding him there until the convulsive throes and struggles for life churned the black water to foam, as the monster plunged, and squirmed, and gasped in death agony.

She awoke suddenly with a shudder, cold and clammy with horror. Branches of the great oak, heavy with rain, were screeching against the roof. Drop—splash— trickle—continually the dreary sound, with now and then the same moaning screech upon the roof, which she continued to hear. She slept again at length, but she awoke suddenly in the morning with that dull, undefined feeling of anxiety and burden at taking up life again.

The air was alive with sound. The sun was rising big and red, the birds were twittering and pluming themselves; or flitting with exultant song from tree to tree, shaking glittering showers from twig and branch. Sunshine and flashing rain-drops made all nature radiant. A contrast that seemed to deepen the gloom at Aliena's heart as she thought how soon she was to say good-bye to all these loved surroundings.

And soon the busy sound of nailing and packing was heard through the Castle. Trunks were being exhumed from the attics, where faded relics of past generations had accumulated; the quaintly fashioned garments of olden times; the narrow skirts and stiff brocades; the moth-eaten revolutionary uniforms; the knee-breeches, and queer, old, long waistcoats; the quaintly-carved, slim-legged, rickety chairs and furniture, grown black with age; the faded damask; the old, worm-eaten books; the piles of letters, with big seals of strange devices, grown yellow with age, with words loving or otherwise, like their memories, fast fading to nothingness. Even the yellowed satin wedding-dress of the unfortunate aunt of melancholy memory—all were to be left, much as Aliena had delighted in them.

Carpets began to lie around in rolls, smelling strongly of tobacco; furniture to go into shrouds; curtains to be consigned to boxes; bookcases to become vaults in which their treasures were to be buried. The Castle was to be deserted—to be given up to the fate of war. Home, with all its tender memories, desolate.

CHAPTER VI.

" Tell me the dream and I shall know that you can show me the interpretation thereof. Thou, O King, sawest and behold a great image. This image, whose brightness was **excellent, stood before thee**; and the form thereof was terrible. This image's head was **of fine gold, his breast and arms of silver**, his belly and his thighs of brass, his legs of iron, and his *feet* part of iron and part *of clay.*"
DANIEL **II: NEBUCHADNEZZAR'S DREAM.**

Major Baron could have been seen some days after the scenes depicted, at a late hour at night seated upon the gallery of the hotel in Jackson, in apparently a state of abnormal depression. Thither, after mutually plighted troth, he had accompanied Aliena Graeme, and here they had said farewell. His depression was not to be wondered at, since he had this evening been enduring the sweet pain of parting.

Among the group of officers whom Major Baron had joined upon the gallery was Colonel Harvey, who had been sent to Jackson upon business, going on the same train with Major Baron, Aliena and her mother. Most of the group were smoking, seated with their feet elevated upon the balustrade, their chairs tilted back. Even Major Baron with his usual regard for the elegancies of life was indulging in this Americanism.

"By the way Major," said Captain Wilmer addressing Major Baron, "what became of that lovely creature I saw you flying to cover with, the night of the bombardment in Vicksburg?"

"Of what lovely creature are you speaking?" said Major Baron.

"Possibly Colonel Harvey can refresh your memory," suggested some one.

"Oh! no, Colonel Harvey was too intent upon duty for anything so frivolous as parties. He was watching the Yankees. I thought every one knew that he had the glory of firing the first gun that night. But Baron, you need not pretend ignorance. If you have forgotten I have not. I was in Vicksburg myself that night with a party of ladies from here. They stampeded at the first gun and of course I had to fly with them and was present when you consigned your fair charge, Miss Selwyn, with whispered adieux, to Mrs. Knowland's care," said Captain Wilmer.

Colonel Harvey sat silently stroking his beard with a sense of irritation at the turn the conversation had taken. He interrupted it rather abruptly by saying, "It is rumored that General Johnston is to be here to-night. It is time for the train, I think," and taking out his watch and looking at it he added, "Yes, it is twelve o'clock. Suppose we go and see if he is aboard."

"There is the train now," said Captain Wilmer as the distant whistle was heard.

The hotel faced the railroad track, at only about fifty feet distance, and soon the long white light became visible upon the track, the sparks falling in lurid showers in the darkness behind, and the train came whistling, ringing, jarring and thundering on to the platform.

"Let us go and see who is aboard?" proposed Colonel Harvey. "It is said that General Johnston is urging reinforcements for Vicksburg and that we will have warm work there soon. I see there is an unusual number of soldiers on the train."

In the flickering light of the pine torches illuminating the platform, they could see the throng of soldiers who had been packed and jammed in the train, pouring out at every door, yawning and stretching on the platform; relieved at the possibility of once more straightening themselves, and at the prospect of uncramped sleep even, upon the ground.

"I'll be doggoned if I would n't consider the top rail of a fence an uncommon luxury now, in the way of sleeping accommodation," said one of the soldiers, emerging from the car, and going through wonderful gyrations in the way of stretching, relieved at finding his joints still capable of movement.

"You are about right there," said his companion. "I feel as if I had been tied into a double bow knot until there was not stiffening enough in me to make the ends stand out"

"You stand out of my way there. It 's loose tackling that 's moving my lower limbs just now, they are stretched out of all gear from folding up too tight," said another stumbling against the last speaker.

The crowd of soldiers that continued to tumble and scramble out in confusion, soon began to look as wonderfully out of proportion to their limited means of conveyance as the articles from a necromancer's hat to its size. The ladies' car was also crowded with soldiers, principally officers. Now and then a woman's face began to appear.

A young, pretty, rosy-cheeked woman leaned with such conscious pride upon the arm of a youthful looking officer, into whose face she smiled beamingly, that it was apparent they had been married within the Mosaic period of military exemption. If his patriotism did not permit him to urge this plea his strength of will was evidently not equal to enforced separation.

A care-worn woman, pale perhaps from sleepless anxiety, possibly going to nurse a sick or wounded husband, was assisted, by volunteers, to the platform, her baby fretting in her arms, at this disturbance of its slumbers, at so unwonted an hour of the night.

"General Johnston has not arrived, it seems. We might as well go back," said Colonel Harvey as the cars seemed emptied of passengers. And they were about to return to the hotel when a woman apparently alone appeared on the platform of the ladies' car.

Major Baron, with his accustomed gallantry, stepped forward to assist her from the car. As she turned, facing the light, he gave a start of surprise, withdrawing his hand as he caught sight of the beautiful, girlish face, with its straight, delicate features, clear olive complexion, black hair and great, startled black eyes.

"Cecil!" she exclaimed, starting forward with a wild impulse of affection, her beautiful face lighting up with a tender glow as she saw him.

But, checked by his manner, she crimsoned, becoming conscious of the presence of others, to which her surprised delight had evidently made her oblivious. Major Baron, remembering himself, again proffered his hand to assist her; saying in an under-tone, in which surprise and annoyance, not to say indignation, were evident, " Zara, what are you doing here?"

" I must see you," she said, in a low, supplicating tone ; glancing back nervously as she spoke.

" I will see you again," he said in the same suppressed tone, stepping back abruptly, as a slouching, sinister-looking, middle-aged man, encumbered with a basket, shawls and satchel, came out of the car.

The man glowered at him from under his heavy, black

eye-brows as he passed on, saying in a harsh under-tone
to the girl, " Zara, what for is it, that man is here ? "

" I don't know, father," said the girl in a low, musical
voice, as they moved on.

" Who is your friend?   She is certainly dangerously
beautiful," said Capt. Wilmer to Major Baron.

" She is the wife of one of my soldiers," said Major
Baron, evidently embarrassed, stumbling out a falsehood
in his perplexity.

" More is the pity for her husband," said Colonel
Harvey in a hard tone, having overheard the few words
that had passed between Major Baron and the girl.

Though irritated by Colonel Harvey's tone, and evident implication, Major Baron felt it incumbent upon
him to swallow the affront silently, if such were intended.
Major Baron was not such a neophyte in secrecy as he
may appear upon this occasion.   But the most self-
possessed is at times liable to be thrown off his guard.
He could keep a secret.   A manly virtue in which he
prided himself.   Though possibly he had never arrived
at that higher standard which makes secrecy no longer
necessary.

The party separated as they entered the hotel.   Colonel Harvey ascended to his room in a state of disgust
for Major Baron.   A disgust which the moral standard of
men hinges usually rather upon truthfulness than upon
the observance of some other of the Mosaic laws.   But
this feeling was intensified in him by the remembrance
of her with whom he knew that Major Baron had that
evening parted upon the car ; as well as by the thought
of the beautiful, frightened girlish face, whose love had
evidently been repelled by Major Baron's rebuff.   This
had stirred within him that innate desire to protect
which helplessness arouses in every truly noble, manly
nature.

Major Baron, later, joined Capt. Wilmer and others in
a game of cards.   They were " making a night of it "
preparatory to taking the early morning train for Vicks-

burg. Their flushed faces and noisy hilarity as they jostled and crowded upon the morning cars made it quite evident how they had been spending their time. Colonel Harvey, who was also returning, avoided them by taking a different coach for Vicksburg.

Aliena had made her an image, " fair to look upon," whose brightness was excellent as Nebuchadnezzar's vision, but " his feet were of clay."

CHAPTER VII.

" Ay, thou 'rt awake, yet dreamst. Where now the hours
That round thy brow with flow'ry garlands play'd ?
The days, when unrestrain'd, thy yearning soul
Freely explored the heaven's o'er arching blue ? "

GOETHE : TORQUATO TASSO.

The cars failing to make connection at Chattanooga, as Mrs. Graeme and Aliena were pursuing their weary journey, they were compelled to get off in a drizzling rain, and go to the hotel. Here, with the other unfortunate travelers, they were crowded into a small, steamy, reception room, until after some delay rooms could be secured.

When Mrs. Graeme entered her room, she sank into a chair with a look of weariness of body and mind that made Aliena apprehensive. But at the hideous sound of a gong, she made the effort to descend with her daughter to the lower floor, where they were ushered into the low-pitched, dimly-lighted, dismal looking supper room.

Here, long, narrow tables, covered with dingy table cloths, and spread with thick, coarse delf ware, stood at intervals along the large, gloomy room. Above the tables, suspended by hinges from the ceiling, which permitted them to move back and forth, were large, square fans, formed of cloth tacked upon light frames; which may have, at some remote period, been white. The fans were connected by cords passed over rollers into the hands of a sleepy-looking negro boy, of about fourteen. He, lazily pulling and permitting the cords to roll back, continuously moved the fans, performing the double office of keeping the guests cool and of ridding them of the Egyptian plague of flies that would otherwise have afflicted them.

This monotonous exercise proved so lulling to the boy, that he was constantly alternating between a state of semi-somnolence, which scarcely stopped the movement of the fans, and a startled, wide-awake, upward glance to assure himself that they were again in motion, which created the impression that he was given to ejaculatory prayer. A habit that had caused him to have an unduly pious expression.

The crowded tables were surrounded principally by soldiers, though here and there could be seen a sprinkling of civilians, clerks and others. Most of them were eating, not only as though their lives depended upon the food taken, but upon its being consumed in the shortest possible space of time.

Seated at the same table to which Mrs. Graeme and Aliena were assigned, and just opposite them, was a family party; consisting of an old man, his wife, daughter and granddaughter.

The old man, who was apparently more than seventy years of age, was thin to emaciation; with small, keen, round, restless, black eyes, that seemed to have absorbed all the vitality left in his body. His thin, gray hair was carefully arranged over a high, narrow forehead; his cheek bones had an unnaturally prominent look, and his skin a yellow, deathly pallor.

To the left of him sat his wife. Her white hair was smoothed back over a broad brow, under a cap scarcely whiter than the hair it covered. Her skin was comparatively white, soft and unwrinkled for a woman of seventy; as were her velvety looking hands. The unnatural whiteness and regularity of her teeth suggested the assistance of a dentist. The whole expression of her face, and of her pale, steel-blue eye, for one was evidently sightless, was like that of some sister of mercy, whose will was constrained by holy vows.

On the other side of the old gentleman sat his daughter, a widow by repute, of about thirty. Her rigidly sleek, black hair was arranged in the prevailing mode, with broad plaits on either side of her face, carried back partly across the ears, which, despite this confinement, where they were exposed to view set off from her head in a particularly alert way. Nature, as though to assist the activity of her faculties, had left off eye-lashes; which gave her small, round, quick-moving, black eyes an uncommonly wide-awake look. The necessity, grown out of the want of lashes, of winking the eyes frequently seemed to have been compensated by the ability she possessed of accomplishing this action with the most astonishing rapidity. Her glistening complexion was somewhat tawny and without a tinge of red; her teeth were long, white and regular except the eye teeth, which were sharpened, like a squirrel's, to an incisive point. Her thin nose had a labored, apoplectic way of dilating at times inconsonant with the thinness of her person; which, as nature made it, was wiry and angular, without the burden of superfluous flesh to hinder the briskness and activity of her movements; characteristics equally conspicuous in her thin, angular hands.

At her side sat her daughter, a scowling child of about seven, with an unnaturally old, unchild-like face; whose hair, eyes and complexion were all of nearly the same sallow hue.

These particulars were not all noted at the time by either Mrs. Graeme or Aliena; though there was little apparent to the eye which this family failed to discern in the other party.

Mr. and Mrs. Bledsoe, and their daughter, Mrs. Skinker, were engaged in wiping their knives, forks and spoons upon the table cloth, the table being without napkins, as Mrs. Graeme and Aliena took their seats opposite them. Having finished this operation Mr. Bledsoe took up a dish and handing it to his wife, said in a tone of exaggerated politeness, evidently intended for others:

"My dear, will you have some of this chipped beef? You will find it a very nice relish."

Mrs. Bledsoe thanked her husband with an air which implied that she felt a sense of unworthiness of so great a boon; and slowly helping herself she rolled her pale, steel-blue eye heavenward, indicating by her expression that she not only felt grateful to Mr. Bledsoe, as an instrument, but that she would be committing a heinous sin if she did not thank her Heavenly Father for permitting her the privilege of eating chipped beef.

"I would like a little of that beef whenever ma is done with it," Mrs. Skinker snapped out, glancing at her mother's heavenward look.

Mrs. Bledsoe rolled her eye upward again with a look of resigned hopelessness of reward in this world for her Christian patience and forbearance as she handed the dish back to her husband, who passed it to his daughter. Mrs. Skinker having helped herself put some of the beef upon her child's plate.

"Ma, I don't want any of that beef," said the child scowling.

"You eat what I choose to give you," said Mrs. Skinker snapping her eyes.

The child, still scowling, made no reply; but watching her opportunity to get rid of the obnoxious article, or, perhaps, to resist the will of her mother, she gave her plate a tip, as Mrs. Skinker turned to help herself to some hot cakes upon the other side, emptying the contents upon her lap or on the floor as the case might be.

Mrs. Skinker, detecting the child in the act, turned

suddenly, and snapping her eyes viciously gave the
chair in which her daughter sat a sudden jerk backward
which sent the child's chin forward against the sharp edge
of the table. And with a shower of winks that seemed
to snap off in galvanic sparkles from her eyes, said:

"Arista, go to my room and stay there until I come."

Suppressing any sign of emotion, Arista started suddenly and hurriedly out of the room. She stumbled in
her rage against a tall, refined looking gentleman in a
surgeon's uniform, who was entering the room at the
time. He stooped over her saying something in a low
voice.

"My dear, said Mr. Bledsoe to his daughter, as Arista
left, "do let the child have her supper."

Deigning only a look of indignation at her father,
Mrs. Skinker seemed to let off the extra energy accumulated by anger not exhausted in snapping her eyes
in snapping at her food.

The gentleman in the surgeon's uniform came on and
approaching the table, drew back his chair to seat himself a little below Mrs. Bledsoe. He bowed as she
turned and spoke to him, with that grave and elegant
deference of manner toward a lady, and that an old one,
which indicated the best breeding.

At sight of this gentleman Mrs. Skinker, with a much
improved expression of countenance, leaned forward and
bowed graciously. Mr. Bledsoe broke the awkward
silence that had fallen upon their party by saying in a
suave tone, as he offered the dish of beef to Mrs. Graeme,
"Allow me, madame, you will find it very nice."
This little speech was accompanied by an interlude of
coughing.

"Thank you," said Mrs. Graeme, as she took the dish
and helped herself to a small portion, though she would
gladly have remained unnoticed. And, remembering
Mrs. Skinker's rebuke to her mother, she returned the
dish promptly.

"You cannot have traveled far or you would have a

better appetite?" said Mr. Bledsoe interrogatively, as he received the dish from Mrs. Graeme, with a slight bow and bland, insinuating smile.

"At present only from Montgomery," Mrs. Graeme responded.

"That is a beautiful and charming place," Mr. Bledsoe continued.

"I was there so short a time I can scarcely pronounce upon it."

"You do not live there then?" he persisted with another little interlude of hacking cough.

"No, sir, I was detained there by sickness, my home is in Vicksburg," said Mrs. Graeme wearily.

Ah! I am glad of an opportunity to hear something from that place. It is the center of interest just now," Mr. Bledsoe continued with renewed zest.

Mrs. Graeme, wearied and sick, felt like groaning aloud at this persistent catechising, but constrained by politeness she replied, "I really know nothing more than the public as to Vicksburg."

"I have a number of army friends there. I have been engaged in running the blockade for the Confederacy. Doing what little my strength permitted for our country, furnishing supplies for the army. My name is Bledsoe, you may have heard of me. My wife, Mrs. Bledsoe," he continued, waving his hand in an impressive manner toward his wife, "and my daughter, Mrs. Skinker," he added, going through with the same impressive movement of the hand. "We know how to feel for refugees. We have experienced what it is to be torn from home and set adrift among strangers, and we would be happy to be of any service to you."

"Yes, my dear." said Mrs. Bledsoe in a most motherly tone. "My heart yearns toward those driven from home at this time. I know what it is to leave the luxuries of home, and to be torn from loving friends to endure the sorrows and hardships of exile for the sake of our suffering land," and casting her eye heavenward and then resting it meekly upon her folded hands she paused, as though engaged in silent prayer.

Mrs. Skinker snapped her eyes viciously at this moment. It may have been at her mother's silent invocation, or it may have been, that leaning forward, she not only caught sight of her mother, but that she saw a pair of intense eyes resting in sympathetic glance for a moment upon the two ladies opposite. Following their direction with her own eyes they assumed a hopelessly unforgiving expression, as she was forced to acknowledge to herself that Aliena was beautiful, young and patrician in appearance.

" I am sorry for you if you expect to remain in this place," she said spitefully rather than sympathetically, addressing Aliena.

" We are only passing through," Aliena replied in a low, musical voice ; the tones of which probably reached the ears of the gentleman beyond Mrs. Bledsoe, as he again raised his eyes for an instant to her.

Mrs. Graeme and Aliena now rose, almost supperless, from the uninviting table, gladly escaping to their own rooms.

" I am not feeling well to-night, daughter. I must lie down, but don't let me keep you here, if you can find it pleasanter elsewhere," said Mrs. Graeme wearily.

" No place could be pleasant without you, mother," Aliena replied, looking lovingly and anxiously at the pale, worn face before her; and putting aside Mauma's proffered assistance to her mother in getting ready for bed, she rendered that service herself. The thought flashing painfully through her mind, what a weary world this would be without a mother's love.

Aliena sat beside her mother's bed smoothing back the soft, brown hair from her feverish forehead with the light magnetic touch of her cool, caressing fingers, until Mrs. Graeme insisted upon her retiring for the night. And kissing the feverish brow Aliena said good-night, and went to her room, which opened into her mother's.

CHAPTER VIII.

> " She still took note that when the living smile
> Died from his lips, across him came a cloud
> Of melancholy severe, from which again,
> Whenever in her hovering to and fro
> The lily maid had striven to make him cheer,
> There brake a sudden beaming tenderness
> Of manners and of nature."
>
> TENNYSON : IDYLS OF A KING.

At sunrise the following morning when Mauma came to awaken Mrs. Graeme, preparatory to resuming their journey, she found her tossing with fever, as she had done all night. Mrs. Graeme, aghast at the thought of being detained sick in this place, insisted upon making the effort to rise, but she sank back in bed almost fainting.

Aliena was not less pained than her mother at this detention, though that thought was as nothing compared with her anxiety as to her mother's illness. But endeavoring to assume a cheerfulness she was far from feeling, she said, " You will soon be well I hope, mother, and a day or two here will not be so bad, if you will only try to get well," and she kissed her mother's brow lovingly.

Aliena insisted upon sending at once for a physician, and Mauma was sent to make inquiry concerning one. She soon returned with the information that there was a distinguished Confederate surgeon in the house, whose services might possibly be secured, for whom she was immediately despatched.

Aliena recognized at once, in the tall, quietly elegant, intellectual looking gentleman who was soon ushered into her mother's room, the possessor of the intense eyes whose sympathetic glance had met her's the evening before at the supper table.

As Dr. Leigh entered the room with that grave, calm air of self-possession, he might have been thought to be more than thirty years old, though when his face lit up, as it did at times, with his rare smile, which seemed to break like sunshine over his whole face, he appeared much younger.

Greeting Aliena with quiet ease, he moved to where Mrs. Graeme lay, and took her white, limp hand for a moment in his. Asking but few questions, he apparently took in at a glance at the sad, suffering face before him, the state of the case. Seating himself for a few moments in conversation with Mrs. Graeme, he rose, gave the necessary directions, and bowing, left the room. Aliena's anxious eyes followed him wistfully, and unwilling to be left thus in doubt, hoping that he might by word or look alleviate her anxiety at the apprehended illness of her mother, she walked on after him into the hall.

Dr. Leigh, hearing her footsteps, turned and awaited her approach. She looked anxiously into his face for a moment, hesitating to ask, but said at length, "Dr. Leigh, mother is not ill, I hope?"

"No, she is not ill," he said, looking into her sorrowful eyes as though desirous of sparing her pain.

"Do you think she will be able to travel in a few days?" she continued, impelled by the painful anxiety which Dr. Leigh's cautious answer had increased.

"I shall do everything in my power to have her well as soon as possible," he said, and looking at the troubled face before him, he added: "The strong point in treatment must be, I think, the keeping your mother as calm and cheerful as possible, otherwise I cannot promise that she will be up for many days."

Aliena felt keenly this constructive rebuke, and her mind running quickly and painfully over not only her present trouble but the many others she was trying to bear silently for her mother's sake, the sensitive nerves about her mobile mouth quivered, and her voice faltered as she answered as simply as a chided child, "I do try to look cheerful," and two big tears she could not restrain rolled from under the long lashes over her white cheeks. She brushed them away quickly, but not before they had been seen.

"Pardon me if I seemed unkind, but that your mother's condition is the result of mental rather than of physical causes must be my apology," said Dr. Leigh in that low, clear, self-sustained, yet sympathetic, voice; which, as much as his appearance, indicated culture, refinement, and firmness of purpose; and bowing he left her.

<hr>

CHAPTER IX.

"And having both together heaved it up
We 'll both together lift our heads to heaven;
And never more abase our sight so low
As to vouchsafe one glance unto the ground."
SHAKSPEARE: HENRY VI.

Mrs. Skinker, managed to ply Mauma with questions, who, not above the amiable weakness of family servants generally, enlarged upon whatever facts she thought calculated to swell the importance of her mistress in the eyes of strangers. Mrs. Skinker consequently thought it worth the while to proffer her services in the sick room and dropped in as if by the merest chance, when Dr. Leigh was there, bringing some little delicacy secured through the steward. She generally managed to keep upon terms with such parties.

Mrs. Bledsoe also gained access to Mrs. Graeme's room, where she lay suffering more in mind than in body, and, taking the feverish hand between her own cool, velvety ones, stroked it affectionately; asking in motherly tones the privilege of doing something to alleviate her suffering. Giving Mrs. Graeme to understand that she would feel aggrieved if deprived of this opportunity for good work, she cast her eye heavenward in benediction when leaving. Even Mr. Bledsoe tapped softly at the door of the sick-room with kind words of inquiry, or left a flower as a token of sympathy.

Mrs. Skinker, who had timed Dr. Leigh's visit to Mrs. Graeme one evening, awaited him in her little so-called parlor, intending to waylay him in passing, as he was obliged to do. Here a lounge had been substituted for a bedstead, for Mrs. Skinker's accommodation. Arista having been crowded into the room with her grand-parents, and some other additional furniture secured through the chambermaid, who, for a trifle, had been induced to denude other apartments for this purpose, thus enabling Mrs. Skinker cheaply to indulge in the luxury of a private reception room.

She was enticingly arrayed upon this occasion, though somehow the scarlet bows with which she had adorned herself at her throat and upon the top of her head sug-gested the idea of a crowing hen. To while away the time she was reading a sensational, yellow-backed novel. But hearing Dr. Leigh's footsteps in the hall she quickly substituted a small volume of poetry for the novel, which went into retirement under the lounge cover, and rising walked to the door, holding the volume of poetry in her hand, with her finger between the lids as though suddenly disturbed in reading it.

"Doctor, how is dear Mrs. Graeme?" she said as he approached. "I have been feeling so anxious about her."

"She is still very ill. I cannot see that she is improv-ing," he replied.

"I am very sorry to hear it," said Mrs. Skinker, and heaving a mechanical sigh she continued, "Is n't she a charming lady?" And don't you think Miss Graeme beautiful?"

"They are very elegant ladies."

"Don't you think Miss Graeme is a beauty?" Mrs. Skinker reiterated.

"Beauty is a relative term," Dr. Leigh said vaguely.

"I don't know what you mean by that?" persisted Mrs. Skinker interrogatively, but as Dr. Leigh showed no disposition to enlighten her she continued, " It seems strange they should be traveling without a protector as they are doing."

Dr. Leigh, apparently gazing into vacancy, was thinking that it was scarcely possible that such ladies could ever be without a protector, but said nothing. Mrs. Skinker, more than ever determined to get an expression of opinion from him, continued:

" Do you think it is proper for ladies to travel alone? It seems strange that they could not have found some one to take charge of them, though pa says he never met them in society in Vicksburg."

" I imagine they chose not to go into society," said Dr. Leigh with a tone of hardness in his voice, which Mrs. Skinker seemed to understand too well to continue the subject though she snapped her eyes rather viciously for the first time during the interview.

But changing the subject she said with a forced smile of affability:

" This is such a sweet book, I have been reading Lucille, I suppose you have seen it. Won't you come in? I want to show you a passage that I think beautiful," she said, opening at the passage which she had selected for this occasion.

" I have never read it, but excuse me this evening if you please."

" Just read this one little piece," she persisted, rather thrusting it upon him.

Dr. Leigh took the book and proceeded to read. Mrs. Skinker moving close to his side. The sense of her nearness produced such a feeling of repulsion that Dr. Leigh could scarcely take in any other thought, and he quickly returned the book, expressing himself vaguely, at random. Arista running into the room interrupted them at this moment, saying, " Ma, can't I have some candy?"

" No, you can't have any now. Go to your grandmother's room," said Mrs. Skinker curtly.

"I 'll go there and I won't come back any more until Dr. Leigh is gone if you 'll give me some candy," said Arista.

The telegraphic lines about Mrs. Skinker's eyes were put in rapid motion by this speech, but Mrs. Bledsoe's entering proved an agreeable diversion. Arista taking advantage of her opportunity, prowling stealthily about the room, discovered the paper of candy protruding from its hiding place behind the old-fashioned mirror upon the mantle. Giving it a pull the impetus was too great, and the candy came with a rattle, as of hailstones, pell-mell over the floor.

Fortunately for Mrs. Skinker her back was toward Dr. Leigh as she confronted Arista. Her countenance would not have been conducive to the furtherance of any schemes she might have had in reference to that gentleman. Under cover of Mrs. Bledsoe's anxious inquiries as to the health of Dr. Leigh she said in a hissing under-tone:

"Arista, did n't I tell you to go to your grandmother's room? Go there and stay until I come."

Arista did not dare to remain when her mother spoke in that tone, with the snapping accompaniment going on with her eyes; and rising from where she was gathering up the candy she sullenly left the room. Dr. Leigh succeeded in releasing his hand at length from the feline caresses of the old lady and, saying good evening, left.

He walked on down the dimly lighted hall and turned into the still darker side hall to descend the steps, and upon the stairway he stumbled against a soft heap, which proved to be Arista.

"Why, Arista, what are you doing here alone in the dark? I hope I did not hurt you?" he said as the child commenced to sob, in the revulsion from the sullen. fierce wrath she had been cherishing, overcome by the tenderness of Dr. Leigh's tone and manner, a tenderness to which she was so unaccustomed.

"I just hate ma!" she gasped out. relapsing into rage.

"Don't talk that way," Dr. Leigh said in a voice as much of sympathy as of rebuke.

"Well, I do hate her! And I wish I was dead—I do—I just wish I was dead."

"Arista? Arista?" Mrs. Skinker's voice was heard calling in tones much less pleasing than those to which Dr. Leigh was accustomed from her, though they were none of the sweetest at best.

The child cowered under the sound as though it had been a blow, but she moved slowly back to certain punishment.

CHAPTER X.

"Art thou awakened from a dream, and is
The fair delusion suddenly dissolved ? "
GOETHE : TORQUATO TASSO.

One of the first duties to which Aliena attended after her detention in Chattanooga, if so cold a word as duty is allowable, was to write to Major Baron. Words tremblingly chosen, "like apples of gold in pictures of silver."

Major Baron had mounted his horse for a ride with Lilian Selwyn when Aliena's tender missive was handed him. He recognized the graceful, flowing hand, but before he opened it he took out his watch, and seeing that it was time for the ride he consigned the letter to his pocket for future delectation. And spurring his horse he was soon with Lilian, going over, perhaps, the same ground over which he had ridden with Aliena.

He returned from the ride too much fascinated to resign a twilight *tête-à-tête* upon the gallery with Lilian for camp duty, and accepted her invitation to remain. He had opportunity while she was exchanging her dark riding habit for a soft, transparent white muslin with the pale blue ribbons, which caught loosely back her golden curls, to have read Aliena's letter. But with sorrow be it confessed, he had forgotten it. And that poor little missive, if it could have had ears to hear, or a heart to feel, how the little thing would have trembled and fluttered and thumped against his heart where it lay, while his beat calmly on without the quickening of a pulsation; at least by what lay near it.

Happy, fortunate Eve, to whom was first whispered vows of love—in that there was no other woman to whom they could be whispered.

And the stars peeped out, and pale, faithless Luna looked coldly down upon them. And a little later the tender missive that lay above Major Baron's heart might, for some reason, have been heard to utter a faint out-cry as he was saying good-night.

So days went on. Major Baron's camp duties were now more rigidly enforced, yet he did not fail to find time for relaxation, to which the reader has some clew. Not neglecting graceful letters—letters full of vows—of these he was not niggardly.

Aliena's replies were delicate but trustful; the fullness of her heart cropping out in true womanly fashion.

People in love are wonderfully interesting, not only to each other but to the world in general if it can only pry into their secret hearts, listen to their vows of love, know of their hopes and fears, their bliss and woes.

Love is that fabled fountain of perpetual youth, from which if one be barred the next most interesting thing is to take a position commanding the fountain and watch the pilgrims from the whole earth coming, more eager to drink of its Lethean water than those other pilgrims to be dipped into the fountain that " the angel came down at certain seasons to trouble." Nor is the transformation at times less marvelous; the moral leprosies cured, the blooming out into perfect manhood or womanhood. His must be a gross nature indeed that is not purified by its waters.

4

Day after day passed and Mrs. Graeme still lay there prostrated by low, wasting fever, without apparent desire to live, or recuperative energy to overcome disease. Dr. Leigh could not but be impressed by the refinement and culture of the two ladies thrown as by chance upon his care, and he came to ministering to them, not only as a physician, but as a friend. He endeavored to cheer both the patient and the tender, untiring nurse, by bringing flowers, reminders of sunshine, fruit to tempt an appetite he could not restore, or books, which, if they could not bring forgetfulness, might brighten the lonely hours of self-forgetful watching with which Aliena unceasingly tended her mother.

In the long intervals of stillness in the sick room Aliena not only essayed to read, to quiet her mother's anxiety in regard to herself, but she endeavored to constrain her mind to the thoughtful reading of the books brought by Dr. Leigh, that she might discuss them intelligently with him. She soon found that no superficial reading would enable her to do this with one who not only absorbed the thoughts the book contained, but adorned them as Murillo did his Madonnas with myriad angelic after thoughts.

In these discussions Dr. Leigh sometimes lost that grave, preoccupied look his face usually wore, and at times it lighted up with an enthusiasm which seemed to transfigure it.

On more than one occasion Dr. Leigh found Aliena reading to her mother in soft, low tones which soothed and tranquilized by the lulling sound, if not by the sense conveyed. He was loth to disturb her when thus engaged. Her voice had a peculiar charm for him—the soft waves of sound fell soothingly upon his ear like the echo of some sweet, forgotten melody. And as she moved quietly and gracefully around, lovingly ministering to her mother, his eyes unconsciously followed her, and he found himself silently studying her expressive face, her beautiful, sensitive mouth. and her tender, fathomless eyes; over which hung a sadness which he felt was not altogether the result of her present apprehensions in regard to her mother's illness.

There came to him, too, at times, a vague feeling as of an impossible memory of Aliena, as though in some strange responsive way she had always formed a part of his life.

CHAPTER XI.

"And beaming tenderly with looks of love
Climb not the everlasting stars on high?
Are we not gazing into each other's eyes?
Nature's impenetrable agencies.
Are they not thronging on thy heart and brain
Viewless, or visible to mortal ken,
Around thee weaving their mysterious reign?
Then call it what thou wilt. Bliss! Heart! Love! God!"
GOETHE: FAUST.

Dr. Leigh, leaving Mrs. Graeme's room at a late hour one evening, said to Aliena: "The indications, as to your mother's illness, are, I think more favorable. If she can get a good night's rest I hope the crisis shall have past and that I may be able to pronounce her convalescent in the morning. I need not caution you to be careful, as I know that everything possible will be done."

Mauma moved noiselessly around after Dr. Leigh left, arranging everything for Mrs. Graeme's comfort during the night; having done this, she went to where Aliena was seated lying languidly back in an easy chair, and said in a low tone, "Honey you go and lie down now and get some rest, if mistress wants you I'll be sure to call you. You are looking most like a ghost, and if you don't take care you'll be gettin sick in this dreadful place."

"I could not possibly leave mother to-night," said Aliena firmly.

"I should think I could do everything for mistress. I 've done it before you was born into the world," said Mauma, evidently a little hurt.

"Of course you could, Mauma. I am not afraid to trust mother to you, but it is not necessary for both to be up. You know you have been untiring in nursing her, and you need rest yourself. Remember you are not as young as you were when I was a baby. Go on to bed, and I will call you if anything happens," said Aliena with a faint effort at a smile.

"Well, be sure and wake me up if you want anything, honey, you know I could easy set here in this chair and get all the sleep I want."

"Thank you, Mauma, I 'll be sure to send for you if I need you."

"Well, I hope mistress will be better in the morning. Good night, honey. God bless you and mistress," and with her usual courtesy Mauma left the room.

Aliena, left to herself, felt more depressed than she had been willing to acknowledge, but moving to the door opening into the hall she locked it, and went into her own room to make herself more comfortable for the night's watching before her. As the night was warm she laid aside her black dress, putting on a white *robe-de-chambre*, dainty with lace and embroidery; and loosening her hair let it fall in masses of rippling waves around her. Returning to the sick room she seated herself again by the table where stood the light, shaded from her mother's eyes, and took up the watch to note the time. But seeing that her mother was restless, and fearing that even these slight movements disturbed her, Aliena took a book from the table to make her watching seem more natural, and rested back ·in the chair apparently reading, to lull her mother's anxiety in regard to her.

It was only a form, her mind was busy revolving the painful contingencies that hung upon this night in the crisis through which she knew her mother was passing.

She glanced up occasionally, to see if her mother was sleeping, still seeing the restless wide-open eyes. They closed at length, opening at the slightest sound, but after an interminable time, as it seemed to Aliena, to her intense relief, she heard the low, regular, though feeble breathing, which to her acutely listening ears betokened sleep. She drew a long breath of relieved anxiety, though almost afraid to breathe even for fear of disturbing the prayed-for sleep, which alone she knew could restore her mother.

The house was still and silent now; every one seemed to have retired for the night. And Aliena, dropping the book to her lap, prayed in her inmost heart that her mother's life might be spared. Her thoughts reverted to another life imperiled by shot and shell. She thought of the past, of all the dim, uncertain future before her. It may have been for hours that she sat thus, her hands clasped in her lap over her scarcely whiter robe, disclosing by their fixed grasp the nervous tension of her mind as she kept anxious weary watch.

The sound of footsteps in the hall struck painfully upon her acute hearing, causing her hands to tighten in their clasp—but she felt a sense of satisfaction as she recognized Dr. Leigh's firm, yet elastic step going to his room beyond. He had been detained at the hospital.

Mrs. Graeme, awakened by the sound, said feebly, "Daughter, what time is it?"

Aliena looking at the watch, said softly, but in the cheerful tone she always tried to assume in the sick room, "It is a few minutes after one. It is time you were taking your draught."

"Give it to me, and come and lie here by me, daughter. It seems to me I could sleep if you were here by my side," said Mrs. Graeme, unconscious of having slept at all. Having taken the draught, and seeing the traces of anxiety in Aliena's face, she continued feebly, "I am feeling better to-night, daughter."

"I am so thankful," said Aliena, leaning over and pressing her lips to the white brow before her.

"Lie down by me now," said Mrs. Graeme.

Aliena thinking it best to indulge her mother's wish, lay down by her side, with no intention however of sleeping. But soon her apprehensions were again relieved by hearing the low, regular breathing; and exhausted by the many weary nights of watching, relieved by her mother's resting, and lulled by the stillness, she unconsciously dropped asleep. She awoke with a nervous, guilty start at having been thus overcome, hearing at the same time, the sound, as she thought, of the bolt turned with a click in the lock. But listening she heard nothing. And finding to her relief that her starting had not awakened her mother, she concluded that it must have been a dream. Determined not to sleep again, she lay with her eyes wide open, afraid to move lest she might awaken her mother. But the relief that hope had given, and the exhaustion from her long continued anxiety and watching, at length again overcame her. Unwittingly, the long lashes drooped, and lay upon the white cheeks—and she slept.

Suddenly Aliena was again startled to consciousness by creaking sounds as of footsteps upon the floor. She opened her eyes. Her heart leaped to her throat as through the door from her room came a man, stealthily approaching. He hesitated at the sound his footsteps had produced, then came stealing on into the room. Paralyzed by fear she lay perfectly still, scarcely breathing. The man moved on towards the table upon which lay her watch, set with brilliants, and put out his hand to take it. The light shaded from the bed fell full upon him.

In this short interval of time, as when one is drowning, myriad thoughts passed through Aliena's mind, but her mother's critical condition held precedence over everything else, even her sense of personal danger. Remembering Dr. Leigh's injunction, she made no outcry.

Sliding softly from the bed, she put her hand upon the bell pull. It gave in her hand.

The man's face turned full upon her at this moment, paralyzing motion. In her agonizing fear that instant seemed unending; but, grasping the watch, the man turned and fled from the room as stealthily as he had come. Clutching the bell cord she essayed again to ring. The wire had been cut. She waited in an agony of uncertainty and trepidation, fearing the man's return, feeling as though ages passed in the dread of his re-appearance.

Suddenly the thought of Dr. Leigh came to her mind. Gliding, in terrified apprehension, softly into the hall, fearing lest she should encounter the man, and in agonized dread of his re-entering her mother's room in her absence, she sped on to Dr. Leigh's door and gave a quick rap.

He was sitting reading, though it was past two o'clock. Apprehensive as to Mrs. Graeme, the thought of her came instantly to his mind. He moved quickly to the door; and opening it, Aliena's white, terror-stricken face met his view.

"Come"—she gasped, sinking to the floor before, in surprise, he could prevent it.

Astonished and shocked, he stooped and raised the insensible girl in his arms. His first impulse was to take her into his room ; but thinking again he bore her on to her own room, the door of which was standing wide open. Here laying her upon the bed he sprinkled water in her face. With a quick gasp and a long drawn inspiration she opened her bewildered eyes. The look of terror that came back into her face, alarmed Dr. Leigh by its intensity. Thinking at once that something fatal had happened to Mrs. Graeme, he moved to the door opening between the rooms. Here he saw her lying so death-like that he concluded she must have died suddenly. Returning to Aliena, his face full of the intense sympathy he felt, she caught the expression.

and, starting up wildly, tottered to her mother's room, followed by Dr. Leigh.

At this moment Mrs. Graeme awoke. Fortunately Aliena's face was in the shadow. Mrs. Graeme asked quietly, "What time is it?" Aliena sank into a chair and Dr. Leigh answered quickly, though in a low tone, to anticipate Aliena, "It is early, but I thought I would come and see how you had slept."

"I slept very well all night. I feel better this morning." Mrs. Graeme responded with an invalid's unconsciousness of time.

"Go to sleep again, that is the best thing for you," said Dr. Leigh, and seating himself by the table he took up the book Aliena had laid down, and assumed to be reading.

His eyes could not but wander to the pale face before him, upon which the impress of terror still lingered, deepening painfully at times, as her mind dwelt upon the scene of terror through which she had just passed.

Perceiving at length that Mrs. Graeme again slept, Dr. Leigh asked in a low tone, "What was it that alarmed you?"

"A robber," Aliena whispered, glancing at the door open between the rooms, the look of terror coming startlingly back to her face. Fearing to awaken Mrs. Graeme, nothing more was said for some time. Dr. Leigh, seeing Aliena's face grow even paler, if possible, said at length,

"You must lie down."

"I cannot," she said, glancing again with terror at the open door.

"I will sit here and watch. You must rest," said Dr. Leigh, in something of a peremptory tone.

"Is n't the door of my room open?" asked Aliena, feeling that it was impossible for her to summons the strength and courage to see for herself.

"I will see," said Dr. Leigh, rising and moving noiselessly into Aliena's room, scarcely glancing around at what he felt to be sacred ground. Here, even in this uninviting hotel, Aliena had environed herself with an air of taste, a sort of fragrance permeating the room. Locking the outside door Dr. Leigh returned, and seeing from Aliena's face her continued apprehension, he said to her, "Lie down there on the lounge," motioning to one in the room. "You must rest if you cannot sleep."

Aliena, scarcely able to sit up, felt the necessity herself for rest. And rising, she moved toward the lounge and sank upon it. Dr. Leigh again took up the book, and sat there apparently reading. Aliena lay at first with her eyes wide open. But gradually lulled by the stillness, the sense of protection, and the relief of mind as to her mother, and exhausted by loss of rest, she sank to sleep. She started nervously as she did so, the same frightened look coming back into her face, but seeing Dr. Leigh sitting there and her mother still sleeping quietly, her expression changed to a look of quiet rest, and she again slept.

Dr. Leigh sat with the book in his hand, thinking rather than reading.

"This girl is capable of suffering martyrdom for one she loved," and a possibility he had long negatived came to his mind. "Is happiness possible to me? Have I wasted all the best, the profoundest feelings of my nature? Or is there capability out of the ashes of the past to plume a bird, strong of wing, buoyant in courage, that may soar to bathe its plumage in the very atmosphere of Heaven?"

He gave a sigh—a curious thought came to his mind, "Ah! if this girl, lying there with all the mind, the sensibility, the affection apparent in her, with all her possibilities for happiness or woe, had only died in my arms, instead of fainting. There could be no change then, eternally she would be to me whatever ideally I made her." And the strange thought became almost a wish, the imagined culmination gave him satisfaction.

Sitting there forced by circumstances as it were, into

the position of a protector, he felt that it was sweet to stand in that relation toward such a woman.

He could not restrain his eyes from wandering now and then to the graceful form outlined in its delicately rounded perfection, in the clinging white robe; the soft cheek resting upon one pink tipped white hand, while the other fell gracefully upon her person; her glory of hair falling like a shining veil around her; her long, dark lashes resting upon her pale cheeks. The deep red of her exquisite lips alone attesting that she needed not Pygmalion's thrice tried spell to make her start to life.

The time appeared so short to Dr. Leigh that he was surprised, when, through the open window he saw the first faint tinge of dawn grow red upon Lookout mountain, and gradually spread like the life tint in the statue, in roseate hue over the graceful form and lovely face before him.

Feeling the air chill as it came across Aliena from the open window, he took a light white shawl that was laying near him, and spread it over her. Quietly as this was done she awoke. A grateful smile came to her face, and the delicate color deepened, as, rising to a sitting posture she said softly and apologetically, "I did not think to keep you watching so long. You must be very tired. But I was so exhausted I slept longer than I expected."

"I could not be tired while you could be induced to rest. You needed sleep almost as much as your mother."

"But that I knew you were watching I could not have slept. I will send for Mauma now."

"I will go and send her to you," he said.

When later that morning Dr. Leigh returned to see Mrs. Graeme he found her more improved even than he had dared to hope. Words were scarcely necessary to communicate this to Aliena. One of those rarely illuminating smiles lit up his whole face as he said, "I think your mother will be well enough for me to take the other patient up Lookout mountain this afternoon."

CHAPTER XII.

"Fields, groves and flowery vales; above them all
The golden sun, in splendor likest Heaven,
Allumed his eyes."

MILTON: PARADISE LOST.

Though it was only the last of May, the atmosphere was heavy and warm in the valley of the Tennessee that afternoon, as Aliena and Dr. Leigh drove up Lookout mountain. It constantly freshened into that delightful vitality peculiar to mountain air as they ascended, the beautiful valley disclosing more and more to view.

Aliena, relieved from apprehension as to her mother, experienced an exquisite feeling of exhilaration in the revulsion. This with the fresh, mountain air brought the delicate rose tint to her cheeks, deepened the red in her beautiful mobile lips, and lit up her dark eyes.

Her happiness must have been contagious, for Dr. Leigh's face seemed to have lost that abnormal look of sadness, which had of late been less habitual; and growing animated in conversation, his intense eyes glowed with a sense of happiness, the more striking from its rarity. His eloquence was stimulated by Aliena's eloquent listening—a faculty she possessed in an eminent degree. Her eyes, her mouth, her whole face, in the delicate play of sympathetic, sensitive nerves, mirroring the sentiment expressed as clearly as a mountain lake its beautiful surroundings.

Having ascended the mountain they drove as near as possible to the Point of Rocks; from there they walked to where the rock juts out in a sheer precipice, high above Chattanooga and the beautiful valley of the Tennessee; as, with its silvery, sinuous line stretching and winding for miles before them, it lost itself in the soft blue-gray haze in the distance. The sun was about setting, and the rays of light, spreading out from their grand center, seemed crowning him with a dazzling halo as he sank from sight.

Dr. Leigh instinctively took his hat from his head as they stood gazing in silence for some minutes at the scene before them.

"I scarcely wonder at times that the devotees of Ormuzd confound the emblem with the Creator, and worship the sun," said Dr. Leigh at length, breaking the silence. "It seems to me that if I were a heathen that is the god I should adore."

Aliena took an inspiration almost as deep drawn as when aroused from the swoon of the night before, as Dr. Leigh's voice recalled her thoughts.

"I think if I were a Parsee I should make a sort of Holy Virgin of the moon, and pray to that for intercession," she said. "I should almost fear to approach a god of such glorious grandeur as the sun."

"Did you ever think of the God-like attributes of the sun?" said Dr. Leigh.

"I don't know that I ever did," Aliena replied.

"I was thinking just now, as I looked at that God-personifying sun with his halo-crowned head, of how he adorns the earth and sky with tints the most delicate as well as the most gorgeous; such as it never entered into the imagination of man to conceive, much less to depict. Of the lightning rapidity with which he scornfully flings off the artist's work, in the counterfeit presentment of nature. That without him there can be neither animal nor vegetable life. That when his revivifying rays are withdrawn, the pallor of death becomes the precursor of dissolution. That at this temporary withdrawal all nature sinks to mock death to be resurrected at his reappearing to renewed life; all nature singing then its sweetest matin hallelujahs. That the very earth itself, subservient to his will, revolving continually around him, dragging her satellite with her, moves onward forever in his slow, silent, eternal course throughout immensity."

Aliena looked into Dr. Leigh's glowing face, as he stood, with uncovered head, gazing as he spoke far off at the scene before him. His form even seemed grander with the theme, and her voice took almost a tone of reverence as she replied,

"Don't tempt me to become a convert to Ormuzd by your eloquence, for I feel in a fit frame of mind to act more foolishly, perhaps, than Peter desired to do upon the mount of transfiguration."

"And from the same cause. It is not my words that have wrought upon you. It is the sense of the sublime, which in its highest form is inseparable from worship. The contemplation of objects in themselves so grand as to produce a sense of humiliation in the lack of capacity for their appreciation, necessarily suggests a Creator so above, and beyond the power of man to conceive of, as to cause him in that supreme moment, to feel like falling in humility and adoration before the God made faintly visible in his works."

"The greater the capacity for perception and appreciation, the more God-like man becomes," said Aliena, looking with a curiously mingled expression into Dr. Leigh's face, lit up as it was with the intense sense of the sublime. Something in her tone jarred upon Dr. Leigh, and he did not speak for some moments.

Letting his thoughts drift on, he asked at length, "Do you think it possible to find the same pleasure in the contemplation of objects, however grand in themselves—alone without sympathy?"

Aliena glanced at Dr. Leigh's saddened face now turned to her, and hers grew sad as her thoughts reverted with a guilty feeling to Major Baron, shut up to privation and danger, to whom she had been so oblivious in this evening's enjoyment—one of those gems the brighter for the blackness of its surroundings—and she replied sadly, "No, I think it impossible to enjoy anything in the highest degree without sympathy—alone—if there is such a thing possible as being alone in its fullest sense."

" What do you mean ? You do not believe in spiritual presence ? "

" If you mean angelic presence, I do. The Bible certainly teaches the ministry of angels, and it is delightful to think that even now we may be surrounded by angelic hosts. As to the spirits of departed loved ones, I do not know what to believe. Though I can scarcely think it possible that they are permitted to revisit scenes likely to harrow them with pain. I was thinking of something, however, scarcely less tangible than even spiritual presence. The being alone does not seem to me to depend upon actual presence. There is, I think, an invisible, inexplicable bond, which distance has not the power to sever. A subtile spell, or influence, by which we are constantly held in intercommunion with those we love. Possibly even malign influences may thus be brought to bear."

" Since the very lightning has been tamed and made to do the bidding of man, and is constantly driven in delicate traces ; and one may sit and hold communion with the antipodes of the earth, it does not require a great strain upon the imagination to think that the subtile influences of personal magnetism may hold the mind and heart in sympathy. A sympathy as real, if as intangible, as that by which the needle is held in its mysterious devotion to the pole. But I think you are wrong in using ' those,' the plural. In its highest sense sympathy can exist only between soul and soul. The human soul is of dual unity, incomplete and maimed otherwise," said Dr. Leigh, looking earnestly into Aliena's face.

She relapsed into silence, thinking somehow doubtfully of the power of being held in inter-communion, in its highest sense, with one of whom she thought ; but she instantly banished the traitorous doubt.

Dr. Leigh seemed to have forgotten the scene before

him in a curious speculative study of the far-away
expression that had come into the eyes before him.
Becoming conscious of this Aliena's eyes met his, apparently reading her thoughts, and the delicate color over-
spread her face, her white throat, and even her shell-
like ears. With a suppressed sigh she said, " Is it not
time we were returning ? " and taking a lingering farewell look at the valley before them, they turned to go.

Aliena's heart saddened as they descended the mountain and she thought of taking up again the burden of
life. And as they entered the valley and the twilight
deepened, there seemed to come a proportional reaction
to Dr. Leigh from his exaltation on the heights. A
feeling that though seated by the side of Aliena, they
were as far asunder as though seas divided them.

CHAPTER XIII.

> " If impious war—
> Arrayed in flames, like to the prince of fiends,—
> Do with his smirch'd complexion, all fell deeds
> Enlink'd to waste and desolation."
>
> SHAKESPEARE.

It is useless to depict the scenes of that memorable
day in May, when Vicksburg, astounded and paralyzed,
saw the little army that had gone out to confront the
enemy and prevent a landing below return—defeated
by the hordes that had been launched against this devoted place. And the appalling certainty fell upon all
that they were shut up to the horrors of a siege, the
dangers of which must be shared alike.

No thought was at first entertained, but that the
victorious army would advance and take possession of
the place ; and thus achieve an easy conquest.

All were terror-stricken. But night came on, and
still the enemy had not appeared. With the dawn

courage revived. Preparations were hurriedly inaugurated to meet the new exigencies. The spade rather than the gun now absorbed the energy of the besieged. Earthworks were strengthened. Caves were excavated in the hillsides. Those dank, dark vaulted arches where, when the heavens rained shot and shell, women and children took refuge.

Day after day passed, and the tired, ill-fed soldiers in the sun-scorched trenches, stood heroically to their guns. And hope revived. Wild rumors of gathering strength outside, with which in combined assault the city was to be rescued, buoyed the soldiers, and cheered the hearts of all until they grew strong again. And, remembering that the eyes of the world were upon them, they stood ready to meet death rather than to surrender.

Grown accustomed at length to the continuous firing, even women scarcely quailed under ordinary bombardment. And mirth, and even jollity occasionally lessened the tension of the times. Major Baron, now not only separated from Aliena, but cut off from communication with her, did miss those sweet endearing missives for which he had looked with pleasure. But trusting her love implicitly, no anxious thought in that direction disturbed his mind. He dwelt with satisfaction upon the yearning love and prayers which he believed followed him in his peril.

As he stood by his guns with the whizzing and roaring of shot and shell, offensive and defensive, going on about him, his thoughts took a more serious turn; as will those of the most hardened under danger. Not that Major Baron should be included in that number. Yet upon " the palimpsest of memory " arose some scenes in life he would gladly have had obliterated. And a sense of unworthiness oppressed him at times in the face of eternity, as it were. But in the relaxation following this tension his views, as is natural, also relaxed; and self-complacency coming to the rescue re-asserted its sway. He thought, as was natural, that after all he was quite as good, if not better, than the majority of men. A young man must sow his wild oats; he had not sowed more than the usual crop; and if he had not quite finished, in some cases at least, he could fall back upon the manly refuge, " the woman, she tempted me."

When not feeling quite at ease in mind he found Lilian Selwyn's society soothing; she being amongst the number shut up in the besieged city. There were constant opportunities afforded her now for appealing for sympathy and protection. In fact Lilian had learned to take a sort of secret satisfaction in the sense of danger, as a means of warfare of her own, in which, not unnaturally, she found solace for apprehension. Living in some luxury, as Lilian did, there were other inducements to Major Baron to seek her society beside her personal charms. He was indebted to her for many little luxuries preferable to soldiers' fare in a besieged city; it being the good fortune of some, not only always to find "soft raiment," but "the wine and milk" of this life. So even under present emergencies, Major Baron was still himself, and the little bird, if he had been malicious, might have whispered of "many a vow and ne'er a true one."

Major Baron occasionally visited Castle Hill, roamed in its grounds or gathered flowers from conservatory and garden, by permission—the German gardener having been so instructed. One should take it for granted that these flowers exhaled to his imagination the thought, " As the lily among the thorns so is my love among the roses."

On one occasion however, when there was a comparative cessation in firing, Lilian Selwyn ventured at his request to accompany him in one of his rambles at Castle Hill. Here his taste for the beautiful made him adorn her with flowers; and they floated in the little boat; and lingered in the twilight.

"Cecil is such a sweet name," the little bird heard Lilian say, lingering caressingly upon the name.

"It is very sweet when you say it. Won't you call me that again?" Major Baron asked with a lingering, audacious look.

She was very close to him, he had just assisted her from the little boat, and still retained her soft, white hand in his.

"I have no business calling you that," she said returning his look bewitchingly.

"But you will," he said.

She looked up, smiling, into his ardent eyes, and said with a lingering, caressing tone, "Cecil Baron."

Her mouth was very near. It looked so temptingly sweet that the sound was cut a little short in some way —apparently not distasteful to either party.

"Won't you say it again?" he asked, gazing at her ardently.

"Not if it is going to be stopped that way," she replied, glancing up coquettishly, a pretty glow suffusing her face.

A shell went whizzing over-head, and striking not far distant it exploded with a deafening concussion. The evening firing had begun. Lilian had improved in nerve since the night when she had taken flight with Major Baron from the ball during the bombardment. Scarcely a moment intervened and another shell struck even nearer, and exploded with a frightful concussion which shook the ground.

"For mercy's sake let's get away from here," said Lilian, clutching hold of Major Baron, forgetful of coquetry, now really frightened.

"I think from the sound that shell must have exploded in the Castle," said Major Baron. And they moved rapidly on toward her father's cave; the firing growing more and more fearful.

"What on earth possessed you to walk so far? Your father and I have been almost crazy about you ever since this firing began," said Mrs. Selwyn, who was on the look-out for them at the entrance of the cave.

Lilian, too much out of breath from fright and haste to answer, disappeared in the dark, cramped vault; amazed at her own temerity. And Major Baron returned to his guns, while the firing went furiously on.

The following afternoon Major Baron went again to Castle Hill, alone, to see what damage had been done the evening before. He was beginning to feel a sort of proprietorship there. The unclipped shrubbery and hedges began already to have a wilder look of luxuriance, adding, if anything, to the beauty of the deserted place.

The German woman, coming to answer the unusual sound of the door-bell, peered curiously around one of the turrets. Seeing who it was she came forward with alacrity, saying, "Good-eben, Major Baron, dot is you is it? We hab haf von ter'ble time yest-day eben. We vas taut dot we vas kilt dis dimes, shure."

"I came to see if there were any killed and wounded."

"How is it dot you knows dot die shell hab sthruck us?" the woman asked. In her surprise confounding her identity with that of The Castle.

Waiving a direct answer, Major Baron said, "You know we had a sharper time than usual yesterday evening, and I did not know but that The Castle might have been struck. It has been before, and it is a prominent place."

"We did hab von fer-ful dimes, sir, but tank die Lordt dot we vas not hurted. Vait til dot I can go rount and open die door, unt I vill show you sometings, how it toret up tings fer-ful, sir," the woman replied, disappearing around the turret.

Major Baron had time to look about him while she went for the key. The great white magnolia blooms were filling the air with fragrance. The mocking birds from their nest in the magnolia were learning to fly. A wild, yellow cat, hiding under the clump of azaleas was stealthily lying in wait, its head resting upon its paws, pretending to sleep, but watching the delicate coveted *morceau* with deceitful, blinking eyes. One of the young birds dropped almost to the ground, and the eyes of the cat emitted a sort of flame as he watched his opportunity to spring upon it. He was restrained possibly by Major Baron's presence; or by the angry screams of the old birds as they swooped down again and again to protect their young. After renewed efforts the young bird soared, on feebly fluttering wings, to the branches of a pomegranate, that stood near; thus escaping its ambushed enemy.

A spider of unusual size had spun its web from the banksia rose, that had ceased to bloom, to a hydranger near, which was covered with masses of pale blue flowers. The geometric lines of the web were assuming rainbow tints in the sunshine. The edge of the web having been broken by Major Baron, the spider was vigorously engaged repairing the damage done; running hither and thither, drawing out the lines and clamping them with wonderful celerity and skill.

Leaves had gathered upon the portico; drifted by the wind they lay in little heaps against the columns and sides of the house. The sound of the bolt withdrawn and of the key turned with a clank, resounding in the silent, deserted house, recalled Major Baron's thoughts, and the door being opened he entered. The locked up air had a close, dank smell. Major Brown halted in the rotunda, looking around. From habit he took off his military cap and ran his fingers over his hair. He certainly looked very handsome as he stood there flooded by the rich, warm light that fell upon him through the stained glass of the rotunda. Turning into the southern hall the woman unlocked another door, and they entered the parlors. What a scene of destruction here met his eyes?

The shell, entering from the west, had shattered the great mirror in the front parlor, splintering the ebony table as it passed on down into the wine cellar below, where it had exploded. The fragments, thrown back, had burst again into the room, leaving a great chasm in the floor, striking in wild confusion all around.

The chandelier was shattered to pieces; a portion of the shell had struck full upon the picture of the dripping girl upon the sea-beach, imbedding a large portion in the wall beyond. Splinters of wood, fragments of shell, of plaster, of the mirrors, and of the chandeliers were strewn over the floor and over the shrouded furniture.

Turning at length sadly away from the wreck of the rooms so changed since those halcyon days, he had spent in them, Major Baron directed the woman to close the house again.

Standing once more upon the portico he heard the dreary sound of lock and bolt with a sort of ominous shudder. He remembered a time when he had smilingly plead here against being shut out of Paradise. Instead of leaving, he again seated himself upon the steps under the banksia rose.

The yellow cat was still on guard. A successful spring soon crowned his efforts in spite of the screams of the swooping birds. Major Baron did not move to the rescue, though he averted his eyes as he heard the crunching of the soft bones; while the parent birds moving frantically hither and thither, uttered their wild cries of distress. The spider was peeping out of the tunnel in his main fortification, dubious as to coming to the front again for repairs, while his enemy sat calmly smoking beneath another rent he had made.

All the sweet and bitter memories of the past came back to Major Baron's mind as he sat there; the time from when he had first met Aliena in Italy, his renewed acquaintance when ordered to Vicksburg, and all the happy days since then until her departure as his affianced bride. He felt now as then how incomparably above and beyond all the women to whom he might have said words of love, she seemed in delicate, trusting, self-sacrificing affection. He wondered that he had been blessed with such love from such a woman, "unspotted from the world." And his better nature pleaded with him to be worthy of her love.

Not that his conscience troubled him. If conscience it might be called, in one to whom his own pleasure was the law of life, a law restrained only by a sense of honor, as the world calls honor. There was a little festering spot of which he also thought now; this troubled him at times. But a cordon of guns separated him from this source of annoyance; there was comfort in that.

As to Lilian Selwyn, he considered that pastime. "I cannot hurt her," he thought. Living in the present was his motto, and he reveled in his honey as he gathered it; he was not wont to look into the future for care.

Throwing away the remnant of his cigar, Major Baron walked on, mounted his horse, and rode slowly and sadly down the winding graveled road and out of the grounds. As he left the gate he met Colonel Harvey on horse back, going in the same direction.

"One would imagine the Graemes were at home to see you coming out of this gate," said Colonel Harvey.

"I could scarcely wish them back again since I have seen the wreck and ruin in the Castle."

"Why, has anything happened there?"

"A shell exploded yesterday in one of the parlors, demolishing things generally. Miss Graeme might have met death if she had been there."

"Death is not the worst fate that can befall one," said Colonel Harvey as he turned into one of the forts, leaving Major Baron to his own reflections.

Major Baron's thoughts reverted for some reason to the night in Jackson, when the startled, pleading eyes had been raised to his in gladness and surprise, mingled with pain and fear as his outstretched hand had been withdrawn. And to the wail of love and anguish in the utterance of his name, " Cecil," then, which no more mellifluous tones could now obliterate from memory.

" He is a confounded puppy," Major Baron said to himself angrily, in thought of Colonel Harvey, for what reason he could not exactly have defined. And digging his spurs violently into the sides of his horse he galloped on to barracks. The evening firing had begun.

CHAPTER XIV.

" By the stern brow and waspish action
Which she did use, it bears an angry tenor."

Dr. Leigh and Aliena had not visited Lookout mountain without the knowledge of so alert a lady as Mrs. Skinker, and not liking the turn events were taking she determined upon reconnoitering the ground. Paying some extra attention to her toilet, still retaining the favorite scarlet top-knot, she waited until she heard Dr. Leigh go to Mrs. Graeme's room; then taking a little bowl of jelly, procured as usual from the steward, she started herself in the same direction.

Here, tapping at the half open door, she entered without waiting a summons. Apparently too much interested in the patient to notice any one else, she stepped briskly to the bedside. with that energetic movement which always startled Mrs. Graeme, and kept her nerves in quivering motion as long as Mrs. Skinker was in the room.

" Here is some jelly I have brought you. I hope you will be able to relish it. No doubt you will since you are so much better. I was delighted to see that you were well enough for Miss Graeme and Dr. Leigh to leave **you** this evening," said Mrs. Skinker in that quick, sharp voice whose metallic ring was as startling to Mrs. Graeme as her manner. "Thank you," Mrs. Graeme gasped feebly, with a feeling of oppression which was partially relieved by Mrs. Skinker's leaving her bedside and approaching Dr. Leigh and Aliena.

"I hope you enjoyed your drive this afternoon," she said, including them both in her remark as she had done in her bow with a smile which showed the incisors.

Dr. Leigh was not habitually anxious to respond to Mrs. Skinker's remarks, but upon this occasion he volunteered to reply. "It was a very pleasant afternoon," a remark that might have applied indefinitely to the meteorological condition of the atmosphere, or to the drive itself.

"Did you go up the mountain?" she continued.

Dr. Leigh, having had some experience in Mrs. Skinker's faculty for catechizing, seeing that she was bent in that direction, abandoned the conversational arena, leaving Aliena to reply. "Yes, madam," Aliena said laconically, feeling no desire to enlarge upon the subject to one in whom she felt she could scarcely expect to find æsthetic sympathy.

"Don't you think it a pretty view?" Mrs. Skinker persisted.

Aliena experienced the sensation she might have done from a cold douche at this remark, and, hesitating to reply, Dr. Leigh came to the rescue, saying,

"I scarcely think the term pretty most applicable to that view."

"That depends perhaps upon the sentimental condition of those enjoying it," said Mrs. Skinker with a forced smile which again showed the incisors. And she treated herself to a little shower of satisfactory snaps at this home thrust.

Dr. Leigh glanced at Aliena, but relieved at the unconscious look upon her face he made no reply, as he had been tempted to do. But addressing her he gave some directions for the night in regard to her mother, and left.

He had intended to offer to watch with Mrs. Graeme to prevent farther apprehension upon Aliena's part, either in regard to her mother, or to the reappearance of the robber; but he was prevented by Mrs. Skinker's presence, and by her last remark. A fact which would have afforded her satisfaction if she could have been aware of it.

She continued her questioning after Dr. Leigh left, but found it impossible to extract anything from Aliena, who was unconscious of her drift, and perfectly self-oblivious in her replies.

Mrs. Skinker was about to leave when it occurred to her to ask, " Miss Graeme, did you hear anything fall in the hall last night?"

Aliena could truthfully have said that she did not, having been unconscious of that sound. But a vague idea of her having fallen coming to her mind, with the remembrance of finding herself afterward in her own room; and the thought that she must have been carried there by Dr. Leigh, which occurred to her for the first time; together with the evasion made necessary by Dr. Leigh's having suggested to her not to speak of the robbery, caused the color to deepen in her face as she replied, " I did not hear anything fall."

Mrs. Skinker's keen eye detected the embarrassment and evasion at once, and her suspicious mind set to work to unravel the mystery—and saying good-night, she returned to her own room. Here she again met Dr. Leigh, whom her father had stopped in consultation as to his health. Mr. Bledsoe was more feeble this evening than usual. The hectic spot on his cheeks had deepened in color, his respiration was hard and labored, and the pain and oppression were evidently more unendurable.

Mrs. Bledsoe was sitting with her hands meekly folded in her lap. Arista, taking advantage of her mother's absence, had been rummaging in one of the bureau drawers, from which she had taken out and arranged upon her person sundry articles of tawdry finery which had not improved her appearance. Having wet and plastered her hair back from her face, and tucked up what she could screw to the rear of her head with a large comb, she had put on a faded artificial wreath, from under which, on each side of the unnaturally old face, streamed Medusa-like false curls.

As Mrs. Skinker entered the room Arista caught sight of her in the looking-glass, and turning guiltily around she certainly presented a comical appearance. Mrs. Skinker, however, did not see the ludicrous side of the picture. Restraining herself as much as possible, on account of Dr. Leigh's presence, she exclaimed in a tone in which her state of feelings cropped out in spite of herself, "Arista, what on earth are you doing there ?" and, endeavoring to smile as she passed Dr. Leigh, she made a swoop at the head of the child, bringing off curls, flowers and comb with some of the natural hair, in a manner not unattended with pain to the forlorn looking little elf; and in an incredibly short time, she had the articles back in the drawer.

Arista stood this like a stoic, feeling assured that but for the presence of Dr. Leigh, she might not have escaped so easily.

"Ma, what possessed you to let Arista act so," said Mrs. Skinker in an under-tone, under cover of Dr. Leigh's conversation with her father.

Mrs. Bledsoe only heaved a sigh of put upon resignation, folded her hands, and cast her eye heavenward with greater meekness ; which always exasperated Mrs. Skinker and set her eyes to snapping. But she restrained herself from saying anything more to her mother, and watching her opportunity, in a pause in the conversation between the two gentlemen, she struck in deftly :

" Doctor, did n't you hear something fall in the hall last night? It seemed to be up at your end of the hall."

"At what hour was it?" Dr. Leigh asked, to give himself time to evade Mrs. Skinker's unexpected question.

"I don't know exactly what time it was. I had been asleep, and woke with the sound as of something heavy falling, and I thought I heard footsteps in the hall."

"I think I did hear something of the kind before I went to sleep," said Dr. Leigh, with an assumed air of indifference.

Mrs. Skinker, being on the alert, felt quite assured by Dr. Leigh's answer and manner that he knew more about it than he chose to tell, and would have continued her inquiries but that he arose to leave.

The room door had stood open during this visit and conversation, and Dr. Leigh, after giving some directions to Mr. Bledsoe, professionally, left the room. As he did so, notwithstanding the dim light in the hall, he caught the glitter of a pair of keen eyes looking through the transom over the door of a room nearly opposite. He walked on, revolving this incident in his mind.

The numerous engagements of the day, at the hospital and upon the mountain, had not prevented Dr. Leigh from making such inquiries as would not arouse comment, with the view of obtaining a clue to the robber of the night before. He had hoped that the fear of detection had caused the man to leave the same night, the constant moving hither and thither which the times necessitated making it easy to elude suspicion. But the sight of those glittering eyes under such suspicious circumstances caused him to think instantly that this might be the robber. He had refrained from giving any evidence of having seen the eyes as he passed the room, but walking on to the office, he inquired as to who was occupying that apartment.

The clerk referred to his book, and replied, "John Smith."

Dr. Leigh looked at the register himself, and found

the name written in a fine, bold hand ; which somehow seemed familiar to him.　A good name to avoid identity, Dr. Leigh thought.

"How long has he been here?" he asked.

"He came yesterday evening on the eight o'clock train, and has been in bed sick ever since, I believe.　I suppose he has called you in to see him?"

"It is very well to know with whom one has to deal," Dr. Leigh responded evasively.

Supposing now that this man, whom more than ever he believed to be the robber, would not leave his room until time for the train at eleven o'clock, the first going out, Dr. Leigh determined to assure himself as to his leaving.　Returning with this purpose, as he ascended the steps in the side-hall and turned into the main one, he saw, in the partly open door of the room where the glittering eyes had peered above the transom, a man's head peeping out, evidently reconnoitering.　The man must have turned his head in the opposite direction at the moment Dr. Leigh appeared ; as, seemingly assured of his opportunity, he moved swiftly and noiselessly across the hall toward the open door of the room where the Bledsoe party were still assembled, from whence could be heard Mrs. Skinker's voice in excited conversation.　She and her mother were having a little tilt in reference to Arista's late procedure.　Dr. Leigh now felt assured that this was the robber, and, knowing Mr. Bledsoe's enfeebled condition, and that he was in no state to cope with so stalwart a person, he moved rapidly to the rescue.

"My God!" he heard Mrs. Bledsoe exclaim as though aghast.

"Jim Skinker?" ejaculated Mr. Bledsoe in a tone of scarcely less horror,—while Mrs. Skinker must have been struck dumb, as she uttered no sound.

"You don't give me a very affectionate welcome, after such a long absence," he heard the man say as he closed and locked the door quickly.

Dr. Leigh halted, astounded at what he had heard. He could not at first make himself believe otherwise than that the recognition of the parties was a mistake of his own imagination, since Mrs. Bledsoe had told him that her son-in-law was dead. But he understood now why the handwriting had appeared so familiar to him. A signature by the same hand, of Dr. Leigh's own name, had cost him some thousands of dollars ; the discovery of which, had some years before caused the flight of the unfortunate man.

He waited for some moments expecting an outcry, but hearing nothing that could be construed into a call for help he moved off, with the unpleasant consciousness of having unwittingly acted as a spy upon those to whom he had intended only kindness.

Mr. Skinker, after locking the door, calmly surveyed the horror-stricken group. Even Mrs. Skinker had a more subdued look than one could have thought possible, while Mrs. Bledsoe seemed to have petrified with her hand clasped, and her eyes rolled heavenward.

"Come here Arista and speak to your father?" he said, holding out his hand to his child who shrank, cowering behind the chair of her gasping old grandfather. "Its a very hard case when a man's own child is turned against him," he added with a touch of nature.

"What are you doing here?" Mr. Bledsoe gasped faintly.

"I'm in a devilish tight place just now. It was accidental, my stumbling upon you, but it is d—d lucky. Don't think I have fallen in love with you Eliza, your voice has n't changed much since I saw you, from what I caught of its tones with your mother, and I can't see that your beauty is improved either. That expression on your face is quite natural," said Mr. Skinker tantalizingly, incited to the last remark by the look of glowering hatred upon Mrs. Skinker's face. He continued, bowing with a mock air of deference to each as he spoke. "I thought that my affectionate pa-in-law, and my venerated ma-in-law might prefer making me a little present rather than be subjected to the possibility of some developments which my presence may bring to light."

"Eliza, take the child out of the room," said Mr. Bledsoe.

"No you won't," said Mr. Skinker, standing before the closed door.

"For God's sake let the child go," said Mr. Bledsoe dreading what she was to hear.

"Do you think she would blab?" asked Mr. Skinker.

"Arista go to your grand-ma's room, and don't you speak to any one before I come," said Mrs. Skinker in a tone that assured her quondam husband that she would be obeyed, and he turned the key and opened the door wide enough for the child to squeeze through, glancing back as she did so with a look of terror at her father, as though darkness and banishment were nothing compared with her fear of him.

"Now, the sooner we transact this little business the better for all parties," said Mr. Skinker, relocking the door. "It is important that I should get away from here as soon as possible, unless you are particularly anxious to have me stay, and I advise you to curb your affection and let me go, and ask no questions either. 'Where ignorance is bliss 'tis folly to be wise,' you know. But I have got to have some money, and that right away, and the least said the soonest mended."

"How much will do you?" asked Mr. Bledsoe resignedly, evidently wishing to avoid farther information.

"Three hundred dollars in Confederate money and a hundred in gold or greenbacks might do; and I will pledge myself not to stop within Confederate lines longer than is necessary for me to get away."

"I might let you have the Confederate money, but it is impossible for me to get the greenbacks," said the old man.

"You can give me an order upon some one in Federal lines."

"I can't do that," said Mr. Bledsoe, shrinking from committing himself upon paper to this man, even if he could have commanded the money.

"Don't drive me to resorting to what I did last night," said Mr. Skinker recklessly.

Mrs. Skinker's mind immediately reverted to the sound in the hall the night before, and to the possibility that he might have knocked some one down with the intention of robbing. Aghast at the thought of the disgrace likely to attach to them from his presence, and from farther developments, together with the plans likely to be disconcerted, by the knowledge of his existence, she exclaimed.

"For the Lord's sake pa, give him the money."

"It is something new to have you on my side, Eliza," said Mr. Skinker. "You are not falling in love with me I hope." Mrs. Skinker glowering upon her husband, made no reply.

"I might possibly get the greenbacks, but it would require time," said Mr. Bledsoe.

"Well, give me Confederate money instead, and I will take my chances for exchange, but I must have ten to one. Make it ten to one and I will go."

"I shall have to go and see if I can raise it," said Mr. Bledsoe, rising wearily, and with difficulty; coughing as he moved toward the door.

"I will go with you," said Mr. Skinker.

"No, stay here, and I pledge my word to return as soon as I can secure the money," said Mr. Bledsoe, the fear that his son-in-law might encounter Dr. Leigh coming to his mind.

Mr. Skinker permitted the old man to pass out, looking unusually worn and feeble as he moved slowly on leaning heavily upon his cane. and, locking the door behind him, said, "Eliza, who was that man in here before I came? His voice and appearance reminded me of Dr. Leigh."   Mrs. Skinker, scowling at her husband, made no reply.

"Don't imagine I am jealous," he continued tauntingly. "If any man is —— fool enough to want you he can have you, and welcome.   I couldn't wish sweeter revenge upon my worst enemy.   If you and my venerated ma couldn't make things lively for him, I don't know who could, your temper would drive any man to the devil," and he laughed a sardonic laugh.

"My temper!" exclaimed Mrs. Skinker, in a hissing tone, livid with rage.   "Don't try to put your deviltry upon me.   When I first laid eyes upon you, you were a fraud—a swindler and a gambler, and living by false pretences.   But for ma I would never have been fool enough to marry you.   And now you try to put your rascality upon me.   God knows I never spent your money.   And pa has had to give you more to hide your villainy than you ever spent upon me and your child.   And now you come here, when you see that pa has one foot in the grave, and take the very bread out of our mouths.   I hope to the Lord that this is the last time I shall ever set eyes upon you."

"That wish is one of the few things we ever agreed in.   I can assure you that is mutual.   Don't imagine I am here because I wanted to see you.   I happened here, and being in the room nearly opposite, recognized the sweet tones of your voice quarreling with your mother, and as I was in a tight fix I concluded to give you the privilege of paying something to get me out of your neighborhood."

Mr. Bledsoe's step could now be heard approaching, and tapping feebly at the door, his son-in-law opened it suspiciously, wide enough to permit him to enter.

He sank into a chair gasping for breath, and, dropping his hat and cane upon the floor by his side without a word, extended the package of money to Mr. Skinker; who received and counted it in a business way.

Depositing it in his breast pocket, Mr. Skinker rose,

saying, " I hope your temper may improve before I see you again, Eliza. I think if that wish is to be fulfilled we are not likely to meet this side of Jordan. By-by, ma, don't sniffle when I am gone," and leaving the room he crept softly through the hall on down the stairs.

Instead of taking the cars, however, as Dr. Leigh had supposed he would, Mr. Skinker went to a livery stable near, where the evening before he had seen a beautiful thorough-bred horse, which he had greatly admired. Having learned, through the hostler, to whom it belonged, it being Alert, Aliena Graeme's beautiful riding horse, he now presented a forged order for the animal.

The groom brought the horse out, and Mr. Skinker mounting, rode rapidly off, saying as he left, " Alert, you and I had better make quick time out of this place."

Hard as it was for Dr. Leigh to believe that Mr. Skinker had sunk so low, he could not but believe, from Aliena's description, from the handwriting upon the register and from the other suspicious circumstances, that he and the robber were identical. Determined to assure himself that the degraded man was gone, he drove to the depot for that purpose, but unavailingly as we know.

Having returned to the hotel after the train left, Dr. Leigh retired to his room. Annoyed by his uncertainty as to the movements of the supposed robber, and at the apprehension he feared Aliena was enduring, he determined to sit up. He was thus sitting, reading, at a late hour of the night, when a hurried step and rap upon his door startled him into renewed anxiety as to Aliena or her mother.

Opening the door a servant accosted him, saying, " Dr. Leigh, Mrs. Bledsoe says please come there quick —Mr. Bledsoe is dying. He looks monsus like it sir," the negro added of his own volition.

6

CHAPTER XV.

> "Sleep hath forsook and gi'en me o'er
> To death's benumbing opium as my cure,
> Thence faintings, swoonings of despair,
> And sense of Heaven's desertion."
>
> MILTON: SAMSON AGONISTES.

Aliena Graeme had for some reason reacted from the state of exaltation she had experienced upon Lookout mountain. It may have been that the angel of death was with black, brooding wing, hovering over and darkening the dismal place, where a remorseful man lay dying; causing the most indifferent to shudder and tread softly before the great mystery of death enacting here.

Though Aliena found occupation in ministering with tenderest care to her mother in her tedious convalescence; yet, when she could, she stole away from time to time to visit the dying man, to whom her presence seemed especially grateful. But there were moments of stillness and inaction when her mind dwelt with corroding pain upon matters concerning herself; in which was mingled a curiously remorseful feeling.

Aliena's gentle manner, sympathetic voice, and magnetic presence seemed to have a wonderfully soothing effect upon Mr. Bledsoe; and he came to looking anxiously for her brief visits. She was not surprised therefore when one night she was summoned to his dying bedside.

She could not but be awed as she entered the dimly lighted room and approached the dying man, about whom she had a dim consciousness that others were grouped. Mr. Bledsoe appeared to have grown years older in the short interval since she had seen him last. The hectic spot, which had at times relieved his death-like pallor, was gone. His emaciated features had lost every vestige of life except what was concentrated in his sunken, restless, burning eyes.

"Child," he gasped in a hoarse whisper, as Aliena approached his bedside, "are you a Christian?"

There was something strangely weird and startling in being brought thus to confront this great question, coming as it were from the other side of the tomb. It had such a profound significance, that Aliena hesitated to reply.

But Mr. Bledsoe did not await an answer. "As a little child," he continued in that labored, sepulchral whisper, his eyes rolling more restlessly than ever. " Get the bible there," he said, motioning to his wife, who moved to the table upon which it lay, though truly seldom read. " Give it to her," he added pointing, with his long, fleshless finger to Aliena. " Look, find it, ' You cannot serve God and mammon,' read it to me. The time is short."

Aliena took the book with trembling hands, and turned to the place. But she hesitated to read, as she might have done to pronounce doom upon a criminal.

"Read it child, read it. I have no time to lose," he gasped.

Dr. Leigh's eyes resting upon her seemed to strengthen her to go on. And Aliena read in an unnatural tone of dread and awe: "No man can serve two masters; for either he will hate the one and love the other; or else he will hold to the one and despise the other. Ye cannot serve God and mammon."

"'He will hold to the one.' Yes," gasped the dying man. "I have held to the one. It is a straw in a drowning man's hand. I am sinking down—down—down—" and he rolled his head from side to side, his eyes moving despairingly from face to face as though seeking help or consolation. "'Ye cannot serve God and mammon.' I have held to the one and despised the other. It is too late—too late," he said in a despairing tone, gasping for breath. And struggling to raise himself, his eyes seeking Dr. Leigh's appealingly, the blood gurgled in his throat and flowed from his mouth.

Dr. Leigh raised him, but there was no hope in his eyes in answer to the appealing look.

When he could speak he gasped again, addressing Aliena, " I am dying, child. I know it. Pray for me—pray for me."

Aliena, transfixed, bowed her face in her hands, praying silently from the depth of her heart.

" Pray—pray on—pray for me—there is no time to lose," he gasped wildly. " No time to lose."

Moved by his frantic entreaties, with the restless, dying eyes fixed upon her in despairing appeal, Aliena sank upon her knees. And, buoyed by some strange, mysterious power, she prayed in a low voice vibrant with awe, reverence and fervent desire:

" Lord God, before whom angels bow, and seraphim do veil their faces, yet who stoopest to hear the faintest cry of thy stricken ones, look down in thy infinite love and compassion upon thy servant whom thou hast afflicted. Give him strength according to his days. If his time on earth be short, do thou grant that his faith be strong. Hear thou, O Lord God, in Heaven, thy dwelling-place, and hearing, answer his grief-stricken. penitential cry. Thou who didst send thine only Son to bear the sins of the world upon the accursed tree, to whom came the cry of agony, ' Eloi, eloi, Lama sabachthani,' hear the forsaken cry of thy servant, and shine in upon him with the light of thy Holy Spirit. the Comforter, whom thou didst promise to send. Blot out, O Lord, our Heavenly Father, his sins and iniquities from the book of thy remembrance. Clothe him in the spotless robe of thy righteousness. If according to thy holy will, spare his life, good Lord. But if his days on earth be ended, do thou grant him an abundant entrance into that blessed abode where, with saints, and angels, and archangels, he shall cast his blood-bought crown before the throne, crying ' Alleluia ! salvation, and glory, and honor, and power, be unto the Lord our God, for the Lord God omnipotent reigneth.' Amen."

"He is gone," said Dr. Leigh solemnly. "Take her from the room," motioning to Mrs. Bledsoe, who had tottered to her feet with a dazed, helpless look. Aliena put her arm around the old woman and led her from the room.

Late as it was when Dr. Leigh retired that night to his room, he found it impossible to sleep. Accustomed as he was to death, that of Mr. Bledsoe, with its incongruous surroundings, had moved him strangely. Illumining the scene to him, came the vision of Aliena's kneeling form. He heard again and again the tones of that low, musical, pleading voice, pulsating with feeling; until in imagination, she seemed to rise above the humanity of her surroundings; and as if borne upon angel's wings to hover about him in sweetest benediction, mingling at length in his dreams.

CHAPTER XVI.

"Weighs the spread wings, at leisure to behold
Far off th' empyreal heaven extended wide;
With opal towers and battlements adorned
Of living sapphire—
And fast by hanging in a golden chain
This pendent world."

MILTON: PARADISE LOST.

Lookout mountain had seemed to Mrs. Graeme's fevered imagination "the shadow of a great rock in a weary land," while, lying sick in body and in mind, she had caught glimpses of it through her window. She had longed for its cool, invigorating air, and for its clear, icy springs. And now that she had grown stronger she had determined to leave Chattanooga for a temporary stay upon its summit. She felt that there she might regain her strength sufficiently to resume her journey once more.

As Dr. Leigh accompanied Mrs. Graeme and Aliena to the carriage which was to take them to the mountain, Hugi, wild with delight at recovered freedom from necessary confinement, bounded around them.

Aliena, stroking the dog's head as he fawned upon her, said, "It is hard to say which enjoys freedom most to-day, Hugi, you or I."

Dr. Leigh looked curiously at Aliena as she said this. She may have read his thoughts, as, looking back toward the dingy old hotel she said with a sigh, "It is sad that in this life pain and pleasure should be so commingled. It seems impossible to leave any place without regret, no matter how repulsive it may have seemed at times. Much as I have longed to be on Lookout mountain, yet I cannot leave this old hotel without a pang."

Dr. Leigh made no reply unless the quick look of mingled pain and pleasure could be construed as such. Assisting them silently into the carriage he bade them good-bye. Looking after them for some moments as they drove away, he turned and went back to his dreary room.

How often in life do we gaze with anxious longing at some height, whether real or imaginary, bathed in sunshine, on which imagination depicts one's self disporting in bliss, not less illusive than the phosphorescent flicker of the dark valley below. So it was with Aliena, who, with change of scene had hoped to find renewed happiness. Yet after the first great pleasure in seeing that her mother bade fair to be restored to her usual health through the exhilarating mountain air, the solicitude and occupation of the sick room gone, she sank back to a feeling of isolation and loneliness more profound even than in Chattanooga. A feeling that tinged the beautiful in nature by which she was surrounded with unnaturally somber hues.

Leaving her mother when she could she walked alone to points of interest, either beautiful in themselves, or commanding views of the valley; especially to the Point of Rocks, which seemed to have taken a firm hold upon her heart. Here, seated, poised as it were in air, she gazed at the scene spread out before her with that feeling of oppression that a too intense perception of the sublime sometimes produces. Feeling as though she were a waif, floating in immensity, with a great God above, the Creator of worlds, to whom she seemed but an atom, too insignificant for especial care and protection, drifting as an atom might in ether, helplessly at random, tossed hither and thither by blind chance.

She wondered if He who said " Let there be light," and the great suns came forth, with their trains of worlds, and satellites, and wild flaming comets could be looking down upon her yearning heart. Holding it, by infinitesimal, electric bonds, in live sympathy with the Great Life Giver. And the yearning may have been a prayer, which with curiously wonderful power moved the Great Heart above ; as she usually returned strengthened for the duties of life.

Dr. Leigh came at first ostensibly to visit Mrs. Graeme, but he continued his visits, at intervals, when she could no longer have needed his care. He went with Aliena occasionally, when he could command time from hospital duties, to see objects of interest upon the mountain. The waterfall, the lake, the city of rocks, or more aptly the Mausoleums of the gods. Entering this last through the apparent ruins of a gigantic overarched gateway, guarded perpetually by monster images in stone, Dr. Leigh and Aliena walked in awed silence through the still, deserted streets ; along which one might well imagine a solemn procession, in the days when the "sons of God took to themselves the daughters of men, and there were giants upon the earth ; " moving to some grand requiem of nature, conveying to their resting places those who had fallen in defense of this great old bulwark. Here they may still be lying, where the eternal rocks uprear their heads in monumental gloom.

Rumors from the front of the contemplated falling back of the army, soon became rife; causing Dr. Leigh to think painfully of his final separation from Aliena, which would thus apparently be made inevitable. This thought recalled in full force those feelings he had been endeavoring to combat, and made him hopeless of the possibility of success in stifling them. He found that in reality, the bond which held him had acquired new strength, that it fettered him more firmly even than when he had last permitted himself to analyze his feelings.

The position of protector to Aliena had at first been thrust upon him by circumstances, but he had continued to assume this position even after their removal to Lookout mountain, when it had apparently been unnecessary. It had now become to him a sweet privilege, one that he could not willingly bring himself to surrender.

Dr. Leigh had rashly and persistently put himself in the way of having the chains which bound him more firmly riveted by constant companionship with Aliena. Here the latent depths of her nature had been stirred and evolved by communion with all that was beautiful in nature, and in sympathetic companionship with one, whose profound perceptions and intense emotions aroused her to even greater depths of feeling than she might otherwise have attained. Associated as she had thus become, with all that was beautiful by which they had been surrounded, the impress of Aliena's charms had become even more enduring in this remembrance.

It is not strange, then, that though Dr. Leigh had promised to keep Mrs. Graeme posted as to the movements of the army, as affecting her own, that he should have hesitated until he felt constrained to do so by the rumors rife as to the contemplated retreat of the army.

Reckless now, at the prospect of separation Dr. Leigh could not forego the happiness of seeing Aliena. And that afternoon, as soon as his hospital duties would permit, he drove to Lookout mountain.

CHAPTER XVII.

"All heaven and earth are still, though not in sleep,
But breathless as we grow when feeling most,
And silent as we stand in thoughts too deep;—
All concentrated in a life intense,
When not a beam, nor air, nor leaf is lost
But hath a part of being."

BYRON: CHILDE HAROLD.

At Lookout mountain, Dr. Leigh soon proposed to Aliena to walk to the Point of Rocks. A spot indissolubly connected in his memory with her glowing face, as she had stood there with him the evening of their first visit, radiant with a sense of enjoyment that had seemed to flash out in sentient beauty in her face, and to pervade her whole being.

Hugi, who also seemed to have accepted Dr. Leigh as a friend, joined them, keeping in advance; his great intelligent eyes looking as though he thoroughly appreciated his opportunity for æsthetic enjoyment.

They walked slowly at first, but, inspired with that buoyancy of spirit natural to Aliena before the evil days of sorrow, she quickened her steps, which aided in producing an exhilaration that added to her beauty. Moving with that flexible grace which characterized her every motion, she climbed the massive rocks, or bounded from stone to stone; Dr. Leigh quickening his movements with corresponding animation.

Hugi evidently enjoyed this much more than the staid pace at which they had started. He leaped and bounded on before them, or turning retraced his steps with equal rapidity; speeding over the ground and rocks with a grace which made him a picture of canine beauty, his great eyes appealing now and then to Aliena for word or caress of approval.

Reaching the Point of Rocks, Aliena took her favorite seat at the extreme verge, Dr. Leigh seating himself beside her.

He could not but feel oppressed with the thought which came over him now, that it might be for the last time that he was enjoying what he felt to be the greatest privilege that earth could afford him. The undivided companionship of her for whom, of all the world, his whole being yearned, surrounded as they were by everything in nature to incite to grand and elevated thought.

It was as though in the voyage of life, when his bark had been shattered and stranded when bruised and torn until life seemed a burden, he might gladly have laid down; that he had awakened to consciousness, not solitary and alone, but transported to a sun-capped height, and to the companionship of a woman perfect in his eyes as was the first woman, fresh from the hands of her Creator. A happiness more exquisite than that of Paradise itself, in that he had known disappointment and suffering.

Dr. Leigh's experience in life had taught him a self-abnegation rarely found in man. Aliena's happiness was pre-eminent with him. Passionately as he yearned to possess her, to carry her as a ewe lamb in his bosom, she must gladly nestle there. Oppressed more with these thoughts, than with the view spread out before them he did not speak.

They sat silent for some time. The soft air was coming in fitful waves to them from below. Far away was the lovely valley of the Tennessee, the sunlit mountain-tops outlined in dazzling gold near the horizon.

“ It is delightful at times to feel that one lives,” said Aliena at length, in a tone of exquisite satisfaction.

“ You say that as though you might sometimes have doubted the fact. I scarcely supposed that you could ever have thought otherwise,” said Dr. Leigh.

Aliena looked at him earnestly and with some surprise, as she replied, “ Did you think it possible for me to have lived, even as short a time as I have done, without occasion to doubt that fact ? ”

“ I had hoped so, at least, and I still hope the times are exceptional when life is not a happiness to you. Though my experience seems exceptionally the other way,” he added sadly.

Aliena had so rarely heard Dr. Leigh allude to himself, that unconsciously she had almost lost sight of the fact that, despite the strength of his apparently self-sustained manhood, while caring for and sympathizing with others he too might feel the need of sympathy and tenderness. His tone as much as his words pained her. And she said earnestly :

“ I thought you could always find pleasure in life, if only in the happiness of others—you seem to give yourself up so entirely to that object. I am sure I cannot tell what we should have done without you, and I can never forget that I am probably indebted to you for not being desolate indeed in mother's death,” said Aliena, her sympathy and gratitude giving her voice and manner unusual warmth as she spoke.

“ I experience now one of those exceptional moments. If my life has conduced to a moment's happiness to you it has not proved altogether a failure.”

There was a depth of feeling in Dr. Leigh's voice that struck painfully upon Aliena, and glancing around from the scene she met his impassioned eyes fixed yearningly upon her. The delicate pink came suddenly to her face and white throat as the painful thought flashed through her mind. “ He may care too much for my happiness.”

Dr. Leigh saw the sudden flush that beautified her

face, as well as the look of pained tenderness that accompanied the thought—as for an instant her beautiful, sorrowful eyes met his, and he felt that she comprehended him.

But Aliena, endeavoring to banish this thought, as a coinage of her imagination, said, "How is it possible that a life of high intent, with the capability for doing so much for humanity, can be a failure? Look at what you are doing, not only for our country, but for each individual in your hospital work. And, if personally you are as good to them as you have unfailingly been to mother and myself and to the other sufferers that I have seen you with, you can have no right to think life a failure."

Dr. Leigh felt that Aliena was trying to comfort him in the only direction that seemed open to him, and he replied in a voice full of pathos, "A life of duty is certainly the highest possible. But whether a life of duty—coldly duty, is possible to man—is doubtful. The heart thrown back upon itself slowly suffers petrifaction. A mechanical act, of goodness even, has no charm. The warmth of vitality alone can give the power truly to succor and comfort."

"But I cannot think it possible your heart could ever undergo petrifaction with the constant attrition of good deeds wearing against what, at its worst, could only be a superficial hardening. It must give way and allow the kind, warm, palpitating heart to come to life again," said Aliena in a voice tremulous with feeling.

Dr. Leigh felt now as though there was scarcely petrifaction enough to prevent the fullness of his heart from crying out, or to keep him from passionately clasping her to his heart. But reading a negation in the sad, tender face before him, he said, "I shall strive to keep alive whatever there is of good in my heart. I shall need it. My profession gives me opportunity for duty, at least. I shall count it as amongst its privileges to have made me know you. If I should falter in duty at any time, it will strengthen me to think I have done what you would have commended."

"You are so far beyond me in goodness that it pains me to think how unworthy I am of such an estimate. But I shall try to bring myself to a standard worthy of your appreciation," Aliena replied, her voice faltering, and tears welling to the tender brown eyes, as a sense of wrong in some way done to Dr. Leigh pained her heart.

"It seems almost profanation for you to rank yourself as you are doing," said Dr. Leigh in a low, pained voice, noting the suffering mirrored in Aliena's sensitive face.

She turned once more toward the scene before her, to which she was evidently now oblivious; a sad, far-away expression clouding her face.

Both were silent for a time. Aliena said at length with a sigh, " I thought we were going to be so happy here this beautiful evening, lifted so far above humanity," and she glanced down at Chattanooga far away in the valley, " with this delightful air to breathe, and with everything beautiful in nature surrounding us. And yet I feel wretched—and I don't know why."

" There are visible and invisible deaths. In spirit we unconsciously kneel beside invisible death-beds. Pray to God that the dead may sleep tranquilly in their graves; and not start constantly to life, phantoms paralyzing energy," said Dr. Leigh in a tone of such profound earnestness and sorrow that Aliena shuddered at the vague emotion produced.

Her voice trembled as she replied, " Dr. Leigh, you are nearer being cruel to me than I thought you could be. It makes me shudder to hear you talk that way. I feel as though haunted by ghostly phantoms now."

" God forbid that you should ever be cognizant of a death like that," he said with profound sadness. " But forgive me if I am selfish, and cruel to you. It is the last thing I intended."

" I should rather ask you to forgive me for saying

what I did. I know you do not want to be cruel to me. But—but—" she said with a quiver about her mouth and a pathetic tremor in her voice, and the big tears escaped from under the long lashes and rolled over her white cheeks.

Dr. Leigh, instantly forgetting his own pain in Aliena's, said with infinite tenderness, "If I have caused that feeling I shall never forgive myself. As God knows my heart my desire is for your happiness beyond everything in this world."

Aliena knew now to what death Dr. Leigh referred. His voice and manner left little room for doubt. The profoundest depths of her heart were stirred by the pain she felt his great heart was enduring, and her own feeling was too deep for utterance.

The sun was setting big and red in the hazy air. The full moon coming up shed a subdued light that mingled with the twilight. Hugi hearing hounds baying upon the mountain sped off to join in their pursuit of the deer.

It seemed to Aliena that an interminable time had intervened since Dr. Leigh had spoken. Interminable in the pain and remorse with which she was tortured at thought of the sorrow she had unconsciously caused. So poor a return for all his goodness to her. Apologetically she wished to fall at his feet, to bathe them with her tears, to implore his forgiveness, to tell him of her plighted troth. To Dr. Leigh the time seemed not less interminable, measured by pain, since he felt assured that hope was gone.

He first broke the silence. "Will you remember," he said, "that no time or circumstances can make me regard your happiness less. And will you promise me that if you should ever need a friend you will allow me the privilege of acting as one?"

"It does not need that I should promise you that. Nothing could shake my trust in you," said Aliena earnestly.

“ But promise me, nevertheless,” he said.

“ I do trust you, and always shall, and should I ever need a friend I will gladly call upon you,” said Aliena with a quivering voice, raising her sorrowful, trustful eyes to his.

Dr. Leigh driving in the still moonlight from the height, real and figurative, to which hope had lured him, endeavored to stifle the anguish he felt. An anguish that even the calmest philosopher has found it hard to endure. The dreariness of life oppressed him. He thought of the Point of Rocks where the slightest volition could have made it easy to plunge into futurity. “ It is the part of manhood to live,” he thought, “ to act. I must wrap my mantle about the rankling wound, and go on enduring. Some bane follows my existence. I have not the power to kindle love. I have borne the pain of disappointment before. I must bear it again. Though I never loved as I do now. That was a passionate first love it is true, but my judgment, the inmost depths of my being cry out for the love, the tenderness and sympathy which I might find here. But I must find refuge in duty. Duty? it is crying for bread and getting a stone. Yet I shall try to live upon it.”

And he drove back to his hospital and to duty going attentively through each ward, seeing that each patient’s wants were cared for, with even more of the feeling of brotherhood to humanity than ever, before abandoning himself to a night of sleepless agony.

CHAPTER XVIII.

> "Long as you're false and he believes you,
> Long as you trust and he deceives you,
> So long the blissful bond endures."

And still the wearisome firing went on in Vicksburg, day after day and night after night. Lulling perhaps, comparatively, for hours during the day, but kept up steadily at night, and especially during those early hours of the morning, from two or three to five, hours of watchfulness, apprehension and duty, the most tiresome and exhausting.

Hope, which from day to day had buoyed the hearts of the besieged, grew fainter and fainter. The lack of proper food was telling, not only upon the body, but in dispiriting effect upon the mind of even the boldest. Though they suffered with fortitude, and even pretended to make light of their privations.

"Good-morning, Colonel," said Colonel Sturdyvant, meeting Colonel Harvey one evening. "You are getting as lean and hungry looking as a greyhound. Can't you come around and take breakfast with us in the morning? We are to have some fresh steak. You look like a few pounds' might not come amiss."

"I am beginning to be a little wolfish," Colonel Harvey responded. "I shall be on hand unless a shot or shell has done for me. At what hour do you breakfast?"

"At nine, guns permitting. I shall tell our cook to put your name in the pot, so be sure to come."

Accordingly, the next morning, Colonel Harvey was punctual to time at Colonel Sturdyvant's quarters. They were decidedly more comfortable than the sort of wigwam of brush, of which Colonel Harvey boasted. The former, with his brother officers, having taken possession of a luxurious home, vacated by a citizen, near their fort. Major Baron, who was one of the mess, was present. His handsome face and vigorous form were in apparently good condition in spite of privation, he looked little like he was on short rations.

When breakfast was announced, Colonel Sturdyvant led the way to the breakfast-room, doing the honors. Here a table with plates for twelve was set out in something of home style, if a meal under the supervision of men can ever be said to be in home style. Upon one end of the table was a smutty-looking tin coffee-pot, containing so-called coffee. A concoction from a compound of coffee, in infinitesimal proportion, and parched meal, to be sweetened with burnt sugar, to carry out a supposed illusion as to that fragrant berry. The coffee, even in the small proportion expected, fell short, from the nimble, flagitious fingers of the negro cook, who, not liking his mixed, with prudent fore-thought retained what he wished for his own purposes, before making it for the mess. Two plates in the center of the table were piled with biscuits, having a curious gray tinge, caused by the flour being mixed with meal made from beans. Two other plates contained what is familiarly known as corn dodgers; a bread made of meal mixed with water, formed into small pones and baked slowly, a process by which they became so hard as to make them a dangerous missile, to which fact they are possibly indebted for their name.

At the end of the table, opposite to where the coffee-pot stood, was placed a scanty dish of fried bacon and another of tempting looking steak, so Colonel Harvey thought, at least.

Colonel Sturdyvant took his place at the head of the table, and proceeded to help from the dishes of meat before him. Colonel Harvey as a guest was of course first attended to.

"Colonel, will you have some bacon or some of the steak?" he asked.

"I will take some steak, thank you. I have been on bacon until nature rebels," said Colonel Harvey with a freedom warranted by the times.

7

"The *rebel's* nature is getting starved out of me pretty rapidly," said Captain Berry facetiously, a dapper looking young officer who was also one of the mess.

"I have a notion to punish you for that villainous pun, by not letting you have any of the steak," said Colonel Sturdyvant.

A remark which was followed by more laughter, as Colonel Harvey thought, than it seemed to warrant. He noticed, also, that singularly the officers appeared to prefer bacon to the steak, though that was of a very inferior quality and small in quantity; yet one or two who had taken steak ate gingerly of it; even Colonel Sturdyvant, who had advanced boldly to the attack, had stopped with one mouthful.

"You must be more accustomed to fresh meat than we are up at our end of the line, you don't seem to appreciate steak," said Colonel Harvey.

There was an exchange of glances and a repressed tendency to smile, which Colonel Harvey noticed, and he added, "It is true our beef is not very tender just now, but we cannot expect Texas cattle to keep as fat upon the scorched Bermuda grass that is left upon these hills as upon Texas grass which reaches to their bellies. They are not sensible enough to accommodate themselves to circumstances, and refuse corn. But to one who has been as long as I have on half rations of rusty bacon and bean bread, this is not so bad."

This was more than some, who were in the secret, could stand, and laying down their knives and forks, they burst into a chorus of laughter, in spite of Colonel Sturdyvant's signs to the contrary, who said, trying to keep his countenance, "I am glad you like the steak so well, Colonel."

Colonel Harvey put down his fork, with the *morceau* which he had been in the act of transporting to his mouth still on it. He looked quizzed and dubious for the moment, for rumors of mule steak had circulated

through camp, though he had not imagined it sufficiently
in vogue to be introduced in such high quarters as yet.

"Is this mule?" he asked dubiously, stroking his
beard, and looking a little aghast.

Such a hilarious peal of laughter followed this question, that it did not need Captain Berry's reply as he
sang out in a quizzical tone above the noise, "Here's
your mule," to inform him of the fact.

Recovering from his first feeling of repugnance and
not to be outdone, Colonel Harvey said:

"It is better than rusty bacon any way, and I will
pledge myself to eat mule steak for the balance of my
days rather than surrender Vicksburg," and he put the
morsel in his mouth and applied his fine teeth vigorously
to its mastication, amidst a round of applause.

"It is only an idea after all," said Colonel Sturdyvant.
"It is not as bad as the bean bread." Encouraged by
this several of the officers tried the steak, but all soon
broke down in the patriotic effort.

Major Baron had not brought himself to mule steak
yet, or in fact to partaking largely of anything else
upon the table, Colonel Harvey wondered under the
circumstances that he looked so fresh and in such good
condition. Commenting upon this fact, Captain Berry
responded for Major Baron:

"Aha! you let Baron alone for that sort of thing.
Don't believe he is living on as short commons as he
lets on. You may rest assured he has some 'underground' arrangement."

"What is the use of a man's being good looking if he
can't make it pay?" said Major Baron smiling, self-
complacently and twirling his mustache.

"You are a lucky dog. You always manage to get
ahead of the rest of us, particularly if there is a woman
in the case," said Colonel Sturdyvant.

"Did I say I got any advantage?" said Major Baron
with the same air.

"The conceited puppy," thought Captain Berry,

whose mind reverted jealously to Lilian Selwyn. "It would be a good thing if some shot or shell spoiled his good looks, and took the conceit out of him."

The firing having increased, the meal was cut short and the party separated for duty.

There was a lull in the bombardment about the middle of the day, and Major Baron, looking exceedingly trim as well as very handsome in his closely fitting uniform, buttoned over his fine form, mounted his horse and rode off. His horse even was looking more spirited and in better condition than was usual at this time. Owing possibly to tact in foraging in the servant who tended him, as well as in the master. The horse apparently divined his destination as he stopped, seemingly of his own accord, in front of a cottage of irregular design, with gables running up here and there, and little galleries jutting out on all sides, over-run with vines and surrounded by flowers. As the servant who answered the bell ushered Major Baron in, he glanced complacently at himself in the mirror of the rack as he placed his hat there, and walked on into the dimly lighted luxurious parlor.

Lilian Selwyn must have been expecting him, as she was risking something in being at home instead of in their cave, as she usually was. Besides, she was in a fresh and charmingly becoming toilet. She wore a sheer white muslin dress, sprinkled apparently with her favorite blue convolvulus, so perfectly were the flowers painted upon the organdie. Her golden curls were tied loosely back with pale blue ribbon, that corresponded in color with the flowers of her dress. In her bosom were two or three creamy fragrant tea-rose buds. Taking her hand in salutation Major Baron seemed in no hurry to release it, as they seated themselves upon one of the little damask cushioned sofas.

Gazing at Lilian's face and person with rather an audacious look of fixed admiration, Major Baron said, "You are looking as fresh and lovely this morning as the morning glories with which you are sprinkled. Burrowing under ground would seem to be your normal condition."

"Maybe I don't burrow, as you call it, so much as you would think. I am getting quite brave under fire now. I am not nearly such a coward as I was the night we ran away in such a fright from the party. Though mamma and papa think it dreadful that I will expose myself to danger as I do. But you mustn't keep telling me that I am lovely, and all that sort of thing, or you will make me believe you think it, after awhile," said Lilian, looking coquettishly into Major Baron's face and casting her eyes down with prettily assumed coyness.

"You know already that you are beautiful. It is not necessary for me to tell you that fact. If you don't believe me, just make a looking-glass of my eyes and see for yourself," he said, moving nearer to her, and proffering his eyes as a mirror. Lilian, with a pretty, coquettish air, leaned forward and smilingly gazed into his blue eyes.

"If that is not a beautiful picture it is the fault of the mirror," he continued, possessing himself again of the soft, white hand. But Lilian, repulsing him, rose and seated herself in a chair at a little distance from him.

"Come back here," said Major Baron, half pleadingly and half commandingly, retaining his half lolling position.

"I shan't," she said, glancing up coquettishly, and taking a rose from the vase on the table by her side, she pulled it to pieces, leaf by leaf.

"If you will come back, I will promise to be very good and not to love you a bit, if I can help it, and to think you ugly, if I possibly can."

She raised her eyes, glancing reproachfully at him, and dropped them again, and still pulling the rose to pieces, made no reply. Major Baron, now rising, approached, and bending over her said, in his tenderest, most supplicating tone, "Come back, Lilian."

"I won't," she said, with another coquettish glance.

But taking her hand with gentle force, he drew her, not unwillingly, back to her seat by his side.

"Don't," she said, shying off for some reason.

"Oh! I thought you said Cecil," he responded, smiling. And moving away a little, he continued, "Now, don't you see how good I am." And he went on to tell her of the breakfast of that morning, and of the practical joke perpetrated upon Col. Harvey.

"I am sure after such a breakfast, you must need a lunch," said Lilian, rising.

"Not if it is to deprive me of your company," said Major Baron, taking her hand and gently restraining her.

"I am coming right back," she said, seemingly not displeased.

She did return in a few moments; and almost simultaneously the servant announced the lunch. It was temptingly set out, and simple as it was, it comprised luxuries unknown in camp.

Lilian poured out the fragrant, steaming mocha herself, and Major Baron did ample justice to the viands set before him. And notwithstanding the sound now and then of a shot or shell, sometimes alarmingly near. Lilian devoted herself to ministering to his wants with wonderfully improved nerve. They had returned to the parlor and resumed their seats, when the door-bell again rang, and Captain Berry, twirling his mustache, was ushered into the room. Rising to meet him, Lilian did not return to her seat by Major Baron, but gauging the distance, seated herself about equally distant from each. Revolving in her mind that, while Major Baron was much the handsomer, more charming and elegant of the two, and in a pecuniary sense, being the only son of a wealthy Louisiana planter, decidedly the better match; but that Captain Berry was in earnest, while she was by no means so sure of the other.

Major Baron, concluding that his chances for entertainment were lessened, Lilian being much more piquant *tête-à-tête* than she was likely to be now, soon retired.

Her conversational talent did not equal her personal charms, as may have been discovered.

Captain Berry took a long drawn breath of relief as the door closed on Major Baron, and rising took the seat vacated by him, saying in quite a matter-of-course way as he twirled his moustache:

"Now, Lily, tell me what that conceited fellow has been talking about. Has he been making love to you?"

"Charlie, you are so jealous. You are always imagining that men are making love to me."

"How can a man help being jealous, Lily, when he hears that you are running the risk of getting shot, strolling with Major Baron at Castle Hill while a bombardment was going on."

"At Castle Hill, Charlie?" exclaimed Lilian with well feigned astonishment. "Who could have told you such a thing?"

"It does not matter who told me, if it is true?"

Catching at the "if." in this remark, Lilian said. "I am not going to deny it. If you think no more of my constancy than to believe everything you hear, and are going to torment me about every idle report we might as well quit."

Lilian understood well how to hold her vantage ground. Captain Berry, thoroughly alarmed at this threat, was willing now to compromise upon almost any terms.

"Well, Lily, tell me that you love me a little, and I will promise to try never to doubt you again."

"Try? I don't have to try not to doubt you. I am tempted to tell you I don't love you a bit."

"Let's make friends, Lily," said Charlie humbly. "You know I am the biggest fool extant about you; and it is because I think you the prettiest and sweetest thing in the world that I can't help getting jealous sometimes. Everybody in camp thinks that Major

Baron is a fortune hunter any way," added Captain Berry maliciously.

Lilian being herself dubious as to Major Baron, thought it best to make up with Captain Berry. And assuming an aggrieved air, he had to sue humbly for pardon before he was taken into favor again, when he relapsed more desperately than ever.

Major Baron had had large experience in love affairs. His generally overlapped in such quick succession, that according to homœopathic principle, like curing like, his happiness was scarcely likely to be seriously jeopardized by any one of them. Yet his heart did revert to Aliena truly in a certain sense, despite the defections already hinted. A man does not expect to be held by the rules he would consider binding upon the woman he loves. Major Baron would have laughed to scorn the idea of rejecting so-called loving advances; or of neglecting honeyed opportunities. He was sufficiently posted in feminine character not to be seriously duped by Lilian; he did not think it likely that he was the only recipient of favor. Perhaps the same little bird, plumed by masculine self-complacency, that not infrequently whispers stories, the knowledge of which might be surprising to at least one of the parties interested, had been whispering to him. Yet he found it pleasant to be with Lilian, who had, as we have seen, more ways than one of making herself agreeable at this time.

Major Baron was getting tired of war. Though not lacking in physical courage he was wanting in that persistence in purpose, and power of endurance necessary to make a true soldier. In fact, by inheritance, by nature, and by practice he was a Sybarite; preferring compromise to self-sacrifice, his own ease to rigid principle.

Riding from Lilian's fascinating presence as he passed the castle, he thought, with some longing of the time, when, as master of that beautiful home, he might sit at ease and allow Aliena the happiness, as he believed she would consider it, of ministering to him. In all his thoughts of life, and especially of married life, which he usually dated in his mind at some rather remote period, when life should have lost something of its piquancy, it was of what he was to be the recipient, and not of how he might make life charming to others upon which his mind dwelt.

Accustomed to being loved, he was somewhat satiated by the ordinary routine of passion. But there was a rare and delicate charm about Aliena. She was unlike the women he had met. There was the freshness of unexhaled dew about her, the transparent purity and trustfulness of a child; and, beyond this, he felt that she had profoundly a woman's heart, its instinctive delicacy, its trustfulness and its depth of feeling.

There was something, however, in these characteristics, charming as they were, that made him instinctively draw back at times with the feeling, that being himself of the earth, earthy, he could never satisfy the ideal longings of her soul. Yet there was to him in Aliena's untried capacity for feeling, in her refined ideality, and in the intensity of her nature a fascinating piquancy.

Let us not say that her wealth and elegant surroundings had influenced him, though doubtless he dwelt with satisfaction upon them, as well as upon her aristocratic descent, if such a term be allowable in a democratic country; though even here an aristocracy of intellect, culture, and merit may be admissible. If he ever intended to marry, and the indefinite duration of the war made that necessarily seem a thing of the future, certainly no more charming and lovely bride could be found. Living, as he did, in the present, it was sweet to be loved.

To be loved—that was the idea. Whether he knew anything of love, in the true highest sense of that word, is another question. According to his own standard he had scarcely known a time when he was not loving some pretty woman, more or less, and now he was loving more, he thought. And this was the love Aliena was getting.

Neither Lilian Selwyn nor Major Baron must be taken as types of the men and women to be found in this devoted city at that time.

If Lilian absorbed in the honey-tongued tributes of her sybarite lovers, found no time for other less agreeable offices, there were women oblivious to danger and to self, who did. Like good angels, they ministered to those exhausted by unceasing duty in sultry trenches, under a burning sun; comforted those who, wounded by shot or shell, were falling all around them, and being carried off to hospitals; and hovered around the hard pallets of the sick, the wounded and the dying. These women, facing danger and famine, unmurmuringly, bore comforts to the suffering, of which they deprived themselves; and endeavored by words of sympathy to strengthen the living for life, and to make the valley less dark to those who, shivering on the brink, went down into that cold stream across which they might hope to find "rest upon the other side of the river."

CHAPTER XIX.

> "With gentle voice
> Close at mine ear one called me forth to walk.
> I rose as at thy call but found thee not;
> To find thee I directed then my walk;
> And on methought, alone, I passed through ways
> That brought me on a sudden to the tree
> Of interdicted knowledge."
>
> Milton : Paradise Lost.

"I have finished looking over pa's papers," said Mrs. Skinker to her mother, laying a paper from her hand upon a pile on the table by which she sat, "and from all I can see to the contrary, there is nothing but starvation ahead of us."

Her mother made no reply, but commenced moving her body back and forth, uttering a sort of piteous moan.

"Ma, for the Lord's sake stop that whimpering and listen to me," said Mrs. Skinker in a hard incisive tone. "It is narrowed down to this—we must do something for a living, or we will soon not have even our clothes left to cover our bodies; for they will be taken for our board."

"What can I do, Eliza?" asked the tremulous old woman in a helpless tone.

"You have got to do something, that is a well established fact. Do you know I've told you often enough, that Dr. Leigh is going up that mountain every few days? It is no use trying to blind ourselves with the idea that he is visiting Mrs. Graeme. She is up and going about. Joe, our new waiter, who was hired at the Mountain House, says that Dr. Leigh went walking or driving with Miss Graeme nearly every time he went up there, and that he could not keep his eyes off of her. So you see the only chance is to bring about a rupture between them."

"Eliza, don't try to make me a worse woman than I am," said Mrs. Bledsoe, in a subdued tone, casting her eye at the obstructing ceiling, and letting it fall meekly upon her hands.

"Worse than you are? You are precious good all of a sudden. It is late in the day for that sort of thing. You goaded pa on for mammon all the days of his life, until he went down to his grave in despair. And what have we got now?"

Mrs. Bledsoe started up, twitching and trembling all over, put out her arms to balance herself, and tottered to her feet. Her distended fingers were working aimlessly in the air, her eyes rolling wildly.

"What have I done? Don't try those tricks on me

because I want you to do something to keep our souls in our bodies. Existence is all I am indebted to you for. You owe me something for inflicting that upon me. I tell you now you need never expect love from me. You have made my life a misery, and whatever I may do for you is solely because I can't help it. You need not try to drive me to perdition as you did pa."

Mrs. Bledsoe, more and more frantic, was tottering to and fro in the room as her daughter snapped out at emphatic intervals these cruel words.

Gathering strength, she now moved wildly from the room—her pale steel-blue eye rolling frantically, her teeth clicking and chattering in her head—as, with distended twitching fingers, she moved on through the hall to her room. A lady, whose room she passed, seeing the frantic old woman rushing thus wildly along, put her baby from her arms, and, in kindness, followed her to her room, where she was moving like a caged lioness to and fro in the same wild, strange way.

Approaching Mrs. Bledsoe timidly she said with an anxious look of sympathy, "What is the matter? Has anything happened? Can I do anything for you?" but Mrs. Bledsoe making no reply continued her frantic movements.

Awe-struck at the appearance of the white haired old woman, but full of sympathy, the would-be benefactress ventured nearer, asking again, "Can't I do something for you, Mrs. Bledsoe?" Without stopping the frantic old woman put out her hand with the open palm against the breast of the other and hurled her with unnatural strength against the wall.

Stunned and terrified, glancing back to see that she was not pursued by the maniacal old woman she fled to Mrs. Skinker's room, where she sank almost breathless into a chair, gasping out, "Your mother—go to her."

"Don't worry yourself about ma, there's nothing the matter with her but temper," said Mrs. Skinker, calmly, but, rising she went to her mother's room.

Here, finding that her mother had locked the door, Mrs. Skinker put her mouth to the key-hole and hissed through it, "Open this door, ma. Do you hear me? Open this door." Mrs. Bledsoe made no reply and her daughter could hear her still moving frantically back and forth.

Rattling the door Mrs. Skinker placed her mouth again at the key-hole and hissed, "Open this door I tell you."

"I am going to throw myself out of the window," said the frenzied old woman.

"No you wont. Open this door," again hissed the daughter in a hard, imperious tone, and after a time the click of the lock was heard, and Mrs. Skinker entered the room and shut the door behind her.

Whatever transpired there must have had a calming effect upon the old woman, as she appeared at the tea-table that night with more than her usual look of resigned piety.

Mrs. Skinker had learned that her mother was more pliable after these attacks. The following day at dinner she said to Dr. Leigh with an unusually affable smile, showing the incisors, "Doctor, have you any messages for your friends on the mountain? I thought a drive would do ma good, and we may see Mrs. Graeme and her daughter."

"The drive will benefit her no doubt. I have some letters for them. I will be glad if you will be kind enough to hand them to Mrs. Graeme," he replied.

"Certainly," said Mrs. Skinker with great affability, receiving the letters, handling them with evident satisfaction.

"Will you be good enough to see ma to the carriage, Doctor? We are going immediately after dinner," said Mrs. Skinker. Dr. Leigh accordingly assisted them with Arista into the carriage, and they drove off.

"Dr. Leigh did not mention that there was a letter for Miss Graeme," said Mrs. Skinker, squeezing and eying the letters with great interest. "Hers is in a gentleman's handwriting, but I think it is an old man's. Possibly it may be from Vicksburg, run out 'underground' and remailed, but that is scarcely probable now. Mrs. Graeme is from Athens, Georgia, it looks like a business letter. It is a hotel envelope. I don't think there is much of anything in it.

"Ma, won't you let me see them?" said Arista, imagining there must be some unknown charm about the letters.

"You just dare to say letter on the mountain and you'll never want to say letter again while you live," said Mrs. Skinker letting off a shower of snaps from her eyes.

Arriving at the quiet hotel upon the mountain, they sought Mrs. Graeme's room, where, upon the gallery of a retired wing of the house, they found her and Aliena seated. Rising as the visitors approached, surprised at seeing these recently bereaved ladies, Mrs. Graeme advanced, and proffering her hand said cordially, "How do you do Mrs. Bledsoe? I am glad to see you."

"My dear, I am so glad to find you up. I was afraid from Dr. Leigh's continued visits that you were still ill, and I made the effort to come and see you. I know that my dear husband would have wished me to do so," said Mrs. Bledsoe with an incipient show of grief, but catching her daughter's eye she seemed to recover herself, and pressing Aliena's hand she took the chair proffered by her, continuing, "Thank you my dear. Bring your chair close here and sit by me. I am so glad to see you looking so well. Either the mountain air or something else has almost brought the roses to your cheeks."

Aliena seating herself as requested, Mrs. Bledsoe took her hand in both of hers stroking it with velvety feline caress.

But as the conversation progressed Mrs. Skinker evidently grew restless and impatient, and she soon said, "Mrs. Graeme do you think you have regained your strength enough to go to the Point of Rocks? I am anxious for ma to visit it, she has never seen the view from there, and we had proposed after seeing you to go there this afternoon."

"I doubt whether I have sufficient strength yet, to venture upon so long a walk," said Mrs. Graeme.

"We can drive to within a short distance of the Point and the walk will be nothing then," persisted Mrs. Skinker.

"If your mother is willing to undertake it I suppose I might," Mrs. Graeme responded reluctantly.

The party accordingly entered the carriage and, driving as near as possible to the Point, they got out to walk the remainder of the distance.

"Take my arm Mrs. Graeme and I will assist you, ma can come on with Miss Graeme. Run on ahead Arista," said Mrs. Skinker, and they started off to walk.

Mrs. Bledsoe followed slowly, leaning heavily upon Aliena's arm. Aliena sighed unconsciously, possibly at the painful remembrance of the visit she had last paid to the Point of Rocks, and Mrs. Bledsoe said, "What are you sighing about, my dear? It is bad enough for old, sorrow-stricken women like myself to be sighing."

"Don't you suppose that young people have sorrows as well as old ones?" said Aliena sadly. But penitent the next moment for obtruding her troubles upon the afflicted old woman she added, "It seems selfish, however, for me to be thinking of any unhappiness I may have when you are good enough, with your great sorrow, to be thinking of others."

This reply diverted Mrs. Bledsoe from the purpose of her visit for the moment; but since the outburst of the day before, her will was more than usually subservient to that of her daughter. The thought of facing Mrs. Skinker in case of failure strengthened the mother's resolution to go on, and she said in her most maternal manner, "I have thought of you frequently lately, my dear, and I have been feeling that I owed it to you to tell you something; painful as it is to me to do so."

Aliena's heart bounded with a sudden pain. Her constant state of anxiety and incertitude kept her intensely alive to any undefined. unpleasant communication. Impressed with Mrs. Bledsoe's manner she awaited, in intense apprehension to hear what it should be.

"Dr. Leigh has been coming here frequently to see you since you have been on the mountain. Has he not, my dear?" Mrs. Bledsoe asked.

"Yes, he has been a good many times to see mother," Aliena replied hesitating, trembling with fear. Her hands growing cold and her eyes dilating, as this question gave her a possible clew to the topic Mrs. Bledsoe wished to discuss.

"To see *you*, my dear? Excuse me, this is not mere idle curiosity."

Aliena could not but think, now that her attention was called to the fact, that for sometime Dr. Leigh's visits could not have been altogether to her mother. The memory too of his last visit, with the conversation at the spot they were approaching, flashed sorrowfully upon her mind. This thought pictured itself so plainly upon her face that it needed nothing more to convince Mrs. Bledsoe that her daughter's fears were not without foundation.

"He probably intended his visits for me, as well as for mother." Aliena replied, adding apologetically, "Mother's sickness seemed to throw us upon his protection and care."

"Those relations sometimes prove dangerous, my dear, between charming young ladies, and agreeable gentlemen," said Mrs. Bledsoe, watching Aliena's expressive face.

The thought that this might have proved too true, brought the tell-tale tide to Aliena's face under Mrs. Bledsoe's gaze.

"I don't want to ask you any questions. my dear," the old woman continued with assumed delicacy, having discovered all she wished to know. Dropping

Aliena's arm she halted, and taking her hand in hers, stroked it caressingly, while seemingly the claws through the velvety exterior were digging into Aliena's quivering nerves, the old woman continued. " Dr. Leigh has been our physician here, he is a talented man, and my husband had him in attendance. He did all he could for my husband, I have no doubt, and we feel under obligations to him." Mrs. Bledsoe almost broke down at this review of Dr. Leigh's kindness, though she had not stated that all this was done without other compensation than the sense of gratification in the alleviation of suffering, But strengthened by the thought of her daughter's indignation in case of failure, and of the stake for which she was playing, she continued, " I thought that these facts being known to you, my dear, might have had some influence in forming your opinion of Dr. Leigh. As a physician, this of course, does not matter; but," and she stroked the hand in a still more feline way, as she continued, "looking at Dr. Leigh in the attitude of a lover, to you, my dear, as a lover—it appears in quite a different light."

Aliena, turning white and then red, was trying to collect her thoughts so as to be truthful and at the same time non-committal ; and yet, without rudeness, to prevent Mrs. Bledsoe's making what she felt was to be some painful disclosure. But as she hesitated, the old woman continued, still stroking her hand caressingly, " I am very sorry to pain you, my dear, but I feel it my duty to tell you," and she cast her eye heavenward with one of her most resigned looks of piety, " that as a man and as a husband, Dr. Leigh is not one to whom I can stand quietly by and see you sacrificed."

" I have no idea of marrying Dr. Leigh. He has never asked me to marry him," Aliena gasped out quickly, interrupting Mrs. Bledsoe, hoping to stop further communication.

Aliena's agitation more than ever determined Mrs. Bledsoe to continue, and she went on, " I knew Dr.

Leigh before he was married—and knew his wife, poor thing! I am pained to say it, but her father forced Dr. Leigh to marry her, for very good reasons, they ought to have been married sooner. She only lived a few months after their marriage. There was a great deal of talk—there was something very mysterious about her death. I only tell you what everybody knows where he lives. I feel that I must tell you this, painful as it is, I owe it to you, my dear. I do by you as I would by my own child."

Aliena, gasping, withdrew her cold, trembling hand, shrinking instinctively from the touch of Mrs. Bledsoe, as she would have done from a viper, much as she had heretofore reverenced her supposed truthfulness and piety, and deeply as she had sympathized with her in her grief.

"My dear," said Mrs. Bledsoe in a wounded tone, "I suppose I shall get no thanks for doing what my love for you has impelled me to, but I have done it for your good."

"May God forgive him, if this be true," Aliena gasped out, bewildered between the implicit faith she had in Dr. Leigh, and the apparent impossibility that the seemingly pious, afflicted old woman beside her could, untruthfully, so murder character.

"I am sorry that you should have told me this, Mrs. Bledsoe," Aliena felt impelled to say, in a strange, unnatural voice. "Dr. Leigh has been exceedingly kind to mother and myself. I have been very grateful to him." Thinking this sounded like desertion, she added, "I *am* very grateful. He has never said he loved me. There is no possibility of our being more to each other than friends. It is painful in the extreme to me to have my faith shaken. Friendship cannot exist without trust. He and I are soon to separate—it would have been a great happiness to have parted without a shadow upon our friendship."

"My affection is always making me do something

that I ought not to do," Mrs. Bledsoe whimpered out, in a tone of wounded feeling.

"I thank you for your kind intentions. Excuse me if I have said anything I ought not," said Aliena coldly, in the same unnatural tone of voice.

"You must have walked slowly, we have been here some time," said Mrs. Graeme, as Mrs. Bledsoe and Aliena slowly approached, both looking painfully depressed.

"I suppose we did," said Aliena, in a weary, preoccupied way. And regardless of forms, she walked on to where she had sat when last here, seating herself with her back to the rest of the party.

This was the first time she had ventured here since the evening she had spent with Dr. Leigh. She felt now as though she could scarcely restrain herself from groaning aloud. Dr. Leigh's words came to her mind with renewed force and pain. "There are visible and invisible deaths. We unconsciously kneel beside these invisible death-beds." What if she were kneeling beside one now? some evil spirit whispered. Here, in a spot sacred to friendship, where all nature was so beautiful, where she had given her pledge of trust. Other words of Dr. Leigh came back painfully now, too, with startling and perverted meaning, to her memory. "Pray to God that they may rest tranquilly in their graves, and not start to life—phantoms, paralyzing energy." And as if an emanation from the evil one, warping and distorting their meaning, she thought, "My God! could he have meant the ghost of a wronged and murdered wife?"

Mrs. Skinker had to call a second time before Aliena became conscious of the summons; so profoundly was she absorbed in thought. "Miss Graeme, I am sorry to cut short your enjoyment," she said, with a satisfactory smile, disclosing the incisors as she caught the expression of the white, fixed face that was turned toward her, continuing, "You seem so absorbed in the view that it is a pity to tear you away, but we must be going."

Aliena rose mechanically, oblivious to everything around her, and they walked back to the carriage. Mrs. Skinker accompanied her, now doing all the talking.

Aliena could scarcely bring herself to submit to Mrs. Bledsoe's affectionate farewell and pantomimic benediction at parting.

When she and her mother sat once more alone in the twilight upon the gallery, there was a prolonged silence. Aliena said at length with a sigh,

"Mother, do you think Mrs. Bledsoe is a good woman?"

"Certainly I do, daughter. Why do you ask?"

"I always thought so, but this evening I felt a sort of natural repulsion to her."

"You ought not to give up to such feelings, my child. She seems to be an exceedingly pious, good woman."

"The wrong is possibly in myself," said Aliena, sighing wearily.

"Is there anything the matter with you, daughter? you seem out of spirits," said Mrs. Graeme anxiously, watching Aliena as she sat looking utterly weary and wretched.

"I don't feel well for some reason," said Aliena, rising and retiring to her room to avoid questioning.

CHAPTER XX.

"Misleads the mazed night wanderer from his way
To bogs, and mires, and oft through pond or pool
There swallowed up and lost."

SHAKESPEARE.

Mrs. Bledsoe's feelings were not of an enviable nature as she drove with her daughter and grandchild down

Lookout mountain that afternoon. Mrs. Skinker, however, was apparently in an unusually amiable frame of mind.

"Ma, did you tell Miss Graeme," Mrs. Skinker asked as soon as they started, too impatient to await the volition of her mother, who sat looking jaded and feeble with her hands folded in her lap.

"Yes," said Mrs. Bledsoe, with a groan that under ordinary circumstances would inevitably have caused an explosion of temper upon the daughter's part. But she restrained herself at present.

"What did she say? How did she take it? Did she seem worried?" asked Mrs. Skinker, eagerly.

"It is hard to say," her mother responded mournfully.

This response was too much for Mrs. Skinker, her temper could not stand everything. "Ma, for the Lord's sake stop that higgling, and tell me if you are going to. Don't let me have to use a forty-horse power to pump a little information out of you," she exclaimed angrily.

"Eliza, will you let me have a little peace until I can collect my thoughts?"

"I wish you would go on collecting them then, and try to let me hear from you this side of Christmas, if possible."

"Well, I told her. I don't know whether she believes it or not. She was dreadfully shocked; that I could see. I am almost certain Dr. Leigh has given her to understand—you know what?" said Mrs. Bledsoe, nodding her head mysteriously at Arista.

"Arista, don't you want to get out and ride with the driver? You will have a nice time out there." Mrs. Skinker condescended to say, in her anxiety, to get rid of the child so that she might hear undisturbed what her mother had to communicate.

"No, I don't want to go with the driver, I want to hear what you and grandma are talking about," said

Arista, moved by curiosity as well as a spirit of contrariness.

"You are going whether you want to or not," said Mrs. Skinker, her eyes snapping violently.

"I know what you want me to go out there for. You want to talk about Dr. Leigh and Miss Graeme, and you don't want me to hear. I am going to tell him that you and grandma were telling Miss Graeme something about him."

"You just tell him that and I'll whip you within an inch of your life," said her mother, with a perfect storm of snaps, continuing—"Driver, stop a minute and take Arista out with you. She wants to be where she can see."

The carriage was stopped, and Mrs. Skinker taking hold of the child's arm helped her to the driver's seat; leaving the impress of the five amiable fingers upon the flesh. But Arista made no outcry. She said nothing until the sound of the wheels covered her voice.

"Ma told a lie," she said then to the driver. "I didn't want to get out here at all. I wanted to hear what they were telling about Miss Graeme and Dr. Leigh."

"Aint you afeered to talk that way, Miss? To call your mar a liar? The devil always gits little gals what calls thar mas liars," said the negro driver.

"No I'm not ashamed. I want the devil to get me."

"Laws a marcy! Miss. I neber heern a white chile talk like that. You aint never seen the devil I 'low, or you wouldn't say that, and you wouldn't never want to see him no more neither, I know."

"You never saw him either?" the child said interrogatively—diverted from her angry train of thought by the negro's words and manner.

"Yes. Miss, I 'low I is, and I don't neber want to make his quaintance no more, not as long as I live."

"Where did you see him? What did he look like?" asked Arista, eagerly.

"It was before I come here. It was down in the low country. I was gwine along one night with a fine fat pig, in a sack. It was jest a roastin size. I'm powerful fond of roast pig, and I was thinkin until my mouf was farly waterin how I was gwine to eat pig and hot ash cake that night. I was monsus grub struck, and it was as dark as pitch, and I was jest a puttin ground behind me. It was nigh on to midnight when I come outen the path in the woods and struck into the big road and was makin a bee line for home. Just then I heerd a orful rumblin and a roarin, and I stopped a minnit to listen. And I did n't hear nothin more, but thinks I to myself this here nigger had better git up and git. And I struck inter a kind of dog trot. Bout that time I heerd the roarin agin, a comin towards me like, and I turned around to look. Thar come a light just then, and what should I see but the devil hisself—my har farly stood on eend when the light shined his eyes. They was as big as good sized saucers—just a blazin with light. And I seen his horns a standin out, and his tail a switchin round. He was as high as a middlin sized sapplin. Just then I heerd him roar agin, and I seen him slash his tail around, and make fur this nigger, but perhaps he did n't git up and git. I dropped that sack, pig and all, and you oughterer seen me put ground behind me. I made tracks for sartin. It began to rain before I got home, and you'd a thought I was a young lime kiln to a seen me a steamin when I got into the cabin. I ain't never been through that bottom after dark sence. And it 'pears like to me that I ain't hankered as much for pig."

"Did he say anything to you?" asked Arista, deeply interested.

"I never stopped to hear nothin, but for nigh on to a mile thar was a powerful smell of sulfire and brimstone."

"Well, what did Dr. Leigh give her to understand?" asked Mrs. Skinker eargerly, after ridding herself of the child.

"I think from what she said, and I don't believe she would tell a story—"   •

"I declare to goodness you are equal to 'cousin Sally Dillard,'" Mrs. Skinker snapped out, interrupting Mrs. Bledsoe in spite of herself. "Can't you tell what it was Dr. Leigh gave her to understand without all that stuff about her not telling a story? I believe she would tell a lie as soon as anybody else if it suited her. I don't see why you imagine she is any better than the rest of the world. And according to my experience they'll all do it, if it suits their purpose better than the truth. Have you found out yet what it is that you were going to tell?"

"Eliza, I am not going to tell you at all if I can't tell it my own way," said Mrs. Bledsoe, folding her hands resignedly, venturing on a faint show of silent prayer.

Mrs. Skinker, in her anxiety to hear, was at too great a disadvantage not to subside at this threat. She bit her lips, breathing in a labored apoplectic way as her mother sat tantalizingly silent.

"I told her the story," Mrs. Bledsoe said at length; "she tried very hard to stop me, but I saw in her face, and knew from what she said, that there was something between them, and I determined not to be stopped."

"Do you think they are engaged?" asked Mrs. Skinker, still breathing heavily. "She listened to me, evidently aghast, and when I had finished she looked as white as a sheet. She said then that he had never told her he loved her, and that they could never be more to each other than friends. I suppose she meant after what I had told her. And that she was very sorry I had told her anything. That it was extremely painful to have to give up a friendship. From that I know she intends to give him up."

"Do you suppose it possible for her to tell him," asked Mrs. Skinker, her spirits evidently improved by the last part of the report.

"You know, Eliza, you made the story as you did because

you thought she could not tell him, so it is your fault if she does. You know a great many did say his wife died with a broken heart on account of being made to marry him," said Mrs. Bledsoe as though to excuse herself to her own conscience. As they drove up to the hotel Dr. Leigh, who was about entering on his way to tea, seeing them, approached the carriage to assist them out.

" I had such a nice time," said Arista as he lifted her from her elevated perch. "Joe told me about his seeing the devil, and what he looked like. Ma did n't spite me a bit by putting me out there so she and grandma could talk about "—Arista stopped suddenly, as she caught the look her mother darted at her, which might have suggested his Satanic majesty himself.   .

Mrs Bledsoe came to the rescue by saying to Dr. Leigh in her most motherly manner, " My dear, allow me the support of your arm ? I am feeling feeble. The trip was almost too much for me to undertake," and taking his arm she walked into the house, and on to the supper room, leaning affectionately upon him. Mrs. Skinker had in the mean time whisked Arista off to her room. It was not likely after what transpired there that she would soon venture so boldly, in her mother's presence at least. Locking the child in her room supperless, Mrs. Skinker hastened down to the supper table.

Here, a little out of breath, she seated herself by her mother. " We had a charming drive," said Mrs. Skinker, " we found your friends astonishingly well. Mrs. Graeme is a monument of your skill. We had expected to find her in bed, as you continued your visits so frequently. But she actually walked to the Point of Rocks with us," and leaning forward she watched the effect of her words upon Dr. Leigh who was seated below her mother.

He made no reply, and Mrs. Bledsoe added, " The young lady was not looking so well, however. I think she must be pining to see her lover."

"What lover?" asked Dr. Leigh eagerly, dropping his knife and fork.

"The young officer—Oh! but I must not tell secrets. I thought of course she had told you. You and she are such good friends," the old woman said with a wicked smile, as she looked at Dr. Leigh, whose face had become suddenly deathly pale.

"Are you not well, Doctor?" Mrs. Skinker asked maliciously, her nostrils vibrating and her eyes snapping.

"Yes—no, I am not feeling well," said Dr. Leigh, pushing his chair back, with ill-concealed impatience to get away, restrained by a sense of politeness.

Mrs. Skinker kept time to the vibrating of her nostrils by snapping her food vindictively. Though it seemed to Dr. Leigh she was eating with unusual deliberateness.

The supper being finished at length, Dr. Leigh accompanied them to the foot of the stairs, and bowing, was about to leave, but Mrs. Bledsoe again asked his support upstairs. Thus compelled, he walked on with her, declining somewhat abruptly her invitation to come into her daughter's parlor.

The knowledge of Aliena's engagement was the happy inspiration of the moment to this astute old lady. But she soon argued herself almost into its belief. "What else than an engagement to another could make it impossible that she and Dr. Leigh should ever be more to each other than friends—all the men of any account are in the army; she would not, with her beauty and money, be engaged to an ordinary man, *ergo*, she is engaged, and to an officer," argued Mrs. Bledsoe. She was a keen old lady, with a fine faculty for divination. Her white hair, venerable appearance, and pious air would have made her invaluable in the mystic sisterhood of Delphi. A Pythia not needing the divine afflatus.

CHAPTER XXI.

> "Evil into the mind of God or man
> May come and go so unapprov'd and leave
> No spot or blame behind ; which gives me hope.
> Be not disheartened then, nor cloud those looks
> That wont to be more cheerful and serene."
>
> Milton : Paradise Lost.

Since the conversation with Aliena at the Point of Rocks, and the information that Mrs. Bledsoe had given him as to her engagement, Dr. Leigh had refrained from seeing her. The pain which this announcement had caused confirmed him in the determination that, in absence, lay his only hope of freedom from suffering.

Except when engaged in actual duty, he endeavored to fill up his time with unintermitting study, either of subjects scientifically connected with his profession, or which, philosophically considered, might answer as a clew out of the Labyrinth in which he found himself involved. Endeavoring to recover at least that self-control and poise which would make duty less galling, he held up before him that quaint old mirror of the mind, Burtons' "Anatomy of Melancholy." In the light of its erudite pages he tried calmly to analyze his own perturbed mind and affections with doubtful conclusions. Having become acquainted with a cultivated German, an associate surgeon, Dr. Leigh renewed his knowledge of that language. They read together often until past midnight. Schiller's more passionate writings were unfortunately selected, and, carried away as Dr. Leigh always was by the creations of this great author, he experienced the ill-effect of his passionate delineations. They served responsively to keep alive feelings, which, if he could not bring himself entirely to banish, he had hoped to hold sufficiently in abeyance to prevent that sway likely only to be disastrous in result.

In spite of his efforts to the contrary Dr. Leigh seemed to have relapsed into an even more fixed and

melancholy abstraction than when he was first called
to minister in that dreary sick-room, which had become
to him a hallowed temple of love.

Rumors from the front soon, however, assumed such
significance that he felt it incumbent upon himself to
see Mrs. Graeme and Aliena once more, that he might
comply with his promise to let them know when it
should have become necessary for them to seek safety
elsewhere.

The sore pain he experienced in thought of a final
separation from Aliena was not indicative of a sound
convalescence. But Dr. Leigh was not unaccustomed to
pain ; and his heart suggested that this was likely to be
his normal condition. He need not, therefore, shrink
from duty in consideration of this fact.

It was a warm day in June when he once more ascended the mountain. He became more hopeful as he
neared the spot, perhaps under the revivifying influence
of the scenery, and of the mountain air. But the
thought of being once more with Aliena was fraught
with such pleasure to him, despite every other circumstance or contingency, that this of itself made his heart
throb quicker with happiness.

As he reached the top of the mountain and made an
abrupt turn, commanding a beautiful view of the valley,
his attention was attracted by a quick bark of recognition, and Hugi came bounding forward into the road,
jumping from side to side in front of his horses, thus
attesting his delight at seeing him. Looking in the direction from which the dog had come, Dr. Leigh saw
Aliena standing at some distance from the road, her hat
off, the sunlight making a glory of her beautiful hair.
Aliena, at Hugi's bark, turned and recognized Dr Leigh.
She bowed to him in the distance, but he was fortunately too far away to see the color that surged to her
face and almost as quickly died out, leaving her deadly
pale.

He checked his horses, handed the reins to his servant,

and getting out started toward her. Aliena instinctively walked to meet him—a throng of emotions agitat-
ing her at being thus suddenly brought face to face
with him once more. Her obligation for kindness—
their friendship—his possible love—their last painful
interview—the dreadful story Mrs. Bledsoe had told;
all flashed upon her in quick succession; but she determined as quickly to give no sign of change, whatever might be her belief.

The delicate color tinged her whole face as she met
him. She hesitated at first to extend her hand in salutation, but scorning herself for this apparent endorse-
ment of the horrible story Mrs. Bledsoe had told, she
offered her hand.

Raising her eyes for the first time to Dr. Leigh's face
she met his sad, steadfast eyes fixed upon her; and indignant at herself for want of trust, she put her hand
confidingly in his. She relapsed into shyness, however,
as he asked her to get in and drive with him to the
hotel; but entering the carriage. she seated herself as
far as possible from him.

Dr. Leigh could not but note the change in Aliena's
manner. Attributing it to their last conversation at the
Point of Rocks, he felt embarrassed himself, and an
awkward pause ensued. Chilled by a manner so unlike
her usual confiding one, and so little like that with
which she had parted from him, he said formally,
"Miss Graeme, I came this evening in compliance
with the promise to your mother, to tell her that, in all
probability, our army is to fall back from the front.
In that case this may not be a safe place for her to remain."

Aliena, sensitive to manner and tone, as well as to
more subtile influences, could not but be impressed by
Dr. Leigh's coldness; and she replied in something of
the same tone.

"I know mother will be obliged to you for your
kindness in remembering us, and for the trouble you

have taken to come and give us this information. I am
sorry we should prove such a tax on your goodness."

Dr. Leigh, annoyed and surprised at Aliena's tone
and manner, which were even more objectionable to
him than the words themselves; and hurt if not indignant at the word "tax," replied in an equally frigid
tone. "Have I in any way, given you reason to suppose that, whatever I may have had it in my power to
do for you could be a tax? The word tax to my mind
conveys the idea of an exaction, not of a free-will offering. If I should have been so unfortunate as to have
conveyed such an impression, I have been extremely
unhappy in my manner, or in my choice of terms."

Notwithstanding the chilling way in which this was
said, Aliena's sense of the possible injustice she had been
doing Dr. Leigh made her penitent. And feeling that
she was apparently ungrateful for his kindness she said,
in a softened tone, "Pardon me, if I have seemed to
show a want of appreciation of your constant goodness
to us. It is hard always to know and to do what is
right. If I only make use of the wrong word sometimes, you will forgive me?"

Dr. Leigh not only lost all feeling of resentment, if
such it could be called; but, in the revulsion, was in
danger of going too far the other way.

"I should rather ask your forgiveness for a speech
almost rude, I fear," he said, "but pain may make one
so morbidly sensitive as to shrink unduly from even apprehended unkindness. I wish you to believe, and I
think you do, that to be able to contribute to your happiness is one of the greatest pleasures of my life. One
which requires magnanimity in me to relinquish it, as
I must do when I come to tell you that which may
make it impossible for me ever to enjoy that privilege
again."

There was a perceptible shrinking back in Aliena's
tone and manner as she replied. "I must believe that
it is a pleasure since you are so unfailing in kindness."

"Could you attribute no higher motive?" said Dr. Leigh, in a chilled tone.

"Whatever the motive, mother and I have been the gainers," Aliena replied in an assumed tone of lightness that jarred upon Dr. Leigh.

She felt a pang as soon as the words had left her lips. Glancing at him, she saw Dr. Leigh's steadfast, troubled eyes fixed upon her in astonishment and pain; not so much at the apparent want of appreciation of what he had intended to convey as at the inexplicable change in her whole manner.

Dr. Leigh made no reply, and Aliena, shrinking from the continuation of a conversation likely to result only in pain, felt a sense of relief as they drew up before the hotel. Here they joined Mrs. Graeme on the retired gallery in front of their room.

Dr. Leigh having given the information which induced his visit, Mrs. Graeme at once determined to leave Lookout as soon as possible. She arranged to stay in Chattanooga the night previous to taking the early morning cars for Athens, Georgia, in which place she had some time since resolved eventually to take refuge.

Mrs. Graeme's manner toward Dr. Leigh, always one of marked kindness and deference, was tinged with unusual warmth upon this occasion. As he left, after a very short visit, she thanked him, not only for his kindness in this instance, in coming to give her the information as to the movement of the army, but for saving her life, perhaps, and for his many acts of continued kindness to them; both during her illness, and since their stay upon the mountain.

Aliena, seating herself upon a low stool in the twilight, leaned her head wearily upon her mother's knee after Dr. Leigh had gone.

"Daughter," said Mrs. Graeme, stroking her shining hair tenderly, "it seemed to me that you were very cold and distant in your manner toward Dr. Leigh this evening. I know you must feel grateful to him for his kindness to us. at a time too when we most needed it ; and you cannot but think highly of him, but it is well to show one's feeling sometimes. We may not always be so blessed in friends."

"Do you think I seemed indifferent ? It would certainly distress me if I thought so, or if Dr. Leigh believed me ungrateful. I am beginning to think it is very hard to do right," said Aliena in a tone of profound sadness.

"I am sorry to have said anything about it, my child, if it distresses you. It seems to me that you have not been as equable and cheerful lately as when you first came on the mountain. I hope nothing troubles you ?" said Mrs. Graeme, tenderly.

"It would trouble me very much to distress you, mother," Aliena replied, looking up into her mother's face with a faint effort at a smile, continuing, with a tremor in her voice in spite of her effort to seem cheerful, as she laid her head back upon her mother's knee. "But don't scold me this evening, mother. I feel as though a little petting would do me more good than scolding."

CHAPTER XXII.

> "I live not in myself, but I become
>   Portion of that around me ; and to me
>   High mountains are a feeling."
>
> BYRON : CHILDE HAROLD.

The following afternoon Aliena went out for a farewell walk, as she was to leave Lookout mountain the next morning. Her steps turned, instinctively, toward the Point of Rocks. Here she took her accustomed seat and gazed with an oppressive feeling of sadness at the scene before her.

> "The earth outstretched immense, a prospect wide
>   And various."

Now that she was to bid farewell to it, perhaps forever, a painful sense of its loveliness came over her, as it had never done before.

Lookout had now become as it were a part of her life ; and true to life was associated in memory with both the painful and the pleasant. Looking, as we believe, for the last time upon anything, be it loved or otherwise, how wonderfully the mind tones down whatever there may be of the unsightly or harsh. How it brings out the beautiful curved lines, the softer tints in coloring, disclosing beauties perhaps unseen before. The painful in association, if not dying out, lives only in shadows that brighten sunshine ; to which memory even clings with a subdued pleasure.

Seated here memory brought in review to Aliena her first visit, set in its gloomy surroundings, those dreamy evenings spent alone with nature, the last painful interview with Dr. Leigh, and the shuddering horror of the evening with Mrs. Bledsoe. Here, too, she had lived over in memory other scenes momentous to her for happiness or woe. Here in imagination she had breathed the soft air from the Mississippi, surveyed hill and valley and "inland sea," with the mellow glories of its sunsets, had coursed with quickened blood upon Alert, had floated upon the little lake in the fragrant April air, had stood again under the swaying banksia rose, been sprinkled with its fragrant petals, listened to vows of love with a vague pain at the memory of that time. Here, too, imagination had torturingly depicted him to whom she was plighted in every condition contingent upon a starving, besieged city. With all this came now an undefined sense of remorse, of fixed pain and of woe.

With an effort, she recalled her thoughts and gave herself up to the enjoyment of her surroundings, with which she was so soon to part. The evening breeze was coming in fitful gusts, warm and luxurious, from the valley below, fragrant as with new-mown hay, alternating with currents of fresher mountain air. The floating clouds, taking on the changing hues of sunset, tinged mountain and valley with pink and purple in softly melting tints. The crescent moon came out, with the star of love nestling in its lap, and star after star began tremblingly to peep out, yet Aliena lingered, loth to go. The deepening twilight warned her at length that it was time to leave. She rose with a sigh, and taking a lingering farewell look, in her pained heart, she said good-bye to Nature, and to all the sweet associations of this spot. Thus closing forever, as she felt, this sweet and bitter chapter of her life's history, she stooped and took a tuft of the gray moss from the heary old rock, touching it tenderly as she carried it with her.

"My child, I had begun to be uneasy about you," said Mrs. Graeme, as Aliena appeared.

"I have been saying good-bye to Lookout," said Aliena sadly, continuing after a pause, "It seems strange how I feel about every place to which I go. I thought it would break my heart to leave home. I was sorry even to leave that old hotel in Chattanooga, and here, blown like a waif upon this mountain, like some parasitic plant I seem to have put out clasps that hold me so firmly to these old rocks that it tears my heart to get me away."

"It is well to find something for the heart to cling to wherever we go," said Mrs. Graeme.

"I don't know whether I think it well or not,— between the happiness and woe of positive feeling, and the nothingness of the negative, it is only a balance after all. Sometimes I feel tempted to wish I had not the power to feel," said Aliena sadly.

"My child, I am astonished at you for having such a thought. A well regulated capacity for feeling is the greatest possible boon."

"It may be. But the getting the heart into that well regulated condition must be a work of time, of philosophical culture, and of sore experience. I sometimes despair of that happy result."

"If your father could only have lived, you would have found it easier, no doubt," said Mrs. Graeme mournfully.

"Ah! if? Yes, his calm strength might have made many a pathway easy," said Aliena, with such profound sadness as sorely to disturb her mother's mind, dwelling as she did upon the loss to her daughter as well as to herself of that calmly poised, self-reliant mind upon which they could depend now only through memory.

CHAPTER XXIII.

" Though on his brow were graven lines austere
   And tranquil sternness, which had ta'en the place
   Of feelings fierier far, but less severe;
   Joy was not always absent from his face,
   But o'er it in such scenes would steal with transient grace."
BYRON: CHILDE HAROLD.

Mrs. Graeme and Aliena drove from Lookout mountain the afternoon appointed, to Chattanooga. The sun had not set when they arrived at the hotel, and Aliena, having laid aside her hat in her own room, went restlessly to the parlor. Here, attracted by a beautiful child, dimpled and fair, with soft rings of silky hair, in the arms of its nurse, she took it and moved to the window to divert it by looking into the street. Putting aside the crimson curtains that fell in a rich background behind them, she stood here; the child finding diversion more in clutching at her shining hair, of which the last rays of the setting sun were making a halo, than in objects in the street.

Here, Dr. Leigh, coming toward the hotel, caught sight of Aliena at the window, and glancing into the street her eyes met his. Raising his hat, he crossed the street and came on to join her.

Aliena's heart beat quickly as she heard his footsteps in the hall, and as flushed from the walk, his face glowing with a glad smile of welcome, he approached.

"A devout Catholic might have been tempted to fall upon his knees and say a few Hail Mary's, if he had caught sight of you as I did from the street," said Dr. Leigh, extending his hand in salutation.

"I am certainly very glad that no devout Catholic was subjected to such a temptation then," Aliena replied, smiling, the color flooding her face.

"You ought to be glad at least of the power to inspire such an impulse."

"I think in this case I ought rather to be glad of the omnipotent power of public opinion, which would have prevented the adoration of a very unworthy object; especially in so public a manner."

"That a woman's face is capable of suggesting the ideal Madonna ought to plead for him, even before that inexorable bar, public opinion," said Dr. Leigh, looking into the clear depths of the eyes before him with an exquisite sense of happiness in Aliena's presence which made him oblivious to everything else.

The baby ceasing to find Dr. Leigh an interesting study, or to be entertained by the conversation, began to indicate that fact by vigorous efforts to get from Aliena's arms to the nurse. She checked him long enough to take a parting kiss from the little wide-open moist mouth.

Becoming conscious of Dr. Leigh's eyes fixed upon her, Mrs. Bledsoe's revolting story came painfully to her mind. Penitent at this thought she said, "How can you reconcile prayer to the Madonna with the charge, which I sometimes think is true, that woman is harder and less forgiving in judgment than man?"

"That the Madonna is so constantly appealed to, is, I think, in itself a reputation of such a charge. In fact I believe it is oftener charged that woman is not only prone to forgive, but to admire and even to love the most audacious sinners," said Dr. Leigh.

" If there is truth in that charge, it must arise from their seeming heroism. From the God and man defying audacity, abhorrent as it is, that great sinners sometimes assume, which gives them a certain fascination, a sort of dazzling grandeur like Milton's Satan, for instance," said Aliena.

" I believe cowardice is the one unpardonable sin with woman," said Dr. Leigh.

" I can't see how there could be, with man or woman, any grand heroic ideal without perfect courage," said Aliena.

" Certainly not. But is it always the highest courage that is most admired by woman? That courage which alone can make a man a hero in any true sense of the word, moral courage. The courage to conquer self—to live for the highest possibilities of man's nature, and not for what is lowest and basest. The god-like element. not the animal. Or is Rochester a true type of a woman's hero? A man, oblivious not only to what was elevated and grand, but even to man's first duty. The protection of the woman he loves, even against himself. One who could repay such love, so exquisitely depicted, as that of Jane Eyre, by utter selfishness, deception, and basest contemplated wrong. A sort of wandering satyr, unblushing in confessed shame, who was miraculously to be transformed by the power of love, and that of the most brutish form into fitness for the love of such a woman as the heroine of that story."

Aliena stood listening eagerly with glowing face as Dr. Leigh spoke. Suddenly the light died out from her face for some reason, as he ceased, and apparently unconscious that an answer might be expected she turned from him with a sigh, and gazed into the darkening street. Becoming vaguely conscious that Dr. Leigh was studying her face she moved unasked to the piano, and seating herself ran her fingers softly over the keys, gliding at length into the chords, if chords they may be called, preluding Balfe's *"Du bist mir nah und doch so fern*," music which like "the rapture of life does not arise unless by the confluence of discords with the subtle concords." She sang in a low, vibrant voice the words to which the music gives intense utterance in vague yearning pain.

Dr. Leigh had never heard Aliena sing before, and as he stood as though transfixed with his intense passionate eyes fixed upon her in the deepening twilight, Aliena felt as if she were under some strange spell. As though all the world had become motionless, transfixed, and that she must go on thus forever.

She gave a shuddering start as the gong sounding for tea jarred upon her, painfully breaking the spell.

When later in the evening Mrs. Graeme returned to her room from the parlor, she found Aliena seated by the window, her face supported in her hand, her eyes fixed upon Lookout mountain, outlined black in the distance against the sky.

"You left the parlor very unceremoniously daughter, Mrs. Bledsoe and Mrs. Skinker left good-night for you, and said they would try to be up in time to see us off in the morning, and say good-bye," said Mrs. Graeme.

"I would be glad never to see those people again. I wish they would not trouble themselves to say good-bye to me," said Aliena with strange bitterness.

"Daughter, I would not express myself so harshly if I were you," Mrs. Graeme said gravely but gently.

"I have no faith in either of them," Aliena continued in a bitter tone.

"You should not judge harshly my child. Mrs. Bledsoe is an afflicted old woman, and apparently a very pious one. As to Mrs. Skinker you cannot expect every one to come up to your own standard, and it takes a variety of people to make a world."

"The less I see of the world then the better," said Aliena with continued bitterness.

"If others do wrong you cannot remedy it by doing wrong yourself. Try to practice charity, my child. It is wrong to allow one's self to be carried away by prejudice," said Mrs. Graeme, and seating herself by another window she sat silently absorbed in thought.

Aliena, penitent at having as she feared, troubled her mother, soon rose, and approaching put her arms tenderly around her, and, trying to smile, said, " Mother, don't let my foolish whims trouble you, I am like the weather I suppose, the better for a little thunder gust," and kissing her tenderly good night she retired to her own room.

Dr. Leigh, having gone to his room after tea, had taken up a book with the intention, if possible, of preventing his mind from going over the same weary round, coming always to the same dreary conclusion, which had tormented him of late. But soon hopeless of fixing his thoughts upon the book, he laid it down and started to the hospital. Having gone the rounds here he was returning to the hotel, when raising his eyes, longing for another glimpse of Aliena, he saw her at that moment bending over her mother, tenderly kissing her good night. A profound sigh escaped him. Regardless of his steps, he stumbled against some one moving on before him.

" Pardon me," he said, as a beautiful girlish face with great startled black eyes turned toward him.

" It is I who should say pardon. I was—"

" Zara, what for is it that you do not keep up. I cannot that I attend to you and all the things," interrupted a gruff voice, from a slouching, sinister looking man who was walking on ahead.

" I am coming," she said in a peculiarly musical voice, hastening her footsteps.

" That voice is singularly out of accord with that of her companion," Dr. Leigh thought. " I should judge from it that she was refined as well as young and beautiful." And his thoughts wandered, as they were too prone to do, to another, whose voice came to his mind, flexible, rippling as sunshine upon water, full of pathos, capable of expressing the deepest emotion, sympathetic, changing, sensitive as the delicate nature of which it was an index.

Re-entering the hotel, he returned to his room, filled with the gloom of the thought that, after to-night, he might never again be under the same roof with her whom he loved her, for whom his whole being longed.

CHAPTER XXIV.

> Friar. "I 'll give thee armor to keep off that word,
> Adversity's sweet milk, philosophy,
> To comfort thee though thou art banished.
> Romeo. Yet banished ? Hang up philosophy,
> Unless philosophy can make a Juliet."

Dr. Leigh was up early the next morning; he had, in fact, scarcely slept at all. Hearing a woman's voice in the hall, supposing it might be Aliena, he stepped from his room to meet her. But instead, he encountered the same beautiful girl he had met the night before. She was apparently foreign, either Spanish or Italian, with great black eyes, waving, silky black hair, straight, delicate features, and a clear olive complexion.

She was accompanied by the same middle-aged man, also foreign in appearance, whose heavy, overhanging black brows gave his deep-set black eyes a particularly disagreeable, sinister expression, which was not improved by his unkempt black beard and hair.

"Which way is it that you turn to go?" said the man, addressing the girl in a gruff voice.

"I did not notice." the girl replied in clear, musical tones, which Dr. Leigh also recognized as the same he had heard the night before. Stepping forward, with that air of quiet ease which always characterized his bearing, and with that deference natural to him in addressing a woman, he said "Allow me to show you the way," and he walked on with them to the side hall in which were the steps.

The man made no acknowledgment of this courtesy, but the girl thanked him in a low voice, her face crimsoning as she met his eye, and drawing up the mantle which had slipped from her shoulders, she moved on. Dr. Leigh now went on to the parlor, where he found Aliena, awaiting her mother. Proffering his hand in salutation, he said, " And you are really going ? "

" I am sure you ought to know, since you banished us," said Aliena, with the sickliest ghost of a smile that vanished with the color from her face, as she raised her eyes and caught the look of fixed pain upon the face before her.

" That I have done so shows how much more I have thought of others than of myself," he replied in a low voice. And longing for some word to illumine the dead blank future before him, he continued, " Have you no word of regret at parting ? "

" It would be strange if I felt no regret, when you have been so unswervingly kind to us, forlorn as we would otherwise have been," she said, her voice faltering. And remembering what her mother had said about her seeming ingratitude, she continued, " Let us hope to meet again, and that I may be better able then to show how truly I do appreciate your goodness."

" If I could only be oblivious myself to the pain of parting, I might seem less forgetful of the debt I owe you. In restoring my faith in woman ; and in brightening my stay here into an oasis in the dreariness of my life—into which it must again lapse."

Mrs. Graeme joining them, they walked on silently to the breakfast room.

As they left the dingy, low-pitched room, with its rows of long tables, and its quaint old fans, which the unnaturally pious looking negro boy was still droning on, Aliena lingered behind and placed in the boy's hand a sum of money which served to keep him awake for at least the remainder of that day.

As Aliena walked on to the carriage she went over painfully in her mind the time from when by an apparent chance they had been brought to a painful halt here until now. It was with a sore, vague pain that she felt it was all ended now.

Entering the carriage which awaited them, they were driven to the cars. Here they had scarcely more than time to be seated when the signal for departure sounded. Dr. Leigh looked yearningly into Aliena's eyes, but spoke no word of farewell as he pressed her hand in parting.

Aliena's eyes sought Dr. Leigh as the cars moved off. He stood waiting with his hat lifted as they swept by. Her heart throbbed as she caught the look of repressed agony in his pale face, his compressed mouth, and his intense longing eyes. And they were gone.

Aliena drew her veil over her face. It was well, perhaps, that Dr. Leigh could not see the quivering lips and the great silent tears which forced themselves from under the long dark lashes and dropped upon the listless hands lying in her lap.

They sped on through the dense cloud of silvery mist that softly rose and fell in great restless billows upon the crystal water of the Tennessee, until before the rising sun it rolled rapidly away, disclosing the beauties of the valley, as they swept on beside the river or crossed and recrossed its sinuous line, over wide-spanning bridges, while islands in emerald greenness appeared in the far-spreading river; and sun-capped mountains loomed beyond in the distant blue gray haze.

Aliena, aroused to consciousness of her surroundings by the beautiful scenery through which they were passing, was attracted at length by the beauty of a girlish face at some distance from her in the rear of the same car. Leaning forward to where her mother sat, she said, " Look at that beautiful girl at the back of the car, mother. Is n't she lovely? She reminds me of Guido's exquisite Beatrici Cenci we saw at the Collona palace."

"She is beautiful indeed. But the man with her is far from being agreeable looking," said Mrs. Graeme.

"The girl is so lovely I had not thought of him," said Aliena.

The next day they changed cars from the main road to a branch road leading to Athens as a terminus, and Mrs. Graeme and Aliena began now to experience that anxious, restless feeling incident upon arriving in a strange place, with the prospect of an indefinite sojourn among strangers. The beautiful girl and her less pre-possessing companion they observed, had also changed cars, with the same apparent destination. Aliena's quick sympathy had been elicited by the shrinking manner of the girl, and, as she thought, the rather tyrannical air of the stronger party.

As they neared Athens, the rolling country that met her eyes rejoiced Aliena with a touch of home; though it assumed marked characteristic features, distinctive from the black soil of the Walnut Hills, in the red clay, glistening with mica as with diamond dust.

***

CHAPTER XXV.

"All weary and o'er watched,
Take vantage, heavy eyes.
Fortune, good-night; smile, once more turn thy wheel."

Arriving at Athens, Mrs. Graeme and Aliena drove from the depot, as is usual. through the least attractive portion of the place, and halted in front of an unpre-tentious looking hotel, which stood at the corner of a square. Ornamental iron galleries, fronting upon the streets, relieved the monotony of the building.

A tall, stout man of about forty, compactly compressed into a suit of black cloth, upon which was the shine of wear rather than of finish, came forward to meet them, as the carriage stopped, preceded by a strong odor of musk. His rigidity of movement was possibly due to the difficulty experienced in moving his compressed joints, if joints there were. For no more angularity denoted that fact than if he had been constructed upon the principles of a mammoth doll—the cloth sewed first and filled in afterward.

Colonel Decca, the landlord, why colonel nobody knew, accosted them in a choked voice, and assisted Mrs. Graeme and Aliena from the carriage.

The usual group of loungers and loafers were gathered at the corner, to see the daily advent, if there were any such, of strangers in this quiet place. The thick veils of these ladies preventing satisfactory information as to their faces, surmises were resorted to.

Loafer number one.—" The one with the trim figure and springy step is young, I know."

Loafer number two.—" Yes, by jove, there is style about the way she moves. And did you see the dainty little foot and gaiter?"

Loafer number three.—" They must be from the 'low country' by the look of that old negro woman; you can tell that by the tie of her head-handkerchief."

Loafer number four.—" What a splendid dog! There is nothing more graceful or prettier in dog flesh than a greyhound."

In the meantime Colonel Decca led the way upstairs to the parlor, where, seating the ladies, he requested their names and residence, in a more choked voice than ever, consequent upon the exertion of ascending the steps, and, promising to send a servant to show them to their rooms, he retired. Before assigning them rooms he went to see the baggage of the travelers, the gauge of their status to a landlord. From these he determined to send them the keys to the best rooms vacant in the house. He now proceeded to register their names, while loafer number five looked over his shoulder, and returned to the corner with the desired information.

Tired, and consequently the more dispirited, Mrs. Graeme and Aliena were glad to get to their rooms, which, as Aliena was delighted to see, had an out-look upon the University grounds, a street only intervening. Scattered picturesquely here and there, under the grand old oaks and elms, the forest growth of centuries, were the University buildings. Some of them, coeval with the institution itself, quaint and old, were overgrown with ivy—others more modern and ornate seemed garishly new.

As Aliena stood at the window the chapel bell struck six, with an ominous sound of warning as it seemed to her, as she counted the deep, slow, solemn strokes.

Loth to give way to their feeling of loneliness by remaining in their rooms, Mrs. Graeme and Aliena having rid themselves of the dust of travel, again sought the parlor. Seated at the piano, hammering vigorously upon the few chords that constituted the accompaniment to a popular ballad of that time, was a young girl of about sixteen, who was singing verse after verse of Lorena in a vigorous, unmodulated tone, with all the energy not exhausted by the accompaniment. She was quite pretty, with regular features, black hair, and blue eyes. She was evidently in that trying state, too overgrown for a child, yet not quite a woman. Her hair in the same doubtful status was hanging loose upon her shoulders.

Near the piano sat a quiet, gentlemanly looking young man of twenty-four or five. He was apparently less interested in the music than in the sport of some children, who were rolling and tumbling over each other in the center of the room. They were laughing and chattering in their noisy play, in a way that would have neutralized less vigorous sounds than those of the performer and songstress.

The young girl, having sung six verses of Lorena, ceased her musical efforts and began a rather giggling conversation with the young man. The children losing the inspiration of the music, and the cover that it had given to their noisy sport, lapsed suddenly into comparative quiet, casting furtive glances at Mrs. Graeme and Aliena, with an occasional remark in a low tone, followed by a bashful snicker, as though but just aware of the presence of strangers. But Col. Decca soon coming in announced tea and ushered them into the supper-room, after which they went to their rooms, a prey to that feeling so often experienced by travelers, that the hoped for happiness at the terminus of a journey is not less illusive than the bag of gold at the foot of a rainbow.

Mrs. Graeme, looking worn and weary, soon retired for the night, and Aliena went to her own room. But instead of seeking sleep she seated herself at the window and sat watching the occasional forms moving in the dimly lighted street, or disappearing with a clash of the great iron gate into the shadows of the campus. She pictured in imagination their aims and ambitions, their hopes and disappointments, their homes and loved ones—with a sore, aching pain at her own heart.

A more utter feeling of loneliness came over her as even these forms ceased to appear, and everything was still except the distant sound of falling water, and the monotonous cry of a "whip-poor-will," repeated over and over again in the distance. She raised her eyes, gazing upward at the stars in their slow, ceaseless motion, vaguely fancying the twinkling far-away stars to be the weary sleepless, blinking eyes of some lost, lonely spirit, moving eternally on in silence and solitude.

She thought with heart-longing of home. Of the hand now moldering in the dust, that could never more be outstretched to draw her back to the ark of love from her heart-sore wandering. She wondered if at the old hotel at Chattanooga there might be one gazing in loneliness and sorrow at the same eyes looking down in pity from above. And with a guilty pang she thought of one cordoned by guns, suffering and in peril. She gave herself up despairingly to remorse—to pain and sorrow, to home sickness and heart-longing for loved ones and objects.

The old chapel bell startled her in the stillness, clashing midnight. And striving to thrust aside torturing thought, she sought sleep.

The following afternoon Aliena induced her mother to drive with her. Colonel Decca appeared as they were about to enter the carriage to assist them in. He was preceded as usual by the odor of musk, and looking, if possible, more compressed in his worn, shiny suit of black cloth. Aliena shrank instinctively from the touch of his clammy hand, proffered to assist her into the carriage, though Mrs. Graeme accepted the assistance.

Owing to the altitude of the place, and to its nearness to the mountains, the air was charmingly fresh and sparkling. They drove on, through streets over-arched by forest trees, past beautiful homes dotted here and there upon the sloping hillsides, in the midst of the forest growth left standing, now interspersed with hedges, plats of flowers, graveled walks and drives winding gracefully through grounds adorned, perhaps, with statuary and fountains.

The next day was Sunday, and, walking to church, they entered the vestibule of the large but unpretentious looking building. Here they were met by the sexton, a tall, thin, pompous-looking, old negro man, dressed in clerical black. Recognizing the fact that they were strangers he approached with a formal military salute, adopted in compliment to the times, and with a second wave of his hand to his head, he said, addressing Mrs. Graeme,

“ Mum, I reprehend that you are strangers.　Would you desire that I mout resignate you a pew, mum ? ” and he gave another flourish of his hand to his head, bowing as he did so.

“ If you please,” Mrs. Graeme replied.

But as he was about to enjoy what he considered one of his greatest privileges, that of “ resignating ” pews, an old gentleman, who had just entered, approached.

There was something particularly striking in the appearance of this gentleman.　He wore his hair, which was almost perfectly white, in natural curls to his shoulders, over a dress coat of finest cloth, which might suitably have been of velvet, with *point d'Alençon* ruffles instead of the conventional linen cuffs and collar, which showed at his wrists and above his white brocaded silk neck-kerchief.

Mrs. Graeme and Aliena recognized him at once as Judge Massey, whom they had met in Italy.　Mrs. Graeme's heavy crêpe veil and Aliena's development into womanhood had prevented his knowing them at first.　But he greeted them with evident pleasure as they made themselves known, though with a grave, dignified formality which was natural with him, and invited them to take seats in his pew.

Promptly at the moment when the vibrations from the great bell ceased to resound through the church, the minister rose, in the simple but beautiful white marble pulpit, and stood with his hands raised to invoke the divine blessing.

His striking figure was made more effective by the background of rich crimson velvet hangings.　His tall venerable form was squarely and muscularly built, his white hair surmounted a high broad forehead, and his gray eyes had not lost that look of an eagle's, which was natural to him, though he was more than seventy years old.

He had an awed look of reverence in ministering in divine things, as though entering the Holy of Holies.

As of one called to declare the whole testimony of God, who has dedicated his life to the service of the Divine Master, and who stands as it were in the vestibule of that Upper Temple into which he must soon be called to render an account for the deeds done in the body.

The solemn sound of the organ and the singing accorded well with the other services, which were conducted with simplicity and with an air of profound consciousness of responsibility for souls.

So impressed and absorbed were Mrs. Graeme and Aliena in the services as to be oblivious to everything else until the benediction was pronounced. Strangers as they were, they had not escaped the eye of the minister, who called the following day, as did Mrs. and Miss Massey to see them.

Mrs. Graeme found herself conversing with unusual freedom, not only with those she had known before, but with the fatherly old man, whose deep interest and sympathy in the hardships and sorrows to which, by war, they had so recently been subjected, stimulated their recital.

"My daughter," he said earnestly, as he was leaving. "remember that there is One who has promised to be a husband to the widow and a father to the fatherless. One who does not willingly afflict, who cares for you as no earthly parent could, whose minister I am ; and if I can serve you I shall feel it a privilege to do so."

10

CHAPTER XXVI.

" Living in shattered guise, and still, and cold,
And bloodless; with its sleepless sorrow aches,
Yet withers on."

The great storm of war which was sweeping with
relentless fury over the country was scarcely felt in
Athens, except in anxiety as to loved ones in the army.
Torn and tossed as Aliena's heart and mind were by
the agonizing pain of uncertainty, banished from home
and from loved ones, with Vicksburg constantly and
fearfully imperiled, the seeming want of interest here
jarred upon her. But, finding she could have opportunity daily to mingle her prayers with those of others for
her country, for the soldiers enduring peril and hardship
in its defense, and for the longed for white-winged messenger of peace, she went alone to the gothic, ivy-grown
chapel in the University grounds. Here she bowed in
heartfelt supplication, not only for others but for herself, torn as she was by distracting, conflicting emotions.

The quiet earnestness of this service did seem to calm
and strengthen her sorely troubled heart. And coming
out she strolled on through the quiet streets, seeing
with a throb of mingled pain and pleasure flowers
which, like familiar faces in strange surroundings,
brought with them tender recollections of home, their
odors more than sight, even bringing throbbing memories of the past, its sorrows and its pleasures.

Aliena one afternoon leaving the chapel to which she
now daily resorted, met Jennie Foster, the songstress
from the hotel, accompanied by Mr. Marsden, who had
been seated by the piano upon a former occasion, and
by the children, with whom Aliena had now become
fast friends. They had started for a stroll in the cemetery in which they invited Aliena to join; she gladly
accepted their invitation, and they resumed their walk.

They soon came in view of this beautiful spot, and, walking on entered through an imposing iron gateway, the gloomy place. The cemetery was triangular in form, occupying the space lying between the Occonee river and a small tributary branch. Higher up the river moved in noisy rapids, falling here and there with a roaring sound over the ledges of rock to the lower ground; were, under great overhanging trees and vines. it scarcely seemed to move at all, growing black in its slugglish flow onward in the dark shadows.

The brook went leaping, flashing and sparkling on under less dense, but overarching trees, between rocky banks covered with clinging mosses, lichens and ferns; breaking into white foam over rocks; or rippling on with babbling sound to its junction with the river; the two streams keeping up together unceasing musical chords in the murmur, tinkle, splash. and roar of the falling water.

Jennie and Mr. Marsden had gone on before; the children, charmed with the wild flowers, or enchanted with the pebbly bottomed leaping brook. lingered upon its banks; while Aliena, strolling on, was soon separated from them.

Following one of the winding graveled pathways, she found herself at length upon a hill-top which commanded an extended view. It was the highest point in the cemetery, as she discovered when taking a sweeping view of the scene.

To the forest growth of pines, oaks, and cedars abounding here had been added larches, hemlocks. deodars and other evergreens; and mingled with the wild flowers which grew in rich profusion were others which, carefully tended, enhanced the natural beauty of the place.

Aliena from her elevated position could see, here and there, above the trees, the grander monuments with their caps gleaming in the sunshine. Above them all. at some distance, rose a rarely beautiful mausoleum.

A gothic temple, exquisite in outline, of purest Italian marble, which, as she afterwards found, marked where a young wife and child lay. Under the overarching canopy above the vault stood in deathless marble the figure of the wife with her child in her arms. Above the columns supporting the canopy were life-sized personifications of Faith, Hope, Charity and Religion, while between them rose the delicately tapering spire, which, mounting aloft, was capped by the flame of the altar of love.

Aliena having looked around seated herself upon a rustic seat with her back to the sun, gazing at the solemn but beautiful view of the rolling hillsides, the valleys, and river. Before her was the Occonee overhung by the gnarled old vine-covered trees which almost obcured the black water. Beyond could be seen glimpses of the great hoary rocks that formed its precipitous banks. She watched the shadows growing blacker and blacker upon the water, until it seemed to assume a weird mysteriousness in consonance with the gloomy surroundings, a somber contrast with the white, sun-capped, foaming falls higher up the river.

Superstitious thoughts may unconsciously have tinged her mind as she started nervously as a bird rose near her, and with a sudden whir flew across the black water, disappearing on the other side of the river amid the branches of one of the gnarled trees that were dipping down into the water.

Becoming conscious that the sun had set and that the full moon was rising beyond the gray rocks across the river, casting still blacker shadows upon the water. Aliena looked around her with an unpleasant sense of loneliness at seeing and hearing no one. No sound broke the stillness but the falling water and the mournful monotonous cry of " whip-poor-will," down by the river.

Walking to the other side of the hill she caught sight of her party, anxiously awaiting her at the gate, and hastening her footsteps she soon joined them.

"We were beginning to think that some ghost had spirited you away," Jennie said as Aliena rejoined them.

The children, either tired, or depressed by the growing darkness and their gloomy surroundings, or by the allusion to ghosts, walked on in silence.

Aliena was too much engrossed in thought, especially of the contemplated surrender of Vicksburg, rumors of which had been depressing her all day, to feel like talking Jennie alone seemed irrepressible, as, with Mr. Marsden somewhat in the rear, her voice could be heard in animated, unflagging tones, she apparently doing all the talking.

"I am so glad to-morrow will be the Fourth of July," said Jennie, in an enthusiastic tone, as she joined Mrs. Graeme and Aliena upon the gallery after tea.

"Why? Do they regard its celebration here now?" asked Aliena.

"I don't mean what you think, perhaps. But it is Commencement day here."

"Commencement? I thought all the students were gone into the army?" said Aliena.

"Yes, they are, but they are so used to having it that we are to have music and an oration, any way. Don't you intend to go, Miss Graeme? Everybody goes."

"I don't know that I care to go," said Aliena sadly, her thoughts reverting to other subjects more absorbing to her mind.

"Not go?" exclaimed Jennie in surprise, "why every one goes who can."

Aliena could not but smile at Jennie's look of astonishment. She had such ideas of the importance of this grand culminating event of the year, that Aliena's indifference struck her with amazement. But weary of the sadness, the homesickness, and the monotony of her life Aliena said, smiling,

"Jennie, I believe I will go if you will promise to be my chaperone?"

"I chaperone you?" said Jennie, amused at the thought, adding as though she enjoyed its absurdity, " I'll do it," and so it was arranged that they should go.

Little did Aliena imagine what would be transpiring in that devoted city, to which her prayers turned daily upon the eventful morning which was about to dawn.

Long before the appointed time for the exercises in the chapel, groups could be seen wending their way thither, and the clanging of the iron gate could be heard announcing their entrance into the Campus.

Jennie being inexperienced in elaborate toilet, and over-anxious as to success at her chrysalis age, was slow in making her appearance. She joined Aliena in the parlor, at length, however, looking slightly flushed from anxiety and flurry in getting her hair put up in a coil for the first time, but very pretty and fresh, in a white muslin with pink moss buds apparently sprinkled over it, and a straw hat with corresponding moss buds clustered at one side. As they left the hotel, Mr. Marsden. who had been in waiting, joined them. And falling in with the stream of people still moving toward the Campus, they entered the crowded chapel.

It had not occurred to Aliena to ask who was to be the orator of the day. Now, turning to Jennie, she inquired who was to be the speaker.

" The Chancellor," Jennie responded, with an air of reverence which Aliena attributed to her university breeding.

After the preliminary exercises, of which music finely rendered constituted the principal part, the orator of the day arose. He was a pale, intellectual looking man of about forty-five; his hair, already tinged with gray, brushed from his forehead, showed his finely shaped brow. The brilliancy and intensity of his black eyes seemed almost out of unison with his pale, calm face.

His voice was at first apparently weak, and his manner somewhat formal, and he hesitated at times for a word, which was too fitly chosen not to indicate thorough preparation. But warming with the subject he seemed to change, even physically. His voice had no faltering sound now, but rang out as clear as a trumpet, or sinking in low distinct tones vibrated with profoundest emotion.

His words came with apparent spontaneity, and with a perfect adaptation for clothing the grand thoughts he expressed—holding his audience in wrapt accord with himself, not only by his eloquence, but by his personal magnetism.

As he finished there seemed to be a simultaneous deep-drawn inspiration throughout the audience, and a rustling of fans, and a general change of position—as though awakening from the spell he had thrown over them.

Aliena did not wonder now at the tone and manner with which Jennie Foster had pronounced the words, "The Chancellor." A manner which she found afterward to be the reflex of the general sentiment of the community, founded not only upon his intellectual greatness, but his equal goodness.

The day after Commencement, Mr. Marsden proposed to Aliena to go with him and Jennie to the University Library. Ascending the winding oak stairway in the vestibule of the building, they entered the beautiful room used for this purpose.

At intervals, upon either side of the great room, and projecting at equal distances, were dividing partitions; against these, back to back, shelves filled with books reached to the ceiling; thus subdividing the main room on two sides into cosy, well-lighted compartments, each provided with tables and chairs. The main undivided hall extended the whole length of the room. Here were hung portraits of the distinguished men who had been connected with the University, or other Georgians of historic note.

Since the disbanding of the students for a military career the library had been comparatively deserted;

and it was with a feeling of rare pleasure that Aliena discovered the treasures collected in this quiet room; and thought of the resource it would be to her in her loneliness. Roaming from alcove to alcove, she saw with delight the names of authors whose works were scarcely to be found elsewhere. Taking from one of the shelves a rare old book, she sank into a chair, so absorbed that Mr. Marsden and Jennie wandered on, entertaining themselves as they chose until ready to return.

CHAPTER XXVII.

"Th' adventurous bands
With shudd'ring horror pale, and eyes aghast,
Viewed first their lamentable lot."

The days dragged wearily on in the besieged city. The insufficient provisions had become poorer in quality, and more and more scant. The soldiers on half rations of unpalatable and unwholesome food, doing double duty, under a fiery sun, were dropping exhausted in the stifling trenches.

Even Major Baron had tried mule steak now. Though he found ways still of ekeing it out, and means of keeping comparatively comfortable.

The garrison, though worn out, and to a certain extent dispirited, yet held on with determined pertinacity —hoping against hope. All thought of rescue had died out in the minds of the soldiers, despite the constantly repeated false rumors to the contrary. These now scarcely stirred a heart beat. Rifles, in the hands of sharp-shooters, and cannon, and mortar, still plied their warfare; day and night, and night and day; over and over again, in wearing, ceaseless continuance.

Horses and mules, tottering skeletons from want of food, were shot to end their misery. These skeleton forms, thrown into the Mississippi, floated to the enemy's lines below, telling the tale of suffering and woe. One never to be forgotten day, when, almost a century before, the Goddess of Liberty had looked down, smiling upon a little band of rebels signing a Declaration of Independence, a sullen silence brooded over the doomed city.

" What does it mean ? " suppressed voices asked.

" They say the city has been surrendered," came in more subdued tones.

" It is not so ! It cannot be ! " half famished men and women said aghast.

And even women longed and prayed to hear the sound of guns once more, as a joyful thing.

But no sound came. The dismal, brooding silence continued. A little group of horsemen might have been seen moving silently and secretly to the rear of the city. Under the shade of a tree outside of Confederate lines another group awaited them. There the terms of surrender were signed.

To the credit of the foe, be it said, no joyful demonstration marked their oncoming. Silently they took possession of the doomed place, where against fearful odds a small band, suffering privation and hunger, had so long stood heroically by their guns. No voice found utterance for triumph when the little army stacked their guns, and the officers grimly surrendered their swords, which a gallant enemy returned. And the prisoners, having taken an oath not to serve again until exchanged, sorrowfully turned their backs upon the defenseless women and children and upon a place they had so long and so hopelessly defended. Leaving buried upon the hillsides thousands of their brave comrades in arms who had succumbed to sickness or fallen in the trenches. The women who had uncomplainingly endured the hardships of the siege, now came out of the dank, dark caves where they had found refuge from the firing, and fearfully returned to their homes, to protect them, if possible, from pillage.

Major Baron having endured the mortification of surrender under which he was chafing, went to pay a final visit to Castle Hill. Here the old German gardener and his wife had remained, faithful to their posts. Wandering sadly and sorrowfully through conservatory and grounds, Major Baron went once more to take a farewell look at The Castle. Here he seated himself for the last time, in sweet and bitter retrospection, upon the steps of the portico, under the twining banksia rose.

The mocking-birds, if any were left, had flown away from their nest in the magnolia tree. Few birds of any kind could be heard now. The guns had driven them away. One could be heard singing in a sequestered spot down by the lake. And a dove could be heard moaning in the distance. He rose at length to walk through the grounds—he thought as he walked on of the weary time since he was here with Aliena, a time so long in events, and of the humiliation he would feel in meeting her after the surrender.

He startled the peacocks from their cover, under the clump of azaleas; they half flew and half ran, uttering their discordant cry. They had become wild and strange from neglect, and from the firing.

At sight of the lake the thought of another than Aliena obtruded upon him. He remembered his stroll here, the row on the lake, the caressing intonation of his name, and the sweet way in which the sound had been cut short. And he determined to see Lilian, and learn her plans for the future.

Thinking no time better than the present, which in its bitterness and humiliation, hung so heavily, he returned for his horse, and rode down the graveled road, under the tinkling silver poplar, and out of the gate forever.

Lilian was not looking as dejected as Major Baron

had anticipated, considering the fact of the day's surrender. She was not clad in sack-cloth and ashes ; but was, in reality, looking quite fresh and lovely. He found her in the parlor with Captain Berry, who was also looking more cheerful than might have been expected. He had just learned from Lilian the comforting intelligence that the family were to go into the Confederacy.

Lilian wore a pale, peach-blossom pink organdie, with tea rosebuds of the same color in her bosom. The guns had not shot away her vanity, nor the surrender of her native city abated her desire for admiration.

Captain Berry left, reluctantly, having an engagement. But Major Baron felt no inclination to take the seat vacated by Lilian's side. Being physically a brave man, and having undergone danger, and some privation, at least, incident to the siege, he was sufficiently impressed by the portentous events of the day not to be so much under the spell of Lilian's beauty as to forget these facts. Her gala attire jarred upon his sense of fitness, and her tone of levity upon his feelings. The more so, perhaps, because of having found her dispensing her smiles to another.

There was a look of pre-occupation about his face, and a tone of hardness in his voice that Lilian had never seen or heard. This served gradually to check the flow of pretty little nothings, and even the airs of coquetry with which she was wont to arouse him to a sense of her charms. To these he was usually sufficiently alive. In her own mind they were not to be overshadowed even by the events of this day.

Falling upon another expedient to arouse Major Baron from the slough of despond in which he seemed sunk, Lilian excused herself for the moment, and left the room. She soon returned, bringing upon a silver waiter a decanter of wine, and glasses.

" The servants have all gone wild, and are off. There is no knowing whether they will ever return," she said explanatorily, setting down the waiter. "Here is some old Port that mamma has been saving in case any of us were shot ; but there is no use to save it now, and the Yankees may take it. So we might as well enjoy it." And pouring out the wine, she handed him a glass.

With all his ordinary elegance of manner Major Baron delighted in playing the Grand Mogul where he could. He relished the idea of a heaven of indolent ease, with houris in fragrant robes in attendance. And he permitted Lilian to wait upon him with a sort of royal condescension. Receiving the wine he took it at a draught.

"Let me fill your glass—it will do you good?" said Lilian.

"Thank you," he said, as it was replenished. Lilian now placing a tête-à-tête table within reach of Major Baron, with the wine upon it, seated herself near him. He lolled back in his favorite seat, on the little satin cushioned sofa, with Lilian by his side, sipping the wine.

She had no farther cause to complain of his indifference to her charms. Though apparently unconscious herself of any other exciting cause, his heightened voice and flushed face attested the potent influence of the wine which he continued to sip.

Having been informed by Lilian of her contemplated removal into Confederate lines at once, he promised to accompany her. Becoming sensible of the effect of the wine, at length he concluded to leave.

Mr. Selwyn, Lilian's father, was a merchant, who was so absorbed in the almighty dollar that his influence in his family was scarcely felt; like many others of the same class, he thought that when he had provided for the physical wants of his family. his duty was amply performed. He belonged now to that hungry horde, always developed at a time like this. who consider it their privilege to prey upon the necessities of a people. Having put a paid substitute in the Confederate army, he gave his own energies to the safer and more congenial pursuit of getting money. Rashly caught inside the lines of the besieged city, he had been compelled to endure some of the hardships and perils of war.

His wife, as a girl, had been more remarkable for her beauty than for some other qualities. Lilian, as her father constantly told her, being the counterpart of her mother when he first saw her. With her freshness Mrs. Selwyn had lost her beauty, and was now an inefficient, dowdy, complaining woman. They had lost three children, between Lilian and the two younger remaining ones, of five and three years, respectively.

Lilian had, of course, been the more petted and indulged on this account; absorbing the affection, not only of her parents, but of a maiden aunt, who, only a few years before, had married to the astonishment and annoyance of Mrs. Selwyn. She thinking it less onerous, perhaps, to marry a widower with eight children than to retain the position of drudge in the household of an inefficient sister.

Major Baron, unaccustomed to yielding his own will, keenly alive to the mortification of the surrender, without courage for endurance; did not allow the soothing and cheering influence of wine, or of something stronger, to subside. And, but for the interference of friends, he might, through his rashness, have gotten into serious trouble with the demoralized men, and Federal soldiers with whom he came in contact during the brief interval of his stay in Vicksburg. In fact it must be confessed that he knew little of what transpired during that time. or on his route to Jackson.

The necessary preparations for travel were made by Auguste, his servant, who preferred the soft berth of a valet to a self-indulgent man, lavish of money, with the prospect of a nomadic life, which suited his taste, rather than freedom, with the uncertainty of an unprovided future. He therefore voluntarily accompanied his master.

"Lil, that Major Baron you have been talking so much about, has rather familiar manners, I think," said Mr. Selwyn to his daughter, *en route.* He having until now had no acquaintance really with that gentleman, except through Lilian's eulogies. Adding, "I don't think you ought to permit him to be so free and easy with you. The fact is I believe he has been drinking too much."

Captain Berry's jealousy being aroused, he scowled at Major Baron in such a way that, being in just the state of mind to be more than willing to take up any gauntlet, Major Baron gave him to understand, in rather incoherent terms, that it would afford him satisfaction to take his life's blood, proffering that gentleman the opportunity to have this kind office performed for him.

Colonel Harvey, who was present, going into Confederate lines, now interfered, upon the lady's account rather than from any interest in the parties themselves. And Colonel Sturdyvant resorted at length to the doubtful expedient of inducing Major Baron to take another drink, which, if it did not elevate him to the standard of a hero, had the desired effect of quieting him, at least. In this condition, he was kept in the back-ground until he arrived in Jackson—Captain Berry being thus left in quiet possession of the field.

As far as Lilian was concerned, she was happily of that tranquil turn of mind that prevented her afflicting herself in regard to one gallant, while comforted by the presence and flattering attentions of another.

By this happy absorption she was also oblivious to the sufferings of the dispirited, dusty, tired soldiers; who, on foot, under the burning sun, toiled on over a parched country, made a desert by the enemy, into the confederacy, there to be set aimlessly adrift.

Auguste took charge of his master on his arrival at Jackson, and got him to a hotel. Here it was to be hoped that he would awake to clearer ideas of propriety, as well as of other things.

Late in the following morning he aroused with a throbbing headache; feeling altogether wretched and out of sorts. Auguste appeared soon afterwards; in fact, he had looked in several times to see if his master was awake.

"Auguste, hav n't I been making a confounded fool of myself?" Major Baron asked.

"I should n't wonder if you has, marster," Auguste replied.

"I feel like it, certainly. Go and get me a cock-tail."

"I fetched you one some time ago, sir, but they don't have no ice in the Federacy, and I thought I'd best have you one made fresh. I'll fetch you another in a minnit," said Auguste, disappearing. He did not mention that he had taken the drink himself which he had first brought, But his master was accustomed to those little liberties.

Having by the aid of the cock-tail internally, and the use of cold water externally, gotten himself into a condition to do so, Major Baron, who had not been wholly unconscious of what had transpired *en route*, determined to see Lilian and make the proper amends. He did not, however, as seriously fear the result of any misconduct upon his part, with regard to her, as he would have done with a more nicely sensitive nature.

Lilian received him with a gracious smile, which set him at ease at once, and coming boldly to the front he said, "I was afraid I had made a fool of myself coming from Vicksburg. The surrender was too much for human fortitude to endure. I have come to apologize, and to do any penance you see fit to inflict provided it does not banish me from your favor and presence."

"Papa thought you were a little free in your manners and Capt. Berry got aggravated—"

"Capt. Berry may go to the Plutonian regions for all I care. And I shall tell him so the first chance I get," said Maj. Baron, interrupting Lilian, indignantly. His blood being by no means quite cool yet.

"Please don't," said Lilian entreatingly, alarmed at what she had done, and moving nearer to him she put her hand on his arm, and, looking up beseechingly into his face, continued, "I don't know what possessed me to tell you that. Do please promise me not to say anything to Capt. Berry about it."

"There is no resisting you. I will do anything you ask," said Maj. Baron, ardently putting his arm around Lilian and drawing her to him. And the compact was sealed in a way not likely to have been oil upon the waters to Capt. Berry if he had been present.

Mr. Selwyn, who soon entered the room, was at first distant and formal in his manner toward Maj. Baron, who, the more assiduous in his efforts to please from that fact, soon overcame all coolness by his tact.

Before he left it was with the understanding that he was to go on with them as far as Montgomery, where the Selwyns were to remain, while he was to continue his journey to Georgia, "upon a matter of business," as he told Lilian.

"Good morning, Colonel, your face is as long as the moral law," said Maj. Baron to Col. Harvey, whom he encountered walking restlessly to and fro upon the gallery of the hotel when he returned.

"If it is no longer than the moral law of some persons, I know it is not an index to my feeling," said Colonel Harvey, coldly, stroking his beard and moving restlessly on in his promenade.

CHAPTER XXVIII.

"The land which once was mine
And still is hallowed by thy dust's return."

Colonel Harvey, cast adrift as he was by the contingencies of war, experienced a feeling of isolation, such as he had not felt since, self-banished, he had six years before sought a home amongst strangers. He had not heretofore been able to come to the determination to revisit scenes so fraught with pain to him, but now, in his humiliation at the surrender, his heart turned toward this desolate Mecca, of home. Grave, self-forgetful and self-reliant as he had seemingly become in these years of sad experience, he had not the less been liable to that weakness which has for the time shorn even Samson of his strength.

From boyhood he had loved a beautiful cousin, whose pink and white complexion, spoiled-child manner, and child-like want of regard at times even for the rules of syntax, had made her fascinating. His love was reciprocated, but her parents discerning the supposed advantage of her alliance with another had favored this suit. She was easily persuaded to the change. Her childish volatility, with her other child-like qualities having made the transition seemingly easily. Filled with the glamor of the wedding, its orange blossoms and its costly gifts, rather than with the solemn realities of a plighted troth, she had kept the knowledge of her approaching marriage a secret from her cousin. She had continued to receive his visits and caresses when her footsteps were almost upon the altar, upon which she was to lay, it was to be supposed, the offering of a heart wholly her husband's.

"George, what are you saying good-bye for; as if I were going to die instead of to be married? I shall be lonely in that big house. I hope to see you often then. You must not be angry with me, but love me a

11

little any way, and come to see me sometimes," said
Lutie, as they were parting after she had made this
crushing communication to him.

"Love you a little? I can do nothing else but love
you, and that is why I say good-bye," George Harvey
gasped in reply.

"You know it is not my fault. You are so poor,
George, and mamma and papa say we would starve to
death while you were waiting for clients."

"I could never starve while I had your love."

"Poor George!" she said tenderly, moving nearer to
him, "why did n't you make a heap of money and then
we could have married."

"Don't talk to me that way, Lutie. You drive me
mad. I can work for you, starve for you. Only wait,
and we can marry yet, if you will."

"No, it is all fixed now. I can't marry you. But
you can come to see me sometimes. And it cannot be
wrong for us to love each other a little, when we are
cousins."

"It will be a horrible sin for you to marry a man
without loving *him*."

"I do love him some. He is very good to me, and
gives me such beautiful things. But somehow I don't
like him to pet me," and she looked regretfully into
her cousin's face.

"Will you persist in driving me mad?" he exclaimed.

"George, don't talk that way to me, or I shall think
you hate me," she said, nestling closer to him, and
he clasped her in his arms, kissing her passionately, and
tore himself away ; brushing by her future husband as
he was entering the house.

George Harvey did not go to the wedding, but he did
meet his pretty cousin accidentally a short time afterwards, fresh and beautiful in her bridal array, leaning upon her husband's arm. He would have avoided her, but
leaving her husband, she moved impulsively and delightedly forward proffering her hand.

" Why, howd'y do George, I am so glad to meet you. It has been such a long time since I saw you," and looking at her husband, who had proffered his hand also, she said with more of awe than of love in her manner. " Don't you think cousin George might come to see us sometimes ? when we have always been such good friends ? "

" Certainly, I shall be glad to have your cousin visit us," her husband replied.

George looked at her in her pretty bridal array, and his heart longed for her, and her sweet words. But to his honor be it spoken, he loved her too well to trust himself, and never went.

Thinking drearily of her that night as he sat gazing into the firelight in his solitary room, the warmth of her greeting having stirred within him all that he had striven to forget, and with it remembering the magnanimity of her husband, as he imagined, not doubting but that she had confided her former love and troth, he determined to write a line—just a line—to put himself right in the course he thought proper to pursue. To prevent her believing as she had said she would, that he hated her.

He moved to the table. Here he sat dipping his pen into the ink, and splashing it impatiently from its point, but without commencing. He was puzzled how to begin. It had been easy enough in other days. All the sweet endearing terms of those times came back to memory, but these he could not use in addressing the wife of another.

He commenced at last, " Mrs." He tore the paper to pieces and cast it into the fire. He began now without address. " Since I met you this morning my heart" —he struck out heart and put " mind has been torn with conflicting emotions." Reading this he crossed " torn " and substituted " troubled."

Laying down his pen hopelessly he gazed again into the fire, giving himself up remorselessly to thought.

His heart was truly "torn with conflicting emotions." The same sense of right that had restrained him from going to see her, now determined him not to write. Then the warmth with which she had met him—the remembrance of his last visit to her, when she had nestled to his side confessing her unchanged love, the sweet image of her loving face then upturned to his—the passionate kisses, all left him in a mad conflict with love and duty.

Hating her husband at one moment, and pitying him with his better nature the next, thus wrought upon, he recklessly determined to write as he felt. He might, as he thought, at least express himself, and in imagination have the satisfaction of her knowing his feelings. He had no difficulty now.

Wildly dashing off his thoughts, he wrote:

"MY EVER LOVED LUTIE:—

The sight of you this morning which I had prayed God to withhold from me forever, as you leaned upon your husband's arm, drove me almost wild. When, leaving him, you came forward with that sweet, childlike impulsiveness, always so irresistible in you, and put that precious little hand in mine, which I had never thought to clasp again, I felt madly like taking you in my arms, as in other days, and tearing you away from duty, if such it can be called, when you belong to me by the divine right of love, and carrying you off to the ends of the earth, so that you might be mine. I cannot endure it. It maddens me to think of you as the wife of another, when you have told me that I have your love. Don't hate me for this or for anything else. If I do not come to see you it is because I dare not. If I should see you I cannot say what wild thing I might do. For that reason I stay away. Will you not believe that it is because I love you too well that I cannot come. If I listened to my own mad heart I should be with you now. Only write me one line, one little precious line to tell me that you do not hate me.

Yours ever,   GEORGE."

Having wrought himself to desperation in thus recklessly giving vent to his feelings, in the mad impulse of the moment he folded, directed, and sent this wild effusion.

In answer he received this reply:

"DEAR GEORGE:—

I got your note. I don't know what makes you talk so to me. I cried myself to sleep last night when I got it, and I kept waking, sobbing in my sleep. *He* wanted to know what was the matter, but I couldn't tell him for fear he would be mad with me. I didn't tell him before and now somehow I can't. But I don't know what makes you talk so, and why you won't come to see me, and be good friends like we used to be. It is so lonesome and dull in this great big house without mamma and papa, and you are mad with me, and nobody loves me like they used to. His sisters come sometimes and bring their children. I would rather see the children than them, they seem so elegant and proper. At first he was always wanting to pet me, but I don't like him to do it, and he don't seem to love me like he used to, and I try to be good for him too. Now sometimes he looks so grave at me that it scares me, and he seems so old, though he is only two years older than you. I feel like I was getting old myself, though I will not be eighteen until next month. What a charming time we had my last birthday sailing on the bay, and the first thing I saw when I woke up in the morning was the beautiful flowers you sent me, and the sweet little note. Oh! but I ought not to say that now, I suppose, but I'm so lonesome. Sometimes he bows to me like I was company, and says good-morning and goes off. and stays most all day, and I don't know what to do with myself. But when he comes back, he always brings me something pretty. He used to bring me books at first, I am sorry, but I don't like books. And I can't feel glad to see him when he looks so solemn. If I ask him if he is mad with me he says "No, my darling, what have I to be angry about?" and I don't know, but I feel like I have been doing something wrong. I think so often of the merry times we used to have. It seems to me we never had any trouble finding something pleasant to talk about. And what nice long walks we used to take, and how sweet the air was from the sea. I ride there sometimes, but it don't seem the same. I can't go sailing now, I don't know why but I don't feel like it. Don't think he is not good to me. But he reads such awful hard books about 'physics' and 'metaphysics' and 'concepts' and 'entities,' I believe he calls it. And he used to look so grave at me when he found I was asleep while he was reading out loud. But he don't read to me any more now, I suppose it is because I am stupid. He drew what he called a diagram to show me the difference between 'deduction' and 'induction,' to impress it on my mind, but somehow I always forgot. And when he asked if that was induction or deduction. the 'in' arrow was sure to pop into my head instead of the 'de' arrow. That reminds me of when you used to try to teach me to shoot with a bow and arrow, you told me that I would make a better cupid than a Dinah, (Diana,) for the cupid's bow of my mouth shot straight to your heart. Though I am sure I would not have hurt you for anything in the world. You used to fix my hand, and show me how to hold my bow, and how to shoot. And one day when I hit right in the center of the mark—Oh! me! I reckon I ought not to think about that now. But you don't mind hurting my feelings, or you wouldn't write me such a letter, and say you won't come and see me. There, I hear him coming upstairs, and I must stop. So good-bye until I see

you, which I hope will be soon, my dear, naughty old
George.   LUTIE."

Of course he could not but answer this letter. He
replied: "I feel more than ever assured that my only
hope is in absence. I must fly. I am going away. If
the soft sea-air gently touches your pink cheek, believe
it an eternal farewell. I must get away somewhere—
anywhere—to the ends of the earth; away from this
misery. I saw you only a few evenings since from the
far corner of the theater. I could not endure it. I
rushed blindly out, unconscious of everything but of
the bottomless abyss that separates us—as profound
and as horrible as that between Dives and Lazarus. If
I must be as wretched as the one, God grant that you
may not be less happy than the other. Possibly absence, time and work may banish the memory of you
and of my once hoped for happiness."

To this she replied that he was still cruel; he need
not go; or if he would that he might have come to say
good-bye. That even *he* could not have minded my
giving one little farewell kiss to so dear a cousin as
you.

In reply to this he wrote that he thanked God that
he was too far away when this letter reached him to be
tempted to go back upon his determination never to see
her again; feeling that he might not have been able to
tear himself away. That he would give his life if,
rightfully, he might have had the "one little good-bye
kiss." Asking her not to write again, to keep open a
wound the pain of which he felt he had not the fortitude to endure.

Not a year after her husband laid her in the tomb, a
wretched, contrite man, in that he knew her married
life had been a joyless one. Looking over, afterward,
everything connected with her preparatory to putting
them forever from view, he found, carefully tied together, not only these letters received, but copies of

those written in reply. Reading the topmost letter he could but go on. And what a picture was unfolded to his view?

Sleepless and hopeless, almost maddened by this discovery, when sorrow had done its worst and time had assuaged the pain, and he had become comparatively calm, he took the letters his wife had received, enclosed them with these lines and sent them:

"MR. GEORGE HARVEY,

Sir: Enclosed you will find your letters to my wife. I might have been a worse man under the same temptation. You know that I was ignorant or I should not have defrauded you of the right to her love. She is gone to her great account. A merciful God will not judge her harshly.   HAMPTON LEIGH."

And such had been Dr. Leigh's wife.

CHAPTER XXIX.

"O Fleeting joys
Of Paradise, dear bought with lasting woes."

The cloistered buildings of the University, hid away under the grand old forest growth of oaks and elms, had had a charm for Aliena from the time when she had first caught sight of them from her window at the hotel, and heard the old chapel bell toll the hour of her arrival.

This feeling had grown upon her, as in the dimly lighted chapel she had found strength and solace in prayer. Here also, her troubled heart had found utterance in the plaintive music as fluttering and beating against the obstructing arches it seemed to soar on struggling wings for that higher, nobler life of perfect faith, in whose beatitude no pain is mingled.

In the library she had found oblivion at times, in poring over books whose eloquence stirred the heart, or whose rhythmic lines lulled with more soothing power than that wonderful weed, which, bringing to the mind visions of ecstatic bliss, has not the power to prevent its sinking back into no less fathomless depths of black despair.

In the quiet and seclusion of the library she had held converse with the real princes of the earth. Princes who still hold sway when other monarchs have sunk into oblivion, or been buried in the dim records of a dead past. Princes who did not scorn to come, obedient to her call, as the slave to the ring, unfolding treasures richer than ever magic power disclosed.

In these deserted cloistered rooms Mrs. Graeme and Aliena now sought a refuge. Soon the marvelous hieroglyphs, representing nothing " in heaven above, or in the earth beneath, or in the water under the earth," which college students delight in inscribing, disappeared from the walls. Floors disfigured by rough usage were covered. The deep window frames in the massive walls, grotesquely carved by the chiseling tools of would-be Phidias, Praxitiles, or Michael Angelos, were draped in damask—part of the furnishing of Phi Capa or Demosthenian halls, dismantled for Confederate purposes.

Halls where incipient Ciceroes, or Caesars, had " flouted their banners upon the outer walls ; " and frothed, and fumed. lashing themselves to mimic furies in their cramped arenas ; preparatory to those grander ones, where, in imagination, they swayed senates and conquered worlds.

These arrangements having been completed under Aliena's supervision, Mrs. Graeme was ushered into what was to be their home for an indefinite time. As she entered the little parlor she was deeply moved, as facing her she saw her husband's portrait which had hung in the library at home. Beneath it, upon a bracket, stood an antique vase filled with lilies and trailing vines. Here and there little articles of vertu brought with them gave an air of taste and refinement, even under circumstances so unpropitious.

In spite of Aliena's effort at cheerfulness in taking possession of their new home, as twilight came on, an undefined feeling of gloom—of heart-longing for loved voices, forms, and surroundings, came over her, which she found it impossible to throw off. Gliding quietly from the room, where she had been seated with her mother, she moved through the hall to the wide, deep-arched, old-fashioned doorway leading into the grounds. Here, seated upon the steps, her hands lying listlessly in her lap, she leaned wearily back as though partaking bodily of the heart-weariness that oppressed her.

Light, like the hope in her heart, faded, and the shadows of the great trees grew black about her, like those upon her heart. Memory and imagination held their sway.

Aliena rarely resigned herself to thought, and she struggled against it now; but she felt powerless to combat it this evening. She thought remorsefully of Major Baron, as she had so often done since the surrender of Vicksburg. Many weary days had passed since then, and yet she could hear nothing from him. The clanging of the far off iron gate suggested prison bolts and bars. She wondered, if still living, if he were languishing in prison? or if he could have forgotten her?

The sound of footsteps in the distance made her think with a sort of guilty, helpless pang that, while others might be reunited to those they loved, she seemed forever separated by irrevocable fate.

The steps drew nearer. She discerned the gray uniform of a soldier in the dim light. She started to her feet with a great heart-throb, gasping out " Major Baron ! " And his strong arms enfolded her.

CHAPTER XXX.

"Then plainly know my heart's dear love is set ;—
And all combined save what thou must combine
By holy marriage—"

SHAKSPEARE.

From day to day Major Baron could be seen wending his way through the Campus to where, with Aliena, as Othello with Desdemona, he found never ending themes of conversation,

"in battles, sieges, fortunes ;—
Of moving accidents by flood and field ;
Of hair-breadth 'scapes i' the imminent deadly breach ;
Of being taken by the insolent foe."

With which, as with the Moor, love, revivified by Aliena's presence, mingled in all his talk. Soon regardless of everything else, uncertain as to his stay, which might at any time be cut short by his exchange, Major Baron urged a speedy marriage. To this Aliena would not consent. Appealing to Mrs. Graeme, she, in view of her own precarious health and the unprotected condition in which her death would leave Aliena, not only consented, but urged these reasons upon Aliena, who finally consented that a day should be fixed for their marriage before Major Baron's return to the army.

That evening as he was about to leave, Major Baron said to Aliena, "I have a request to make of you. I hope you will grant it. It does not seem suited to our happiness that you should wear mourning. Will you promise to let me see you in white to-morrow evening when I come again? I can fancy you then my bride." Aliena's eyes sank as she caught the ardent look and heard the tone with which he dwelt upon the last words, and she replied with profound sadness.

"It is hard for me to put aside my mourning. I can scarcely realize that in a few short days my father will have been dead two years—two weary years. But if

you wish it, I will do it. To-morrow, too, will be my
birthday," she added with a sigh. "I shall be nineteen
then."

"Mauma, what became of that white dress, the India
swiss I had at home?" said Aliena the following morning, remembering her promise to Major Baron.

"I fetched it along, honey. You never wore it but
once, that day that marster had all them big officers to
dinner to meet President Davis. There was just thir-
teen at the table that day, and marster was the last to
set down. I remember that particuler, for I asked
Washington about it, and sure enough marster was took
before the year was out. Not that I believe in them
sort of things neither, honey, but the Lord has curus
ways of makin his will known." Aliena sighed at this
reminiscence revived by her mention of the dress, feeling the more loth to put it on. Mauma continued.

"I brought it, honey, though it 'peared like to me
you want never goin to wear nothin but black no more.
But I heard mistiss say that the lace on it was worth
its weight in dimuns. You know mistiss never did 'pear
like she keerd for jewelry and sech likes, but she always
had a hankerin for fine lace. I fetched that satin
along too, honey, what marster bought for mistiss when
we was in the old country. You know mistiss was too
sick to wear it, and it ain't never had scissors put to it.
That 'pears like a mighty nice young gentleman that's
comin round here so much, honey. And I didn't know
but what you might want it for—"

"Never mind about the satin," said Aliena quickly,
"but I am going to wear that swiss this evening.
Please have it ready for me, Mauma."

"I'm powerful glad to hear it, honey, though it 'pears
like sometimes that the Lord don't intention for folks to
take off mournin. There's Mrs. Horton, I heerd her
tell mistiss that she had been wearin black for nigh on
to ten years, and that she had quit tryin to git it off,
for as sure as she done it the Lord sent some affliction

upon her, and she had to put it right on again. And ever sence she come to that delusion there had n't been a death in the family."

Aliena showing no disposition to continue this depressing conversation, Mauma went off in search of the dress. Taking it from one of the large trunks, she opened the blue paper in which she had carefully pinned it, to prevent its yellowing, and shaking out the creamy folds a faint odor of violets filled the room. A fragrance which became more distinct, as smoothing its transparent folds and cob-web lace she passed a warm iron over it.

When Aliena returned from the chapel service that evening and entered her room, she shivered strangely as her eyes fell upon the fleecy white dress upon the bed. And her courage almost forsook her at thought of putting it on. Full of melancholy thought she proceeded, however, to do as she had promised.

Aliena could not but feel a sense of satisfaction as, completing her toilet, she surveyed herself in the mirror. Creamy tea roses nestled in her bosom and at her waist, and mingled with the curls which fell from the masses of golden brown hair. The lace of rare and delicate design lay in soft folds about her gracefully poised white throat, about which as about her face tiny rings of shining hair crept out.

The soft trailing of Aliena's dress as she passed through the dimly lighted old hall, with the delicate fragrance that seemed always to environ her, announced her coming to Major Baron as he awaited her in the parlor.

She halted in the doorway as she caught the look of impassioned admiration with which he greeted her appearance, the delicate color suffusing her face.

He rose and came forward to meet her, saying as he surveyed her, "Still my queen." And taking her pink-tipped fingers in his, he led her, as he might have done a queen, to a seat under her father's portrait. Here, seating himself beside her, his manly person set off to advantage in his uniform, his glowing face lit up with admiration and love, the trailing vines and flowers of the antique vase crowning them from above ; it would have been difficult to have found a more charming picture.

Taking a jewel case from his breast-pocket, Major Baron unclasped and opened it.   It seemed to leap into flame as the light fell upon a bracelet of curious, antique design.   An emerald serpent, with its glittering diamond eyes that lay coiled upon the white satin cushion.

" Let this, a bridal present from my father to my mother, who died before I could remember, be the pledge of our betrothal," said Major Baron, raising Aliena's perfectly molded arm and clasping it there.

Aliena shivered strangely as he did so.   It might have been at the touch, or it may have been at sight of the perfectly represented glittering serpent upon her arm—or some more mysterious influence even may have moved her.

" You wear it willingly, I hope ? " said Major Baron, looking curiously into her face as he perceived the tremor.

" We are pledged," Aliena said in a strange, unnatural voice, turning deathly white.

" Will you wear it always until you give me the right to claim you as my own ? " he continued, chilled, however, by her tone.

" I will wear it always," she replied, in the same unnatural voice.

Major Baron taking a singular looking key from his chatelaine, adjusted it in the clasp, locked it with a soft click, and replaced the key upon his chatelaine, saying :

" To-day, your birthday, must hereafter mark, not only the day that gave you to brighten the world, but the brightest day in our calendar, until that other day that seems so distant now, when I shall claim you as my bride."

Aliena, lifting her sad, beautiful eyes to the portrait looking down upon them, said solemnly, "I ought to find happiness in the thought that through him I first knew you. And if the spirits of the loved are ever permitted to hover around those dear to them on earth, I pray that his may be bending in benediction above us now."

Impressed by the solemnity that tinged Aliena's manner, not only now, but during the whole evening, Major Baron, when he rose to go, bent in almost reverence, barely touching with his lips the taper fingers he took in his shapely hand, as he bade her good-night.

He took out his cigar case as he walked on under the trees in the Campus, intending to smoke, but finding it empty, and thinking that he might be able to procure some better cigars than those to be had at the hotel, he strolled on down the now almost deserted street.

The only lights at first visible were in the windows where the great sapphire, topaz and ruby colored globes marked the druggist's. He came at length in sight of a light in an insignificant looking shop at almost the terminus of the street. In the window was the inevitable savage warrior smoking the calumet of peace, typical of a tobacco shop. Here with the usual surroundings were pipes, cigars and tobacco of all sorts.

Moving on, with the intention of entering the shop, before reaching the door Major Baron caught sight through the window of something which seemed suddenly to paralyze motion. It was the beautiful girlish face, with the great, startled black eyes that had so attracted Aliena's admiration upon the cars; with the sinister face of the man who had accompanied her. Major Baron as he halted aghast at this sight, was not only near enough to see, but to catch the sound of the voices. His painfully alert ears even distinguished the words in the stillness.

"I saw him, sure, again to-night, with his cursed handsome face. He was clasping a bracelet on the arm of the beautiful girl we saw on the cars. It shall be the worse for him. I swear to God, Zara, it shall be the worse for him, if it is that he does not marry you," the man hissed between his teeth.

"Let me see him, father. Let me only see him. It must be that he has come to see me. He has promised to marry me. He has followed me here. I have not despaired. He must pity me," the low, musical voice said pleadingly, the sound dying out in a wail; and she put her hands to her face and sobbed aloud.

"I swear to God he shall marry you," the man hissed —repeating more venomously, if possible, "I swear to God he shall," and his face assumed a diabolic look in his rage.

Major Baron, recovering himself, staggered back from the shop, and walked rapidly up the street, pursued in thought by this Nemesis that had thus unexpectedly tracked his footsteps to this secluded spot, at a time when of all others he adjured the presence.

Coming again in view of the towering oaks and elms where under their shadows, in one of the old cloistered buildings, a white-souled form kneeled, consecrating him and her own troubled heart to God in prayer, Maj. Baron groaned in spirit as he hurried on.

Returning to the hotel he contented himself now with the cigars to be found there.

Instead of going to his room he went out upon the deserted gallery fronting the University grounds. Here he smoked his cigar ineffectually as far as his perturbed mind was concerned. No Lotus weed had power now to tranquilize to Lethean stillness the scorpion stings with which conscience lacerated the breast of this Priapus, in face of what he had just seen and heard. He tremblingly realized, brave as he was physically, how cruelly " conscience doth make cowards of us all."

But for the promise of marriage which he had so passionately urged upon Aliena, only the day before ; and for the troth so solemnly renewed this evening, a

time that from the pain since endured seemed to
stretch into the dim past, he would have fled affrighted
as much at thought of exposure as of vengeance.

Tormented by doubts, without the apparent possibility of a tenable conclusion, Maj. Baron sat possibly
for hours in fruitless, perplexing thought. At length
crunching his unlit cigar between his teeth, which he
had long since unconsciously allowed to go out, he
threw it from him into the deserted street, and retired
to bed. Here he tossed in sleepless wretchedness until
exhausted he sank to troubled sleep as gray dawn crept
slowly and drearily over the horizon.

CHAPTER XXXI.

"Nay curs'd be thou since 'gainst his, thy will
Chose freely what it now so justly rues,
Me miserable! which way shall I fly
Infinite wrath and infinite despair?
Which way I fly is hell; myself am hell;
And in the lowest deep a lower deep
Still threat'ning to devour me opens wide
To which the hell I suffer seems a heaven."
MILTON : PARADISE LOST.

"Marster, Miss Zara and old Varja's here. I seen
him last night," said Auguste to Maj. Baron the morning after the latter had himself so unexpectedly become
aware of that startling fact.

"Where did you see them?" asked Maj. Baron,
nervously anxious for information in regard to them.

"I was a walkin' down street last night, just after
you went into the Campus, and I seen Varja comin'
towards me. I knowed him before he got nigh me, and
I dodged around a corner. You know he's kinder
savigerous lookin', but I watched him until I seen him
go past, and go into the Campus."

"You keep out of his way," interrupted Maj. Baron sharply, in a state of nervous irritation which quickly silenced Auguste.

Lounging in the office of the hotel after breakfast, which had an outlook upon the street, Maj. Baron endeavored to interest himself in reading the war news. But even the stirring events of those times could not absorb his thoughts, or prevent their tormenting him with constantly recurring anxiety, as to the unexpected complication in which he found himself involved.

His eyes as he sat here were attracted to the street by the driving up of a stylish looking team and phaeton. In this was a young man in the uniform of a Confederate colonel, with a little more than the regulation amount of gold lace. Throwing the reins to his servant, the young man sprang from the carriage and entered the office.

"Why, how do you do, Baron?" he exclaimed in a delighted tone of surprise, as he caught sight of Major Baron. And coming forward he shook hands with him in an enthusiastic way.

There was something about the sort of roll in the springy walk, and in the easy devil-may-care manner of the young man, that indicated the sailor and the cosmopolitan. He was a little above medium height, with dark hair, a somewhat prominent aquiline nose, clear gray eyes, and a carefully trained black mustache and side whiskers.

"I am charmed to see you, Massey," said Major Baron in delighted surprise, his voice and manner indicating more pleasure than one might have expected at the time. "Where did you spring from? I had no idea of meeting you here."

"Have you forgotten that this is my home? I am here on a short furlough, and I am delighted to meet you once more, old fellow. I hope we may have a chance to renew some of our Mediterranean reminiscences, and have a good time generally together. This is my first visit home since I went into the army, at the beginning of the war. But how on earth did you happen to bring up in this quiet out-of-the-way little place?"

"I had the misfortune to be surrendered at Vicksburg, and am a vagabond upon the earth for the time being, floating around on parole."

"I would like to be floating around myself—literally, upon the sea, I mean. You might as well try to make a Christian of a Jew, as a land-lubber of a sailor,

'A life on the ocean wave
A home on the rolling deep'

forever for me."

"One scarcely connects the idea of home with a sailor. I remember now that Miss Graeme told me, that this was your home, but I had really forgotten it."

"What Miss Graeme are you talking about?"

"Don't you remember the Graemes that were on board your vessel with me on several occasions, at Nice?"

"Of course I do. Was n't there a pretty, brown-eyed, soft-voiced girl in the party, not quite grown?"

"Yes, with her father, a tall, elegant looking man, and an invalid mother. They were there for Mrs. Graeme's health."

"Certainly, I remember them. The girl was about in the chrysalis state, wings beginning to show and flutter. I fell half in love with that girl, with her tender, dreamy brown eyes, and a mouth as sensitive as a mimosa. Where did you see them? And what has become of them now?"

"They are here, refugees, at least the mother and daughter are, in the University buildings."

"You don't say so, that is delightful. I wonder mother and sister have not found them out—but possibly they have, and not told me. I only arrived yesterday. I was just beginning to wonder how I was to kill time. She must be about eighteen, now. She has plantations also, if I remember rightly. That might cover a multitude of sins even. But this lovely creature in the bargain? I'll pitch right in—provided you are not in before me."

"You have not changed much I see since I saw you. I thought time might have cured you of some of your rattling nonsense before this."

"When did you don the garb of a saint? According to my remembrance that was not your normal condition when I saw you last. It strikes me that there is something of the midnight oil tinge about you—but I know it isn't study, unless it is the study of that most intricate problem that ever puzzled the brain of man—a feminine heart in a pretty form. 'Tell me in sadness who it is you love?'"

"You forget that I am recently from sultry trenches, bean bread and mule steak. You must not expect me to look as fresh as a 'buttermilk ranger,'" said Major Baron with a sickly effort at a smile.

"Since you deny the soft impeachment suppose we go over at once and call upon Miss Graeme? There is no time we can be sure of but the present. My furlough is short and I must be like the little busy bee. Don't think I mean anything personal, but I feel that I am wasting time talking to a man. I have been with 'villainous bearded pards' until I am tempted to forswear the society of man forever. I have made a vow that if I ever get out of this war I will either set up a millinery establishment, or open a boarding school for young ladies exclusively," said Colonel Massey.

"I have not told you that Miss Graeme lost her father two years ago. He was killed at the battle of Manassas," said Major Baron.

"I am sorry to hear that. I remember to have seen a notice of the death of a Colonel Graeme and of his gallantry upon the battlefield of Manassas, and I wondered at the time if it was the same person. Whatever became of your friend who was traveling with you in Italy? I have forgotten his name."

"Seldon? He is in the Yankee army. Does n't that seem strange?" said Major Baron. And drawing on his gloves they walked on toward the Campus.

"By Jove! That must be the siren singing now. And never did

> ' Mother Circe and the sirens three
>   Amidst the flowery Näiades
> Culling their potent herbs and baneful drugs,
> Who, as they sung, would take the prisoned soul
> And lap it in Elysium,'

sing a sweeter song. It is an Italian one too as I live. It carries me back to the billowy waves and soft air of the Mediterranean. What glorious times we had there. That must be Miss Graeme herself, and that is one of the memories of that land of song she has revived. I don't wonder that Ulysses had to be tied to his mast and his ears stopped with wax, if the sirens ever uttered sounds as sweet as that," said Colonel Massey as they arrived at the door.

Aliena rose from the piano as they were ushered into the room, and not only recognized Colonel Massey, but moved forward and greeted him with such evident pleasure as charmed him. A salutation to which he responded with even more than his usual enthusiasm.

"Don't let our coming stop your music," said Colonel Massey after a few greeting remarks had been interchanged. "Nothing could have more charmingly reminded me of the days when we were together upon the Mediterranean than the song you were singing. It flooded me with memories of those times."

"I am indebted to Major Baron for recalling it, and if he will join me I will sing it with pleasure," she replied.

Major Baron had seated himself a little apart, and seemed to have sunk into an abstracted mood, but he rose now mechanically, and without replying, walked to the piano with Aliena. And soon his rich tenor voice was mingling with hers in the song.

Major Baron, standing by Aliena's side, faced the open window where the curtains were drawn partly aside to admit the air.

Suddenly his voice faltered into a discord. Looking up at him Aliena was surprised and shocked at the fixed look of terror depicted upon his blanched face as he stood, as though transfixed, with his eyes riveted upon the window.

Following their direction she saw, between the curtains, the sinister face of a man, his eyes glittering like a tiger's ready to spring upon his prey, as he peered into the room. The man moved on almost instantly.

Aliena, turning to Major Baron, whose face still wore a strangely terrified conscience-smitten expression, asked:

"Who was that horrible man? What could he have wanted here?"

"I am sure I can't tell," said Major Baron with painful embarrassment.

"His expression was murderous as he peered in," said Aliena.

"It was all lost upon me," said Colonel Massey, "I was too much absorbed in the music to have seen him, even if I could have done so where I sat. Let me get a sight of the impudent intruder," and moving toward the window he looked out and added, "His back looks mild enough. I suppose he was passing through the Campus, and it is not to be wondered at that your music drew him, as it might have done the very stocks and stones. For never

> 'Did Thracian shepherd by the grave
> Of Orpheus hear a sweeter melody.'"

This proved a fortunate diversion for Major Baron, as it gave him an opportunity somewhat to recover himself.

"I met that man on the cars as we were coming here from Chattanooga," said Aliena. "I was struck then with the sinister expression of his face, and with his disagreeable voice and manner; the more so from the contrast with his companion, a beautiful girl, about seventeen. She reminded me of the Beatrici Cenci, in the Colonna palace," Aliena said, and looking up at Major Baron she was again strangely and painfully impressed by the look of conscience-smitten embarrassment depicted in his face. And a feeling of contempt flashed through her mind, in spite of herself, as she connected this with the terror-stricken expression it had worn while the peering face scowled in at the window.

The conversation, drifting to other subjects, devolved principally upon Col. Massey, who seemed at no loss for topics of interest, in reminiscences with which he went on in spite of the abstracted expression in Aliena's face.

As they were about leaving, Aliena, who could not but observe Maj. Baron's silence and depression, as well as his unusual pallor, feeling that in her mind she had possibly been doing him injustice, said, addressing him,

"Are you feeling well to-day Maj. Baron? It seems to me that you are looking pale."

"Yes—no, I am not feeling very well," he answered, truly in a certain sense at least, his face reddening like a girl's, as he met her scrutinizing look. And bidding her good-morning they left.

"Look here, Baron," said Col. Massey as they left the house, "that was a confounded shabby trick you were trying to play off upon me, making me believe I had an open sea and nothing to do but sail into port, and drop anchor. You are in love with that girl yourself; I never saw you regularly spooney before. I am a little dubious about entering against you. I may not find it easy sailing after all. Somehow you always seemed to have the knack of getting away with

women. I shouldn't wonder if that is the secret of
finding you here in this quiet little out-of-the-way haven.
You'll be a lucky dog if you get her. I would be
willing to 'forswear villainy and vice' for the balance of
my days for such a prize."

"I am glad you are so easily driven off. I am willing to accept the situation. Though you flatter me,
I fear, and I could never expect to win if you really
entered the list," said Maj. Baron with a sickly effort
at badinage.

"Don't let's go back to the hotel. Get in with me,
and I'll drive you around and show you some of the
beauties of our place," said Col. Massey, as they were
crossing the street to the hotel where he had left his
phaeton.

"That will be an improvement upon loafing around
the hotel," said Maj. Baron. "I have been giving
myself up to a sort of *dolce far niente* since I came here
and have seen very little of your place. I needed rest
after what we had to undergo at Vicksburg, but I am
getting restless with inaction I suppose. I am a sort of
bird of passage any way."

Returning to the hotel, after driving for some time,
Col. Massey said as he was about leaving, "Baron, we
are to have the fatted calf at our house Wednesday
evening, in honor of the returned prodigal, with a
dance and all that sort of thing. Gen. Carleton has
halted here, passing through, with part of his division;
we expect it to be rather a brilliant affair. Can't you
come and bring Miss Graeme? I want you to know
my family. Though I don't pretend to much modesty,
and consider myself a pretty fair specimen. I am by
no means the best of the clan."

"I shall take pleasure in becoming acquainted with
your family, and will do my best to induce Miss Graeme
to accompany me to the party, though I can't promise
for her." And saying good-morning, Colonel Massey
drove off.

CHAPTER XXXII.

"You are no surer, no,
Than is the coal of fire upon the ice,
Or hailstone in the sun.
Lo, here upon thy cheek the stain doth sit
Of an old tear that is not washed off."

SHAKSPEARE.

The same feeling of annoyance and apprehension returned with redoubled force to Major Baron, when, having re-entered the hotel, he found time for thought in his own room. The scowling face of Varja, as he had recklessly peered in at the window, had not been calculated to lessen this feeling. Seating himself wearily, Major Baron's contracted brow and compressed lips indicated his sorely anxious thoughts.

He sat here for hours, perhaps. Having reached the conclusion at length, that his only hope for safety from exposure and vengeance lay in Zara's love and interposition in his behalf, he determined to seek an interview with her, doubtful as was the prudence and expediency of this step.

With this purpose in view he now wrote to her:

"ZARA:

I am here to see you. I should have done so before but for reasons I will explain when we meet. Be in the cemetery, near the large mausoleum at sunset. C.
JULY 17, 1863."

The drive of the morning had brought him in view of this spot, and from its seclusion it had suggested itself to him as the place for this meeting, least likely to attract observation, or if seen to arouse suspicion.

Ringing for Auguste, he asked, "Have you seen Varja this morning?"

"Yes, marster. I seen him come up the street and go into the Campus just after you and that gentleman in the Colonel's uniform went in there."

"Here is a note I wish you to get into Miss Zara's hands without her father's seeing it. If you can't do it yourself without being seen by him, and I want you to keep out of his sight, get some one else to do it. But be sure that it is put into her hands. Here is some money."

"Yes, marster, I'll see that it gets there, sure," said Auguste in a sprightly voice. A tone as much the consequence of the satisfaction in engaging in a surreptitious affair as of the possession of the money placed in his hands.

"Auguste, I shan't need that brown cloth suit of mine, you can have it. You are looking rather shabby."

"Thank you, marster," he replied with a military salute.

"And I want you to get me the handsomest bouquet and some of the finest peaches and grapes to be had, and have them here before sunset."

"Yes, marster, I'll have 'em here. The finest to be had in this legion of country," said Auguste, and waiting to see if his master had any farther commands, he disappeared.

Major Baron tried to pass away the time until evening by sleeping; more to rid himself of thought than because he had scarcely slept at all the night before. But he found sleep impossible. Rising he took a book, hoping to find relief in that, but failed equally.

Auguste came at length with the flowers and fruit, and with the assurance of the safe delivery of the note to Zara. Major Baron then wrote to Aliena:

"I am sorely disappointed in not being able to be with you this evening as I had hoped, but I am not feeling well. I send the flowers and fruit to represent me. If the flowers do not say everything that is beautiful and sweet to you, they are recreant messengers. I shall envy the grapes and peaches the privilege of being pressed to the sweetest lips that man ever hoped to possess. I will see you to-morrow, until which eternity,

Lovingly and truly yours,

ATHENS, July 17, 1863.   CECIL BARON."

Auguste, having been despatched with this note, and with the flowers and fruit, Major Baron started by a circuitous route toward the cemetery, not daring to go through the Campus. Happening upon a path that led him by a retired way over some stiles, he walked on toward the mausoleum. It was almost twilight, when, guided by the towering spire, he made his way to the designated place of meeting.

Zara, who for some time had awaited Major Baron, had, as she thought, heard footsteps approaching and had moved out to view. But failing to see any one, and awakened to renewed fear of observation, though it was late for loiterers, she seated herself, almost crouching in the tall grass, behind the tomb. Hence at first Major Baron failed to discern her. Starting again nervously as his footsteps announced his approach, and catching sight of him now, she rose to her feet. Trembling with emotion, she awaited his approach.

"Oh! Cecil, I thought you would never come," she gasped out as he drew near. And throwing herself upon his breast, she clasped her arms around his neck, sobbing convulsively upon his shoulder, as his arms coldly supported her.

The feelings that surged through the breast of Major Baron may be more easily imagined than described, as he stood thus stonily clasped by arms whose caress had once had so different a power. He raised the beautiful, tear-stained face at length and kissed her on the brow. Zara's heart sank within her as she felt how coldly.

"Oh! Cecil, it was so long—and I could not see you, or let you know where I was. How did you find me here?"

"It does not matter how I found you, does it? so I am here," said Major Baron.

Both started guiltily at a sound, as of a twig stepped upon and crackling under foot.

"Come, let us walk on," said Major Baron in a sup-

pressed tone, and they took the path leading down to
the river.

"Does your father know anything?" he asked.

"Yes, I could not help it," she replied, laying her icy
hand on his arm and looking into his face with an appealing, frightened expression in the great, black eyes.

"He is so violent it frightens me. Try not to cross
his path, Cecil. He was wild with rage to-day. He
says he saw you bending over a beautiful young lady—
singing love songs with her. Do not arouse my father.
I cannot tell what he may do. You could not desert
me, Cecil? You could not desert me now?"

"You must quiet your father. Tell him I have
come to marry you. You can keep him from doing
anything rash."

"Then you have come to marry me, my darling?"
she said, clasping his arm with both her hands, and
looking up beseechingly into his handsome, stony face.

"Yes, to marry," he answered coldly.

"When? my noble, good Cecil, when?" she asked,
clinging to him.

"I cannot say what day yet, but soon. I must be
ready to take you away. I am obliged to be here for
a while."

"It must be soon," the girl said, turning scarlet in
the twilight.

"I must go now," he answered stolidly.

The sound of the falling water around them—the ripple, gurgle, splash and roar, with the deepening and
dying wail in the pines, that the evening breeze brought
to him in the twilight, surrounded as he was by the
ghostly-white tombs, added to the heart-sickness that
oppressed Major Baron, as they retraced their steps.

"We must part here," he said as they reached the
stiles

"When shall I see you again?" Zara asked.

"Thursday, here by the river. You had best go
now," he said, as Zara halted looking into his face, per-

haps for a different parting, and she moved slowly and sadly on. He waited until she was lost to view, and then followed, stealing back in the darkness to the hotel.

Zara walked on alone with a sorely aching heart—despite the reiterated promise of marriage. Thinking of his manner, which she knew too well not to mark the change. Heart-sore she entered, through a side door, the room in the rear of the shop.

In a few moments she saw her father come into the shop through the front door; where only the dim taper kept burning to light cigars, was yet lighted. He came on into the room where Zara was in the act of striking a light.

"Where is it that you have been, Zara?" he asked abruptly, in a fierce tone. Zara saw the demon look lowering under his eyebrow, and she knew she must answer truthfully.

"I have been to meet him. He is to marry me. It will be soon."

"What day?" the father asked, through clinched teeth.

"He wants to take me away. He has some business. He must attend to that first. He cannot say what day yet."

"I tell you, Zara, if it is not soon that it is done he shall wake up in hell. I swear to God he shall wake up in hell."

"Father," said Zara in an entreating tone, moving towards him, and putting her hand on his shoulder, "Have pity upon me, I love him."

"Is it that he pities you?" he said, throwing her hand off fiercely.

"Your mother gave her life for you. You are my all. And he comes with devil's arts. I don't want that I see him. If it is not soon that he marries you he shall wake up in hell. I swear to God he shall wake up in hell." Varja hissed through his clinched teeth, grinding them in his rage.

Did the flowers sent speak beautiful things to Aliena?
If they spoke truthfully the violets, tea roses, and
jasmines must have exhaled mournfully circling incense around the altar of a dead love, over which the
grapes poured a funeral libation, while nodding fuchsias
and fairy bells tolled a requiem.

CHAPTER XXXIII.

*" At my poor house look to behold this night,
Earth treading stars that make dark heaven light."*
                                        SHAKSPEARE.

The following evening Maj. Baron paid his accustomed visit to Aliena. He was looking sufficiently
jaded and depressed to confirm what he had written,
that he was not feeling well. Having little desire to
converse, he soon asked Aliena to sing. He regretted
the request the next moment as he thought with apprehension of the sardonic face her voice might again con-
jure to the open window. But, walking with her to the
piano, as he returned he silently closed the blinds, and
seated himself lolling wearily back in his chair while
she sang.

It may have been her own mood, or Maj. Baron's
may unconsciously have affected her, but Aliena too
seemed for some reason to prefer singing, and she went
on from one song of profoundest sadness to another,
singing with unwonted pathos.

He made his visit shorter than usual, almost forgetting to ask, as he had promised Col. Massey to do, if
Aliena would go with him to the party.

"I suppose you are invited to the Masseys for
Thursday evening," he said listlessly as he rose to leave.

" Yes, Col. Massey and his sister called yesterday and invited me."

" Will you allow me the pleasure of escorting you there ? " he asked indifferently, hoping really that she would decline.

But something lately seemed to have inspired Aliena with a strange spirit of recklessness. This must have come over her now, as hesitating for a moment, to Maj. Baron's surprise she replied, " Yes, I will go."

Mauma was thrown into an intense state of delighted excitement, when Aliena the next morning announced her intention to go to the party. " What are you goin' to wear, honey ? " she asked.

" The same swiss I wore the other evening, I suppose, I had not thought of that."

" Laws a marcy ! honey, it would never do for you to wear that dress. You've done worn it twice already. And there's that satin I told you I fetched along ; that could easy be made up in time for the party, and the lovely lace overdress that mistiss bought in the old country for your comin out dress, you know she never could desist lace ; and the handkerchief and the pearl handled fan just to match, and mistiss dimuns. That would just look lovely ? " and Mauma's face fairly glowed with delight at the possibility of seeing Aliena thus arrayed.

" I might as well wear the lace and satin, I suppose," said Aliena.

" I'm powerful glad. honey. That 'll be somethin like. You ain't had nothin but sorrer and tribberlation these last years of your life noways, honey ; and I know the Lord must have some good in store for you. I did think you was gettin sorter perked up, before we left home, but it 'pears like to me since we got inter this great old, hanted house that you've been monsus onrestless in yer mind. It don't never do to shut young folks up like they was in a nunnery, where they can't have no reversion."

When Major Baron called for Aliena the evening of the party, he found her looking lovely, in the soft, creamy satin, which, training in graceful folds, gave a statuesque appearance to her exquisitely rounded form, draped as it was with gossamer *point de Venice* lace of rare design, caught here and there over the satin, with dewy lilies of the valley. The pure white of her rounded arms and bust veiled with the lace scarcely contrasted with the pear-shaped pearls pendent from her ears and suspended about her throat. The pearls had been a bridal present to her aunt, of melancholy memory, whose portrait, hanging in the dining-room of the Castle, Aliena was said so strangely to resemble. These, partly veiled by the lace, rose and fell with the soft breathing with faint iridescent shimmer. Sprays of the same dewy lilies nestled at her bosom, and in her golden brown curls; and, with roses and fuchsias, formed the exquisite bouquet, which, with her lace, fan and handkerchief she carried in her hand. The jeweled serpent glittering upon her arm was the only colored ornament she wore.

Professor and Mrs. Layton had, at Miss Massey's suggestion, proffered to chaperone Aliena, and being announced, Major Baron wrapped a fleecy white shawl about the lovely girl, and going out they joined the other couple in the carriage. They soon entered the beautiful grounds of the Masseys, and through its winding carriage drive, came in view of the imposing house now flooded with light.

The colonnade in front of the house, reached by a broad flight of steps, extended not only across the front of the main building, but around the sides, thence spreading out before the wide wings. Both pedestals and capitals of the columns as well as the massive cornice were elaborately adorned with carvings of lotus leaves and flowers.

Through the grand doorway of the great hall, and through the lace draped ample windows, open to the floor, the light streamed out upon the colonnade. Here, ladies in gracefully flowing trains, and gentlemen resplendent in the gold lace, stars and bars of their military uniforms, promenaded in couples in constantly interweaving lines.

Professor and Mrs. Layton with Major Baron and Aliena having entered, moved through the thronged rooms to pay their respects to the host and hostess. Judge Massey received them with that courtly dignity and grace which was natural to him. Mrs. Massey welcomed them cordially, but in her calm, dignified way, which was as unlike her son's manner as was her appearance in her quaker-colored silk and white lace head-dress.

"I am delighted to see you," said Colonel Massey, approaching Aliena, as soon as he caught sight of her. "I had begun to fear you would play us false, and not make your appearance. When can I have the pleasure of a dance with you? I have been reserving myself for this privilege."

"I am not likely to be burdened with engagements as you may imagine, as you and Major Baron are the only acquaintances I have here. Unless I except your father and Prof. Layton, who is scarcely likely to unbend the dignity of his portly person, to say nothing of his profession, by 'capering in the nimble dance,'" said Aliena smiling.

"I don't know about Prof. Layton, but I am sure if father thought he could have the honor of your hand he would at least walk a stately minuet with you. But I shall claim the privilege of representing him upon this occasion. Major Baron, I suppose, lays claim to the first dance. The next is a waltz, can I have that?"

"I have a prior claim to that also," interposed Major Baron quickly.

"The set after, then?" said Colonel Massey.

And receiving an affirmative answer he hurried off to secure a partner for the coming quadrille.

13

Major Baron proffered his arm. and, as they walked on to take their position for the dance, he said to Aliena,

“ Pardon me for asserting a claim to the waltz that I did not possess, but I could not endure the thought of seeing you waltz with any one else.”

“ I had not intended to waltz. If I should waltz with you now, I must with Colonel Massey.”

“ Your waltzing with me is quite different, you can give him some excuse if he asks again.”

“ I shall certainly tell him only the truth if I give him any excuse,” said Aliena, coldly, and the music commencing she moved off in the dance.

“ I am so glad to see you here,” said Miss Massey. approaching and offering her hand cordially to Aliena as the waltz ended. “ Let me introduce Captain Brandon?” she said, introducing the gentleman upon whose arm she was leaning. “ Have you seen Pres? I know he would have been disappointed if you had not come. But there he comes now.”

“ Why, Nell, I scarcely knew you. I was wondering who it was that seemed to know Miss Graeme so well,” said Colonel Massey.

“ It seems odd, but between the sea and the war I don’t think you have ever seen me in evening dress since I was out of pinafores,” said Miss Massey, who was looking quite radiant, flushed from the dance, in a peach blossom, pink silk and roses to correspond.

She was wonderfully like her brother in appearance, with the same somewhat aquiline profile. which they inherited from their father, dark hair, gray, spirited eyes, fine teeth and complexion. She was decidedly *distingué* in appearance, with a fine form and bearing, and something of dash in her stylish person.

“ This is my set,” said Colonel Massey, holding out his hand to lead Aliena to their position upon the floor, as Miss Massey’s partner came to claim her.

“ I did not see you in the waltz?” he continued as they moved on.

"I was not there," Aliena replied laconically.

"I am really disappointed. I understood that you were to waltz with Major Baron, or I should have claimed you myself."

"It was a mistake," she answered in the same laconic style. Something in her tone prevented his continuing the subject.

Colonel Massey's contagious spirits, the exhilaration of the dance, or some more subtile influence which had of late made Aliena less equable in spirits than was natural with her, must have conduced to the unnatural gayety which seemed to possess her for the time. This showed itself in her lustrous eyes and in her heightened color, making her almost dazzling in beauty and adding a piquancy and brilliancy to her conversation which drew around her a throng of admirers during the whole evening.

Having finished their dance, Colonel Massey claimed Aliena for a promenade upon the colonnade. As they walked across the brilliantly lighted rooms, her color suddenly left her for the moment, surging back in delicate pink, as in the distance she saw Dr. Leigh, who had just entered the rooms.

He bowed as his eyes met hers, his face lighting up in delighted surprise at seeing her here, as well as at the dazzling transformation in her appearance.

"Where did you know Dr. Leigh?" asked Colonel Massey, seeing her recognition.

"Mother was extremely ill at Chattanooga, and I think he saved her life."

"He is one of our most distinguished surgeons and physicians; you were fortunate in having him with your mother. He has been sent here to open some hospitals I hear, on account of the retreat of our army in Tennessee. He only came yesterday. Mother has known his family always. He belongs to one of the most historic families of South Carolina, and is an elegant gentleman, though I need not tell you this, as you have no doubt discovered that fact for yourself. I am a little surprised that he accepted the invitation for to-night. I had heard that since his wife's death he never went into society. I have a vague sort of remembrance that there was something unusually sad and painful connected with his married life. You knew, I suppose, that he had lost his wife?"

Aliena made no reply, but shivered strangely, leaning heavily upon Col. Massey's arm.

"I fear the night air chills you after dancing. Shall we go into the conservatory?"

"No, no, let me stay here," said Aliena.

"I am afraid if you were to ask me to give you your 'quietus with a bare bodkin' in that tone, I should scarcely be able to resist, much less to do anything so agreeable to myself," said Colonel Massey, continuing their promenade.

The music commencing, Aliena was sought by her partner for the dance. As she took her position Dr. Leigh approached her. He came forward with that quiet, self oblivious ease which always distinguished him. His superiority seemed instinctively accorded him by the admirers by whom Aliena was surrounded, who were seeking engagements to dance. Dr. Leigh was not in his surgeon's uniform, as she had been accustomed to see him, but wore instead the conventional suit of black cloth, which seemed to accord particularly well with him.

The dance was about to commence, and he had scarcely more than time to ask for a promenade with her after the quadrille, which she promised,

When Dr. Leigh returned to claim Aliena for the promenade she almost shrank from complying with her engagement, and she scarcely more than touched his arm with her gloved hand as they moved out upon the colonnade.

While Dr. Leigh had seen Aliena in the garish light, brilliant in beauty, moving with exquisite grace in the mazes of the dance, she had seemed to him a thing apart. He could scarcely realize that she was the same gentle girl, who, in mourning garb, had ministered with loving grace by the bedside of a sick mother. Or who had sat in quiet, dreamy happiness beside him upon the Point of Rocks, drinking in the beauty of the lovely view it commanded; permeated as it were with the sense of the beautiful. One imbued with that rare and inexplicable charm of sensitive, delicate, silent sympathy. These memories scarcely seemed consonant with her present dazzling beauty, her gayety, and her brilliant artificial surroundings.

But getting away from the crowd, the glitter and glare, comparatively alone with Aliena, in the subdued light, the influence of her presence reasserted itself. Taking her hand as it lay lightly upon his arm he drew it farther, feeling an almost irresistible desire to retain the soft hand in his own, as he realized the exquisite loveliness of the girl, draped in that soft cloud of lace, shimmering with satin and pearls, and fragrant with dewy lilies. He remembered the time when he had carried her in his arms, with a longing once more to fold her to his heart.

"I had so associated you with the sort of nun's garb, with the tender offices of the sick room, and with the dreamy happiness of the solitary haunts of nature; that this brilliant transformation almost bewildered me at first. I am only beginning to realize that you are yourself. And that you still carry the same tender, womanly nature with you, transfigured as you are," said Dr. Leigh.

"It seems almost as hard for me to realize that I am myself to-night. Suppose we consider that we have suffered a metempsychosis and start anew," said Aliena, impelled by the same reckless spirit which possessed her this evening.

Dr. Leigh's countenance and tone changed instantly, as this reply jarred harshly upon him. "I do not esteem the memories of the past so lightly myself as willingly to surrender them for whatever there may be in the blank future before me," he replied.

" You implied that you did not like me so well, as I am at present," said Aliena, still strangely jangled out of tune.

" I do not think that what I said could justly be so construed. Though, if you make it so, I will not deny that at present, at least, there seems an imperceptible, subtile something lacking, which permeated you at Lookout, as the fragrance of the lilies you wear does the air we breathe."

" You are truthful, at least, if less complimentary than—" Aliena, glancing into Dr. Leigh's eyes, broke down in this reply, so unlike herself.

" You are looking more brilliantly beautiful to-night than I ever saw you," said Dr. Leigh, looking sadly at her.

The delicate pink suffused Aliena's face and white throat, at this response, which she felt that she had brought upon herself, and she said, " I am sorry to have forced you to do violence to your feelings in a compliment extorted by my foolish remark."

" I assure you that no remark, even from you, could have extorted anything but the truth from me," said Dr. Leigh somewhat haughtily. " I still claim that my remark is not inconsistent with the fact, that there may be a rarer and more subtile charm, somewhat inconsonant with brilliancy, that does not at all times accompany even the most dazzling beauty. It is dependent possibly upon inexplicable psychological conditions which are beyond the power of the most beautiful to command."

" I don't know what I lay claim to to-night—or whether I have a soul at all," said Aliena, in a tone of weariness, not only induced by this conversation, but the consequence of her general state of mind.

Dr. Leigh, annoyed by Aliena's apparent misconception of what he had said, as well as at her manner, which seemed abruptly to dismiss the subject of their conversation, was unwilling again to allude to it.

Aliena felt instantly and keenly a sense of wrong, but the evil genius which seemed to rule her this evening prevented her giving token of this feeling. And the conversation drifted for the few moments before she was claimed for the next dance into the formal discussion of commonplace topics.

Aliena appeared even more recklessly gay during the remainder of the evening. Major Baron seemed imbued with the same spirit as he whirled past Aliena in the waltz. And almost to her own amazement she found herself whirling in a waltz with Colonel Massey, into which she seemed to enter with a sort of wild delight as well as with exquisite grace, in which she was well sustained by her expert partner. As she moved around the room she caught Dr. Leigh's intense eyes fixed upon her with a pained look of wonder and astonishment.

Aliena seemed, in fact, to enter with zest into a flirtation with Colonel Massey, into which he would have been recreant to himself if he had not launched with delighted enthusiasm. When Major Baron sought Aliena to escort her to the supper table, Colonel Massey joined them, plying her with the choicest viands from tables covered with every delicacy, glittering with silver, glass and porcelain of rarest designs; and exquisitely adorned with fruits and flowers.

Despite the exhilaration of the evening Aliena was glad when Professor and Mrs. Layton sought her to know if she were ready to leave. Late as it was, Dr. Leigh, who had not approached Aliena again during the evening, had been held here by some spell. He responded formally to her bow as she passed him going out.

As Aliena was standing leaning upon Major Baron's arm, waiting while Mrs. Layton entered the carriage, she started nervously, as almost at her side she caught sight of a pair of glittering eyes, and a glowering face, scowling upon Major Baron and herself from behind some shrubbery. She felt Major Baron start at the same moment, pressing her arm to his side until the emerald serpent upon it left its impress on the soft white flesh.

He instinctively put his other hand upon his pistol, without which he had never gone since overhearing the conversation between Varja and Zara that night in the shop. The scowling face disappeared almost instantly behind the shrubbery, which had served to obscure his person, but not before Aliena had recognized it as the same that had peered into her window.

Withdrawing her bruised arm, Aliena said in a startled whisper, " Did you see that face again ? "

" What face ? " he asked, glancing around in spite of himself, his face still livid in the light of the carriage lamps.

" I thought you saw it. The same that peered into our parlor the morning when we were singing."

Major Baron assisting Aliena into the carriage made no reply, glancing around again, nervously, however, as he did so.

Aliena felt assured that Major Baron had seen the man, his apprehension was too clearly depicted in his face. And she could not but feel a flash of contempt as she looked at his white, terror-stricken face.

But now away from the whirl, the glitter and the glare of the ball-room; in the dim star-light made darker by the little circle of flickering yellow light which the carriage lamps afforded; she felt a humiliating reaction from the reckless spirit that had possessed her during the evening, from which she could scarcely arouse herself sufficiently to blame any one but herself.

" You certainly made a brilliant début to-night, Miss Graeme," said Professor Layton, " you were decidedly the belle of the evening."

" I always had an idea that belles must feel very triumphant and happy," Aliena responded in a depressed tone.

"Success is presumed always to bring happiness. You can speak experimentally no doubt," said Professor Layton. "Preston Massey seemed quite to have surrendered to your charms, to say nothing of your other conquests."

"The ball-room is the mimic battle field of woman, and the more victims she can count the happier she is presumed to be," Mrs. Layton interposed with a tinge of sarcasm in her voice.

"I cannot lay claim to the victor's wreath then," said Aliena. And the party lapsed into silence for the few moments before the carriage reached its destination.

"You need not wait. I will walk to the hotel," said Major Baron to Professor Layton, as he assisted Aliena from the carriage. And saying good-night they drove off.

Major Baron left alone with Aliena had no desire to renew the discussion of the evening, or in reality of anything else. His thoughts were too much absorbed now in apprehension as to Varja, whose haunting presence had left him in a state of dejection, out of which nothing could arouse him. Fearing that Aliena might again question him in reference to Varja, or that the man might again appear, Major Baron said good-night abruptly, and left.

Standing before her mirror, loosening her shining hair and letting it fall in rippling profusion over her beautiful white shoulders and arms, Aliena thought with a pang, as she saw the sad face reflected there, that the human soul that Dr. Leigh had missed to-night, which for the time seemed to have deserted her, had come back sorrowfully and in penitence now.

Catching the reflection of the emerald serpent in the mirror, with its glittering diamond eyes, her mind reverted with shuddering horror to the glittering eyes of Varja as he scowled from behind the shrubbery upon them with an undefined, but fixed fear and wonder as to why he should haunt her with that look of hatred and malice. The bracelet slipping on her arm as she raised it, she saw, with a vague horror, upon the white arm another coiling serpent, defined in purple upon the bruised flesh.

A shuddering repulsion irrepressibly possessed her at this sight, as with it she connected in memory the livid look of terror depicted in Major Baron's face at sight of that fierce sinister face which continuously haunted them.

CHAPTER XXXIV.

> " Present fears
> Are less than horrible imaginings,
> Whose horrid image doth unfix my hair,
> And make my seated heart knock at my ribs."
>
> SHAKSPEARE : MACBETH.

Aliena was listless and out of spirits the day after the party. She flitted restlessly about, unable to occupy herself or to fix her thoughts upon anything. Colonel Massey called in the afternoon. Her sense of wrong in her course toward him at the party made her at first somewhat shy and constrained in her manner. But his gay, exuberant spirits made it impossible for her to keep up this reserve; and she found herself growing cheerful in spite of herself in forgetfulness of all she had to trouble her.

Late in the afternoon Colonel Massey proposed a stroll. As they started out he said, " A walk in a cemetery is not very inspiriting. but that by the river is about the most attractive we have. Suppose we go there ? "

Aliena, being indifferent, they took the route suggested. Entering the cemetery they strolled on. taking the right hand overshadowed pathway which led by the fern-fringed brook, leaping and glimmering on to its junction with the Occonee. Strolling leisurely along, they came at length to the gnarled trees and tangled vines upon the bank of the river, where wild flowers and ferns especially abounded.

Aliena, leaving the path, had strayed off a little in advance of Colonel Massey, and was gathering the crimson digitalis, growing in profusion here, when she discovered a singularly beautiful flower, one she had never seen before, growing in the very water's edge. Its leaves resembled the amaryllis, but the flower stalk spreading out and bleaching white toward the top, developed into an exquisite flower, pyramidal in shape, eight or ten inches in length, and half as wide at the base of the flower, which looked like exquisitely carved ivory or frost work.

She was stooping, gathering the blooms of the strange plant, when her attention was attracted by the sound of a voice she well knew, saying in an earnest, suppressed tone,

"Zara, tell your father it shall be as soon as—" And, the speaker and his companion moving on, she could distinguish no other words.

The couple had almost passed when she arose from her stooping posture, but she recognized the form, as she had the voice of Major Baron, and with him saw the girl whose beauty had so attracted her upon the cars. Both were evidently so engrossed in the conversation as not to have seen her, even if that had been possible. Aliena's heart seemed to stop beating, with the vague pain which oppressed her as it flashed upon her that this might furnish a clew to the haunting of the father's sinister face.

Colonel Massey rejoined Aliena, after Major Baron and Zara had passed on.

"Look! see what I have gotten for you. Here are some exquisite ferns. You ought to prize them. I came near taking an involuntary plunge into the river getting them for you. Here is some walking fern which is very rare."

"Thank you," said Aliena, abstractedly.

"What is that beautiful white flower you have? I never saw one like it. It looks like fairy frost work; one of their ivory temples, perhaps," said Colonel Massey.

"Nor I," said Aliena absently, her mind still absorbed in thought of Major Baron and his words to the beautiful girl. "Tell your father it shall be as soon as—" "Tell that horrible man—and it shall be as soon as what?" her mind went over and over in efforts to solve the mystery of this speech, as well as that of Major Baron's appearance with the girl in this secluded spot.

"Who was that beautiful girl with Major Baron?" she asked Colonel Massey, despite her instinctive shrinking from this subject.

"When was she with him?" he asked, evidently bewildered by her question.

"As he passed just now."

"I did not see him. He must have passed as I was gathering these ferns. Is that the reason you seemed so indifferent to my offering, after all the perils I encountered in your behalf?" said Colonel Massey. Aliena making no reply, he continued, "What is the matter with you? Is it that beautiful girl? or is it these gloomy surroundings that seemed to have depressed you so suddenly?"

"I must be under a ban. Last night I was too gay, this evening I am too sad," she replied.

"I thought you were delightful last night, and I was not alone in that opinion, it seems, judging from the throng that surrounded you."

Aliena, who was in no mood for badinage, made no reply, and at her suggestion they retraced their steps.

She occupied herself after Colonel Massey had left her at their cloistered rooms, in arranging the flowers and ferns, placing them with the "fairy temple" under her father's portrait. Then seating herself at the piano her fingers wandered softly over the keys into a nocturne, and from that into one of the dreamy German studies of which she was so fond, full of vague, inarticulate pain and heart-longing; but disturbed by the bringing in of a light, and remembering that her mother was alone, she sought her.

Mrs. Graeme was reclining upon a lounge, looking, as Aliena's conscience-smitten heart suggested, more worn and pale than usual. Seating herself by her mother's side, she took the listless hand in hers, and, remembering that the day after to-morrow would be the anniversary of her father's death, she tried to converse cheerfully, on her mother's account, for the remainder of the evening, despite the constantly recurring harrowing thoughts which tormented her.

The next morning, Aliena, in accordance with her mother's request, sacrificed her own feelings by going to see Mrs. Bledsoe and Mrs. Skinker, who had sent cards announcing their arrival, to Mrs. Graeme, who sympathized deeply with them in their grief and loneliness here amongst strangers.

Mrs. Bledsoe and her daughter were even more than usually demonstrative in their apparent delight at seeing Aliena, who submitted with what grace she could command, to the feline caresses of the old lady. Mrs. Bledsoe was looking more saintly, if possible, than ever, in her white cap, over her white hair. Her pale steel-blue eye, as usual, seeking the obstructing ceiling at intervals with a subdued look of resigned piety. Mrs. Skinker was seemingly in a remarkably amiable state of mind, scarcely snapping her eyes once during the visit.

Aliena, making her visit short, was leaving the hotel, when she met Dr. Leigh entering. Her color deepened as he approached. She held out her hand to him in salutation. He touched it formally, and joining her, walked across the street, inquiring in regard to her mother. He opened the Campus gate, held it for her to enter, and, raising his hat, bowed and returned to the hotel.

Aliena found during her absence that Major Baron had called; she had thus failed to see him, and, if possible, to have this tormenting mystery solved.

She had also missed seeing Colonel Massey, who had come to say good-bye, he having been unexpectedly recalled to the army.

CHAPTER XXXV.

" Glared lightnings and shot pernicious fire—
Drove them before him, thunder-struck, pursu'd
With terrors and with furies to the bounds,
And crystal walls—
           headlong themselves they threw
Down from the verge of heaven."
                  MILTON: PARADISE LOST.

The anniversary of Colonel Graeme's death had come, with all its melancholy and depressing influences to Mrs. Graeme and Aliena. It was a day sufficiently depressing from that fact, but nature, as though to add its gloom, seemed to have made the day itself a trying one. It was dull, oppressive and sultry, one rarely felt here, where the altitude and mountain air tempered the heat. The wilted leaves hung drooping on the trees, the flowers bent their heads. The grasshoppers and crickets made a continuous droning sound, and the tree frogs cried aloud. Tiny insects floated in murky circles in the stagnant air. The birds uttered spiritless chirps as they moved listlessly from tree to tree. Aliena devoted herself with more than usual tenderness to her mother during the day, but, depressed by its memories, and by the stagnant lull around her, in the afternoon she sought consolation in the chapel services.

.It seemed to her that the music was unusually touching and plaintive as it swelled in the dim, vaulted arches. The words dwelt upon were full of tenderness and pathos; words to which her mind reverted afterwards in comforting thought.

"Have I been so long time with you, and yet hast thou not known me, Philip?" God-man, mysteriously blended. As God, stooping to a personification, through which the finite mind might grasp the Infinite. The exaltation of humanity in that blending. The infinite God-love in the sacrifice, the tenderness of the rebuke in face of the great atonement about to be consummated. "And yet hast thou not known me, Philip?" Known Him in faith—by divine compassion and condescension, as in profoundest sympathy with humanity. In human form, tempted as we are, and yet without sin. Human, yet so far beyond and above humanity as to be possible only to Divinity. And again the words were reiterated in tones of profoundly moving pathos, which vibrated in her heart with something of the feeling that must have moved Philip, as they were wrung from the heart of the God-man. "Have I been so long time with you, and yet hast thou not known me, Philip?"

Leaving the chapel, still influenced by the physical depression around her, and by the memories of the day, Aliena strolled on. Her footsteps naturally turned toward the cemetery. Entering there, followed by Hugi, who had joined her in the Campus, she wandered slowly on with a feeling of mental and physical depression, in unison with nature, and with the memories which oppressed her.

Taking the pathway that wound up the hill-side in the center of the cemetery, Aliena sank into the same seat she had occupied when she had first visited this beautiful, though gloomy spot. Facing her was the overshadowed river flowing darkly on between the hills, to which the sun had already set. The still sultriness made repose desirable. But, though physically motionless sitting there, her mind was busy tormenting her with torturing thought. A torture to which her surroundings seemed to give intensity. In the still air, the sound of the falling water around came in more distinct, monotonous, and mournful tones. The gurgle, ripple, splash and roar. Now and then the crooning song of the old grave-digger, at work upon a grave, mingled with the minor accompaniment of the falling water with strange effect. Absorbed in thought she sat unmindful of the growing darkness, when suddenly a woman's shriek startled and shocked her to painful consciousness.

Hugi, who had been lying listless at her feet, sprang up, pricking his ears and bounded off toward the river. Aliena recalled him quickly, and alarmed now, not only at the frightful sound in this lonely spot, but at the ominous blackness of the sky, she hurriedly rose and turned to retrace her steps homeward. She found that the clouds which had flecked the sky had gathered, and thickened rapidly. These now grown dense, cumulus, and bronze, in the still, stifling, sulphurous air, were fast closing like fierce battling hosts above her.

Suddenly a blinding blaze of lightning and an almost simultaneous crash of deafening thunder seemed to signal the change, and great pattering rain-drops urged her onward. Crash after crash of near thunder and zig-zag lightning followed with sheets of rain, which driven before the wind, came dashing, blinding, into her face. The dull bronze sky and the unnatural darkness made the lightning more fearfully lurid and vivid.

Retarded by the wind, by the rain dashing in her face, and by the weight of water saturating her clinging clothing, Aliena bent her head to the storm, and labored on. She had left the cemetery behind her and was struggling against the wind and rain when she came nearly into collision with some one moving toward her. She raised her head and a glad smile came to her face, in spite of her terror, with a sense of relief and protection at seeing Dr. Leigh.

He turned, took her hand, drew it firmly through his arm, and walked rapidly on with her.

"What could have brought you out in this fearful storm?" he asked.

"What brought you here, yourself?" she gasped, the wind and rain almost taking away her breath. And an unusually blinding blaze of lightning and crash of thunder made her cling to his arm and shrink closer to his side.

"It is nothing strange for me, but that you should be out at such a time?" he said, looking at her with a curiously mingled expression.

"I came for a walk. I could not endure the house. I was thinking—and—and the storm was upon me before I knew it," she said, hesitating.

She had started to speak of the fearful shriek which had startled her into consciousness of the approaching storm. But for some vague reason she hesitated, and suppressing that fact, she continued, "and the wind and the rain made it almost impossible for me to get on. But it is not so hard now," she said, looking gratefully and restfully into his face. And they moved silently on battling against the fierceness of the storm to the University, where Dr. Leigh left her.

14

CHAPTER XXXVI.

" Come thick night,
And pall thee in the dunnest smoke of hell!
That my keen knife see not the wounds it makes."
SHAKSPEARE: MACBETH.

The evening of the storm, which had found Aliena at
the cemetery, Major Baron had, according to agreement,
again met Zara at their appointed trysting place by the
river, to make final arrangement for their marriage, as
he had promised.

Having become more nervously alive to intrusion
since the re-appearance of Varja, the night of the party—
seeing a small boat tied at the river bank, Major Baron
proposed to Zara that they should cross to the opposite
and more secluded side of the river. They entered the
boat and were in the act of crossing the river as Varja,
who, dogging their footsteps, had eluded observation by
moving stealthily from tomb to tomb, or tree to tree,
came once more to where he could command a view of
them.

Peering from behind a sunken tombstone under the
dense growth of gnarled trees upon the river bank, he
gnashed his teeth in impotent rage. Hissing horrible
oaths in a suppressed tone as he saw that for the time
they had eluded him.

Varja had never had real hope of justice to his daughter. The little hope he might have had, had died out after
what he had seen and heard when Major Baron was
with Aliena. He had therefore determined this evening to learn the truth for himself, and, if convinced that
Major Baron was playing false with Zara, to allow
nothing longer to thwart his vengeance.

This was not the first time that Varja had dogged
their footsteps, as the sound of the snapping twig by
the mausoleum had almost disclosed. Nor were the occasions when seen the only ones when he had kept vigi-

lant watch upon Major Baron and Aliena, or when shut
out from sight, that his keenly listening ears had been
applied for information. Having thus become aware of
Major Baron's duplicity, Zara no longer had the power
to restrain him from vengeance if this evening's interview proved treacherous.

Crouching, watching their receding forms as they
moved across the river, more than ever he longed for
vengeance. His eyes glittered like a serpent's as he
writhed in his impotent rage, grinding his teeth and
hissing horrible oaths.

He drew his pistol, examined, and cocked it. He
pointed and sighted as they rowed on. He muttered
renewed imprecations, as he saw the danger to which
Zara would be exposed should he fire and miss the
mark.

Replacing the pistol, he took from his bosom a dagger. He unsheathed it and drew its sharp edge across
his hand, testing its keen slender point until the flow of
blood marked its edge.

He waited, crouching, it seemed an interminable time,
the deadly purpose growing stronger with time.

Zara and Major Baron, after what seemed an eternity
to Varja, came down the precipitous, rocky bank of the
opposite shore to the water's edge, entered the boat,
and started across. Varja uttered a low, chuckling, demoniac laugh, as he saw them approach. The devil's
heart growing within him, his eyes flamed with the
intense delight of hoped for vengeance.

Major Baron rowed on across, landed, and assisted
Zara from the boat. Stepping ashore himself, as Zara
ascended the bank, he stooped, and taking up the chain
by which the boat had been secured, made it fast to the
shore.

Varja, assassin as he was, yet not a beast of prey,
awaited to face his enemy, his daughter's perjured betrayer. With the dagger clutched in his hand he stood
concealed, with glittering eyes, like a tiger ready to

spring from his lair, until Major Baron turned. Then, with a hissing oath of vengeance, he sprang forward, making a lunge at the heart of the traitor.

The muscular strength of Major Baron would seem to have had little chance to avail against the ferocity of this sudden, terrible onslaught of the lithe, infuriated foreigner. But fear had made him alert.

Throwing up his arm with a sudden, desperate force, at the lunge of the dagger, the blow of the assassin, turned aside, lost its aim. Striking through the thick uniform, against the gold cigar-case in Major Baron's breast pocket, it glanced off, with a flesh wound.

Grappling now in life or death struggle, the skill and and muscle of Major Baron with his greater coolness gave him vantage. Writhing against the restraining grip, Varja's eyes had a demoniac glare as they struggled on.

With the strength of desperation, Major Baron at length wrenched the dagger from the furious man, and made a lunge at Varja. The blood followed the fatal stroke, spouting at each pulsation, covering his antagonist with the crimson gore.

"Damn him to ——," Varja gurgled out as he dropped to the ground struck to the heart. The hue of death settling over his face, his eyes glazing, his teeth clenched.

His soul had gone to meet his God.

So noiseless and sudden had been the encounter that Zara, paralyzed by horror, had scarcely realized what was being done until her father uttering the oath fell to the ground, the life blood gushing from his heart. Then, uttering a wild shriek of horror and grief, she threw herself prostrate upon his body.

This was the shriek which had fallen upon Aliena's ears.

Who can depict the agony of that time? When certain of Varja's death, Major Baron, dragging Zara with him, before that awful storm of blinding lightning, thunder, and driving rain, turned his back upon the man he had slain; leaving him lying prone upon the river bank, stiffening and growing cold, beaten upon by the pitiless storm. And in stony silence, in the black darkness, sought the home of the woman he had wronged, and of the father he had murdered.

Entering through the side door of the dreary house, the spirit of the dead man seemed already to haunt his desolate home.

Zara, by a merciful Providence, stony with grief, could not realize her treble sorrow, her father dead, her promised husband his murderer, herself the cause.

Haunted by his fearful sense of guilt, Major Baron dared not remain. It was all important, as he felt now, that he should not implicate himself. He must leave her. Leave her alone with all this blackness of despair.

Lighting the candle to do away with the horror of darkness, he tried to explain to Zara, cautioning her again and again to divulge nothing in regard to her father's death. In the stunned condition to which horror and grief had brought her, he could get no assurance on her part.

But, not daring to stay longer, or to send comfort in the presence of any one else, lest Varja's absence and Zara's grief should divulge the fearful secret, he turned his back upon her. Leaving her alone.

Alone with all this weight of grief to bear, where everything recalled her father, who, let him be what he might to the world, had loved her, had given his life to avenge her wrongs. His dead face, his fixed staring eyes, his stiffening form haunted her. She saw him as he lay prone upon the river bank.

She could not endure it. She crept fearfully to the door, and looked out into the darkness. The storm continued, though abated in force. The wind drove the rain into her face, and put out the light beyond her which Major Baron had lighted.

Shuddering, yet urged by her yearning love for her father, she moved out into the black darkness of the deserted street. And on—and on, as if pursued by some avenging spirit, she took her way—back toward the cemetery—staggering along in the darkness, the wind and the rain.

The storm ceased somewhat as she neared the cemetery. The clouds, breaking apart, like guilty phantoms seemed to fly before the wind. In the dim light of struggling moonlight and shadow, the tall white columns assumed ghostly forms. A great white marble cross seemed to stretch out its arms—to take weird form and fly toward her with a wild shriek—as an owl, startled at her coming flew up and off with a screech.

Going on into the shadows, the wind shook the rain from the dripping trees in showers over the already drenched form, still she pressed on. On into the darkness, the eternal shadows, to the river bank.

The flying clouds, drifting from across the pale moon, left it shining down upon the white upturned face—the clenched teeth—the glazed eyes—the pool of blood in which her father's life had oozed away.

Throwing herself with a wild shriek upon the inanimate form—God gave her for a time surcease of sorrow.

CHAPTER XXXVII.

> "A pick-ax and a spade, a spade
> For—and a shrouding sheet;
> O! a pit of clay for to be made
> For such a guest is meet."
>
> SHAKSPEARE.

In the early morning the old Scotch grave-digger, who had been stopped by the storm of the evening before from his almost completed labor, returning, trudged on with spade, and pick, and bail toward the lower ground of the cemetery.

Here laying aside his coat, and putting his brawny hands upon the sides of the grave he was to finish, he let his gaunt body down into it with an expertness indicative of long practice; and went to work vigorously bailing out the water.

After the storm of the evening before, the air was alive with the song, chirp and twitter of birds; the buzz and whir of insects; and fragrant with flowers and with the spicy odors of freshened leaves. Even the moist earth yielded a fresh, sweet smell.

The exercise quickening the circulation of the old man's blood, and the ozone vitalized air stimulating him, he whistled cheerfully at his work; or trolled a bar or two of some old-time ditty which he had sung when life was young with him. Having finished bailing he began to dig, throwing out the moist clay spadeful after spadeful, stopping at intervals to wipe his streaming face and brow with a great, red-flowered handkerchief.

He was startled at length by the sound of a faint moan that seemed to come from the grave he was digging. Listening attentively he caught the faint, dismal sound once more. Placing his ear against the solid earth, after a time it came again more distinctly than ever. Unwilling to give way to superstitious fears, the old man took up his spade, and whistling now to keep his courage up, he spaded away vigorously.

Suddenly a voice at his side startled him.

"Good-morning, Mr. McElroy," the voice said. Nothing very startling certainly; but seeing the nervous movement of the old man, Mr. Rogers, the undertaker, continued, "You must have a bad conscience this morning, Mr. Mc., that you should start so at the sound of a Christian voice. How are you getting on with the grave?"

"Oh! that's a' right. It'll be ready in time," said the grave-digger, wiping the perspiration from his face, and leaning on his spade. "I was set back some by the storm yestereen, but I 've maistly caught up, and I 'se soon be done."

"I was afraid the storm would set you back, and I came to see about it. It would never do to have anything go wrong now. The girl makes a lovely corpse, just a neat size. And the coffin is a beauty, blockade or no blockade, if I say it that should n't. It 's my opinion it 's a flying in the face of Providence, any way, to have them metal coffins. The Lord always intended that we should go back to dust sooner or later. And there is no use in rebelling against his will. This is all white, inside and out, with silver screws. Fortunately I had some of that white satin left for lining, and some white lace and flowers. Though for the life of me I can't see how I 'm to get up another first-class funeral without we get some things through from Wilmington. The blockade runners come in piled down with guns and ammunition and the likes o' that for killing, but how they can expect a man to keep on burying and—"

"Do you ken what that girl died of?" interrupted the old grave-digger in a mysterious tone, hopeless of a stop to Mr. Rogers' talk.

"They say she had some kind of fever. As I was saying—"

"I wadna like to cast insinuations," interrupted the old Scotchman again, "but I hae been digging graves now amaist forty-five years, and I hae na heard naething like the woeful sounds I have been hearing syne I 've been digging this grave. I heard it yestereen for the first time just before the storm. It sounded for a' the world like the skirl of a wraith. Leastways like I wad think that wad sound. Heck! there it is again," the old man said in an awe-struck tone, with a startled look, putting his ear against the side of the grave in which he stood. "What did I tell you? Dinna ye hear 't?"

“ I think I did hear something,” said the undertaker, speaking lower, his eyes dilating in spite of himself.

“ Get down in here, and I ken you ’ll hear ’t. It ’s as plain as cock crowing.”

Mr. Roger’s could not but be impressed by the earnestness of the old Scotchman, and, moving to the now deepened grave, he let himself down into it with scarcely less expertness than the grave-digger himself. And placing his ear to the ground he said, “ I don’t hear a sound.”

“ Hist! wait!” said the old grave-digger in a suppressed tone. And both held their ears to the side of the grave listening intently, and sure enough in a few moments a low wailing moan was heard.

“ Heck!” dinna you hear it? What do you think o’ that?” the old man asked with dilated eyes, the other showing scarcely less plainly the effect of the sound upon him.

They listened again for some moments in silence, and again they heard the mysterious sound. Mr. Rogers having had time to recuperate somewhat from his first feeling of superstitious awe, now suggested, “ It does seem strange, but it may be from some natural cause after all. Let ’s look around and see.”

“ Well, we maun look, but it ’s my mind we ’ll nae see whar that sound comes frae i’this world,” said the old grave-digger shaking his head dubiously.

But scrambling out of the grave they began searching carefully around. Coming at length beyond the grave, on toward the denser growth near the river, the same sound reached their ears more distinctly than ever. Here they stopped and listened, and the sound came again after a time from toward the river. They moved on now. looking nervously around as they went. Suddenly the old grave-digger started back with an exclamation of horror.

“ My God!” It maun be the foreigner and his daughter, Varja, wha kept the tobacco shop at the sign of the

Indian warrior. Thae be stane dead, both o' them, murdert," said the old man, aghast at the sight.

There lay the murdered man and his daughter, her head upon his breast, her clothing dripping with water and dabbled in his blood.

They would have believed her dead, but as they came nearer she uttered one of those low, wailing moans. Her eyes were closed, the long black lashes lay upon her wan cheeks, her loosened black hair straggled in silky, waving masses over the murdered man, around whom were her arms in loosened clasp.

The old man stooped pityingly over the beautiful young girl, clinging to the stiff staring corpse, and taking up one of the limp hands, as cold as the dead man's upon whose breast it lay, he said tenderly, "Puir thing! Open your e'en hiney, here's an auld mon, he's rough but he's got a hairt. It's damp here, hiney, just open your e'en and let me help you up," but no response came.

The old man covered the small cold hand with his great rough one trying to warm it, then chafing it as gently as a woman, he said, "Hiney, it's naebody but an auld grave-digger, but he's got a hairt. Open your e'en just a minute, hiney. It's nae use," he said, turning to Mr. Rogers. "She's past my power. Gang and get something to take them up in. I'se stay here until y'er maun come back."

Mr. Rogers having started off to do as the old man had suggested, he lifted the inanimate form of the girl in his arms, as he might have done a child's, and carried her wet, and dabbled with blood as she was, to an old flat, sunken tombstone. Here he seated himself, still holding her in his arms, and moved, back and forth, as he might have done to still a child. When, now and then, she uttered one of those faint moans, the old man tried again and again to arouse her.

" Ye hae nae neither mither nor faither, now hiney, but I've got a hairt, I've got a hairt," and the big tears rolled down the old man's furrowed face, dropping upon the wan form lying there. But no sign of consciousness appeared.

CHAPTER XXXVIII.

"I fled but he pursued. I cried out Death!
Hell trembled at the hideous name and sigh'd
From all her caves and back resounded, Death!"
MILTON. PARADISE LOST.

Major Baron, leaving Zara, had slunk back, in the darkness. dripping with rain, blood-stained from the murdered man, to his room in the hotel. But for the wound, where the deadly dagger had been aimed at his own heart, and the mutilated cigar-case which had turned aside the death dealing blow, witnesses of the horrible conflict. he might have believed the whole fearful drama, a frightful phantasm of his disordered brain.

Passing before the mirror, he started, turning paler if possible. He did not recognize in the wet, care-worn, blood-stained, conscience-smitten image, that confronted him there, the handsome, well-cared-for, self-complacent form which had so lately greeted his vision.

He instinctively changed his clothing to rid himself of the torturing evidences of his guilt, and seated himself, tormented with agonizing fear and remorse. In imagination he still saw the clenched teeth, the staring eyes, the stiffening form of the dead man, lying beaten upon by the storm, at the river's side. He felt the warm blood spout upon him. He heard the muttered imprecation, the gurgle of the dying man, the wild shriek of horror and grief of the daughter—the forlorn girl upon whom he had brought all this weight of sorrow—whom he had left alone with her grief, her horror and her remorse.

He thought, too, of his affianced bride, of their plighted

troth, of his exposure to the world, and to her. Of his punishment by the law, of the scorn of the hooting multitude, of the utter hopelessness of sympathy from living mortal, which his double crime insured.

Could he go on with his marriage? Yet how could he defer it without committing himself? He must fly, he could not face the horrors that menaced him. One only, bare thought of relief came to his mind. There was no one now to uphold the forlorn girl—no one to compel him to marry her. No relenting tenderness made him once think of soiling his escutcheon by such an alliance.

A sound of footsteps in the hall made him tremble. The sweat oozed in great clammy drops upon his brow. The steps passed on.

Could he endure the agony of this night? And of to-morrow? To-morrow, which might bring exposure and shame. And now that Aliena seemed slipping away from him, the beauty of her character impressed him as it had never done before. Its transparent purity, its self-abnegation, its tenderness. He pictured the sweet worship which might have been his—sanctifying to him a home in which his hot blood might have calmed and cooled, under the purifying influence of a wife like this, into fitness for such an Eden of repose.

He thought of the myriad shot and shell he had escaped. And for what? Then he might at least have filled a "patriot's honored grave."

He rose and paced the floor. He strove to get away from himself—his agony—his despair. "Which way I fly is hell—myself am hell." He dared not think. His fear and his remorse had made a coward of him.

He rang for Auguste. Seating himself he awaited with his back to the door. He trembled as he heard his servant's footsteps approaching.

"Auguste, I am sick to-night. Go and get me some morphine," he said in a strange, unnatural voice, as the door opened.

Auguste, returning with the opiate, struck by something unusual in his master's manner, lingered at the door.

"What are you waiting for," said Major Baron sharply, glancing nervously around.

"I thought maybe you 'd like me to stay with you, master, as you was sick?" said Auguste, humbly.

"Go on," said Major Baron, abruptly, unwilling to risk a witness to his agony, much as he longed for human sympathy. Major Baron locked the door after Auguste, opened one of the papers of morphine and swallowed the narcotic. Then throwing himself, dressed as he was, upon the bed he tossed in an agony of mind which the opium had, if possible, intensified. Here he also came to know "the lineaments of those awful sisters—" Our Ladies of Sorrow. "They spoke not. Like God, whose servants they are, they utter their pleasure not by sounds that perish, but by signs in heaven, by changes on earth, by pulses in secret rivers, heraldries painted on darkness, and hieroglyphics written upon the tablets of the brain."

"The third sister, who is also the youngest—! Her kingdom is not large, or else no flesh should live; but within that kingdom all power is hers. Her head, turreted like that of Cybele, rises almost beyond the reach of sight. She droops not; and her eyes, rising so high, might be hidden by distance. But, being what they are, they cannot be hidden; through the treble veil of crape which she wears, the fierce light of a blazing misery, that rests not for matins or for vespers, for noon of day or noon of night, for ebbing or for flowing tide, may be read from the very ground—" "Madonna moves with uncertain steps, fast or slow, but still with tragic grace—Our Lady of Sighs creeps timidly and stealthily. But this youngest sister moves with incalculable motions, bounding with a tiger's leaps. And her name is *Mater Tenebrarum*,—Our Lady of Darkness," Madonna spoke —What she spoke translated out of signs was this;

"Lo! this is he that once I made my darling. Through me it was, by languishing desires, that he worshiped the worm." And thou "turning to Mater Tenebrarum she said, wicked sister, that temptest and hatest, do thou take him, see that thy sceptre lies heavy on his head. Suffer not woman, and her tenderness, to sit near him in his darkness. Banish the frailties of hope, wither the relenting of love, scorch the fountain of tears, curse him as only thou canst curse."

Truly the horrors of darkness—of *Mater Tenebrarum,* encompassed him, he was enduring the agonies of the damned. He rose and recklessly resorted to more of the opiate, this time with greater success. He slept but a sleep tortured with frightful visions.

CHAPTER XXXIX.

"O, she is gone forever.
I know when one is dead, and when one lives;
She 's dead as earth; Lend me a looking-glass;
If that her breath will mist or stain the stone,
Why, then she lives."

SHAKSPEARE : KING LEAR.

In the morning Auguste, having been told by his master that he was sick, went earlier to his room than was his custom. He turned the door-knob softly not to awaken Major Baron, if sleeping, and hearing no sound went back down stairs.

He remained until a rather late hour before returning and was about doing so when his attention was attracted by a confused mass of people moving along the street. Like a line of ants thrown into confusion they were halting here and there in groups, as though touching antennae, and hurrying on in continuously increasing stream down the street.

Auguste, with natural curiosity changed the course of his steps and went hurriedly into the street to enquire the cause of the commotion.

"Old Varja, the tobacco man, and his pretty daughter are murdered. Dead, all cut to pieces, down by the river in the cemetery. Mr. Rogers has seen them, and come up for a cart to bring them in," said the man of whom Auguste inquired, with the usual exaggeration, as well as with alacrity to communicate ill-news.

Auguste was probably more horror-stricken and aghast at this information than any one in the crowd. His acquaintance antedated theirs, and some circumstances connected with them were also known to him, of which they were ignorant. But with that tendency to secrecy inherent in the negro race he kept his own counsel. The white orbs around his dilated eyes, however, attested the horror with which he heard the fearful story.

Returning to the hotel he did not hesitate now to awaken his master, but went quickly upstairs for that purpose. Having been valet to Major Baron for years, Auguste was probably better posted as to that gentleman's affairs than any other living person. He had now an instinctive idea that his master's illness was in some mysterious way connected with this tragedy.

Auguste also began to feel some alarm as to the morphine which he had been sent to purchase. Though he was aware that Major Baron resorted at times to a stimulant, under vexation or annoyance, he had never known him to take a narcotic.

Knocking gently at Major Baron's door without avail, Auguste shook it violently, but without response. Now really alarmed, he shook the door with still greater violence. Major Baron sighed profoundly, and, turning upon his bed, muttered some incoherent words, and was about falling asleep again, when another rattling of the door aroused him to dim, painful consciousness.

He rose to a sitting posture with a bewildered, half-dazed feeling, but with a rush of confused thought and apprehension; at another shake of the door, he with uncertain step walked to the door and opened it.

Auguste was too much absorbed at the time in the startling news he had to communicate to observe Major Baron. But, with eyes still dilated with horror, he gasped out, "Marster, Miss Zara and old Varja's dead. Done murdered, cut all to pieces, down in the cemetery. Mr. Hodges is come for a cart to fetch 'em up. He's gone for 'em now."

Still stupified by the opium, it seemed to Major Baron that he was in a horrible dream. That he was hearing an old, old story. Something from the dim, distant past, which he had known or dreamed an interminable time before, as to Varja's death, which could not be made more horrible. But, in the new, strange addition of Zara's death, there was something that almost made him laugh, a grim, horrible laugh, as the thought of this unexpected and unhoped for deliverance from Zara, and from this witness of his crime, dawned upon his dim consciousness.

Clasping both hands tightly to his throbbing temples Major Baron asked, "How—how do you know? Are you sure—sure it is true?"

"Everybody says so. All the town's done gone down there to see them. I thought I'd come and tell you and see if you wanted anything, and if I couldn't go too?"

"Bring me a cup of coffee," said Major Baron, shifting his hands to the top of his head and clasping them there. He had a vague remembrance that coffee was an antidote to the opiate, he felt as though he were losing his reason.

Auguste returned quickly with the coffee, being incited to unusual alacrity by a wish to gratify his curiosity.

"Can I go now, marster?" he asked.

"Yes, see, and—and come and tell me. Don't tell

that you knew anything of them," said Major Baron, tortured with harrowing dread and anxiety. Hoping, yet fearing that the news of Zara's death might not be true.

Before Auguste had opportunity to get away from the hotel, the cart conveying the insensible girl to her desolate home was on its way back. The old Scotch grave-digger, walking by the side of the cart, where he had placed Zara, had constituted himself a sort of a body-guard.

Auguste soon joined the crowd surrounding the girl, who had been attracted by that morbid curiosity which never fails to draw a throng, to batten like birds of evil omen upon scenes of horror. They were discussing the tragic event as they moved on.

Auguste, peering over the heads of those nearer than himself, could not determine in his own mind whether Zara were dead or not, and he ventured to inquire.

"No, she's not dead at all," said the man addressed with something of disappointment in his tone.

"The likes o that don't die easy," said Sal Slemmins, a shriveled, parchment-dried old hag in the crowd.

"She's puttin on now. Don't you see she is, Sal Slemmins?" said Polly Magraw, another old woman. "I believe she knows what's a goin on this minnit, jest as well as you ur me."

"Jes so, Polly. Maybe she knows more'n she'd like to tell."

"Thars no knowin—who can tell but what she done the killin," Sal Slemmins replied.

"No, indeed, thar aint no knowing for a fact," said the other woman with a dubious shake of the head.

"I dinna believe a word o' it, yer blarsted old hags," said the old grave-digger indignantly.

"In course yer don't," said Sal Slemmins, "jest let a hussy be young and pretty and yer can't find a man that'll believe nary thing agin 'em. But I don't keer who hears me. I believe she knows more'n she'll let

15

on.   And we 'll see what we 'll see," and she shook her head oracularly.

"Shut up yer gab, you blarsted skirling auld vampire, or I 'se mak it warm for some of you, blamed if I dinna," said the old Scotchman still more indignantly.

"Ha! ha! ha!" laughed Sal Slemmins, her shriveled wrinkled face looking more hideous as she disclosed her few remaining snaggled black teeth. "I thought yer was a gettin too fur along in life, Peter McElroy, for to be takin on about a young hussy," and the crowd joined in the laugh. The halting of the cart at the shop door produced a diversion from the talk, for the time. Here the old Scotchman took the insensible girl in his arms, and followed by the crowd, carried her into the room back of the shop and laid her upon the bed.

Looking around and seeing the motherly face of Mrs. Simkins, the shoemaker's wife, who lived across the way, the old man said, "Mrs. Simkins, you 've got a hairt, I trow, come and do something for this puir, faitherless and mitherless young thing. And if thar's aebody here you want to help you, say so. And I 'se blarsted if I dinna hurt somebody if they dinna gang frae here."

The old man's countenance showed that he was too much in earnest to be fooled with, and all except Mrs. Simkins and Mrs. Brown, the saddler's wife, whom she requested to remain with her, left the room, while he having sent for a doctor, stood guard himself, outside of the door.

The women did everything practicable to restore Zara, and she at length gave signs of returning consciousness. Her bewildered gaze and incoherent words however, made the doctor say when he came, that it was likely to be a tedious time, if at all, before she could recuperate from the fearful shock to which she had been subjected.

Varja's body upon the river bank was gazed upon by the prying crowd, until a coroner's jury could be summoned. They in vain sought other clew to the killing than that probably locked in the breast of the insensible girl; who having been found prostrate upon her murdered father's breast, was likely to have been a witness, if not a party to the horrible deed. No footsteps or other signs which might have indicated the guilty author of the crime remained after the flooding storm of the night before.

The possibility of the daughter's having done the deed was suggested. But young, frail, half-dead as she was, with her sorrow and her beauty to plead for her; no set of men could possibly have passed judgment upon her unheard.

The jury returned a verdict, " Killed by stabbing to the heart with a dagger, in the hand of some person unknown to the jury."

CHAPTER XL.

" Not thus our vows confirm'd by wine and gore,
  Those hands we plighted and those oaths we swore,
  Shall all be vain; when Heaven's revenge is slow
  Jove but prepares to strike the fiercer blow,
  The day shall come—that great avenging day."
                                    Homer: Iliad.

The news of this tragic event could not be long in reaching Aliena's ears. Mauma, suddenly entering the room, where Mrs. Graeme and Aliena were seated, puffing for breath, in her excitement, exclaimed with unwonted freedom, " Mistiss. what do you think? That man Varjo, that traveled on the cars with us, with the pretty daughter, is murdered, killed, dead, down in the ceminery. His daughter was with him and she 's gone clean mad and is most dead too, they say—Though some say, she 's puttin' on, because she done the killin'."

“When did it happen?” gasped Aliena, ghastly white.

“Laws a mercy! honey, what’s the matter with you? You are jest as white as a sheet,” exclaimed Mauma.

“When did it happen?” gasped Aliena again, oblivious to what Mauma had said, with a sharp pain, like a knife at her heart.

“I don’t know, honey, they’ve just now found his body and his daughter lyin’ acrost him, covered with blood, some said she was cut to pieces too.”

“I heard her shriek. I was in the cemetery, when it was done,” Aliena gasped, shivering and white.

“You don’t say so!” exclaimed Mauma, ashy with horror at Aliena’s manner, and at the thought of her witnessing the deed.

“I heard the woman’s shriek. That sound startled me to consciousness of the storm. It was just as the storm commenced,” said Aliena, still trembling at the memory, and at the fearful suspicion that had entered her mind.

“Hush, daughter. Don’t mention this, Malvina. You might be summoned as a witness,” said Mrs. Graeme, agitated by Aliena’s manner, and alarmed at the thought of the disagreeable publicity to which her daughter might be subjected.

Major Baron knew that he must come out of his room and face the fearful reality, but he had not at first the nerve to do it. Remembering that the clothes he had taken off might testify against him, he placed his heavy uniform, wet as it was, in his trunk; as well as the mutilated cigar-case which had served him to such good purpose. And locking his trunk, an unusual circumstance, he placed the key in his pocket, until he could more safely rid himself of these accusing witnesses. The slight wound he had received, which amounted to nothing, had already closed.

Auguste found Major Baron still in his room when he returned. He reported to him all that he had seen and heard, with the fact that Zara, though not dead, was "gone clean mad."

Amongst the surmises as to the killing he repeated that in reference to Zara's having done the deed herself. A surmise which Auguste was far from believing. Even this was a relief to Major Baron—anything but the horrible truth itself.

In the afternoon of that seemingly endless day, Major Baron having concluded to leave—to go anywhere rather than face the agonizing possibility of exposure, shame and retribution—determined to go and say goodbye to Aliena.

As he was crossing the street to the University he caught sight of a shabby hearse, with its nodding black plumes, moving slowly down the street. It jostled in its movement, swaying aside the curtains, disclosing to view the coffin within. At this sight his face became scarcely less deathly than that of the murdered man shut up there. And he staggered as he moved on to meet his affianced bride—picturing to himself as he did so the frightful, staring face shut in there—now eternally graven upon his conscience-stricken memory.

Delicately sensitive as Aliena was to the subtile influences of personal magnetism, she could not but be possessed by an irrepressible and fearful repulsion as she caught sight of Major Baron's pale face, contracted brow, and compressed lips; so unlike the easy sensuousness which usually marked his handsome face, and which now so strangely altered him. And the vague, shuddering, accusing thought came back with increased force, that in some mysterious, dreadful way he was implicated in this tragedy.

Aliena could not have been tortured into confessing this horrible suspicion which had taken possession of and constantly tormented her—yet, though hating herself for the thought, she could not rid herself of the fearful suspicion.

Major Baron's avoidance of the mention of Zara,—

his terror-stricken expression at the appearance of her father's face at the window, the continued dogging of his footsteps by Varja, the seeing him with Zara in that secluded spot, almost identical with that where the murder had been committed, the words she had overheard, " Zara, tell your father it shall be as soon as—" all these circumstances though, as she tried to convince herself, insignificant in themselves, taken singly, yet considered consecutively, recurred with constantly increasing and terrible force.

The great tragic event of the day would naturally have been discussed—one that so fearfully agitated this quiet place. Aliena, hoping that her cruel suspicions might be allayed, would have introduced the subject herself, but her tongue faltered and refused to utter the words.

Major Baron, too, felt that his avoidance of this subject was calculated to arouse suspicion; and would gladly have nerved himself to its discussion, but he found it impossible.

Aliena's manner was so transparent that Major Baron felt, as plainly as though words had uttered it, that a great change had come about in her. Alive to suspicion, this re-acted upon himself; and he felt a certain premonition of the loss of what he felt now to be the fairest—the most lovable woman that the world contained. His heart more truly than ever yearned for her love now, when he felt he was isolated, by crime, from human sympathy.

If, as his good spirit plead with him to do, he had, in penitence, confessed all to Aliena, who can tell what a woman's heart might have done. But he did not, and to have seen them part, one would scarcely have imagined it was with the understanding that he was to return in a few short weeks to claim her as his bride.

" Marster," said Auguste, having come earlier than was his habit, to his master's room, as Major Baron was to take the morning's train, " They say they don't think Miss Zara nor her baby will live the day out," and he glanced furtively at his master.

Major Baron flushed scarlet and then turned deadly pale, as he caught the furtive glance of the black valet, who experienced a sense of satisfaction in making this communication, like that of a brutal character in goading a spirited animal and holding him at the same time with a cruel curb. His master had a murderous impulse toward the black creature at this moment. He felt how much freer the slave was of the two.

"Don't you want me to finish your packing, marster," Auguste asked humbly.

"Of course," said Major Baron, with irritation.

"Please sir, give me your trunk key then," said Auguste. He had had an especial desire to repossess himself of this key, not only because his master seldom carried it; but from the fact that Major Baron was wearing a uniform he had thought somewhat shabby in camp, in place of his new and much handsomer one; in reference to which, under the circumstances, he was anxious to satisfy his curiosity.

"Never mind. Go down and see about my breakfast, and have it on the table. I will finish packing, myself," said Major Baron, with evident embarrassment, quailing before the glance of his cringing slave.

A little later Major Baron sped away upon the cars. The rapid motion was soothing to his overwrought nerves, as he left behind him the desolate girl whose life he had blighted, without a word or a line, the untimely little waif whom he had cursed with life, yet whom in his heart he wished might not live the day out, the murdered man mouldering in his grave, and her to whom he was unworthily plighted.

But he could not leave behind him accusing conscience, the avenging sense of guilt. That like a swift-winged Nemesis, pursued him with a speed which no power of steam could outstrip. There, close by his side, sat this grinning demon, eternally there.

CHAPTER XLI.

"O heat dry up my brains! Tears seven times salt
Burn out the sense and virtue of mine eyes."
SHAKSPEARE: MACBETH.

Mrs. Skinker with Arista called some days after the preceding events to see Mrs. Graeme and Aliena. The child amused herself during the call by a romp with Hugi in the Campus. Mrs. Skinker was ushered in before Aliena had an opportunity to have excused herself as she would gladly have done.

"Did you ever know anything so horrible as the murder of that man Varja?" said Mrs. Skinker soon after seating herself. "And they say the woman will never have her reason again. She has been perfectly wild ever since it happened. They think now it is because she killed her father, herself, that she takes on so about it. No wonder she's gone crazy. I have no idea she would ever be hung, however, as they say she is uncommonly pretty. A pretty woman can do whatever she chooses. She might commit murder every day in the year without any danger of being hung as long as only men are on the juries, and have the say so. And I hear Mrs. Layton has gone to that shop to nurse her. I think they are hard up here for something to waste sentiment upon, when they have to take up such people as that."

"I should think it remarkable if in a Christian community no one had the charity to minister to a sick, sorrow-stricken, helpless woman," said Mrs. Graeme, with unwonted asperity.

"*Chacun à son gout,*" said Mrs. Skinker, with an impertinent grimace, shrugging her shoulders, and pronouncing the French execrably. As no one replied Mrs. Skinker continued, changing the subject. "We are thinking of taking rooms in the University. Are there any pleasant ones vacant in this building?"

"I do not know," said Mrs. Graeme wearily.

"Miss Graeme is, if rumor is to be credited, too much absorbed in other things to be posted as to such practical, common-place matters, I suppose. A gentleman in gray, with a major's star, is said to be the bright particular star with her at present." said Mrs. Skinker, showing the incisors in her effort to be facetious. Aliena was too loth to discuss this, or any other subject in fact, to reply, and Mrs. Skinker continued. "There might possibly be another star of sufficient magnitude to arrest her attention. A surgeon general's for instance," but Aliena seemed so oblivious to her meaning that, despairing of gaining any information, she soon rose and left to see about the desired rooms.

"My daughter," said Mrs. Graeme, the same afternoon, to Aliena, as she sat listlessly holding a book in her hand, not a leaf of which had she turned in half an hour, "It seems to me you are acting strangely. It is not a month now before the time, when you have promised to marry Major Baron. Yet you never speak of your approaching marriage; and act as though you were oblivious to the fact. Not that I wish you to marry, my child—certainly not, unless it is to conduce to your happiness—you know the reasons which actuated my consent."

"I don't know what is the matter with me, mother," said Aliena, with profound sadness. "I seem to be under some inscrutable spell, which makes it impossible for me to do anything now."

"You owe it to yourself and to Major Baron, then, to tell him that you cannot marry him, when you promised; nor at all, my child, unless you love him sufficiently to make it, not only a duty but a delight to prepare for an event that should be the crowning happiness of your life."

Aliena made no reply, but sat with her eyes fixed with a stony look upon the floor before her, evidently too hopeless and perplexed for conclusion.

" Are you certain, my child, that you do love him ? It would be a fearful mistake to marry and then awaken to the consciousness that you did not ? "

" I only know that I am possessed by some haunting demon that makes me unworthy to marry any one," said Aliena, bitterly. And rising abruptly she left the room, and taking her hat she started off to walk with a feeling of wretchedness which she tried to still by physical exhaustion. Going by a secluded route, not venturing certainly into the cemetery, of which she could not even think now without a shuddering horror, she came at length to a spot which gave her a view of Athens. She halted here, gazing with a profound sigh, at the scene before her as, with the houses dotted here and there upon hillside and valley, it reminded her of Vicksburg. " Oh ! if I could only banish the cruel time since I left home," she thought. She wondered, if she was thus to be tormented by doubt and want of trust forever. She longed to write deferring her marriage, at least ; but what reason could she assign ? That horrible suspicion ? Though the great throbbing pain of that accusing doubt daily grew in force and became more and more fearful, she could not consent to form it into words.

As night came on she instinctively retraced her steps, though seemingly oblivious to every outward surrounding. Intent only upon stilling by fatigue the demon of suspicion and unrest that tormented her.

Letters came duly from Major Baron, with all the forms and show of affection. But to Aliena they lacked the genuineness of trusting love. She tried to convince herself that the fault lay in herself, and she replied ; endeavoring to write as she had in former days, but she found this impossible.

Day after day passed, and yet she had not the courage, or power to write that she could not marry him, —blankly so, without assigning a reason. Yet each day she became if possible more wretched. She could not read, she never opened her piano, she sat idle and listless when alone, making a pretext of busying herself when with her mother. She scarcely slept a few troubled hours each night, waking habitually long before day, tossing in hopeless wakefulness. Yet she did not complain.

Mrs. Graeme could not but see with pain the restless eyes and wearied look that Aliena wore, making her know that she was still pursued by this "haunting demon," whatever it might be, until she was beginning to look like a phantom herself. Yet after their conversation upon the subject of her daughter's marriage, Mrs. Graeme could not again refer to the subject, feeling that it was a sore problem which Aliena must work out for herself.

After weeks of mental struggle, which seemed prolonged to years, Aliena determined to write to Major Baron, deferring their marriage indefinitely, assigning no cause.

She wrote as tenderly as possible, only accusing herself. "For some inexplicable reason I cannot marry you at the time appointed. I am possessed by some evil spirit which is tormenting me. Some day I may confess it all. It pains me more than words can express to inflict this upon you. Forgive me, forget me if you can. Try to be happy. Do not trouble your mind about me, or about this cruel mystery, but hope and pray for happiness for both in the future."

Major Baron's guilty conscience could not but suggest to him what the evil spirit tormenting Aliena might be—the suspicion of his guilt. And his conscience smote him with renewed and intensified pain. If he had dared he would have flown to her. But there was the dread of that still unexplained mystery, locked up in his and Zara's breasts, which, as he had learned through the newspapers, she had thus far kept secret even in her wildest ravings.

The pain of disappointment in his marriage with Aliena, to which, since that fearful deed, he had looked forward with greater eagerness than ever, was now the more unendurable in that, blood-stained, guilty as he felt himself to be, a vagabond upon the earth, longing for the sympathy which a wife, his through good and through evil report, might give, he was isolated by crime.

Yet there was one sense of relief to him in all his grief and disappointment. He need not return to that dread place, where blood cried out against him from the ground.

Major Baron wrote in answer to Aliena's letter with unwonted ardor, of his love, his sorrow, his bitter disappointment at such a conclusion upon her part. He still urged their marriage—if not when promised, at no distant day. Clinging to hope in the future, he wrote. " But for circumstances beyond my control I should not write at all, but fly at once to you, and learn from your own lips an explanation of this cruel mystery. Painful as is my uncertainty, this is impossible now. But think of the torture I endure. Have some mercy— write to me that there is hope, that I have not forever lost your love."

Days, weeks, dragged their weary length along in agonizing vacillation with Major Baron, who still awaited exchange in Montgomery. Here he lingered, tortured by apprehension of exposure as Varja's murderer—a disclosure which hung upon the secrecy of Zara, of a woman he had so cruelly wronged and deserted. He felt that even now his power over her was such that a loving word might seal her lips. Yet he dared not write. To communicate with her might involve him in the crime.

Now, however, since Zara still lived, he congratulated himself that the onus of deferring his marriage with Aliena had not fallen upon himself, feeling that his marriage with another would doubtless have unsealed the lips of the wronged and deserted girl.

CHAPTER XLII.

" In evil hour thou didst give ear
To that false woman, of whomsoever taught
To counterfeit man's voice; good lost, evil got;
Bad fruit of knowledge, if this be to know,
Which leaves us naked thus—of honor void,
Of innocence, of faith, of purity."
MILTON : PARADISE LOST.

The community were astonished and shocked, in spite of rumors to that effect, when, being sufficiently recovered, a warrant was issued for the arrest of the frail daughter as the murderer of her father. Without friends or means, nothing remained for Zara but imprisonment, if she persisted in silence as to her father's murder. No one had had the cruelty, in her forlorn state, to tell her of her rumored guilt. And her perplexity and amazement may be imagined when she was told that she must either divulge what she knew as to her father's killing, or risk paying the penalty herself.

Zara, in her feeble, sorrow-stricken condition, was stunned and bewildered by this terrible and unexpected charge. Divided in interest for herself and for him she loved, conscious of innocence. believing it impossible that she could be made to suffer for a crime she had not committed—notwithstanding his crime and his desertion, her love sealed her lips as to Major Baron's guilt. And when brought before the magistrate for preliminary trial, she could be induced to say nothing more than, " I never killed my poor, dear father. No, no. I never killed him. I never killed him."

The crowd, drawn by eager curiosity to hear what would be developed in the trial, could not but be moved by the beauty, grief, and helplessness of the wan, frail girl; who, refusing to testify, implicated herself. And with her child in her arms, she was led to prison.

Friendless, shut up in her cell from even the little sympathy and kindness her sickness and sorrow had evoked, Zara's burden seemed more than she could endure. Day after day she looked and hoped in vain for some word or token from Major Baron, until hope died within her. Behind those dreary prison bars, she dared not even inquire in regard to him. Yet, with a woman's heart she tried to believe that he had come, or sent, when she was unconscious with delirium; and that now he had been perhaps compelled to return to the army.

Preyed upon, in the loneliness of her dismal cell, by conflicting imaginings, the memory of what her father had endeavored to make her believe came back to her in torturing force. That Major Baron loved another, that he had never intended to marry her. She pictured him as her father had done, speaking words of love to another, clasping a bracelet upon the arm of the fair girl whom she well remembered, or mingling his voice with hers in " love songs," or even already married to her. She could endure the harrowing uncertainty no longer. And she determined, if possible, to see Aliena, and learn the whole truth—let it be what it might.

Mrs. Layton, remembering the words, " I was sick and ye visited me; I was in prison and ye came unto me," yet ministered by sympathetic words and kind deeds to the forlorn girl; despite the added shame of the accusation of parricidal murder.

During one of these visits, Zara tremulously asked Mrs. Layton if she thought Aliena would come and see her if requested. And being assured by her kind visitor that she believed she would, Zara begged that she would carry a note to Aliena with that request. This Mrs. Layton undertook to do.

Aliena rarely saw visitors now. On that day especially, she would have declined to see even Mrs. Layton, whom she had come to regard highly. It was a day made more gloomy and full of humiliation to her from the fact that it was to have been her wedding day. But remembering what Mrs. Skinker had said in reference to Mrs. Layton's kindness to Zara, she caught eagerly at the possibility of hearing something in regard to the forlorn imprisoned girl, and of getting a clew to the solution of the dark mystery overhanging Varja's death. She accordingly determined to see her.

Aliena's agitation may be imagined when soon after her entrance into the room Mrs. Layton handed her Zara's note. Her agitation increased—her face became deathly white, and her heart seemed to cease to beat, as, in confirmation of her fears, her eyes fell upon the curious, cramped handwriting. Gasping out some excuse—trembling as she rose—she left the room. Going to her own room she unlocked a drawer, and took from it a piece of torn envelope. She pressed her hand to her heart and gasped for breath, as she was confirmed in the identity of the writing.

It was the piece of torn envelope which Major Baron had dropped upon the ebony table one evening at The Castle, which she had placed in a book upon the table when startled by footsteps as she was curiously scanning the superscription. This book had been brought with them, and Aliena, having by chance opened to the envelope a few days before, had again curiously scanned the cramped writing thus accidentally preserved with renewed and painful interest.

Here she felt was another link in the chain of evidence as to the dread mystery. And she tremblingly tore open the note, and read Zara's request with throbbing pain, scarcely doubting now that she could there hear the unraveling of the mystery which tormented her. Resolved to endure this harrowing uncertainty no longer, she determined to comply with the request—to go and see the imprisoned girl.

Endeavoring to calm herself—to still the quick beating of her heart, Aliena returned to the parlor to ask Mrs. Layton to accompany her in her visit to the prison. Obtaining the desired consent they walked silently toward the dread place.

Here Aliena's heart sank and her limbs trembled beneath her as the sound of moving bolts and bars reverberated through the gloomy walls, and she entered the dismal place, hearing the same ominous sounds shutting her in with dread, to whatever might be before her. Moving tremblingly on in the narrow dark hall, she approached the cell in which Zara was imprisoned. Again she shuddered, at the sound of bolts withdrawn as she entered the bare, cramped cell.

Here, upon the only chair the room contained, sat the forlorn, frail girl, her head bowed upon her arms, which rested upon the narrow bed, where lay the little unwelcome waif.

Zara raised her head slowly and wearily, as though numbed to a sense of the misery by its very intensity, as she was aroused to consciousness that some one had entered. Her pale, hollow cheeks and sunken, burning eyes, gave evidence of the suffering she had endured since Aliena had seen her last.

Filled with sympathy for the suffering girl before her, yet trembling with apprehension of what she was to endure herself, Aliena had a vague consciousness that Mrs. Layton was saying something to Zara, who having bowed her head again upon her arms slowly raised it.

And the sound of bolts and bars made her know that she was left alone with the girl.

Aliena experienced a feeling as of dual consciousness, as though she were some one else for whom she felt sore pity as she sank into the seat vacated for her by Zara. Helpless to combat the misery to which she felt she was now shut up.

Zara seated herself upon the narrow bed beside her baby. and said in a low, dreary, hopeless tone, "It was good of you to come. Though I am not so bad as they would make me."

"I don't believe you are," said Aliena in a low, compassionate voice, so faint as scarcely to reach Zara's ears.

“No, not so bad as that, not so bad as that. I never killed him. I never killed my poor dear father.”

“I don’t believe you did,” said Aliena in a husky, unnatural tone of dread and apprehension.

“Yet, but for me he would be living now. He was good to me. I was all he had—all he had—and I killed him. I killed him,” said Zara in a low voice, startling, so full was it of horror and despair. And her face sank to her hands.

“I cannot believe it. You must not say you killed him,” said Aliena, moved with compassion, yet with a vague feeling of relief at Zara’s self-accusing words.

“I must speak,” she said, raising her head with a wild impulse of despair. “I cannot keep silent. It is killing me. I must tell some one. I am tormented. I must know. My father,—my poor dear father saw you often. He listened. It was wrong, but will you tell me? For God’s sake have pity upon me, tell me,” said Zara, rising and approaching Aliena, and leaning beseechingly forward with her hands clasped tightly, she continued piteously, “Tell me—tell me the truth. Does he love you? Did he ask you to marry him?”

“Who?” gasped Aliena.

“Cecil—Major Baron. Did he promise to marry you?” and Zara’s eager eyes seemed to pierce Aliena in the agony of her suspense.

“Yes,” gasped Aliena, pale and trembling; feeling that hope was fast leaving her.

“Oh! My God!” exclaimed Zara, clasping her hands to her head. “My father told me that, but I would not believe it. How could I when he told me different. He promised to marry me. Oh! my poor father! my poor dear father! I killed him. I killed him—and for this. And he left me—left me alone,” and she threw her arms wildly above her head, as she continued frantically, “My poor father! He died for me. I caused it— though my hands never did the deed—and now I am all alone—all alone.”

"Whose hands?" gasped Aliena, leaning forward with eager, staring eyes, her voice sounding as though it came from some far-away abyss—her lips even blanched.

"Cecil's—Cecil Baron's," Zara replied in a strange, sepulchral whisper, leaning toward Aliena with horror distended eyes. Her tone changing to entreaty as she continued, "But don't tell—don't tell—for God's sake don't tell. They will hang him. My darling. My baby's father. My father would have killed him. He wrenched the dagger, and struck the blow. But the guilt was mine—the guilt was mine," and clasping her hands to her face she sobbed out, "And he left me and my poor baby. And not a word—not a line. I don't know where he is, and they want to kill me. But I cannot tell at the trial. I love him. I cannot see him suffer," and approaching Aliena and sinking on her knees she continued beseechingly, the tears streaming over her clasped hands, "Where is he? Give him back to me, my darling. You must pity me."

A shivering horror possessed Aliena at thought of the cruel treachery of this man, one whom she had once thought she loved. She shuddered, recoiling in thought from him as from a serpent's fold. And remembering the glittering serpent upon her arm. she would gladly have snatched it away.

"I could tear my very heart out before I could pledge it to a man I must abhor. I have no claim to such a man," she said, trembling with scorn and indignation.

"He did not mean to kill him," said Zara pleadingly, despite the treachery of the man. "My father would have killed him. He wrenched the dagger and did the deed."

"How can I know that all you have been telling me is true?" said Aliena, suddenly awakening to the thought that, carried away by the passionate earnestness of a woman of whom she knew nothing, she had allowed herself to believe fearful charges against the man to whom she was plighted—charges which **might not be true.**

Zara moved to a shelf, swung from the bare wall, from which she took an ordinary looking dressing-case. Pressing against a concealed spring, a shallow drawer slid out, disclosing a photograph in a gray uniform buttoned over a form that Aliena too well knew—the blue eyes smiling into her face. The duplicate of one Major Baron had given to her. By it lay a ring of brown hair, tied with a faded blue ribbon, which Aliena shrank from touching. Upon the top of a little pile of notes and letters lay the one dated July 17. Aliena read it, well remembering the one that had come to her the same day, with the fruit and flowers, written in the same graceful, flowing, German hand.

"Zara, I am here to see you. I should have come before but for what I shall explain when we meet. Be in the cemetery at sunset, near the large Mausoleum.

"JULY 17, 1873.   C."

She did not care to read others.

She loathed herself as she thought with a shudder of the words of love which she had received the same day, written by the same treacherous hand.

"It is enough," said Aliena in an unnatural voice, rising to leave.

"But you will not tell? I could not but tell some one," said Zara beseechingly.

"I must tell him," said Aliena, shrinking from uttering his name.

"No, no, he must not know that I have told," she plead eagerly.

"But it will be known at the trial," said Aliena.

"No, I shall never tell," she said earnestly.

"Not if they try to hang you?" exclaimed Aliena in amazement at Zara's firmness of purpose, now that she knew his treachery—that he had never intended to marry her.

"No, I love him. I could not see him suffer. I am innocent—they cannot punish me. I shall never tell," Zara reiterated.

Aliena felt at that moment that Zara was to be envied the possibility of dying for the man she loved, unworthy as he was. Anything but living. Living without faith in humanity. Cut off from all the beatitude of loving and being loved, which, without trust, was impossible.

"I must hear from him. I cannot live without. Tell me—tell me where he is?" Zara continued beseechingly.

"If I told you, you could not write to him. Your letter would convict him. I must write to·him," Aliena said, with a shudder at the thought. "I must tell him that I loathe him—that I could never marry such a man. Let me tell him all? I will bring you his answer."

"Write then; say I could not help telling some one. I could not endure the agony. But I shall never. never tell at the trial. They cannot make me. I shall save him. He will marry me then. I know he will marry me then," and hope faintly illumined the sad, sunken, despairing eyes of the girl as she spoke.

A wailing sound from the bed awakened the maternal instinct, and Zara turned toward it. Aliena felt a strange, irrepressible desire to see the child. And approaching the bed, she looked into its face with curiously mingled emotions. It had ceased to cry, and was looking into its mother's face. The blue eyes bore that wonderful resemblance, to be found only in the face of a young child, or in that of death.

A glance sufficed. Aliena turned quickly away, and sought egress from the cell and prison.

CHAPTER XLIII.

"The rock, the vulture, and the chain;
All that the proud can feel of pain,
The suffocating sense of woe."

The stony face that Aliena had worn of late made the change less apparent after the fearful communication to which she had listened in the prison. Yet fearing to trust herself to the scrutinizing eyes, and anxious inquiry of her mother, wretched beyond the power of self-control, she hastened to her room and threw herself upon her bed.

Mauma came after a time to summon her to tea. "I want nothing but rest," said Aliena without turning towards Mauma. Here she remained for what seemed an interminable time. At length assured by the stillness that all had retired for the night, Aliena rose to comply with her promise to Zara. She wrote:

MAJOR BARON:—

I write to you to-day which was to have been our wedding day. That such it ever was to have been seems now a frightful dream. I have this evening returned from the prison, where I went at her request to see Zara Varja, incarcerated as the suspected murderer of her father. She told me the whole horrible truth. She asked me to say she could not keep it wholly to herself.

You will not wonder that I return your letters and picture, and should return the coiling serpent, fit emblem of your plighted troth, but that I await the key to unclasp it. You will return my letters with the key.

It is useless for me to express my horror at this knowledge. My disappointment in you, in humanity, in myself, that it was possible for me to have promised to have been the wife of one capable of the treachery you have practiced. One so linked to crime.

I ask no sympathy for myself.   But for a woman who so loves the man perjured by vows he never intended to fulfill, her father's murderer, who without a word or act of sympathy could desert her and his child to the hooting of a friendless multitude, as to be willing to suffer imprisonment, to be hung it may be, rather than disclose the secret of his guilt, for her I do plead. · You will know without my telling you that it is your duty to come and disclose by whose hand her father's blood was spilled, to take her place in prison, and, if spared to ignoble life, to marry her. And may God have mercy upon you, upon the woman expiating your crime in prison, and upon   ALIENA GRAEME.
ATHENS, Aug. 28, 1863.

Aliena enclosed this letter, and the others she had received from him, with his picture, and sealed the package.

Then laying her aimless hands in agony in her lap, she gazed vacantly, with stony eyes before her, exclaiming, " To-morrow, and to-morrow, and to-morrow—and for this."

She could not endure to think. The room stifled her—the walls oppressed her. They seemed closing in upon her. Catching up the same fleecy, white shawl that Major Baron had wrapped around her the night of the party, she threw it over her head and went out. She plunged into the shadows of the great oaks and elms—walking, walking, walking. To escape from what? From herself—from her yearning heart—crying out for faith lost—for love—for a love she had sacrificed for this.

The great clock clashed midnight—midnight it truly was to her. Black with the blackness of the horror to which she was shut in—black with the pall of distrust of humanity—black with despair. Memory recalled her dream in Vicksburg Etherealized humanity rocking in bliss upon an illimitable ocean of happiness. She saw the black, grinning, ogre face—she felt the talon hands clutching her shrunken, humanized body. Her heart hammered against her side. She saw again the fearful conflict—the horrible squirming and plunging, that churned the phosphorescent waves to lurid foam in his death agony.

The grinning demon seemed truly dragging her down now, down into the deep water into which she had come —sinking—gasping—drowning. Down—down—powerless to rise.

She thought of the wrongs to the girl in the dreary prison—of the murdered man, whose sinister face had haunted her living—who haunted her more horribly dead —of the blood-stained hand to which hers had been plighted.

Hearing footsteps in the darkness she started with affright—her heart fluttered like a snared wild bird's. Emerging from the shadows she saw a man approaching. She had an impulse to fly. But it was too late.

"Aliena, what are you doing here alone, at this hour of the night? Has anything happened?" Dr. Leigh exclaimed in amazement, as he recognized the white-robed figure, and wild, pallid face that met his gaze under the white shawl.

"I wanted air—I could not breathe," said Aliena, facing him almost fiercely. Agitated the more by this encounter.

"You are not well. It is not warm. You must go in," said Dr. Leigh tenderly, surprised and moved by the evident agitation her voice and manner indicated.

"I am not sick," said Aliena, walking on rapidly. Scorning to practice duplicity by seeming assent. "I wanted air. I wanted to be alone."

In spite of the seeming rudeness of this speech, Dr. Leigh said in the same tone, "I cannot leave you here, alone. You must go in."

Seeing her enter the house, Dr. Leigh, sorely disturbed in mind by this encounter, and by Aliena's agitation, went sadly on to see the ill soldier to whom he had been called.

CHAPTER XLIV.

‘ His lightning your rebellion shall confound
And hurl you headlong flaming to the ground —
Yourselves condemnéd for rolling years to weep
The wounds by burning thunder deep.”

HOMER: ILIAD.

Sunday afternoon Auguste, with the inevitable in-
amorata that every place furnished him, was strolling
by the river-side at Montgomery.

“ Miss Rose,” said Auguste to his inevitable of this
occasion, who was Mrs. Selwyn’s colored nurse, “ I wonder what all them colored ladies and gemmen is lookin
at down there by the river? Let’s go down and see.”

“ Certainly, Capen. Though I hope it ain’t nothink
dead. I’m powerful feerd of nothink dead,” Miss Rose
responded, making herself amenable to the charge of
tautology in her desire to give what she considered the
“ quality touch ” to the final letter of “ nothink,” upon
which she dwelt with lingering gusto.

“ Don’t you go to bein feerd of nothin’ while I’m
about, my dear,” said Auguste, straightening himself up
and giving Miss Rose a loving leer, as he assisted her
down the steep bank to the water’s edge: Here, a negro
man, around whom had gathered a crowd of idle stroll-
ers, attracted by curiosity to the spot, was drawing in
with a pole a curious looking bundle floating upon the
water.

The negro succeeded at length in making the haul,
and secured the bundle. It was tied tightly around
with a strong twine, from which depended ragged
shreds of paper, giving it a singular appearance. A
noose with a slip-knot indicated the loss of a weight.

“ Sam, here’s a knife to cut the string,” one of the
“ colored gemmen ” suggested, proffering the knife.

“ Is it you that’s doin’ this job, Ned, or is it me ?
Sposen you hold your hosses. It’s the slowest hoss

that's longest in the medder," said Sam, feeling the dignity and importance of his position.

"Ef you was a hoss you'd stand a powerful chance fur grass, shore," said Ned.

"I made some grass ef I tuk some sass. Look at this piece of twine ef yer darsent-ter look at hemp," said Sam, holding up the twine. Then proceeding deliberately and tantalizingly to pick off the shreds of paper, he at length slowly and a little nervously unrolled the bundle, disclosing a gray uniform.

"I thought least ways it was gwine ter be a dead baby or something lively of that sort, and it aint nothin but a muddy old uniform," said Ned contemptuously, with a sense of gratification at making little of Sam's discovered treasure. Though he in reality partook of the general disappointment at finding nothing more startling.

Sam, however, having an eye to the useful, was very well pleased. He unrolled the uniform, took the coat from the ground and shook it out with seeming satisfaction at finding an apparently new uniform.

But as he turned it around, Miss Rose threw up her hands tragically and uttered a little shriek, exclaiming dramatically, "Oh my! take it away, take it away, there's blood on it. Somebody must a been killt. And there's nothink I can't abide better'n the sight of blood," and she clapped her hands to her eyes and leaned heavily against Auguste.

He, putting his arm lovingly around the young lady, who showed no signs of recuperation, said,

"Never you mind that, my dear, blood ain't a gwine to hurt you, nor nothin else while I'm about. By the time you've done been in as many battles as I have, and desieged besides, you won't mind the sight of blood." Auguste was at first too much absorbed in these tender offices with Miss Rose to observe the uniform particularly. Turning now and looking at the coat as it was held up to view with the blood and cut upon it, he grew ashy in appearance. Withdrawing his arm suddenly from the young lady, who managed to stand without extraneous assistance, he stepped forward and took the coat in his own hands to inspect it more closely. Slily putting his hand into a breast pocket, he drew out surreptitiously a mutilated gold cigar-case. This he had the presence of mind to secrete. And dropping the coat as though it had been a serpent, he turned to Miss Rose looking more ashy than ever at this confirmation of his suspicion.

"What's the matter, Capen? It 'pears like you don't like the sight of blood yourself," said Miss Rose.

"I don't keer about soilin my hands with sich. Come on, Miss Rose, let's go," said Auguste, still showing signs of agitation as they moved off.

Miss Rose, as they pursued their walk, tossed her head, rolled her eyes, and te-he'd in the most approved style. She had possibly taken some lessons from Miss Lilian Selwyn in these arts, as, like all her race, she had the faculty of imitation largely developed. For which, according to Darwinian theory, she may have been indebted to some of her evoluting ancestry. But Auguste was in no state of mind for love-making now. And they finished their walk without her receiving any farther demonstrations from her pre-occupied lover.

Returning to the hotel, full of the discovery he had made, Auguste secreted the mutilated cigar-case, and went to Major Baron's room. Here he busied himself, apparently, in arrangements for his master's comfort. Endeavoring in the meanwhile to summon courage to broach the subject of the disappearance of the uniform.

"You ain't been a settin in here all this evenin, and it so fine for walkin, is you, marster?" said Auguste at length craftily.

"Yes," said Major Baron laconically, and throwing the remains of the cigar he had been smoking out of the window, he continued motioning towards the table. "Look there, and get me another cigar."

Auguste took a cigar from the box upon the table, and handing it to Major Baron, said with a furtive glance, "I don't never see you a usin your fine gold cigar-case no more, marster."

Major Baron's brow contracted and his lips compressed as he took the cigar, and the light obsequiously proffered, and went on smoking in silence.

Auguste was too intent perhaps upon the mystery he wished to solve, to observe the expression upon his master's face, as he continued, "Marster, I should 'er thought you'd a had on your new uniform. It's so much finer than that one, and it Sunday too, and I saw Miss Lilian dressed up powerful fine this evening."

Auguste tried to look artless as he made this seemingly innocent remark. But as he glanced suspiciously at Major Baron he trembled as he caught the fierce glitter of the eyes turned suddenly upon him.

Major Baron's face, at first pale, grew scarlet with rage as he confronted Auguste and hissed out, "You black, infernal scoundrel! You let me catch you meddling with my affairs and your infernal head will be broken before you are a day older."

Major Baron felt as soon as the words were uttered that he had allowed his indignation to get the better of his discretion, and he would gladly have recalled them. But it was too late, Auguste's manner and words had goaded him, in his nervous condition, to a state beyond self-control.

"I didn't mean nothin, marster," said Auguste humbly, fully convinced now that Major Baron had himself caused the disappearance of the uniform, that its condition was in some way connected with Varja's death, and that the blood which he had that evening seen was that of the murdered man.

Auguste now gladly quitted the room, leaving Major Baron to the ignoble thought that he not only had blood upon his soul, but that the knowledge of that fact was in the keeping of the black valet who had just left him. And the murderous impulse born of that thought left its polluting slime upon the soul of him who seemingly had once possessed a generous, noble nature.

Thus does sin follow sin after the corruption of the soul, as vulture after vulture that of the body. And a sense of degradation and humiliation oppressed Major Baron as he sat thinking of the depth to which he had sunk ; that he should tremble and quail before even his own slave.

The following day Major Baron received the letter which Aliena had written. Who can depict the self-loathing with which this once proud man looked upon himself as he read Aliena's cruel words, smitten as he was from his high estate by the downward steps of self-indulgence.

He took sheet after sheet of paper in efforts to answer this letter. Some, full of assumed indignation at her belief of the charges, and of recrimination at her loss of faith in him. Destroying these, he felt it useless to debase himself by farther duplicity, and he wrote confessing all.

"How will this affect her, wrung out as it is by her knowledge of the crime ? " he thought, and he destroyed this also. Despairing at last of answering her letter at all, he took her letters and the key to the bracelet, and without a word to Aliena, or to Zara, enclosed and posted them himself.

If then, like another Judas who betrayed with a kiss, he had gone out and hanged himself, it might have seemed well done. But he did not.

CHAPTER XLV.

> "O, Nature! what hadst thou to do in hell
> If thou didst bower the spirit of a friend
> In mortal Paradise of such sweet flesh?
>
> SHAKSPEARE : **OTHELLO.**

Aliena received the package containing the letters and the key to the bracelet. Major Baron's silence had confirmed his guilt. And with loathing she took from her arm the pledge of her betrothal, and returned it to him. She felt now that it remained to her again to see Zara, painful as it was, and let her know that there was not a line, not a word to comfort her in her sorrow. But Zara took consolation from this fact, from Major Baron's silence. Hope comforted her with the thought.

"He loves me—for this reason he no longer writes to Aliena. I shall never divulge his secret, he will marry me then." And, languishing in prison, this thought strengthened her resolution, and made life endurable.

Days—weeks of agonizing trepidation and dread lengthened to age in Zara's troubled imagination, while she awaited her trial. And still she persisted resolutely in her determination to keep undivulged the secret of her father's slayer.

The day dawned at length when she was to be taken from the dismal cell, where she had been incarcerated into the garish sunlight, before the gaping crowd, awaiting a sight of the sorrowful, frail, friendless prisoner; there to comfort the majesty of the law.

The densely thronged court room was as still and silent as death, as the trembling, wild-eyed girl was led to her place in the prisoner's box. There to await the unfolding of the testimony to substantiate the unnatural crime with which she was charged.

"Aha! I wonder what Peter McElroy 'll say now. I told him she know'd more'n she'd like to tell," said Sal Slemmins, the same wrinkled hag who had scrambled for a view of the insensible girl as she was brought from the cemetery. She was now struggling for a better view of the prisoner in the crowded court room, still gloating over the misery of youth and beauty.

"You blamed old witch you, git out of the way here. Set a thief to catch a thief, they say. And them that is so knowin is them that 's doin—that 's my mind," said Simkins, the shoemaker, whom she was elbowing with her sharp angles. And he gave her a thrust with his own elbow that nearly crushed the breath out of the old woman.

Again there was stillness in the court. And a voice resounded in the hushed room, "Guilty or not guilty?"

Zara's wild eyes looked wilder, as, pale and trembling, she answered in a low voice, that vibrated through the silent room, now still as death, "Not guilty."

Zara's lawyer was not less ignorant of the facts in the case than the prosecuting attorney himself. She had, in spite of his entreaties, persisted in her refusal to tell him more than that she did not kill her father. He was therefore almost staggered himself in his belief of her innocence, as witness after witness was examined, confirming circumstantially her guilt. No testimony pointing to any one else could be produced. While her silence under the fearful charge seemed to point to her alone as the murderer.

The old grave-digger testified to hearing a woman's shriek just before the storm, on the evening when the murder was supposed to have been committed, and to finding the body of the murdered man the next morning, with Zara's head upon the breast, and her arms as though in loosened clasp about it. Mr. Rogers corroborated the latter part of this testimony. Physicians who had examined the body said that its condition indicated that Varja had been dead from twelve to twenty-four hours when found. That he had apparently been killed before the storm. That he was killed by a keen-pointed instrument, which had perforated the heart.

That the wound corresponded with the dagger found at his side. That it was a bold stroke, having penetrated to the handle of the dagger, as the probing of the wound disclosed. That the wound could not have been inflicted by himself.

Mr. Simkins, the shoemaker, testified to coming into the tobacco shop a few days before the killing, and seeing Varja examining the dagger now produced in court. He knew it to be the same from having then examined it attentively. Varja having called his attention to the fineness of the metal and to the workmanship, with the name and place of residence of the manufacturer; telling him that he had procured it in his native country, Spain.

Neighbors testified that upon several occasions they had heard Varja speak harshly to Zara, though none had ever heard her answer otherwise than mildly, at times with tears.

Mr. Sandford, a grocer, testified that while purchasing some tobacco from Varja, not long before the storm, on the evening of the murder, he had seemed impatient. restless, and out of temper.

Mr. Magraw and Mr. Simkins testified that the shop was closed that evening before the storm; and that it was an unusual circumstance for it to be closed at all during the day, or until a late hour at night.

Mrs. Simkins, who lived on the street facing the side entrance to Varja's house, which was a corner one and used as a home as well as a tobacco shop, stated that as she was seated sewing, facing this side entrance, she saw Zara come out of the side door, a short time before the storm of that evening, and go down the street in the direction toward the cemetery. That she remembered it the more distinctly from the fact that she so rarely saw her go out of the house.

That very soon afterward she saw Varja come out of the same door, close it behind him, and go in the same direction. After dark, the storm making it darker except when it lightened, she was looking through the window to see if the storm were abating, when by the lightning she saw Zara and Varja at their door. He seemed to be pulling her into the door. She could not say that it was violently done. It was blowing and raining very hard at the time, and it was so dark she could only see when it lightened. She got two glimpses only by the lightning. She saw a light in the house soon afterwards as she was watching the violence of the storm, but noticed, not long after, that the light was out.

She had never seen men hang around Varja's house unless in the shop, and not often there. That Zara was rarely in the shop. She had never heard any disturbance there; though Varja had a disagreeable manner and appearance, and a gruff voice. She had never seen men with Zara, though she had heard some of them talk of her beauty, and express a wish to know her. She did not know that Zara was married, had never heard her say whether she was or not—had never asked her.

She had heard Varja speak in a harsh, excited way to Zara on several occasions; but had never heard her reply harshly. She had seen Zara on more than one occasion shed tears when her father seemed to be abusing or upbraiding her. She could not say what he was abusing her about, as she could only distinguish words now and then.

She had assisted in getting Zara into dry clothing the morning she had been brought home from the cemetery. She saw no bruises or marks of violence upon her person. She did not think Zara physically strong. She had nursed her while sick. Zara had talked little, while out of her head, only moaning, and occasionally saying, "My poor dear father," or "He's ill," or something like that—could n't understand what Zara meant by the last exclamation.

When Zara first came to her right mind she seemed not to notice anything, but lay most of the time as if she were dead, with her eyes closed. The first thing she noticed was her baby; it was laid by her side, and she looked at it for a long time and then shut her eyes again for some time. Then she asked whose it was. When she was told she closed her eyes again, and the tears rolled down her face. The Doctor came in about that time and said let her alone, and leave the baby there, that it would do her good to cry. She cried a long time with her eyes shut, and she did seem better after that. And two days afterward the Doctor said she might live.

After Zara got better she sometimes cried and said over and over again, "My poor dear father." The Doctor had directed every one not to talk to her about her father, for fear of putting her out of her head again. And she had never heard any one talk to her on that subject, and never did it herself.

The prosecuting attorney did little more than sum up the testimony to the jury, dwelling upon the fact that Varja had no known enemies, or scarcely acquaintances, having been in this place a very short time. And that even in a business way, possibly, from being a foreigner and speaking the language imperfectly, he seemed to hold himself aloof. That the killing necessarily implied a motive. That in this instance it could not have been robbery, as the little money and few valuables upon the person of the murdered man were untouched. That it had been in evidence that he had been harsh toward his daughter. That the deed was not done by himself was evident, though it had been done with the dead man's own dagger.

"The daughter was found with her murdered father, prostrate upon the body. There, from all appearances, she had lain all that terrible night. Her dripping, dabbled clothing stained with the blood of her father, indicating that after a deed so fearful—so revolting to nature. Heaven, as though to avenge the terrible crime, had so paralyzed her with horror as to cause her to fall powerless upon her murdered father's body. Thus divulging to the world the guilty actor in this dreadful drama."

"It is natural," he said, "it is womanly to dwell upon scenes of horror witnessed. To depict each word, each tone, each look. To recount them with shuddering horror again and again. But here there is no crying out against the author of this direful, unnatural deed, this sudden taking off of a father. Nothing but blank silence. What but guilt could thus have sealed a daughter's lips? Her conscience, blackened as it is by parricidal guilt, falters at adding perjury to parricide. A perjury she knew she could never substantiate by facts, therefore she is silent."

"One witness thought she saw Zara and her father re-entering their home after the storm had almost spent its fury. She caught a glimpse in the blackness of the darkness of that fearful night, made blacker by the deed done, by a blinding blaze of lightning, of a man and woman struggling on in that fierce, wrathful storm. But this could not have been Varja and his daughter. The shriek heard by Mr. McElroy doubtless timed the deed. The father was then lying dead upon the river bank. His spirit, perhaps, borne upon the wings of that wild storm, had then taken its flight to the bar of that God before whom he had been made to appear without a voice of warning, or an instant of time to plead 'God have mercy upon my soul.'"

"The daughter, paralyzed with horror by an avenging God, in face of the fearful crime, prone upon the body of her murdered father, must have suffered the tortures of the damned that direful night. A foretaste of that hell whose keenest pang is remorse. A remorse the more intense as the crime was most unnatural."

"There, in that dismal place where the foul deed was done, the buried dead might well have left their graves, have come forth to mock and gibe. Pointing their skeleton fingers at the murderer, shrieking in tones to be heard even above the voices of nature resounding in

that dread storm, 'Parricide, thou didst the deed!'
While the winds catching up the sound, swept it over
the earth, proclaiming in thunder tones, 'Thou didst
the deed, thou didst it.'"

"You may say, 'Who can look upon that frail, beautiful girl and think her guilty?' She is frail, she is beautiful, fair to look upon. But does this free her from
the guilt? So much the worse that God should have
endowed her with an angel's form, which could not con-
done the guilt of the devil's heart within her. Pity 'tis
that guilt should wear so fair a mien."

"Is it true, has it been found in the annals of crime,
that deeds of darkness have been done only by women
as revolting in form as in action? That God has set a
seal upon them by which one can unerringly point the
finger and say, 'This is a murderer, that an assassin,
that a parricide?'"

"No—far from it. Unfortunately the most beautiful
have been most noted for crime, as Clytemnestra,
Beatrici Cenci, Catherine di Medici, Lucrezia Borgia.
Yet I do not say that God has given beauty, that most
prized of all his gifts with woman, that it may belie by
outward seeming. No, thank God, there are women as
beautiful in soul as in person, whose deeds illumine the
sometimes gloomy pathway to that city which hath no
need of the sun, neither of the moon."

"'Lead us not into temptation,' says that model of
all prayer. As is the temptation, so is the fall. Beautiful women, caressed, flattered, pursued, tempted, find
it hard to climb the steep heights, which, though sometimes rugged and bare, are sun-capped at the last. But.
yielding step by step, to the seductive glamour of sin,
they find no lack of helping hand to lead them onward
in their rapid, downward course. The grade is unfortunately easy of descent. And, however dank and
deadly the valley, its repose is tempting, its fruits glittering, though they turn to bitter ashes in the mouth."

"A woman who has, as we are, I fear, bound to believe in this case, taken the one dread step which cuts her off eternally from hope of re-instatement in the world's esteem, stained by a guilt which all the tears of a life-time's penitence cannot blot from a woman's record, deserted by her lover, all her sweet affections turned awry, driven to desperation, taunted by her father, stealthily secures the silent weapon which she alone could have procured, and secretes the keen blade. Followed, watched, upbraided by her father, she turns at length, like a beautiful but fierce panther. The devilish purpose, which irredeemable sin has begotten within her, prompting the deed, she strikes the blow."

" The hellish deed done—nature itself revolting, cries out and divulges the unnatural crime. The wild shriek that pierced the grave-digger's ear on that portentous evening told the story."

" Let no mawkish sentiment prevent your doing your whole duty—what is right—what the law demands. If guilty, you have sworn before high heaven and before Him who is at the last day to judge the quick and the dead, to do your duty—your whole duty, regardless of all beside. To pronounce her guilty if such she be."

" I leave the case with you, and with your consciences, whether according to the law and the testimony, this woman be guilty or not guilty ? "

A depressed buzz went through the breathless court-room as the prosecuting attorney seated himself after this summing up of the evidence which appeared to single out the girl arraigned as alone the guilty party.

The lawyer for the defense arose slowly, and apparently unwillingly. His uncertain voice and hesitating manner impressed the eager throng of listeners with his hopelessness of success in his cause.

He dwelt upon the crime charged, murder. The fearfulness of that crime, the shedding of the life's blood of a fellow mortal. The deeper, doubly-dyed blackness of the crime for which this wan, frail, sorrow-stricken

girl before them was arraigned. The murder of a father
—Parricidal guilt.

He spoke of the patient endurance of woman, an en-
dowment of the Almighty to meet the demands of her
nature. A marked characteristic, known and recorded
for all these thousands of years since God created man,
male and female; clothing her with meekness and gen-
tleness, and him with might and power.

"How many women are reviled, abused, struck, even
cruelly beaten, without outcry, or thought of redress?
Not seeking relief even when the law might grant it.
Meekly enduring not the sweet bondage of love, but
the cruel bondage of fear."

"You have in testimony in this case that this girl was
again and again reviled by her father—taunted and re-
proached, moved to bitter tears. Yet only to tears.
The prosecution has failed to show even a bitter, re-
proachful word wrung from her by abuse. A dumb
meekness of spirit certainly wholly inconsistent with
the crime charged. That of confronting a strong man,
frail as she was, and fiercely plunging a dagger to the
very hilt into his heart. And that heart her father's—
apparently the only one upon the earth, beating in a
human breast, to which she could look for love. Since
even he, upon whom maternity gave her a double claim
to love and protection, seems to have deserted her."

"Even when driven to desperation, determined to
seek vengeance, a woman, feeling her weakness, does
not confront a man, her superior in physical strength,
as she knows him to be. History and observation teach
us that her vengeance is silent, stealthy, secret. Like
Clytemnestra, Catherine di Medici, or Lucrezia Borgia,
quoted by the prosecutor, they choose the insidious
poison. Or, like Jael with Sisera, this frail girl if med-
itating murder, might have crept upon her father while
he slept, and with one fell stroke have smitten him until he died."

"Yet, you are asked to believe that for a few harsh

words of reproach, this helpless girl, scarcely more than a child, was willing not only to sunder the only tie that apparently bound her to humanity, save that of a general brotherhood—a brotherhood now willing, apparently, to hound her on. friendless and helpless to a felon's doom—but to sunder it by boldly confronting this man, who could have crushed her frail body in his muscular arms, or, if he had so willed, cast her to certain death in the black water upon whose banks this foul. mysterious deed was done."

"The blow was struck. It was from the front. It was well aimed—boldly struck. No feeble, faltering hand dealt that blow. It was a life and death thrust."

"It is in testimony that this girl rarely went out. She avoided being seen. On that particular evening she did go, contrary to custom. She went to the cemetery. A spot not usually sought by women alone, at such an hour—unless made sacred as the receptacle of some loved form, when love and sorrow banish fear. Say that she went to enjoy the air, the scenery, or to indulge in penitential thought? It might have been. But it is a marked coincidence that the father also went. The same evening. To the same place. Contrary to custom he seems to have closed his shop during business hours for that purpose. He did not go with his daughter, but followed her. Mark that—he followed her."

"Is it not singular that upon this particular evening, when, after a portentous. stagnant lull, nature seemed to be rallying her fiercest battling hosts overhead, that these two should, almost at the same time, leave the house, and, not as would seem most natural, together, but that the daughter. with thoughts intent on murder, as charged, should start before her father—instead of following *him*."

"But let us allow that she preferred to do the deed then and there, instead, as was most natural, of taking advantage of the ample opportunity, daily or nightly offered, silently to dispatch him at home. Here all that is really known of this frightful tragedy is ended."

"The spot where, upon that beautiful morning, when nature seemed to have been resurrected to renewed beauty and life, the moan of the sorrow-stricken daughter revealed the tragic story to the old grave-digger, is a secluded one. A place given up at times to the encroaching floods of the Occonee. One for that reason seldom used as a burial place. One rarely frequented—not so neatly kept—more rank in growth, and consequently more isolated."

"Yet the father and daughter were found there, together. The father murdered. The fair, frail daughter with her head pillowed through the black darkness of that night upon his breast. Her arms in relaxed clasp about him.

"Is this the attitude of a murderer? Is it usual? Is it natural for a murderer thus to cling to the gory corpse of one whom diabolic hate alone could induce to have deprived of life?"

"On the contrary, is it not a well known fact that the most hardened in crime instinctively flee before the staring eyes and blood-stained forms of those who have fallen victims to their wrath or vengeance?"

"Yet she who, when reviled, reviled not again, murders her father—the only being, apparently, in the world to whom she can look for love and protection, and then remains clinging to the murdered man—the ghastly staring corpse—until life and reason seemed extinct!"

"No. She never did the deed. She did not go to this secluded spot to meet, and murder her father. He followed her there. He it was who was intent upon vengeance. Vengeance upon another. There was one, as we must know, for whom her passionate, untutored heart had made her forget her duty to God—the indignation of a father—the scorn of the world—she went to meet him there. This serpent who had crept into and poisoned their home! Her father knew her object. He followed her. He would have stricken this vile creature to the earth. But this fiend incarnate—this devil's demon—not content with his damning deed, clutches the avenging dagger from the father's hand, and strikes the fatal blow."

Zara, who had at this unexpected, impassioned delineation of the scene, reached forward from her seat with distended eyes, and blanched, terror-stricken face, now uttered a wild shriek and sank back insensible.

While means were being used to recover her, the speaker continued.

"You heard that cry? It was a faint echo of the heart-rending one wrung from the suffering girl as her father fell beneath the stroke of her vile betrayer—her father's assassin. The cry which smote so direfully upon the grave-digger's ears as he plyed his vocation on that fearful evening. Zara, then witnessing the deed that left her fatherless, and friendless, which she cannot now hear depicted without the same wail of woe and horror, fell helpless upon her father's body."

"Look at that blanched face! That insensible form! She has refused to speak, but the secret has been wrung from her. Her wailing shriek, her insensible form has divulged the story. Closely as her lips have been sealed it is all told now. Her betrayer did the deed. She loves him. Yes,—despite it all she loves him, and would screen the dastard. Would save him by the sacrifice of her own life."

"It is useless for me to say more. That mute, unconscious form pleads more eloquently than I could possibly do. Called to face the solemn majesty of the law, friendless—deserted—imprisoned—her life imperiled, she bore it all bravely. But point but your finger at the man she loves and the woman's heart cries out."

"Who this man may be we cannot tell. He, God, and herself alone may know. Yet he is the murderer. He it is who should take her place in the prisoner's box, who should expiate his crime upon the scaffold. But dastard and double murderer as he may be, he has left her—this frail girl, to peril her life, to die for him while he keeps in covert."

"If the law can reach him, I say hang him. Yes, hang him as high as Haman. Make him a scoff to the world as he will be to the devils damned in hell."

"But why say more? If there is one among you so dead to justice, to humanity, as to believe her guilty—to be willing to see her hung—let him hang her. But in mercy let him in the verdict include the wailing waif of this unnatural father. In God's name I say, in death do not divide them."

The hum of approbation that followed the closing of this speech burst out into applause that could not at first be checked. This, arousing Zara from her insensibility. she rose slowly and wearily to a sitting posture. Looking around, bewildered at the noise and the crowd, she bowed her head again in her hands, and sat stonily —apparently as lifeless as a statue.

As the Judge gave the charge to the jury, summing up the law, his voice faltered as, glancing at the frail bowed form before him, he charged them. "If there be a reasonable doubt as to the guilt of the accused, the law demands that you give the prisoner the benefit of that doubt."

The jury now slowly and solemnly filed out of the room. A buzz of anxious whispering went on among the excited crowd left in the court room.

The hum of voices suddenly ceased, and the faintest sound could have been heard as the jury were seen returning. And they slowly filed again to their seats, and an anxious pause ensued.

"Have you agreed upon a verdict?" resounded through the still court-room.

"We have agreed."

"What say you? Is the prisoner guilty or not guilty?"

"Not guilty," said the foreman.

A burst of applause that could not be stilled followed this verdict. The old grave-digger, blowing his nose violently upon his great red-flowered handkerchief, leaned forward, and, grasping the limp hand of the bewildered girl, he almost crushed it in his great brawny hand. Tears overflowed the eyes of the motherly Mrs. Simkins as she moved to the side of the outcast girl.

"That comes of being young and pretty, she'd a been hung ef she'd a got her deserts," said old Sal Slemmins to the grave digger as he passed on out, still blowing his nose violently.

"I wish the law maun get hold of you then, yer blarstit auld vampire," said the old man indignantly, pushing on out.

CHAPTER XLVI.

"Raze out the written troubles of the brain;
And with some sweet oblivious antidote
Cleanse the stuff'd bosom of that perilous stuff
Which weighs upon the heart."

SHAKSPEARE.

All that terrible day of Zara's trial, Aliena sat alone in her room, a prey to conflicting emotions. Already, day after day, since Zara's communication of Major Baron's guilt, Aliena had been considering whether, rather than that the innocent should suffer, it might not become her duty to divulge this fact, as well as those of which she was personally cognizant. The haunting presence before his death of the murdered man, her seeing Zara in that lonely spot with Major Baron, a place almost identical with that where the murder was committed, with the words she had there overheard, "Zara, tell your father it shall be as soon as." Facts which she believed might place the killing where it belonged, upon Major Baron instead of upon Zara.

But the agonizing thought of being instrumental in the disgrace, and in the possible ignoble death of Major Baron, and that too when Zara had taken her own life in her hands, willing, apparently, to lay it down rather than imperil his, made it seem impossible for Aliena to divulge. Thus, unable to decide, not daring to seek comfort in sympathy, or advice, in an agony of incertitude, tormented by the thought that should Zara be convicted her blood would be upon her soul, Aliena sat alone, waiting, yet dreading to hear the result of the trial.

At length she heard the hum of excited voices and the steps of passers-by, making her know that the trial was over. Longing to hear, yet fearing to do so, she sat with bated breath, seeming to have lost the power of volition. She at length heard Mauma's voice in the hall in an excited tone, and would gladly have inquired of her, but her tongue clave to her mouth, and her parched throat refused utterance.

But Mauma, entering the room puffing with excitement, exclaimed, " Thank the Lord! honey, they 've done cleared that poor, young thing. I jest knowd that that man never stood there and let that child stick that dagger clean to his heart. They say some man's done it, and run off and left her to be hung. The white-livered villain ! Laws a marcy ! honey, what 's the matter with you ? " exclaimed Mauma, and catching the fainting girl to prevent her falling, and getting her upon a lounge, she called in affright for Mrs. Graeme.

Agitated as her mother was at seeing her in this condition, she had presence of mind to use the usual restoratives, but without success. Now, really alarmed at Aliena's continued insensibility, she sent for a physician.

The servant dispatched happened to meet Dr. Leigh at the hotel, and returned in a few moments accompanied by him. Dr. Leigh was sorely agitated as he caught sight of the death-like looking girl.

"Poor child!" exclaimed Mauma, as he entered the room. "I was just a tellin her about that young thing's bein cleared, and she dropped right down like she was dead."

Aliena soon showed signs of returning consciousness under the remedies employed, looking around with bewildered expression.

Dr. Leigh refrained from asking in reference to the cause of her swoon, after what Mauma had said. He felt, however, that it must have been some more strongly moving cause than sympathy, alone, with an unknown girl, which had induced it. Her strangely worn face and hollow eyes confirmed him in the belief that her present condition, and the change brought about in her in the short time since he had seen her last, was the result of some sore heart-trouble from which she had probably been suffering when he encountered her looking so strange and wild, alone, at midnight in the Campus.

When Dr. Leigh left, instead of returning to the hotel for tea, he seated himself upon one of the rustic seats in the Campus. His mind reverted with curious wonder and pain to the night when he had encountered Aliena here, and he felt that whatever might have troubled her then had culminated in this evening's swoon. And he sat, trying in vain to solve the problem of her sorrow. His eyes wandered to the light shining from her window, where he knew she lay suffering, while he was powerless, as he felt, to lift the burden of sorrow from her heart. He saw with agony to himself, again and again, in memory, the pleading, helpless look with which her eyes had sought his as she returned to consciousness. The remembrance of that other time came back also, when he had held her, insensible it is true, yet clasped in his arms. He thought now, with yearning love, how gladly he would hold her there, and, if possible, shelter and protect her from pain and suffering.

He sighed as he thought of the misfortune of his having been called to see Aliena, whom he had been endeavoring to avoid, knowing as he did that through absence only could he hope to ensure even comparative tranquillity of mind—he could not say happiness. And now this interview, which had made him conscious that she suffered, had undone all his efforts at calm philosophizing.

The following morning, Aliena would gladly have given way to the languor caused by her swoon, the result of mental rather than of physical causes, and have remained in the solitude of her own room; but she was unwilling to add to the burden upon her mother's already sorely troubled heart. And constraining her inclination she rose, accepting Mauma's assistance in dressing, and had but just completed her toilet when Dr. Leigh called.

She looked more than ever like an ivory statue in the soft white dress she wore, which was scarcely whiter than her pale face as she entered the parlor.

Dr. Leigh came forward to meet her, and taking her transparent hand in his, he looked at it in sad surprise, indicating as it did, even more clearly than her face, by its diaphanous whiteness, how much she had suffered.

"I hope you are feeling better this morning," he said, looking into the pale, tired face before him.

"Yes, I am better," she said drearily.

"You must promise me to go out of these cloistered rooms, to get healthily fatigued in body and mind before you can be really well," said Dr. Leigh, his eyes fixed · tenderly and earnestly upon her.

"I will do anything—anything you tell me," said Aliena with a look of helpless, hopeless weariness.

CHAPTER XLVII.

"O, shame to men! devil with devil damn'd
Firm concord holds: men only disagree
Of creatures rational, though under hope
Of Heavenly grace and God proclaiming peace,
Yet live in hatred, enmity, and strife."
MILTON'S PARADISE LOST.

The death of that great chieftain and Christian hero, Stonewall Jackson, the loss of Vicksburg, the falling back of the army of Tennessee, the defeat of Gettysburg, the depreciation of the currency, the necessities growing out of a prolonged blockade, the hopelessness of the chimerical idea of foreign aid, the evident determination of the North never to cease war until a peace had been conquered, with the numerical disparity between the North and South, had brought about a depression and gloom that re-acted upon all.

Aliena, awakening from the dream that had absorbed her, was the more depressed by the general gloom. Her heart turned now more longingly than ever to home. And her prayers were more fervently uttered, if possible, not only for peace to her own sorely troubled heart, but for that white-winged messenger which might permit her once more to find, as she hoped, a haven of rest in a home made sacred by all the hallowed recollections of the past.

Her grief may then be imagined when she learned that since the occupation of Vicksburg by the enemy it had been deemed necessary to draw in their line of defense. And that in consequence, their beautiful, loved home, The Castle, had been pillaged, destroyed, razed to the ground; even the foundation stones dug up to make way for the earth-work entrenchments of the enemy.

All gone; a home consecrated to love, rich in the memories of the past, around which her life-time's joys and sorrows clustered. Where, trained by a father's tender care her mind had unfolded. Where it had learned grander flights, until in its widening sweep she had held communion in the silent watches of the night with Arcturus, Orion, and the Pleiades, or daring farther had veiled her face before the solemn mysteries of the invisible world.

There too had awakened that sweet and bitter dream of love, of which nothing but pain was left. Memory brought in sad review not only the visions that then made life a beautiful dream, but the ghostly phantoms of disappointment and distrust sprung to life from her cruel experience since. A broken troth, a cowardly fugitive, blackened by perjured vows, against whom blood cried from the ground. A forlorn, betrayed, sorrow-stricken, imprisoned girl in peril of her life, herself, with the glittering fruit turned to bitter ashes in the mouth. And she wondered if all the sweetness of trust and faith were gone from her forever. There was a unison in the desolation of her home and of her heart.

Aliena, enduring the agony of her knowledge of this crime, cut off from sympathy by the necessity for secrecy, felt a more entire isolation than ever before. An isolation made more complete by the distrust grown out of her disappointment; which seemed to cut her off as by a great abyss from humanity itself.

This was a cruel awakening for a girl in the first flush of sensitive womanhood—one delicately nurtured and lovingly cared for. She earnestly sought some way of getting out of self—of being "healthily fatigued in body and mind." Anything to escape from torturing thought.

Mrs. Layton, with others, during this cruel war, had devoted herself to all that was left for woman to do— to clothing the naked, feeding the hungry and visiting the sick and in prison. She became now a beneficent guide to Aliena in inducting her into these kind offices, in which good-work she sought to find oblivion to self.

Looking as wan as the sick to whom she ministered,

Aliena carried succor to the hospitals, supplied through the self-sacrifice of those who could not but continue to give when they had already given father, husband and sons, to a cause they believed to be just.

Here she became an angel of mercy to the sick, the wounded and the dying. To them, when past all human help, she could at least give soothing words and tears of sympathy, making the pathway to the tomb less lonely and dark. Here she was the recipient of messages of love from the dying to dear ones at home—or endeavored to direct their dying gaze to Him through whom "there shall be no more death, neither sorrow nor crying."

In thus ministering, if she did not find happiness, she found at least a calm which made life endurable in the consciousness of making it less dreary to others.

Dr. Leigh came upon Aliena one afternoon in these ministrations, in the hospital. Seated by the bedside of a dying man she was reading from a book of holy meditation suited to his condition. The nerves about the beautiful mouth of the sentient girl, were quivering with repressed emotion; her soft, low voice pulsating with feeling. The heavy gray clouds that had all day obscured the leaden sky breaking away, the level rays of the setting sun glinting in through the hospital window upon Aliena and the dying man, seemed a foreshadowing of the days upon which he was entering.

Dr. Leigh remembered another time when he had thought Aliena a Madonna personified, but, as he looked at the white, Mona Lisa face before him now, it seemed realistic indeed, and the halo that the sunshine made of her golden brown hair seemed a fitter crown since her baptism of sorrow.

Putting his hand upon the pulse of the wounded, dying man, Dr. Leigh said in a low voice, "There is little more for you to endure. Your suffering will soon be ended."

"Thank God," said the dying man, and his eyes resting upon Aliena, he continued, "the valley is not so dark—the angels seem present already—and I will soon be at home."

Aliena, overawed by the expression that had come into the man's face, bowed her head upon her hands. He only breathed a few long-drawn breaths and was dead.

"Aliena," said Dr. Leigh, forgetting himself in the agony, the self-immolation of the girl was causing him, "come away from here. You are killing yourself."

Aliena raised her white face from her hands and looked at the dead man, seeing that he no longer needed her, she tottered to her feet. Dr. Leigh drew her arm through his and they walked on out into the fresh evening air. Neither spoke for some time.

"You are in no condition to over-tax your sympathies as you are doing," said Dr. Leigh at length, his voice inexpressibly full of tenderness. "You must not come to the Hospital again until you have recuperated your strength."

He paused, but Aliena did not speak, and he continued in the same low tone, "Aliena, do you remember that upon Lookout mountain you promised that if you ever needed a friend you would trust me, and permit me to act as such. Something is wearing your life away. Could I not help you? I might at least share your pain?"

"No one can help me," said Aliena despairingly. "I must bear it alone."

"If there should ever be a time when I might, will you remember how gladly I would save you a pang," said Dr. Leigh in a low voice, vibrant with tenderness and pity.

She looked up longingly into his face, but made no reply. Silently pressing her hand he left her at her door.

18

CHAPTER XLVIII.

> " Yes! You saw me on the brink—
>   Beheld it giving way beneath my feet,
>   And saw me tottering o'er the hideous leap
>   Whose sight sent round the brain with maddening whirl."
>   KNOWLES: VIRGINIUS.

Aliena truly needed rest, she had over-estimated her power of endurance. The death she had witnessed had over-taxed her little remaining strength. And as Dr. Leigh left her she sank exhausted upon the doorsteps.

Letting her face drop upon her hands she sat there drearily thinking of the dying man, of the dread mystery of death, of the disenthralled spirit, of the mysterious hereafter. She felt helpless to battle and buffet with life. She had a longing to be away from this weary world.

The clashing of the great iron gate, and the hour of evening possibly, brought back a memory she tried to banish, but her thoughts would revert to the sinful man for whom she had sacrificed so much ; and to the dread secret of his guilt.

She heard footsteps approaching—they drew near. She raised her head. She saw in the dim light a soldier in gray moving toward her. She shuddered, but did not utter a sound, though if a disembodied spirit had appeared before her she could scarcely have been more surprised. Before her stood Major Baron.

" Aliena, my darling," he exclaimed, throwing his arm around her.

If it had been a serpent in whose coil she found herself, she could not have flung it off more loathingly.

" Aliena," Major Baron continued, " is there no remnant left of the love you once professed for me ? "

" How dare you touch me ? or suppose there could be ? " said Aliena, tremblingly.

" If you had ever loved me you could not give me up so easily. I have not found it easy to surrender you."

"I have not blackened my soul with perjured vows, nor dyed my hands in blood," said Aliena, almost fiercely.

"Aliena," said Major Baron passionately, "kill me with words, if you choose. I have deserved it, but I cannot live without you. I have come to humble myself in the dust before you. Listen to me. I love you, I love as I never expected, or hoped to love any woman on God's earth. I love you with all the strong passionate love of a man willing to risk heaven and earth to call you my own. To have you to myself, my very own, to hold you in my arms, as I did when I came to claim you as my bride. I believe you to be the purest, the most lovable woman God ever made. I cannot give you up. I am unworthy of you. I know it. I have forfeited all claim to your love. I was born with a passionate nature, uncurbed and uncontrolled in youth; it has grown with my growth, strengthened with my strength. I never truly loved before. Though with man's grosser nature I have been led away by passion. I know you spurn me for it, but men are not held by the same laws as woman. Before I met you I saw, and thought I loved Zara Varja. I was mad enough to pursue her. God knows I have been punished sorely enough. When, after the siege, I came to see you, as my evil star would have it, I found Zara here. My love for you made me a coward. I feared if you knew all you might spurn me. I dared not risk this knowledge to you. To prevent this I made false promises to Zara. I hoped that I might marry you and take you away in ignorance. But her father listened and found that I was to marry you. He threatened, and I determined to fly. I was going away to prevent exposure and I met Zara that fatal evening. Varja, desperate at the feared desertion of his daughter, way-laid and tried to assassinate me. I wrenched the dagger from his hand, and in self-defense was forced to do the deed. The next morning, as you know, I left for Montgomery."

“ Did you know that Zara was accused of the murder ? ” Aliena asked with unnatural calmness.

“ Yes, I knew it. But the same reason that had made me weak before, made me weak still. I loved you. I could not forfeit your love, by avowing my guilt. And I left with the deed unavowed.”

“ And you deserted that frail girl ? Left her to bear the penalty of your crime ? And you come to me pleading for my love ? ” Aliena said, in the same unnatural voice.

“ I was weak. I was criminal. I know it, but you were my plighted wife. I loved you. I longed for you. My better nature cried out for you. With you I could hope to be all that that better nature makes possible. Without you, I am like a vessel, tempest tossed, without rudder, buffeted by passion. Forgive me, Aliena. my spotless white dove. You cannot know how I have been tempted. With you a heaven on earth, a heaven above is possible, without is hell,” and Major Baron took Aliena’s unconscious hand in his, as he continued. “ My darling, think of the torments of the damned I have suffered, of the remorse, remorse for the sin toward the woman, I once believed I loved—for the blood spilled—for the heaven, in your love imperiled—Have mercy, Aliena, my plighted wife, as you hope for mercy at the last day. With you I am willing to face the world—to avow my guilt—if guilt there be ? Anything you say, so that I may be restored to your love.”

Aliena, weak physically as she was, stunned by the death she had witnessed at the hospital, bewildered by Major Baron’s passionate entreaties. could not at first collect her thoughts to answer him. She thought of the wreck of her own happiness, of her hopelessness, of his pleading words to save him from himself. “ Life cannot be more a wreck to me than it is already,” she thought. “ May it not be right that I should sacrifice my happiness, my life to his, and not drive him to perdition.” But she thought also of his weakness under temptation, and above all of his cruel cowardice in his desertion of a girl, willing in spite of all to peril her life for him ; and, throwing off his hand, she said bitterly, " All these vows and more doubtless you have made to Zara, and yet you come to me thinking I can believe and trust you ? "

" In God's name! don't rank that mad passion with the love I bear to you. In this, every noble impulse of my nature is stirred."

" I am tired, and weak, and hopeless. The mad thought, even as I know you now, has entered my mind to sacrifice myself to you. To crucify every high emotion of my soul to your salvation. Mad as is the thought. I have thought to marry you. In marriage, in any sense in which it can be such, a woman must accept her husband as, next to God, to be held in highest love and reverence. Without love marriage becomes a deadly snare and sin. Instead of working salvation for either, it brings perdition. Every sweet emotion of heart, and mind, and being turned awry becomes a poisonous fang, gnawing into and poisoning the soul. Could I before God promise to love and honor a man false to solemn vows—blood-stained—and a coward? If you had had the manliness to come forward, to avow your guilt—to protect the frail woman whom you left, apparently dying, to the scorn and hooting of the cruel multitude. I might hope for something in the future. But when to guilt you have added the craven spirit of a coward, there could be nothing to hope for, even if I loved you. Now I know I never loved you. I loved an ideal I had created and placed in a form that lacked the spirit to avow itself a man. That could cringe and cower behind a feeble woman, and leave her to an ignoble death—and that woman the mother of his child. If there is any manhood in you go, find the girl you have betrayed, who. in spite of all, still clings to you. Show your penitence by making her your wife. And may God have mercy upon you, though you have shown none."

And Aliena, leaving him stunned by her words, turned and entered the house.

CHAPTER XLIX.

> "I feel the impulse yet I do not plunge :
> There is a power upon me that withholds,
> And makes it my fatality to live—
> My own soul's sepulchre."   BYRON.

There was one thing that Major Baron had not confessed to Aliena in the interview depicted.   It was, that the evening before he left Montgomery, while walking along the street, he had caught sight of the wild eyes and still beautiful, pleading face of Zara.   That. at this sight, as of that of an avenging fury, though certainly the frail, beautiful girl presented no likeness to such a character, he had shrunk, cowering from her ; avoiding her by turning abruptly.   Having returned by a circuitous route to the hotel, he had rung for Auguste.

"Auguste," he said, "I want you to pack up—I am going on the ten o'clock train, be ready before that time."

"Yes, sir." said Auguste, beginning his preparations at once.   "Marster," he continued hesitatingly, stopping the folding of some garment, "Miss Zara come here this evening while you was gone.   She said she must see you.   That I must tell you to come to—"

"Haven't I told you that I wanted to hear nothing more on that subject," said Major Baron, in a harsh, metallic tone, turning red and then white, as he glowered at Auguste, who went on meekly with his packing, saying nothing more.

Major Baron did not go to say farewell to Lilian Selwyn; he left a note of adieu instead, to be delivered the next day, saying :

"I regret extremely that, being called away suddenly by business of importance, I am debarred the pleasure of saying good-bye in person," etc.

Zara had learned through Aliena. having privately sought another interview with her. that Major Baron was in Montgomery.   Not daring to communicate with him by letter, since the warning Aliena had given her, still clinging to the hope that love for her and for his child, and gratitude to her for shielding him at the risk of her own life, might make him marry her, as he had promised to do ; she had determined to go and, if possible, see him. And this was the reception she had met.

Major Baron had all along earnestly desired to see Aliena and plead his cause in person ; hoping that, by his presence, he might accomplish what he could not hope to do by letter. While Zara remained in Athens he had not dared to venture there, especially with such a purpose in view, lest she should avenge herself by divulging his guilt. With what success his interview with Aliena was crowned, we have seen.

Returning to the hotel, after this interview, Major Baron had gone to his own room, his guilty conscience, as well as his bitter disappointment with Aliena, made him shrink from sight. He sat here thinking, until almost phrensied. He sought at length to still the agony of his mind by reading. By chance he had gotten hold of Hawthorne's "Scarlet Letter." Such was the chaotic misery into which his mind was plunged, that at first he found it impossible to fix his thoughts upon anything but his own misdoings—his disappointment and the scorn of the woman he had loved with all the intensity possible to his fallen nature.

He rang for Auguste at length. Having determined to leave in the morning, he wished to give him directions to that effect ; desiring even more earnestly to get away now than he had to come to this place. His coming at all and confronting the memories revived and the dangers risked, gave evidence of the power of the attraction that had drawn him here.

Auguste, however, was not to be found. Surmising easily where his master had gone when he entered the Campus, and supposing that he would remain there during the evening, Auguste had eagerly embraced this opportunity for attending to a matter of interest to himself. Something upon which his mind had been greatly exercised ever since leaving Athens—namely, devoting himself to acquiring information in regard to the killing of Varja.

He had no difficulty in finding some one who gladly recounted to him the story of Zara's arrest as the murderer of her father—her persistent silence, the failure to prove her guilty, with the plea of her lawyer. It was as plain to Auguste as if he had seen the deed done, that it was his master who was the guilty party. He gave no intimation of this knowedge, however.

Major Baron had resumed his efforts at reading, and the fearful story at length aroused his interest. It seemed written to torture him. He felt the Scarlet Letter branded into his very soul as he read on with a fearful fascination. He entered with agony into the remorse of the doubly-dyed, despicable hero of the story.

Auguste came at length. There was something in his unusually obsequious manner and furtive look that told as plainly as words could speak to Major Baron's guilty conscience how he had been spending his time.

"I want you to be ready to take the cars in the morning at seven," said Major Baron.

"Yes, marster," Auguste replied, with a very formal military salute.

"What are you waiting for?" said Major Baron sharply, with a look that evinced the repressed desire to hurl something at his head.

"Nothin, marster, only I thought you might be wantin somethin," and Auguste backed toward the door and from the room in a way that showed that he divined his master's impulse.

Major Baron could read no more now, he could not endure it. He sat there thinking. The great University clock clashed midnight, and still he could not rest. He rose at length and went out into the deserted street.

The waning moon was rising dimly. He walked on in the stillness.

His steps turned with a strange, morbid fascination toward the tobacco shop. It was closed now. But the sinister scowling face that he had seen there appeared again in imagination. He heard again the threatening words, "It shall be the worse for him. I swear to God it shall be the worse for him." He saw the sobbing girl. He felt again the tremor that had seized him then, though there was no sign of light or life there now. His limbs shook under him as he turned the corner and went on past the door, into which he had dragged the dripping, forlorn girl on that fatal night. The dreary home where he had left her alone, with all that burden of sin and sorrow to bear. He moved on down the street, the same which Zara, and afterwards her father, had taken toward the cemetery. With the same strange, morbid fascination he kept on his course toward that solemn, dread spot where the deed had been done.

He came in sight of the great gate. He saw the white cross that had seemed to stretch out its arms to take ghostly form and fly toward Zara. He entered the still, solemn place. He went on by the mausoleum where he had first met Zara. In the dim moonlight the white marble form of the mother with her child in her arms, to whom the temple was sacred, seemed mutely to reproach him with the mother and child deserted. The figures above menaced him. Faith silently, unceasingly pointing upward seemed to call down vengeance upon him from Him who has said, " Vengeance is mine, I will repay." Hope seemed no longer hope, but black despair. He moved on into the shadows of the gnarled trees and tangled vines toward the black river, to the dire spot itself where Varja had lain.

Here the dim light of the cold moon lay like "a white face cloth upon the dead earth." He saw in imagination the ghastly form that never left him now. The clenched teeth, the glazing eyes, the pool of blood. He heard the hissing oath, the daughter's wild shriek. He lived over the horrors of that fierce, wild storm. He heard the voice of a wrathful God in the thunder, he saw his avenging arm in the descending stroke of the glittering lightning.

The boat was still there. He loosened it, entered, and rowed to the middle of the black river. The minor chords were sounding in the roar of the falls above, and in the ripple, splash, gurgle of the smaller stream, mingling with the sigh of the pines. He glanced wildly around. The sweat stood upon his clammy brow.

He had thought to throw himself into the dark water. But sin had made a coward of him.

"Myself am hell, but eternity? Eternity?" The voices of nature seemed to resound it in his ears. He took up the oars and rowed vigorously back to the shore. He trembled as he thought of the deed he might have done. He dared not stop to think. He landed the boat and made it fast to the shore. He shuddered as he thought of the tiger spring, the wrestle for life, that had met him here.

Quickly and fearfully he took his way back by the brook, on through the gate, out of the cemetery. Under the shadows of the great oaks in the Campus he passed the cloistered room where lay a white-souled, suffering girl, her hands clasped above her head, her wide open eyes staring into black vacancy.

He hurried on. He dared not think of the Paradise from which sin had driven him. He re-entered his room. He took his pistol, the same that he had carried since that night when Varja's threat had made him tremble, and going to the window, he hurled it into the street. He laughed a sort of maniac laugh as he thought that he must live now.

CHAPTER L.

"But one was out on the hills away,
    Far from the gates of gold ;
  Away on the mountain, wild and bare,
    Away from the tender shepherd's care,
  Out in the desert he heard its cry,
  Sick and helpless, and ready to die."

                              ELIZABETH CLEPHANE.

The following afternoon Jennie Foster and Mr. Marsden called to see Aliena, whose strength had succumbed to the fearful tax upon her sensibilities of late, and she asked to be excused.

"Tell her we have brought something of hers we found, that I know she must prize. And she will see me for a moment, I am sure," Jennie persisted in saying to Mauma, who had brought the excuse.

Aliena wondered, when she received this message, what it could be that Jennie had found. She could think of nothing she had lost except her watch, stolen in Chattanooga. She could scarcely think it possible that it could be that, but hoping that it might be, she consented to see her.

Jennie, ushered by Mauma, entered Aliena's room with a beaming smile, the picture of ruddy health and animal spirits. Seeing Aliena lying upon the lounge, looking as colorless as the white robe she wore, Jennie's expression changed as she approached her.

"I am so sorry to find you so sick, Miss Graeme, but I have brought you something that I hope will make you well—for I know you must have been distressed at losing it. Mr. Marsden and I were walking in the cemetery, down by the river, to see where that awful murder was committed ; and right by where the boat was tied, I saw this jewel case lying. I picked it up and opened it, and I knew it was yours the minute I saw it. I saw you wear it at the Massey's party. I couldn't but remember it, it is so singular. and beautiful. Here it is," said Jennie, unclasping the case with evident gratification, at the pleasure she thought she was conferring. And the glittering emerald serpent was disclosed to view.

Aliena, white as she had seemed before, grew whiter still. All color left her lips even, as the bracelet was disclosed. Springing to a sitting posture, she clutched Jennie's hand, gasping out, "Where is Major Baron?"

"He came yesterday evening. I saw him when he arrived—but—"

"Where is he? where is he now?" Aliena gasped, pressing her hand to her heart with a sharp pain.

"I don't know where he went, he started off on the cars this morning," said Jennie, in evident bewilderment.

"Are you certain?" said Aliena, feebly, her hand still on her heart, which seemed to have stopped beating in the reaction.

"Why, yes, of course, I am. I called good-bye to him from the gallery, as he was getting into the carriage. Though I don't believe he heard me."

Aliena sank back upon the lounge, speechless for a time. At length, seeing Jennie's anxious, perplexed face, she said, "You were very kind to bring it to me, Jennie, I am very much obliged, Don't think anything of what I do. I am tired and sick."

Jennie having rejoined Mr. Marsden in the parlor, and started back to the hotel, said "I never saw any one act as curiously as Miss Graeme did, when I showed her the bracelet. Any one would have thought it was a sure enough serpent. She scared me. She turned as white as a ghost, and clutched at me and asked 'Where is Major Baron?' I think she must have been out of her head. I was sorry to see her so sick. She is such a sweet young lady."

"She and Major Baron must have had a quarrel. I thought he was a lover of hers from the number of times I used to see him coming into the Campus. He went off without telling her good-bye, I suppose."

“ I would n’t break my heart, if any man chose to treat me that way,” said Jennie.

“ I have no idea you would,” said Mr. Marsden dryly, and entering the hotel Jennie’s vigorous voice could soon be heard singing the inevitable six verses of Lorena, with unflagging interest.

Notwithstanding Jennie’s assurance as to Major Baron’s departure on the cars, Aliena sent to make inquiries as to whether he had actually gone, which was confirmed; and as to his destination, which was found to be Richmond. The following day she sent the bracelet to a friend of her father in Richmond, with the request that he should see Major Baron and deliver it in person, and let her know of its safe delivery.

The pain which Aliena had endured in having been impelled to say what she had done in her interview with Major Baron seemed more endurable now, in the face of the greater agony she felt she had escaped since her apprehension of his suicide.

That evening Aliena sought consolation in the chapel service, which was conducted by Dr. Haydon. His remarks were intended to strengthen faith in prayer. It seemed to Aliena that her heart had never gone out before with such earnestness in supplication to God, and in fervent thanksgiving for deliverance from the torture which Major Baron’s death would have caused her.

As the congregation slowly left the chapel Dr. Haydon approached Aliena, and taking her hand, said in his fatherly way, “ I am glad to see you, my daughter. I have not seen you as often of late as I would like ; but my health and the infirmities of age cut me off from many privileges.- It seems to me that you are looking paler than when I saw you last. I would like to talk with you, and the drive might do you good. Won’t you get in with me and let us drive around for a while.”

Aliena, feeling that a conversation with this godly, old man might fit her better to bear the troubles that weighed upon her, accepted his invitation.

"My daughter," said Dr. Haydon, as they drove on, "I am too familiar with the trials of life, and, as a pastor, with the hearts of those over whom God has seen fit to place me as a spiritual guide, not to know from your face that you have been, and are still suffering with some sore trouble. I do not ask your confidence, my daughter, unless you feel that you would find comfort in it. But I hope I shall never live to be so old as to be insensible to the pain to which the acute sensibilities of youth makes the young especially liable. My greater experience may help me to throw some light, however, upon a pathway necessarily dark and beset with thorns at times, that we may be recalled to the remembrance that this is not our abiding place. It grieves my heart to see these thorns pierce and wound. But so it needs must be my child. But if God should grant me the power to assist the torn and bruised ones along the path of life, it will be worth the while for me to carry the burden of age and infirmity a little longer. You believe, of course, my daughter, in the over-ruling hand of Providence, that nothing has or can happen without divine permission—that the same God who made you, rules over, preserves and protects you; not only in the great events in life, but that the very hairs of your head are numbered? Can you not then trust, not only his infinite wisdom and power, but his infinite tenderness and love? And believe that however dark his Providence may seem, he carries you, as a tender shepherd, in the arms of his love. That 'as a father pitieth his children so the Lord pitieth them that fear him,' that 'he does not willingly afflict the children of men,' that 'though for the present your affliction seems grievous, afterward it yieldeth the peaceable fruit of righteousness,' and that though ye have lain among the pots, yet shall ye be as the wings of a dove covered with silver, and her feathers with yellow gold."

"It is hard to realize always, father," said Aliena, "that affliction is sent by God, and it is harder to endure those we think we may have brought upon ourselves."

"My daughter, all affliction is permitted by God, but if you have done evil in his sight, remember that he is not only willing to forgive, but that he stands at the door and knocks, importuning to be let in. 'Open to me my beloved, for my head is filled with dew, and my locks with the drops of the night.'"

"Dr. Haydon," said Aliena, with evident emotion, "could it ever be right to do what you believed wrong for yourself; if that wrong were apparently necessary for the good of another?"

"My daughter, God's word is explicit. Every sin deserves the wrath and curse of God. We are responsible to Him, for our own souls, and, though we must certainly place no snare in the way of any of God's creatures, yet we must deliberately, and prayerfully do what we believe right for ourselves, before God, and leave the issue calmly and trustfully with Him. We cannot, we have no right to hope for blessing, either for ourselves or for others, if we swerve from what we believe to be right, according to the best light God has given us. And doing this we must believe and trust that his infinite love and his infinite wisdom will make it work for good to all in the end. It will save you many a pang, my daughter, if you will carry in mind a thought of which young persons, in the presumptuous idea of their own power and responsibility, are apt to lose sight. It is that we are very weak, finite creatures, and that God is infinitely capable of controlling and governing all his creatures, and all their actions. And that when we have done as nearly as possible what we believe to be right, we have nothing more to do but calmly to rest in his arms, and leave the issue with Him, feeling that we can lie trustingly in the arms of our Heavenly Father, knowing that we are not left to blind chance, but that He who rules over us will carry us tenderly through all the trials of life, bringing us not only a

precious calm in this life, like that which Jesus brought
to the tempest-tossed disciples upon the sea of Galilee,
but an abundant entrance into that upper kingdom,
where there is joy forever more."

"Will you pray, my dear father, that I may find this
calm?" said Aliena in a voice subdued by reverence for
the godly man and for the great truths he so tenderly
inculcated; which already seemed to bring a foretaste
of the calm she invoked.

"I will certainly remember you, my daughter, in my
prayers, and may God grant you now that peace which
passeth all understanding, and an abundant entrance to
his Heavenly Kingdom hereafter," said Dr. Haydon,
as Aliena left him at the Campus gate; calmed and
strengthened for what might be before her in the dark
future.

CHAPTER LI.

"Have we not heard the bridegroom is so sweet,
O let us in, tho' late, to kiss his feet!
No, no, too late! ye cannot enter now.
No light, so late! and dark and chill the night,
O let us in, that we may find the light?
Too late, too late; ye cannot enter now."

TENNYSON: IDYLS OF A KING.

Zara, having called to see Major Baron, unsuccess-
fully, at the hotel in Montgomery, as we have seen;
after leaving the message with Auguste, asking him to
call and see her, with directions where he might find
her, went away. In her sore disappointment, she wandered from street to street, with the vague hope of
meeting him.

She did catch sight of him, at length, in her foot-sore
wandering. Fearing his disapprobation should she
obtrude upon him thus publicly she hesitated, caught
his eye fixed for a moment upon her, his face blanching

at the sight, when turning abruptly, he hurried from her.

Thus abandoned, chilled by the knowledge that he avoided her, she returned, tired and utterly dispirited, to the dingy, obscure boarding-house where she had found refuge. Here she shut herself in her dismal, cramped room, made more unsightly by its furnishing.

In one corner of the room was a narrow bed, with a blue and yellow checked homespun coverlet and one scant pillow. In the center of the bare, stained floor stood a small, rickety, ink-stained table ; upon which was a brass candlestick, covered with the tallow sputterings and with verdigris, containing a short piece of tallow dip. The patched window was without curtain. Hung from a nail against the discolored wall was a small looking-glass, which had the faculty of distorting to hideous deformity the most beautiful features ; this, with two dilapidated chairs, completed the furnishing.

Here she passed the dreary hours of the night. With the morning grown more hopeful, Zara made her baby as attractive as possible, and with womanly instinct, doing the same for herself, she sat watching and waiting. But Major Baron did not come.

The only window to her room had a dismal outlook upon the small back yard. Through the patched panes of glass she could see in this unsightly rear unseemly piles of potato peelings, egg shells, coffee-grounds, feathers and ashes. In a low spot which had become a receptacle for slops and garbage from the kitchen, some ducks paddled and sputtered delightedly.

An aged, mongrel yellow dog, blind in one eye, tall and gaunt, and without hair in spots, moved listlessly around, dragging himself through the filth watching lazily for the appearance of an unctuous-looking black woman, who emerged from the Plutonian region of the odorous, smoky cellar kitchen with a tin pan in her hand full of garbage, which she scraped with a vengeful air into the reeking puddle.

The drake and the mongrel, making a simultaneous rush for spoils, fought it out here, while the ducks got away with the garbage.

Mrs. Stokes, the proprietor of this establishment, was a brawny, big-boned, red-faced woman, with carroty red hair. The sleeves of her homespun dress were rolled up above her elbows and displayed the muscular development of her great, sun-burned arms. The skirt of her dingy dress was short enough not to impede the energetic movement of her large feet and brawny ankles.

She made violent sorties at intervals into the back-yard, seizing sticks of wood from the disorderly pile, and rushing back into the kitchen as though the mildest object she had in view was the braining some victim for a holocaust.

Emerging again with great slices of meat in her hand, as if flayed alive from the expiring victim, she pounded maliciously upon them with a cleaver or axe on a block used for that purpose; the blood spattering her with each blow, and disappeared again with undaunted will and energy into the dismal regions of the kitchen, from whence denser volumes of smoke issued as the sputtering of grease and sizzing of frying meat went on.

In her forlorn, depressed condition, Zara was insensibly wrought upon by these surroundings. And thus the day dragged its weary length along, and still Major Baron did not come.

Night came at last. Worn with waiting, watching and anxiety, she could endure the suspense no longer. Laying her sleeping baby from her arms, she ventured again to seek Major Baron. With what success we may know, as it was about this hour that he was pleading his cause so passionately with Aliena.

Zara, after subjecting herself to prying eyes, significant glances, and whispered comment, learned, in answer to her questions, that Major Baron had gone—taken the cars eastward for some unknown point.

Leaving the hotel—wretched, forlorn, forsaken—she wandered aimlessly and recklessly on, regardless of direction, along the streets. She passed groups of men who sometimes turned to stare curiously at the beautiful, wild-eyed girl; or a woman, leaning upon the arm of her husband, who gathered her skirts closer to her side as she passed; or a Christian mother, who looked with pitying eyes upon the despairing wanderer, saying in her heart, "By the grace of God I am what I am."

But none of these things consciously moved Zara now. She was too absorbed in her own misery. In trying to work out from the chaos of her mind something—anything upon which to build a hope for the future.

Passing under a gas-light, she was startled by the voice of a drunken man, who exclaimed, "That's a d—d tempting little picture, Tom, I would n't mind kissing those pretty lips."

Zara glanced in affright, with startled eyes, at the insolent, staring man, and hurried on. Becoming conscious at length that she had wandered far out of her direction, she found that she must inquire of some one. Seeing a plain, fatherly-looking old man, with a basket of provisions upon his arm, she ventured to ask, in her low, musical voice, for direction.

As the old man kindly gave the desired information, she heard the same voice that had startled her before, and turning nervously, again caught sight of the brutal, staring, drunken face. Alarmed, she hurried on. Out of breath and exhausted, at length, looking around without seeing the man, she ventured to walk more slowly until she reached the dingy house she was seeking.

Groping her way through the narrow, dark hall to her room, she felt in the darkness for matches, but could find none. Instinctively feeling to know if her baby were safe upon the bed, she sat down, leaning her head on her clasped hands upon the side of the bed; and gave herself up to her benumbing misery.

Becoming conscious at length that the darkness weighed upon and oppressed her, adding to her wretchedness, she took the candlestick in her hand and went out through the dark hall into the back yard, hoping to get a light.

Here she could see a feeble, flickering light, coming from the cellar kitchen. Hearing voices there, she moved on. But catching sight of the dread, loud-mouthed Mrs. Stokes, Zara, with instinctive fear, shrank back.

This muscular, red-faced woman was wielding what seemed to Zara an immense beef bone, eyeing it to see if any meat remained upon it, as she gave her orders for the morning to her sub-cook. "Take this and chop it up fine with them cold pertaters, and pieces of cold pork that you biled with them greens, and them scraps of bread, and pour the soup that was left over them, and make a hash for breakfast," she was saying.

Zara at last catching the eye of the dread woman fixed upon her, fearing either to retreat or to come forward, yet advanced to the door, saying timidly:

"I came for a light, will you please let me light my candle?"

Hesitating to enter, she cast her eyes wistfully at what constituted the light of this gloomy region, a skillet with a piece of burning rag, which, hanging over the side, served as a wick, but scarcely made darkness visible.

"Well, why don't yer come along in and light yer candle. Nobody ain't a henderin you, I reckon. What are you skeered of?" said Mrs. Stokes in a voice which added to Zara's fears. It, like her appearance, being much more that of a man than a woman.

But the thick-lipped, flat-nosed black woman evidently compassionating the timid, beautiful girl, lifted the skillet by its long handle and moved forward to proffer her a light. Making it flicker and flame as she moved on, giving a more weird look to the dismal place, over which she seemed a fit presiding genius, crowned as she was with her big-flowered scarlet and yellow head-handkerchief.

Zara, looking the more beautiful from the contrast with her surroundings, now timidly held out her candle and lit it. And thanking the woman, instinctively she returned to her room.

Here she sat down once more by the bedside. It was useless for her to try to sleep. Her mind was too busy with the memories and miseries of the past. Her love —her downfall—her father's death—her wild delirium —the dismal cell—her trial—her cruel desertion—and now—

The short piece of tallow dip Mrs. Stokes had allowed her had burned down ; it flared and flickered, flared and flickered, more and more faintly, like the hope dying in Zara's heart. It went out. She heard nothing now, but the yeowing and spitting of some cats in the back yard.

This was the same night in which Major Baron was suffering the tortures of the damned, under the shadows in that dire spot in the cemetery. It may have been that some inscrutable, subtile bond, grown out of their love, still held her in sympathy with him.

She could not rest. She must move. She got up and groped her way out into the street. She moved up and down before the house, in the dim moon-light—with her hands clasped before her. Kept vibrating like the needle to the pole—swinging off, but coming back magnetically to her child.

Suddenly an arm was thrown around her, and the same brutal, drunken voice that had already frightened her, drawing her to him, exclaimed, " Kiss me, my pretty dear."

Writhing from his grasp, with the look of a wounded, hunted fawn, she sprang away from him, running, panting with affright, into the house, gladly encountering even the dread Mrs. Stokes in her flight. Here she sank into a chair over which she had stumbled in the darkness. Mrs. Stokes standing in the doorway, where she had encountered Zara, put her arms akimbo in righteous horror and indignation and exclaimed:

"Well! I thought you was in bed and asleep long ago. I hadn't no idee that I was a takin' in the likes o' this inter a decent, respectable house. Lookee here now, mum, you jest take that brat o' yourn, and you tramp. This house ain't intended for sich as you, I'd have you to know."

"Please, ma'am, I—" began Zara.

"None of your please mums to me," interrupted the loud-mouthed woman, who had no idea of compromising. "You jest do as I say, and powerful quick, too, or I'll see if there aint a way to make you," and she opened the door of a room in which there was a candle burning, took it up, and returning, advanced menacingly toward Zara.

The girl cowered, tremblingly, before the big-boned, muscular woman; who raised her voice and her fist at the same time, saying:

"Now I don't want to have no sass, nor no row with you, or I'll have you whisked off to jail before you can say Jack Robberson. But you jest git up from there and take that brat o' yourn, and you tramp."

The big tears were rolling down the wan face of the driven girl. Beset by fears of the threatening woman within the house, and of the brutal, drunken man without. Followed by Mrs. Stokes, Zara re-entered her room. Regardless now of everything else except her child, she took it in her arms, wailing at being aroused from sleep, and, still followed by the red-faced woman, went out into the street, hearing the door locked and bolted behind her.

Looking fearfully up and down the street, she thought she saw the same drunken man moving toward her. And turning in the opposite direction, she ran until she no longer had strength to do so, meeting only one per-

son in her flight—a man who turned and looked pityingly after her, saying :

"Poor fallen creature, let her go. I shall certainly
not assist in arresting her."

She walked on more slowly now, knowing that there
was nothing for her to do, at this hour of the night,
under the suspicious circumstances, but to move on.
No other door she could wish to enter, was more open
to her now than Mrs. Stokes'.

She passed a brilliantly lighted, gilded room, whose
doors were wide open. Splendid gilded frames of mirrors, and of sensuous pictures showed above the screens
fronting the door. Behind these she heard the clicking
of glasses, and the sound of oaths. Footsteps moving
toward the door, she hastened on, meeting a painted,
bedizened woman, who went in there.

She passed another house—"the way to hell,"—from
within whose walls came the sound of revelry. The
door opened and closed mysteriously upon those who
entered there, giving glimpses also of gilded splendor.

Only the doors to sin seemed open now.

Sinking exhausted, at length, upon a door-step, Zara
tried to arouse her benumbed consciousness to the remembrance that there was something for her to love in
her arms—something to live for. But she was too
stunned and weary now to feel any well-spring of life,
of love, or of hope from the poor little unwelcome waif
she carried in her arms.

Worn out, her head drooped at last. Exhausted in
body and mind, she slept. Only for an instant. Startled by voices and steps, she sprang up. Worn as she
was, she hastened on again. Conscious that she was
followed, she tried to run. She was past that now.

Unexpectedly, she came in sight of the river. At
sight of the water a sudden longing seized her. She
longed to rest under its hiding, oblivious waves. To be
haunted by sorrow and sin no more. To be hunted and
driven no longer.

Urged by the footsteps behind her, she moved on. She found herself upon the bank of the river. A great cavernous saw-mill, with its black, mysterious vaults, peopled with horrors by her excited imagination, was before her. By its side lay a raft of logs.

She sped on. Led by a strange fascination ; possibly that of a stronger will acting with inexplicable power upon her. She looked back once more. Affrighted at seeing the forms of the two men outlined black against the sky upon the bank above her, like a hunted fawn she fled, on, down—down to the brink of the river— out upon the raft.

Tightening the clasp with which she held her baby to her breast, she gave a leap into the black water. She went down and the waves closed over them. Possibly it may have been at the same moment that another culprit, affrighted at the hell before him, turned and rowed vigorously back to shore.

"My God! Selwyn," exclaimed Colonel Bond, "the woman is drowning, she has jumped into the river," and rushing on, disencumbering himself as he went, he plunged into the water.

Zara had sunk and risen once, before Colonel Bond could get to where she had leaped in. As she rose a second time, she had been carried by the current beyond his reach, and again she went down before he could swim to her. Allowing now for the current, he caught her as she rose the third time, and, supporting her, the child still clasped in her arms, he with difficulty swam to the shore.

Everything possible was done to resuscitate the mother and child. But it was without avail. It was too late. Life was extinct. And Colonel Bond and Mr. Selwyn, having consigned the bodies to the proper authorities, walked slowly and sadly homeward, as the day was dawning. Feeling that what they had intended in kindness, had possibly hurried, instead of preventing the tragic result.

CHAPTER LII.

" I did dream
That I had murdered her. 'Tis false, 't was but
A dream, think you that I shall not believe
Mine eyes before your **tongue** ?   But there she **is.**"

SHAKSPEARE.

In the morning, before a jury could be summoned, and that inevitable horror, an inquest gone through with, thronging crowds came, with prying eyes, to satiate their morbid curiosity, with the mournful sight of the unknown, friendless girl, and of the child still folded in the clasp of death.

In all this thronging crowd none could give a clew to the identity of the beautiful young creature lying there.

Colonel Bond and Mr. Selwyn appeared before the coroner's jury to give their testimony as to her death. They stated that they had been to a card party and were going home late, and coming upon her seated upon a door-step, her sudden movement, and wild furtive manner, with her taking the direction toward the river had aroused their fears. That following her, they had witnessed, instead of preventing the act they had feared.

Searching the body for some clew for identification, a gold locket was found, secreted from view, suspended around her neck. In this was enclosed a small photographed likeness of a soldier in the confederate uniform. In the same locket lay a ring of brown hair, tied with a faded blue ribbon, and with it a blurred note.

The crowd struggled for a view of these articles as they were disclosed.

" It 's a Confederate Major, and a devilish good looking fellow at that, though the picture is blurred some, by the water," said one of the jurors.

" Zara Varga, that is the address on the note, I believe. That must be the woman's name. Let 's see what is inside," said the coroner, and he began to study

that out. "It is signed C., nothing more. C?—what
does C stand for, I wonder?"

"C? C stands for cruelty, cowardice, and crime,"
said some one in the crowd.

Mr. Selwyn, elbowing his way, at length got near
enough to catch sight of the picture. "My God! It's
Bar—" he exclaimed.

But Colonel Bond, who had also been endeavoring to
get a sight at these articles, discerning who it was,
pulled Mr. Selwyn violently by the coat, thus attract-
ing his attention, and stopping this speech.

"Who did you say it was?" some one in the crowd
asked eagerly, but received no reply, another said,

"I believe them men know mor 'n they let on."

"I never saw or heard of this girl, until I saw her on
the door-steps just before she jumped into the river,"
said Mr. Selwyn in such a tone that no one ventured to
say more.

Colonel Bond sought an opportunity to speak privately with the officer, who had these relics in charge,
and said to him, "You know there is no law to punish
the driving of a woman to suicide. And it might be
worth your while to keep that note and picture private,
until you hear from me again."

The man nodded knowingly, and Colonel Bond rejoined Mr. Selwyn, whom he found gazing at the bodies
with an expression as full of wrath as of commisera-
tion.

"Hanging is too good for that infernal scoundrel,"
said the indignant Mr. Selwyn as they walked away.

"Don't fly off the helve that way Selwyn. Give a
fellow a chance. Don't condemn Baron until you hear
him.

"Hear him? Hear the devil! didn't you see that
writing and his picture? And didn't you see the likeness in that child? I have always heard that likeness
came out after death, but I never saw anything to equal
that. It was wonderful."

"Maybe the girl was some kin of his," suggested the kind-hearted Colonel Bond.

"Kin? the devil! That child was kin. And very near kin too. Just let me hear of that infernal scoundrel's coming near Lil again and I'll make food for fishes, or worms of him. D—d if I don't."

Mrs. Stokes, going to market in the morning, and hearing of the tragedy of the night before, had some feeble flickerings of compunctious thought to flit momentarily across her mind. The possibility of her having had some instrumentality in this tragic event occurred to her and she concluded to satisfy her curiosity. Joining in with the streaming crowd she went to look at the dead woman and child, to assure herself as to whether or not it were Zara.

Even this callous woman started back with horror as she recognized in the beautiful face of the dead, that of the frail girl she had so pitilessly driven from her door the night before. A slight pang troubled even her hardened conscience, as she thought that she had aided in hounding this forlorn young creature on to her death. But the comforting thought as quickly suggested itself that she could now safely appropriate whatever the girl had left in her house. Her greed crowding out the less agreeable thoughts of the wan, pitiful face, the streaming eyes, and the pleading words of the forlorn girl, as she had shut her out, homeless and friendless, into the dreary darkness of the streets that night.

No one coming forward to claim the body of the outcast girl, Mrs. Knowland, whose sympathies had been enlisted by the account given by Mr. Selwyn and Col. Bond, went with tender, pitying heart to see that she was decently interred. She arranged, herself, with gentle hand, the tangled masses of silky, waving hair; and tried to close the eyes now "dimly staring into futurity" under the long, black lashes, while she dropped tears of womanly pity upon the still, cold forms of the mother and child as they were shut up forever from scoffing view, going to see them laid away in the Potter's Field.

"And he cast down the pieces of silver in the temple, and departed, and went and hanged himself.

"And they took counsel and bought with them the potter's field, to bury strangers in."

CHAPTER LIII.

"I loved her, one
Not perfect, nay, but full of tender wants,
No angel, but a dearer being, all dipt
In angel instincts, breathing Paradise
Interpreter between the gods and men."
TENNYSON: PRINCESS.

Since the evening when Dr. Leigh had taken Aliena away from the death-bed of the soldier, she had shrunk from returning to her ministering to the sick and wounded there. Not so much from the pain she endured herself as from an apprehension suggested by her remembrance of Dr. Leigh's words and manner upon that occasion.

Her present life of inaction and uselessness, however, seemed unendurable; and she eagerly sought occupation—at least for the mind—oblivion to torturing thought and memories in books. She went therefore often to the library. Here, in the quietude of this comparatively deserted place, she endeavored to find the forgetfulness she had failed to secure elsewhere.

Lingering in the Library one afternoon, near an ivy-draped window of one of the compartments, endeavoring to catch the last lingering rays of light upon the book in which she had become absorbed, Aliena was startled by the sound of the low, clear voice of some one bending over her who had approached unheeded as she sat thus engrossed.

"I am glad to see you once more, and to find you so pleasantly absorbed. You have deserted us altogether lately at the hospital," the firm, low voice said.

Aliena knew the tones before she turned. The sound brought a flood of delicate color to her face as, with a smile of pleased surprise, she looked up into Dr. Leigh's eyes and said:

"You banished me yourself, I think. You could scarcely expect me to return without permission."

Seeing the delicate color, with the comparative repose, since the time when he had seen her last, so painfully overcome by the death of the soldier, Dr. Leigh said, "I think I can safely revoke my edict now. You can no longer plead that prohibition. I owe it to the suffering soldiers in the hospital to make the banishment as short as possible. What is it you were reading that absorbed you so as I came in?" and, taking the book from Aliena's hand, he read the heading of the page, "'Will and Emotion.' To what conclusion have you come upon so subtle a subject?"

"That, like most abstract questions, it is one upon which it is much easier to theorize than to practice satisfactorily. I am quite sure that, in spite of 'will,' I often let 'emotion' run away with my judgment—let me do all that I can to hold it in check," said Aliena.

"It seems to me that you might safely give the reins to any emotion you are likely to have, without apprehension of wrong, or need for compunctuous repining. It is hard to realize the possibility of your being carried into debatable ground even. The making judgment issue the fiat is the difficult point with me, however. To will, that is the point. There are some emotions so sweet in themselves, and apparently so heaven-appointed that judgment cannot decide to crucify them. Though like Phœbus' champing horses, they may threaten to get the bit in their teeth, and to hurl one to destruction as surely as they did his unfortunate son. Yet I am tempted at times by the glorious vision, to throw the reins as wildly, even if, like him, I fall 'from the Empyrean-headlong to the gulf.'"

"I thought that you were too philosophic ever to allow yourself to be carried away by emotion," said Aliena, faltering with embarrassment as she met Dr. Leigh's passionate eyes fixed upon her.

"No man is capable, at all times, of philosophizing. There are times when 'Will' is powerless to combat 'Emotion'—when it cannot prevent Emotion's beating its caged breast against the bars that hold it, or hinder those bars from wounding sorely," said Dr. Leigh in a voice vibrant with emotion.

Aliena raised her eyes to his with a pleading, helpless look ; her sensitive mouth quivering with repressed feeling. Unable to speak, or to control herself, she dropped her face up m her hands, and sobbed convulsively.

"Aliena, forgive me," said Dr. Leigh, in a voice full of tenderness, as he bent over her. "I was selfish—cruel. I thought only of my own pain, while I would give my life to protect you from suffering. But think of the hope, the despair I suffer. If I have been selfish and reckless it is because I love you, and I can endure the agony of suspense no longer."

"Oh! spare me—spare me," exclaimed Aliena in an agonized, helpless tone, looking up yearningly, yet beseechingly, into his face. "I find life so hard. Don't make it harder for me to endure," and her voice went out in a sob.

"What do you mean, Aliena? look at me, tell me ?" said Dr. Leigh, taking both her hands into his and gazing eagerly and longingly into her tender tear-moistened eyes

"I mean -Oh! have mercy upon me, and help me to forget," she said pleadingly, looking yearningly into his face. And withdrawing her hands she hurriedly left the room.

Dr. Leigh looked after her with an expression of intensest pain, and of sore wonder at her inexplicable words and conduct. And dropping into a chair he gazed drearily into vacancy. At length, as though seeking some clew to her words and acts, he took up the book she had been reading and opened it.

Upon the page where she had read lay a single shining strand of her golden brown hair. He took it up and wound the little coil about his finger, passing his hand caressingly over it. Thinking " What a strange thing is the will of man, when it can be held by a gyve no stronger than this."

<hr>

CHAPTER LIV.

" Kixg Richard.—Where is thy power then, to beat him back ?
Are they not now upon the western shore ?
" Stanley.—   I 'll muster up my friends to meet your grace
When and what time your majesty shall please."

The waves of that fearful storm that was rending the whole country had heretofore broken only in faint ripples upon the quiet little haven of Athens. But now a cloud suddenly lowered upon this hitherto clear horizon, looming and threatening to burst in fury upon the place.

It was rumored fearfully around that a Federal raid in progress, demoralized by plunder, had been met by Confederate troops. That turned aside, balked in their design, hoping to reinstate themselves in public estimation, they were swooping down upon this devoted place. Its undefended state making it apparently easy prey.

The wildest excitement prevailed. Bells were rung. The alarm sounded. All, from a state of seeming security, were thrown into the wildest consternation. The few men left at home, most of them operatives in the government factory for arms, set to work with vigor; improvising the best defense for the place practicable in this emergency.

Couriers came and went. The excitement was as intense as it was unexpected. Those who wished to flee feared to do so ; not knowing where they might encounter the enemy. The inevitable morning of disaster, as it was feared, dawned upon the terror-stricken place. Couriers announced the oncoming enemy. Orders came to hold the place, help was coming.

The sound of firing set the nerves of those waiting and watching in quivering motion. All feared for homes and lives. The firing ceased. A terrible uncertainty ensued. A courier with foaming horse brought hope. Soon the citizen guard appeared. It needed no words to tell that the danger was averted.

The victorious soldiers who had come to the rescue had followed, overtaken, routed, and made prisoners of the plunder-demoralized, over-burdened raiders. The victors soon appeared. Men, women and children surrounded them with every demonstration of jubilant joy and gratitude.

Soon a feast was improvised, where every delicacy the place could afford was spread for the tired, hungry soldiers. A banquet that might have tempted Epicurus himself, even without being served as this was by fair women, radiant with grateful smiles, whose delight it was to do them honor.

At the suggestion of the soldiers the ample feast was magnanimously shared with the hundreds of exhausted prisoners, who were gladly bartering their spoils of silver, gold, and jewels for food.

The joy of this occasion was marred by but one thought, that necessarily some must pay the penalty for success by suffering. Wounded and dying soldiers, Federal and Confederate, were being brought into the hospitals to be cared for. Aliena, for the first time since the evening when her strength had been so over-taxed by sympathy for the dying soldier, now with Mrs. Layton, amongst others, came forward to minister to the suffering.

As they were entering the hospital their progress was arrested by the slow tramp of men, bearing in upon a litter a wounded man. Aliena's face suddenly blanched as in the apparently dead man before her she recognized Colonel Harvey. The men having laid the insensible man upon a couch, turned away to bring in others.

Aliena, seeing that he had swooned instead of being dead, as she had at first feared, proceeded to use restoratives. And before a surgeon could be had she was repaid by a return of consciousness, and a look of grateful recognition from the wounded man.

Dr. Leigh's face lit up with pleasure as in answer to a summons he approached and caught sight of Aliena. But when he came near enough to see the wounded man he became suddenly scarcely less white than the bloodless man before him. With an evident effort to overcome his painful emotion, he offered his hand to Colonel Harvey; who, scarcely less moved, feebly extended his hand to that magnanimously offered. Aliena, feeling her presence no longer necessary, moved away to where a wounded Federal soldier lay.

Dr Leigh labored under a feeling of painful embarrassment in being thus called upon to minister to Colonel Harvey. After making the necessary examination of the wound he said with unusual hesitancy of manner, "Colonel Harvey, I must have a consulting surgeon before acting in your case."

"Do as you think best," said Colonel Harvey; continuing with evident emotion and some embarrassment, "but I wish you to feel assured that I am perfectly satisfied to leave my case in your hands."

"I appreciate your confidence, but I prefer a consultation for my own satisfaction," said Dr. Leigh.

He accordingly not only had a consultation with one

of the surgeons, but another was called in, as he differed from the first. And it was decided against Dr. Leigh's judgment to amputate the limb.

This decision having been communicated to Colonel Harvey, he asked, addressing Dr. Leigh, " Do you think there is no possibility of saving my leg?"

Dr. Leigh hesitated to reply, but he answered truthfully, " I thought there was a possibility of saving it. But as both these gentlemen think differently I have yielded my judgment."

"I am willing to abide by your judgment and take my chances. Life will be worth little to me if I must go through it maimed," said Colonel Harvey.

" I feel obliged to tell you, that both these gentlemen think death inevitable without immediate amputation," said Dr. Leigh.

" I am willing to take my chances; and to assume the whole responsibility," said Colonel Harvey firmly.

" A man who can face the chances for death with such nerve may come through, and I say try it," said one of the surgeons. And so it was decided.

For days Colonel Harvey's life hung in the balance. So anxiously did Dr. Leigh watch the case that he scarcely slept until the crisis had passed; but convalescence set in and life and limb were saved.

Mrs. Layton, who, with Aliena, had ministered to Colonel Harvey at the hospital, now proposed that he should be removed to her house; which was accordingly done. Here he was soon able, with the aid of a crutch, to walk the short distance in the same grounds, to where, in Aliena's little parlor, she was able to while away some of the tedious, weary hours of convalescence in conversation, reading and music; until he might once more be able to return to the field of war.

Dr. Leigh continued his professional care of Colonel Harvey, even after his removal from the hospital. Calling one evening and failing to find him at Mrs. Layton's, at her suggestion he followed him to Mrs. Graeme's rooms in the University.

Both Aliena and Col. Harvey were so engrossed, as he was ushered in, that Dr. Leigh stood unheeded in the doorway, acutely impressed with the scene. Colonel Harvey was seated in an easy chair, his limbs stretched out upon a low ottoman, which Aliena had arranged for his comfort, his eyes fastened upon her as she sat at the piano, singing.

Colonel Harvey had asked Aliena to sing "Savourneen Delish," the song which she had sung at Castle Hill upon the last occasion she had sung for Major Baron there. She had not realized the pain she should endure in the memories evoked by this song, when, in compliance with the request, she had commenced to sing it. As she went on her voice faltered more and more with emotion, until she could no longer command it. A painful pause ensued. She tried to recover herself, but finding it impossible to complete the song, she turned at length. As she did so, she caught sight of Dr. Leigh, and of the fixed, compressed look of pain about his mouth, and in his pale face.

Aliena greeted him in a voice still tremulous with feeling. He responded formally. And glancing from Colonel Harvey to her, said apologetically, "I called at Mrs. Layton's to see Colonel Harvey—she suggested I might find him here."

Dr. Leigh's manner, for some reason, seemed to throw a restraint over all, and after a few formal remarks were interchanged, he rose, and bowing formally, left.

"What can be the matter with the doctor, I wonder?" said Colonel Harvey, stroking his beard.

Aliena's conscious face deepened in color as a possible cause suggested itself to her mind; and she replied with some embarrassment, "You will have to ask him. No—don't—it is nothing, I suppose."

Colonel Harvey, struck with Aliena's embarrassed manner, and with the color that had come to her face, looked curiously at her, noting that the tell-tale color returned under his inquiring glance. He remained silent for some moments, as though engrossed in thought. He said at length, sadly, "It is wonderful how many thoughts may surge through one's mind in a short time —of the long ago—the present—and the future."

"You must have thought rapidly, if all this could have passed through your mind since you spoke," said Aliena.

"There are times when a man's whole record is said to pass in review before him in an incredibly short time. When one is drowning, for instance," said Colonel Harvey solemnly. And studying Aliena's face earnestly for a moment, he continued, "If I ask you a question will you promise to answer me and not consider it an impertinence?" But without waiting for an answer he went on, "Does Dr. Leigh love you?"

Aliena glanced at him with a quick conscious look as she replied, "You have no right to ask me questions involving another."

"That is sufficient," said Colonel Harvey, and gazing before him silently for a moment, he added in a subdued tone, "You have the love of one of the noblest men God ever made."

"I don't wonder you think so, since you believe he saved your life and preserved you from being a life-long cripple."

"My opinion is not grounded upon gratitude alone. Though even that could not entirely bias my judgment."

"What else have you to ground it upon? I did not know that you were friends before," said Aliena with some surprise.

"I cannot say that we were ever friends, though I know him."

"You never mentioned that you had known him before. I wonder that you never did since you pronounce such a eulogy upon him now. Will you tell me upon **what your** opinion is founded?" asked Aliena eagerly, yet with evident embarrassment. Impelled by her intense **desire** to hear of Dr. Leigh's past life.

"It is founded upon my knowledge that he possesses a magnanimity to which few men attain in this world."

"Will you tell me **why you** think this?" Aliena persisted, looking earnestly at Colonel Harvey.

Colonel Harvey hesitated for an instant, then said, "I thought that you condemned, **only a few** moments since, the asking questions involving **another?**"

"I think that prohibition need not apply when what is expected in reply is apparently to be eulogistic."

"Could anything **more** commendable **be said** of a man than that he loved a noble, **true woman?**" said Colonel Harvey, his eyes fixed sadly upon Aliena.

"Of course I will **not question you if you think** it wrong," said Aliena, ignoring Colonel Harvey's last re- mark. But still impelled by the possibility thus unex- pectedly **offered** of having her harrowing doubts re- moved she continued, "You said enough to **make me** think you know something of Dr. Leigh's past life ; and you pronounced him one of the noblest men in the world. I ask you to tell me why you think this? Be- cause—because—I want to know," said Aliena, hesitat- ing, disconcerted at the thought of the dreadful story Mrs. Bledsoe had told her. Yet too much carried away by her desire **to know the** truth **not to go** on now, she continued, "I have been **told** things affecting Dr. Leigh's character. I wish to **have him** vindicated if injustice **has been** done him."

"Will you tell me what these things were?" Colonel Harvey asked.

Aliena's color deepened as she continued, "I can tell you only that it was in regard to his marriage, and his conduct toward his wife."

Colonel Harvey's face became pale with repressed emotion at this unexpected announcement. Evidently going through with a painful struggle, loth to speak upon this long sealed subject, he said at length, however, sadly, "I possibly know more than any other living person in regard to this subject, I will tell you," and with evident emotion he went on to tell the whole story. Of his love for Dr. Leigh's wife, and of Dr. Leigh's magnanimity toward him. He even produced the package of letters, painful as it was, which Dr. Leigh had returned to him after his wife's death, with his note enclosed, all of which with the replies he had had the weakness to keep. These he now permitted Aliena to read.

Colonel Harvey sat with a look of intense pain upon his face, as Aliena read these letters. She looked up at him with a scarcely less pained expression as she finished.

"And in the face of all this," said Colonel Harvey, with profound sadness, "when I was brought here at the point of death, Dr. Leigh could not have treated me with greater kindness, or have tended me more faithfully, if I had been a brother. But for him I might now be moldering in yonder cemetery, or what is worse be hobbling maimed through life. And can you wonder that I say he is one of the noblest men God ever made?"

Aliena sat dumb and motionless. And Colonel Harvey, looking painfully depressed arose to go.

"Pardon me, for reviving memories so painful to you," said Aliena, with deep emotion.

"That memory is a dream of the past now. Life is made up of dreams, I find. Most of them painful," said Colonel Harvey, and taking Aliena's hand in his, and looking at her with a curiously mixed lingering look, he added, "I am conscious that I have contributed to your happiness. I ought to feel repaid. I will some day perhaps. God grant you the happiness you deserve. Good-bye," and pressing her hand painfully he left.

Aliena, alone, gasped for breath, as she thought of the cruel wrong she had done Dr. Leigh, of the weary pain and woe she might have saved him, and herself. if, as her heart had dictated, she had only trusted him. She realized now, longingly, how truly she had loved him through all this dreary time—through all the bitterness of her contemplated immolation of self, in her hopelessness, to her troth to Major Baron.

Oh! how intensely she longed to see him again, to hear once more those words of yearning love, to confess her cruel want of faith, to beg his forgiveness, to lie in the very dust, at his feet. to tell him how truly she had loved him all this weary time. despite her efforts to stifle her love, to hear his longed for words of forgiveness, to see his eyes fixed once more in tenderness and love upon her.

How infinitely more intense would have been her pain and remorse, if she could have known that she should look and long in vain. That without seeing her, or even leaving good-bye, Dr. Leigh would two days afterward leave for Richmond, where it soon became known that he had been made a surgeon-general. A less distinguished surgeon taking his place in Athens.

It had been a farewell too with Colonel Harvey. For some reason he never came again to see Aliena. Some weeks afterward he left good-bye for her with Mrs. Layton; with many thanks for all her goodness to him. Going to rejoin his regiment, despite the protest of the surgeon to whom had been assigned Dr. Leigh's place. He was, as Aliena learned afterward, soon promoted to General, for gallant conduct in the battles around Richmond.

CHAPTER LV.

"But ever and anon of griefs subdued
  There comes a token like a scorpion's sting;—
  A tone of music—summer's eve—or spring—
  A flower—the wind—the ocean—which shall wound—
Striking the electric chain wherewith we are darkly bound."
BYRON: CHILDE HAROLD.

Autumn came. The dark days when nature wept over those exposed to cold and privation in camp and field. Where scantily clad, and hungry, perhaps, the soldiers succumbed to sickness; or wounded in battle, were carried to the rear to hospitals, wanting, owing to the blockade, in the necessities of life and in remedial agents for treatment.

Here Aliena, with Mrs. Layton, again sought, through ministry to others, to find peace for her own sorely troubled heart.

The winter slowly and drearily passed. Spring came again with its song of birds, and hum of life, and delicate changing hues of freshly budding foliage. Its odors of sweet flowers, its soft winds, and drifting clouds; its sunshine and shadow, its dripping leaves, rainbow arches, and melting sunsets, and blushing glow of heat. And with it, its yearning unrest.

And Aliena found it harder to find satisfaction in duty then, than when the days were dark and cold.

Summer passed, and the days of the Confederacy were fast drawing to a close. Since the crippling of its energies by the dismemberment, caused by the surrender of Vicksburg, it had constantly lost ground, and hopefulness. Under poverty, hardship and death, its armies were depleting. The people, as well as the soldiers, were becoming more and more hopeless and dispirited.

To those cut off from home and financial resources by the enemy, the times were even more trying.

And autumn came again in gorgeous array, nature giving out its most glorious tints in dying. The myrtles in crimson and gold, the yellow elms, the brilliant reds of sumach and alders, with the staid yellow browns of grave old oaks, mingled with the dark green of cedars and pines, on the sparkling, mica-sprinkled hillsides and valleys. These, toned by the purple-gray haze of Indian summer, with its soft, yet energizing, life-giving atmosphere, made these later days seem calmer, better, than the yearning, wistful spring-time.

The women busied themselves in getting ready for another trying winter before them. For those at home and those to be exposed to the rigors of this season in the field. The old spinning-wheels had been promoted from the cabin to the parlor. It was the fashion now to spin and weave, to dye and knit. Beautiful fingers devoted themselves to this work; and each home, through love, became an energized factory, providing for father, husband and sons, scantily clad and fed, to be exposed to the rigors of another winter's campaign. And all could feelingly say, " God pity the poor."

The autumn leaves faded and fell. The tears of winter falling upon the dead year crystallized into beautiful robes, and the old year, resurrected into the new year, came forth in dazzling beauty; sparkling with countless gems as though the mortal had put on immortality.

Spring came again, and with it the black, blank desolation of Sherman's march to the sea; marked by smouldering homes and ghostly sentinel chimneys. Athens trembled. But the enemy taking a different route the place was spared.

It is useless to attempt to depict the gloom of the Confederacy when, after four long years of privation, self-sacrifice, sorrow and heroic defense, overcome by numbers, it began vaguely to be hinted that surrender was inevitable. When, at last, the surrender had taken place, the people refused to believe it.

Athens, isolated in position, remained in doubt. News of surrender came at length to officials, but they hesitated to make it known. It was whispered among the people upon the barren red hills around Athens, and the spirit of communism, latent with the poor, took possession of the homes of the "crackers." And from hillside and cabin the sallow raw-boned men and women swooped down like ill-omened birds of prey upon the Confederate stores accumulated here.

"Laws a marcy! mistiss, the Yankees have done come," said Mauma, bursting unceremoniously into Mrs. Graeme's room at an early hour the morning after the sacking of the Confederate stores.

Mrs. Graeme was in bed, too sick to have risen if it had been a much later hour; but Mauma felt that there was no time for ceremony now. The clattering of horses' hoofs and of the soldiers' sabres testified to the emergency of the case. Aliena also heard these sounds, and moving to her window, partially unclosed the blinds and saw for herself men in Federal uniforms demanding his watch from the vice-chancellor of the University, at the mouth of their pistols. Trembling and pale, she closed and fastened the blinds, and endeavoring to appear as calm as possible, went to her mother's room to inform her.

She now hurriedly collected and secreted what jewelry and valuables they had with them, and tremblingly awaited what might be before them.

CHAPTER LVI.

"Thou art left alone among foes, O daughter of Torcultorno."

OSSIAN.

To Mrs. Graeme's and Aliena's consternation, the University was selected by the Federals as their headquarters, and they soon found themselves surrounded by soldiers—close prisoners in their rooms.

Later in the day of occupation by the enemy, Mauma concluded to take a furtive observation. Partially opening the door, as she did so, Hugi bounded out and on in the most delighted manner toward a soldier, who, seated upon his horse, was conversing with a group near the house, and to Mauma's astonishment, ran around and around the man, testifying his delight in every imaginable way. Mauma gazed at Hugi and then at the man in amazement and perplexity at this extraordinary performance of the dog.

" Bless the Lord ! if that don't beat anything I ever seen," said Mauma. " I do declare I believe that dog thinks he 's a nigger, and he 's done gone crazy like all the rest of them."

Calling the dog, unheeded, Mauma closed the door, and fastening it securely, went to seek Aliena.

" Honey, do come here, if you please, just a minnit, and see how Hugi 's a goin' on. I never seen anything like it. The Lord has curus ways of makin' his will known. He done it through his dumb beast to Baalam, and it 'pears like to me he 's a doin' through a dumb brute again."

Aliena, going as Mauma requested, looked cautiously through the partially-opened door at Hugi, who was continuing his demonstrations of joy, in a less excited way. She turned suddenly pale and closed the door, saying in a suppressed tone of terror, " That is the robber who entered mother's room at Chattanooga."

" Laws a marcy ! honey, you don't say so? But how did Hugi come to be so fond of him. I can't think he could a took such a fancy to him that night, even if he seen him," said Mauma, more perplexed than ever. Suddenly, as if a bright inspiration had come to her, she exclaimed, " But maybe the Lord intentioned to make the robber known and is a doin' it by this dumb brute."

" I scarcely think that, Mauma, though it is certainly strange that Hugi should act so," said Aliena, and curious herself to solve the mystery, she took another look. Closing the door suddenly, she exclaimed in a delighted tone, in spite of the circumstances, " Why, Mauma, that is Alert the man is riding ! "

" Well, bless your heart honey ! that's a fact," said Mauma peeping out. " And that is what's the matter with the dog. He always was powerful fond of Alert. I was so busy lookin' at the man, I never took no notice of the horse. And he's lookin' mighty fine, too, honey, considerin' he's been through the wars. Don't never let that man see you though for the Lord's sake. Nor don't let on you know anything about him. Must I call Hugi, honey ? It 'pears like to me I'm a losin' all the sense I ever did have."

" Yes, call him in, Mauma. I should be grieved to lose him too." And Mauma opened the door and called in a suppressed tone to Hugi as requested. He came bounding toward them, then turned and leaped back and forth, barking as he approached Alert, as though communicating the glad news of the long lost found. Aliena called softly to Hugi, in one of his approaches, and he bounded at once into the house, and Mauma closed the door quickly behind him.

Aliena, after seeing this man, felt more than ever as though she were besieged, and it did not need Mauma's caution to prevent her from allowing herself to be seen by him, or by any other of those in whose power she found herself placed.

Mrs. Graeme, too sick to rise, shut up a prisoner, tortured by apprehension, seemed scarcely likely to regain her strength.

" Daughter," she said the following evening, " I am growing weaker and weaker, instead of stronger, shut up in this close, stifling room. I can never hope to be out of bed, unless I can breathe the fresh air. Won't you remove the light from the room, and open the blinds for a while."

Aliena, though in greater terror even than her mother

was aware, since her recognition of the robber, proceeded
to move the light, and cautiously to open the blinds.
As she did so, she caught the sound of voices not far
from the window, conversing in a low tone.

"I 'm a reffergee here, my marster lives in Louisean-
ner. I 'm livin' with some white folks, what tuk me fur
my vittles and clothes," she heard the voice say, which
she recognized as that of Pomp, Mrs. Skinker's servant.

"Are there any pretty young ladies in this building?"
the other asked. And her eyes having become accustomed to the darkness, she discovered the other to be
the soldier whom she had recognized as the robber.

"Yes, Miss Lena, what lives in them rooms is powerful pretty and soft spoken," said Pomp, pointing toward
where Aliena stood, trembling, behind the partially open
blinds. She closed them softly, shuddering at hearing
herself thus discussed. And without comment brought
the light back, and went to ask Mauma to come and
sit with them, feeling some sense of protection in
another presence, beside that of her helpless sick mother.

Aliena now took up a book and endeavored to divert
her mother's thought by reading aloud. This, if it did
not have a lulling effect upon Mrs. Graeme, had upon
Mauma, who, with the negro facility for sleeping was
soon nodding in her chair. Aliena continued to read
as she, as well as her mother, felt that it was useless to
seek sleep as long as they could hear the heavy tramp
of soldiers, and the clatter of spurs and sabres through
the halls of the great building.

These sounds ceased as it grew later, and a profound
stillness at length seemed to pervade the building.
Suddenly a heavy thug upon the floor over-head with
stifled sounds and struggles, startled Aliena and Mrs.
Graeme, painfully. Mauma awakened by the heavy
fall above her, startled, confused and frightened, seemed
to have lost all presence of mind and courage.

"Mauma, do go and see what is the matter?" said
Aliena.

“Lord! Lord! I can’t go there to be killed,” said Mauma.

“I must go myself. I can’t stay here and let any one be murdered!” exclaimed Aliena, taking a candle in her hand and starting as the sounds continued.

“Don’t, don’t go there!” said Mrs. Graeme entreatingly, starting up in bed. But Aliena was gone, and her mother fell back, overcome by debility and alarm.

Aliena moved on rapidly to the main cross hall where a number of soldiers in the dread blue uniform were lying upon the floor, either asleep or feigning to be so. In spite of her terror of them Aliena now appealed to the one nearest the door.

“For God’s sake go up stairs. Some one is being murdered?” she said.

The man waking suddenly rose to his elbow as she spoke, and shading his eyes with his hand from the light she carried, he looked up bewildered at the lovely face above him. Aliena reiterating her request, he started to his feet—evidently but just aroused to full consciousness—and guided by the stifled sounds which still continued, and by the quick barking of a dog, he sprang up the steps, and moved on toward the place from whence came the sounds.

He ran against some one whom he encountered in the darkness, almost knocking him down.

“What in the hell are you about?” exclaimed the man encountered, indignantly, who was moving in the same direction.

“Is it you, Major Swofford?” said the soldier apologetically, recognizing the voice. “They say some one is being murdered up here.”

The stifled sounds had ceased, but the noise of the dog guided them to where he was still barking furiously outside the door of his mistress’ room. As they drew nearer they heard, above the sounds the dog was making, a strange, unnatural laugh; and rushing on they threw open the door.

In the dimly lighted room they beheld the form of a white-haired old woman, crouching upon the prostrate body of a younger woman, her fingers almost buried in the flesh, as with unnatural, maniacal strength she clutched the throat of the now insensible form, whose veins were distended to great cords standing out about her face and throat, which were purple almost to blackness, her tongue protruding from her mouth.

As they entered, the old woman lifted her face, her white, disheveled hair standing wildly out about it, her mouth wrinkled and sunken over her toothless gums, and laughed again one of her strange, unearthly laughs, "Ha! ha! ha! Jim Skinker! You've come to the wedding have you? We'll dance together, but it must be upon the coffin. Your bride is stiff—stiff and cold, but all in white," she mumbled, glancing down. And seeing that the woman was gasping back to life she clutched again at her throat.

The soldier, who had been stultified for the moment by the sight which he had beheld, now moved quickly to the rescue. While Major Swofford, as Jim Skinker called himself, crept from the room, saying as he moved back in the darkness, "It's a d—d pity she did n't finish the job."

As the soldier approached, and put out his hands to grasp the old woman, she sprang aside, and, eluding him, escaped quickly from the room, and fled on down stairs, past Aliena, who had awaited in terror in the hall, out into the Campus.

"She is—my mother—is—is crazy. Don't—don't leave me," gasped Mrs. Skinker, still prostrate upon the floor.

CHAPTER LVII.

> "For brother men
> Can counsel and speak comfort to that grief
> Which they themselves not feel; but tasting it
> Their counsel turns to passion."

The Confederate soldiers were beginning to return to their homes, if they had any left. Foot-sore, for no transportation was furnished them, but infinitely more heartsore.

Preston Massey, who with others had determined to expatriate himself, join Maximilian, do anything rather than surrender, had come to say good-bye to home, and friends, before leaving.

He arrived the night before the occupation of Athens by the enemy as described. He was awakened in the morning, by soldiers standing over him, demanding a surrender, at the mouth of the pistol. Chagrined and mortified, he remained a voluntary prisoner, at home for days.

"Nellie," he said some days afterward, to his sister, "I must go and see what has become of Miss Graeme and her mother. It is dreadful to think of them, shut up, prisoners in the University, given over to the mercies of those—Well, I 'll try not to put myself into a passion. But I can imagine that beautiful, sensitive girl,"—and he broke off again. suddenly sitting, stroking with a forlorn air the stubble of more than a week's growth upon his chin. He continued at length, "I thought I would never shave again, but I suppose I 'll have to."

"I am so glad something has aroused you out of the slough of despond you have been in, Pres. I do wish you would shave and go and see Miss Graeme. I know it is hard upon you soldiers, but no one could expect you to whip the whole world," continued Helen Massey tenderly, with a sigh she could not repress.

"Do you think it would matter, if I went without shaving?" said Colonel Massey, relapsing.

"Pres, please don't talk that way?" said Helen, standing behind her brother's chair, stroking his hair tenderly, as he sat, his whole attitude attesting his utter dejection and hopelessness. "You would feel so much better, if you would only shave and dress yourself nicely. It makes me feel so badly to—to see you this way," and her voice faltered, and the tears she could not keep back, dropped upon the unconscious head she was stroking.

"I'll try and do it, Nellie, if you will only get up a little more cheerful tone of voice," said Colonel Massey.

Helen brushed away her tears quickly, and tried to assume a cheerful tone as she said, "I could be cheerful, I think, Pres—" but she broke down again, as Colonel Massey, who had risen listlessly, turned and fixed his eyes upon her.

"You've been crying, Nellie, you know you have," he said; "if you will only quit that, and try and bear it bravely, I will shave and put on clean shirts three times a day, if you want me to."

"It does me good sometimes to cry," Helen faltered out, and, giving way utterly now, she sobbed convulsively, saying, as she struggled to recover herself, "Don't mind me, Pres. I'll be better soon, and I shan't—I shan't cry any more, if—if I can help it, but— but it is so hard—so hard to have you all come back home this way. And, and I expected you to—to come back with flags flying, and—and drums beating, crowned with—with laurel—and all that." And Helen gave herself up to sobbing again, while Preston Massey left the room with a suspicious movement of the hand to his eyes.

He did shave and dress himself, however, that afternoon, and went to the University to see Aliena. After much unbolting and unbarring of doors, he was gladly received by her, to whom it was a comfort to see a sympathetic face.

When he returned home he depicted in moving colors, to his mother and sister, the forlorn state in which he had found Aliena and her sick mother, barricaded in their rooms, unprotected, surrounded by demoralized soldiers. Applying some epithets to the latter for which he apologized for giving utterance in the presence of his mother and sister.

. "Preston," said Mrs. Massey, " Why can't those ladies come and share our home until they can go to their own? I am sure we would be glad to have them do so."

"That 's a fact. Mother, you always were a trump," said Colonel Massey irreverently, with some of his old enthusiasm. Continuing, "Nell, come and go back with me, and let us ask them to come at once?"

"It would be dark before you could get the carriage and go; and I should be afraid for Helen to go among those dreadful soldiers after dark," interposed Mrs. Massey prudently.

"Pres, I will go with you soon in the morning," said Helen, entering earnestly into her brother's feelings.

"But suppose anything happened to Miss Graeme to-night?" suggested Colonel Massey.

"Preston, is there anything serious between you and Miss Graeme?" asked Mrs. Massey earnestly.

"I have a serious notion of falling in love with her, if you call that anything serious," he replied jokingly, in spite of his depression.

"You ought to think very seriously now before doing anything of that kind, my son. These are no times for falling in love," protested Mrs. Massey gravely.

"Do let him fall in love, mother, if he can; anything but this despondency," said Helen.

"Don't be uneasy about me, mother. I 'll try and not fall in love. But that pale, beautiful, sorrowful face, those sad, pleading eyes, and that sweet, sensitive mouth, are almost too much for a man to pledge himself against; especially when he has been cut off from ladies' society for so long a time. But don't you remember how you used to lie awake of nights about Mary Desseau, and I still live," said Colonel Massey with forced levity.

Early the next morning Colonel and Miss Massey,—the latter closely veiled—as was the custom of the few ladies that moved about at this time—entered their carriage and were driven to the University. Here, after the usual unbarring they were ushered in.

Miss Massey, greeting Aliena affectionately, said, " Come Aliena, mother has sent Pres and myself to take you and your mother home with us. She says it will never do for you to stay here, locked up as you are, surrounded by these dreadful soldiers, that we must bring you back with us ? "

" It is certainly very kind of your mother to think of us, and I am very much obliged to her, but I scarcely think we can go. Mother is not well enough even to be out of bed," said Aliena.

"Can't I see your mother and ask her myself ?" said Helen.

" Certainly, come with me," Aliena replied, and the two ladies repaired to Mrs. Graeme's room.

" Now is n't it too bad," said Helen to her brother when they returned to the parlor. " Mrs. Graeme says they can't go with us."

" Is it because your mother is not well enough to go ? " asked Colonel Massey, addressing Aliena.

" I don't know that it is entirely on that account," said Aliena.

" I don't like to differ from your mother," said Colonel Massey, but I think she is wrong to stay here and keep you among these soldiers. Beside, if she only had mother to nurse and coddle her up, she would get well directly. There never was any one equal to mother at that sort of thing I am sure."

" But so it is," replied Aliena in such a way that he felt it useless to continue his entreaties. And disappointed, they took their leave.

Mrs. Graeme shut up in their cloistered rooms, depressed in mind, and sick in body, truly longed to return to her desolate home.   But now that communication was once more established, a new difficulty arose. None were permitted to take out mail or express matter except those who had taken the oath of allegiance to the United States government.

Constant anxiety and sorrow, the sense of humiliation in the surrender, the renewed memory of her husband's life sacrificed, the silent sorrow of Aliena, with actual privation endured, seemed slowly but surely sapping Mrs. Graeme's life.

Aliena, worn with her own sorrows, helpless as she was, almost frenzied by her mother's condition, could endure this no longer.   And she determined to send, asking for their letters, and, if inevitable, to pay the penalty, by taking the oath.

The Provost Marshal came in person to deliver the letters and administer the oath, instead of exacting, as was the custom, that she should come to his office to take it publicly.

As Aliena entered the parlor to meet him, she stood transfixed, as in the officer before her she recognized Colonel Seldon, Major Baron's college friend.   His emotion was scarcely less painful, as in the lovely girl who appeared, he recognized Aliena Graeme.   She halted in the doorway, and her graceful form unconsciously assumed a more erect pose.

Colonel Seldon moved forward to meet her with an air of painful embarrassment, and proffering his hand, said, "Miss Graeme, I hope that the altered position we hold toward each other will not prevent our meeting as friends.   I can assure you that it would give me pleasure to be able to do you any kindness?"

Aliena put out her hand silently, barely touching that proffered, and withdrawing it said somewhat haughtily, "Colonel Seldon, I sent for my letters, not knowing it was to you.   My mother is likely to die here.   I must save her life if possible.   I have endured all I can. We wish to get back to the ashes of a home, at least," and her voice faltered, but she went on. "As I cannot get means without, I must take the oath," and she grew as white as marble as she continued. "It seems hard that a great nation could not content itself with the humiliation of the men it has conquered, but that the women must be included in that humiliation. If to have given my heart's sympathies to the cause baptized in the blood of my father, makes me a rebel, I have been one. And I must pay the penalty, I suppose."

"I had not counted upon this added pain to be endured. I did not know that it was to you that I came. I will not be an instrument in your humiliation. I shall resign rather than inflict it," said Colonel Seldon, deeply moved, pacing the room as he spoke.

"Your resignation could not lessen the humiliation. I find it hard enough to endure now. Spare me the abasement of having to submit to this before one who might not feel as you do," said Aliena.

Colonel Seldon still walked back and forth in the room with the impotent pain of a brave, sensitive man forced into such a position with a woman. Then taking up the form of the oath, looking away from her and omitting the asking as to her "age, color of hair, of eyes, height, etc.," he read the oath of allegiance to the United States government, to which she made the necessary response.

When he had finished, turning to her he said in a pained voice, "Miss Graeme, you cannot know what I have endured in complying with your request. Each word you were compelled to utter seemed a dagger thrust to me. Compensate me by allowing me an opportunity for kindness when possible," and handing her her letters as well as Mrs. Graeme's, he continued, "It seems hard for me to have to suffer added mortification, but, when your mother is able, I shall be compelled to undergo this again."

"Her death may save you both that pain," said Aliena with faltering voice, and Colonel Seldon left, feeling the more humiliated of the two.

It was hard for Aliena to find, when she opened the letters for which she had paid so dearly, that they did not contain means sufficient for their return home; and that but little hope was expressed as to the possibility of their obtaining possession of their property.

CHAPTER LVIII.

"Of all God's works, creature in whom excelled
Whatever can to sight or thought be formed,
How art thou lost ? how on a sudden lost—
How can I live without thee ? How forego
Thy sweet converse, and love so dearly joined,
To live again in these wild woods forlorn ? "
MILTON: PARADISE LOST.

"It is enough to kill any one to sit here and mope and grieve over the dead Confederacy. We might as well try and throw it off. Professor and Mrs. Layton, Helen and I, and a few other friends are proposing a trip to the mountains and falls in North Georgia. The scenery there is grand; and we have come to ask you to join us," said Colonel Massey to Aliena some weeks after the scenes described.

"Yes, Aliena, you must go, we will take no refusal," added Helen Massey. "It is said to be the loveliest scenery imaginable. I know that you will be more than repaid." Visions of the beautiful floating through Aliena's imagination lit up her sad face at this proposal, though on account of her mother she felt constrained to decline it.

But Mrs. Graeme coming in, Helen repeated the proposition, asking her to try and induce Aliena to go. Looking anxiously at the colorless, sad face of her daughter, Mrs. Graeme did urge her to go, and so it was arranged.

"Nell," said Colonel Massey to his sister as they were driving from the Campus, "I am afraid you were all not as kind to Miss Graeme as you ought to have been, during this dreary time, while she has been cut off from home and friends. She seems hopelessly depressed and sad. I can't think it is the surrender entirely."

"I should n't wonder, if some man were to blame. You know, from Adam down, you men have delighted in throwing your sins upon woman," said Helen.

"That's a fact. I don't mean about that Adam business. I wish to heaven, that for the sake of his unfortunate masculine posterity, he had never given a chance for that everlasting fling. But as to the masculine in this mystery, I remember now that I used to think there was a love affair between her and Baron. Don't you remember the handsome fellow I introduced to you at our party, when I was at home on furlough, the young man I knew on the Mediterranean, a Major in our army; he called afterwards?"

"Of course, I remember him. You don't suppose I could forget so elegant and charming a gentleman as that in less than two years, even if beaux had been more plenty than they were then."

"I wonder if she has been remembering him all this time too? How long did he stay here after I left?"

"A very short time I think."

"Was he ever here afterwards?"

"Not that I ever heard of. If he came, he never called on me."

"I remember now, how strangely agitated she was, when I was telling her about him, a week or two since, of his having turned out a regular vagabond, cashiered for drunkenness and arrested for trying to murder his servant. I do wonder if she has been grieving over him all this time."

The party, as agreed, started a few days afterward

upon their excursion. The night before they expected to reach Toccoa, they were to camp by a noted spring, near a country church; but owing to the rough roads, night was coming on and they were still some miles distant. Darkness came, and yet they toiled on, trusting more to the tired animals to keep the road than to their own sight, they bumped wearily along, swaying fearfully, from side to side, at times.

They were relieved at length, by finding that they were approaching the church. As at intervals, the dismal dirge-like wailing, in that direction, made them aware that " meetin' " was goin' on.

" Here we are at last. There is the spring, in that clump of trees to the right. We will camp here in this open space," said Professor Layton, with a long drawn breath of relief. All gladly got out of the carriages, relieved at having arrived without accident, after the perils of darkness and of the rough mountain roads which had encompassed them. Having completed their arrangements for the night, and had supper, the party concluded to satisfy their curiosity by going to the church, where the sounds still indicated that the meeting was progressing.

There was, to Colonel Massey, a sort of Arcadian satisfaction, in strolling on under the arches of the pines, lit up by their camp fires, in this wild wood, toward the church, with Aliena leaning upon his arm.

The excitement had about reached its culmination, when they arrived at the dimly-lighted, rough, unhewn, log building, which served as a church. As they entered, facing the high plank pulpit, that stood upon a small platform, the preacher, a tall, gaunt, big-boned, sallow-faced man of about forty-five or fifty, was in the height of his excited oratory. His keen, deep-set eyes, under heavy, over-hanging eye-brows, with his long, rusty, unkempt, thick beard, and shaggy hair, gave him the appearance of some wild animal; his baggy suit of rough, brown homespun added to this effect.

Before him, seated upon the sawn log benches, was a motley crowd of men, women and children, in the same tawny homespun, which seemed to accord with their hair, eyes and complexion.

The preacher was declaiming wildly, his long hair flying like a mane about his eyes, as he shook his head, and stamped his feet, and pounded with his great sledge hammer-fists, upon the frail pulpit, with thunderous effect, while he pictured the horrors of hell.

He closed his discourse with an appeal to "mourners," to come forward to the altar, for the prayers of the congregation. Having finished this exhortation, he began in a stentorian voice to sing a dismal hymn, full of threatenings of damnation. He walked, as he sang, from the pulpit to the open space between it and the benches; the congregation joining in the singing with startling effect.

Simultaneously, as it seemed, numbers of men, women and children rose, and as though under some strange spell, rushed forward, and threw themselves upon their knees; or groveled in the straw, strewn for that purpose around the altar. The minister continued at intervals to exhort sinners to come to the altar for the prayers of the congregation, before it should be forever too late; in tones to be heard above the mingled sounds of singing, sobbing, and groaning—the number of "mourners" constantly increasing as the singing went on. At a signal from the preacher, all sank upon their knees, in every variety of posture, from groveling in the dust, to the most erect position. He now began, apparently, literally to wrestle in prayer. His voice indicating as Elijah tauntingly said to the prophets of Baal, as to their god, "He is afar off, or peradventure he sleepeth and must be awakened."

The dim light of the tallow candles added to the weird effect of the scene, as the seething mass of "mourners" writhed, groaned, shrieked and squirmed, upon the straw. While the "brethren" and "sisters" surrounding them,

assisted by exhortations, groans and ejaculatory prayer in
"bringing the mourners through," as they call it.   The
main performance of prayer, by the minister, going on
all the while in a wild sort of cadence, was to be heard
above all other sounds.   The preacher, wiping the perspiration from his streaming face with a large, big-flowered cotton handkerchief, fairly succumbed at length to
the powerful physical as well as mental strain, which
this effort had caused him.   Cold chills of horror were
creeping over Aliena, at this weird performance, in the
dim light, with the sobs, groans and shrieks of the
mourners, going on all around her as an accompaniment
to the prayer.

This was followed by a wild, wailing hymn, to each
verse of which a refrain was added, in which the sound
was swelled and the words dwelt upon indefinitely, regardless of measure.

> "Oh! there shall be wa-a-il-ing
> Wa-a-il-ing—wa-a-il-ing
> Oh! there shall be wa-a-il-ing
> At the judgment seat of God."

After which followed a song of exultation, which, react-
ing upon the excited throng, many began to clap their
hands and to jump, shouting "glory," "hallelujah," or to
utter ear-piercing shrieks, while the wails of the mourners,
as of the lost, mingled in the unearthly performance.

"I can't endure this any longer, take me away from
here," said Aliena to Colonel Massey, in a strange unnatural voice; and rising she put her cold, shivering hand
upon his arm, and they moved from the church.   "It
is well we got away, or I am afraid you would have
been among the mourners," said Colonel Massey, feeling her hand trembling upon his arm.

"Oh! how can you jest about it?   It is fearful, dreadful.   It seemed to me like the wailings of the lost,"
said Aliena still shivering.

"I am sorry I induced you to come since it affects

you so painfully, I had no idea you would be so wrought upon," he added penitently.

Aliena had been even more wrought upon by the excitement at the church than she was conscious of at the time. When all were sleeping in their tents that night, she lay looking up at the stars, with wide open staring eyes; still possessed with the horror of the scene. The fearful groans, sobs and shrieks seemed still sounding in her ears.

With it came a shuddering morbid horror of the hell depicted, less for herself than for others. Her mind reverted to that outcast upon the earth, against whom blood cried from the ground. The dread secret weighed upon and stifled her. She thought of the immolation of self she had contemplated making for one so unworthy. Of the infinite tenderness she had rejected which might now have been hers. Of her cruel distrust—of the crucifixion of her love.

But above all, she thought of the pain inflicted, the wrong she had done, in her want of faith in Dr. Leigh. Her heart was wrung with remorse. The dreariness and desolation of her life seemed crushing her. His words came to her mind. "Will cannot always prevent emotion from beating its breast against the bars that cage it, or keep those bars from wounding sorely." She realized the bitter truthfulness of these words now. And she longed, Oh! how truly, as she had done all this weary time, to see him, to lie at his feet, to beg his forgiveness, to be taken once more to his heart, unworthy of his love as she felt that her distrust had made her.

She prayed to God fervently, as she had never ceased to do, for his happiness, for those who had sinned against him, for that outcast upon the earth, for whom she had sacrificed so much, and for herself that she might be enabled to endure the desolation she had brought upon herself.

"How long? Oh! Lord, how long?" she groaned in spirit. The stars looked down pityingly upon her from above.   The long, dark lashes rested at length upon the white, tear-moistened cheeks.

And peaceful dreams, "as it were angels ascending and descending," came to comfort her.

CHAPTER LIX.

> " Thus in a cloud of flowers
> Angelic rose a virgin to my view,
> And o'er my spirit that so long a time
> Had from her presence felt no shuddering dread,
> Albeit mine eye discerned her not, there moved
> A hidden virtue from her, at whose touch
> The power of olden love was strong within me."
>
> DANTE: DIVINA COMMEDIA.

The travelers, having reached the point nearest to Toccoa, possible for conveyances, left their carriages, intending to walk the short distance to the fall.

The path, which had once been a road, was either overgrown, or so obstructed by fallen trees that they made their way with difficulty through tangled vines and undergrowth; under over-arching cedars, hemlocks and pines; or turning aside, climbed over fallen trees or moss covered rocks, as they constantly descended into the valley.   They were guided, at times, only by the sound of the falling water, which grew nearer and nearer, and more distinct, until suddenly and unexpectedly they came into view of the lovely valley.   And the exquisite waterfall burst upon their sight.

There before them was Toccoa, leaping from the sheer precipice of white rock, more than three hundred feet above them, breaking into glittering, silvery spray before it reached the wide, rocky basin, into which it fell, rippling, dancing, and foaming on in rapids, through the beautiful valley, to their feet.

The warm June air, heavy with the spicy odor of pines and the fragrance of the wild flowers abounding here, was freshened by the falling spray into a delicious humid coolness. The soft air, quickened by the falling water, into a gentle breeze, dashed aside the white spray; or carrying it off in dewy showers, sprinkled into fresher green the luxuriant verdure of the valley. Tall, fringy ferns, mosses and lichens, covered with the fine mist, sparkled like delicate emerald tracery in the shimmering sunlight.

Shut in by the towering, rocky precipices, to this beautiful valley, Aliena felt as though she had been transported to a little fairy world. She did not wonder that the Indians should have named it Toccoa, the beautiful.

As she sat silently absorbed in the view, Colonel Massey, who was by her side, began the recitation of a local poem, descriptive of the scene:

> "In the gray shadows of a mountain wood
> There flows a crystal stream scarce known to song,
> That to its own sweet music glides along,
> Charming the else unbroken solitude.
> Toccoa called, in rhythmic Indian tongue,
> Nor ever yet was name more fitly given;
> No lovelier stream was e'er by poet sung.
> Here forest boughs above it interweave,
> And through the leafy net-work sunbeams stray,
> That dancing, rippling, o'er the water play
> Like golden threads that glancing shuttles leave,
> While on its marge the scented wild flower blows;
> And bright and beautiful the streamlet goes."

To Aliena's mind, the words recited fell far short of painting the exquisite beauty of the scene, by which she was surrounded. She felt out of unison with Colonel Massey, and his somewhat dramatic style jarred painfully upon her. She experienced a sense of relief in no longer hearing his voice. And sitting silent, she felt even more out of harmony with him than she had done before.

"I fear you are disappointed in Toccoa?" said Colonel Massey, at length, looking at the sad, introspective face beside him.

Aliena sighed involuntarily as she replied, "I am disappointed, but not in Toccoa. It is far more beautiful than I could have thought, or imagined."

"In what can you be disappointed then?"

"Only as I seem doomed to disappointment in everything in life. In its not bringing the happiness expected. I had hoped that the sense of the beautiful in nature might be the one exception," said Aliena, gazing before her, at the fall, with a look of fixed, profoundest sadness.

"There may be an exception yet in which you may find the happiness you seek," said Colonel Massey with hesitation and some embarrassment, looking anxiously into Aliena's face.

Something in his tone made Aliena glance around— and catching his expression it seemed to act as a repellant upon her. She said abruptly, "I no longer hope to find an exception."

"Pres, Pres, do come here, won't you?" called Helen Massey from some invisible point near; her voice indicating a dilemma. This fortunately broke the awkward silence which had fallen upon Colonel Massey. Excusing himself, he moved off in the direction indicated by the voice, leaving Aliena seated upon the rock with an intense sense of relief at being left alone.

Her sadness deepened, however, as she gave herself up to thought. To the dull, fixed, hopeless pain which the contemplation of the scene seemed to increase.

The Dead Pan of Mrs. Browning came to her mind. "Pan is dead," she said to herself mournfully. The sighing breeze seemed to echo the words. "Pan is dead." Nature no longer seemed instinct with pulsating life and poetry to her. No neiads disported in fountains, no dryads sighed, wept, or loved in trees, no oreads flitted through mountain and grotto. "Pan is dead," her heart re-echoed.

Her mind wandered with dull, aching pain to a time when life as well as nature seemed redundant in poetry and in happiness. It was all gone now. Lookout mountain came to memory with the deep, calm, permeating happiness of that time. The perfect repose in the companionship and sympathy found there. which, like the prodigal, she had cast away for " the husks the swine did eat."

A strange feeling of rest seemed stealing over her tired heart, tranquilizing it to peace. The tension of her clinging hands relaxed, big tears rolled from under the long lashes, and dropped upon her hands.

" God is good," she said.

" In what is God so good?" said a low voice at her side. It scarcely seemed to change the current of her thoughts. Raising her eyes her soul seemed to leap into them through her tears, as she answered in a voice vibrant with joy and love, " In sending you."

"Aliena, think of what you are saying," said Dr. Leigh in a low voice, startling, so full was it of passionate earnestness.

" I have thought. Oh! so long!" and her head rested upon his breast, as he clasped her close to his heart, while upon her quivering lips he pressed a long, passionate kiss.

" God is good, indeed! Better than I could have hoped or imagined," said Dr. Leigh.

" Pan is not dead," said Aliena.

" No, nothing is dead. Everything is instinct with life, and love, and hope, and happiness," said Dr. Leigh.

Aliena's full heart, throbbing with happiness, pulsating musically, re-echoed, " Pan is not dead." The leaping water, sparkling in rainbow tints of hope, danced and laughed—the falling water had no minor chords now, it sang gayly, " Pan is not dead." All nature seemed to take up the chorus, " Pan is not dead."

The soft air was fragrant with wild flowers, and with the pines. The great rock, over which the water fell, loomed white above them.   The moon rising, the white moonlight gave a look of exquisite *spiritelle* beauty to the scene, which seemed unreal.

The soft breeze swaying aside the clouds of fleecy white mist, into which the falling water broke, carried off portions, that, flying softly into the shadows, appeared and disappeared with the rifts of moonlight, like angelic forms moving and floating in the air.

The myriad tones of rippling, gurgling, falling water, mingling with the sound of the air stirring the pines, seemed to be the music of angelic harps, to which the spirit forms were moving.

"It almost makes me tremble to be so happy," said Dr. Leigh in a low voice, gazing into Aliena's upturned eyes, as he spoke.   "It seems unnatural in its intensity. I can scarcely realize that it is not an ecstatic vision, from which I may awake to see you dissolve away before my eyes, like those etherial forms floating out of the mist; to leave nothing but shadow and darkness behind."

The look of perfect trust, love and happiness in the eyes that met his, answered him as no words could have done.

When they had returned to camp and separated for the night, Dr. Leigh found sleep impossible, so filled was he with the thought, "My beloved is mine.   O my dove, that art in the clefts of the rock—let me see thy countenance, let me hear thy voice.   Thy countenance is comely.   Thou art all fair my love, behold thou art fair.   Thou hast dove's eyes.   There is no spot in thee. Stay me with flagons, comfort me with apples; for I am sick of love.   Until the day break and the shadows flee away, I will get me to the mountain of myrrh, and to the hill of frankincense."

CHAPTER LX.

"So high as heaven the turried hills, so low
Down sunk a hollow bottom, broad and deep,
Capacious bed of waters; thither they hasted
With glad precipitance."

MILTON: PARADISE LOST.

The travelers having the next day reached Tallula, where they camped for the night, were awakened the following morning at gray dawn, by the yelping of a hound, which proved to be the property of their guide. The party, eager for a view of the falls by sunrise, soon gathered around the tall, gaunt, loose-jointed, smoke-dried looking man of about fifty, dressed in the usual walnut-dyed brown homespun. His slouched hat remained undisturbed over his long, straggling hair, as he stood leaning loungingly upon his long rifle; his gaunt, starved-looking yellow hound lying at his feet.

After a tedious, winding, precarious descent—climbing down rocks, creeping through crevices, or leaping down precipitous places, they came into the grand gorge through which Tallula, The Terrible, pours its torrents.

Here rugged granite walls, towering in wild grandeur, a thousand feet above the chasm, hold the river in its onward course, as leaping, surging and writhing, it makes the three great falls, Terrora, Tempesta, and Oceana.

Moving out upon the rock over which the torrent pours, which shook and trembled with the shock of the falling water, Aliena, with Dr. Leigh, looked up far above them to Terrora. There leaping with awful, thunderous roar, it lashes itself to fury against the rocky barriers. Then gathering strength, Tempesta vaults over the wild ledge; and Oceana, surging, foaming and raging, again leaps—making the earth quake and tremble in the triple fall.

Here they lingered in silent, intensest sympathy, filled

22

with the sense of the greatness and goodness of God, visible in the grandeur of his works. Watching the gloriously changing hues of the sunrise upon the floating clouds, the mist and the water—the granite walls —the dark green pines, hemlocks and laurels, with the more delicate hues of foliage.

In the afternoon the party started for another more distant view of the falls from Devil's Pulpit. This rock, sundered apparently by some convulsion of nature from the grand ledge through which Tallula rushes, is upon a level with its highest point. Facing the falls, isolated above the vast chasm, it juts out a sheer precipice of a thousand feet, commanding the view of the gorge, the falls, the rapids below, and of the river; which, winding in and out, is lost to view at last in the great hemlocks and pines in the valley beyond.

It had been the intention of the party to go from the Devil's Pulpit on to the rapids. But the clouds that had been flitting across the sky, adding the charm of sunshine and shadow to the view, had grown rapidly dense. And the opinion was divided as to continuing their walk.

Most of the party decided to return to camp; but Helen Massey and Aliena Graeme, with Captain Brandon and Dr. Leigh, determined to go on. They found the path to the rapids rougher and more devious even than they had expected. But they moved rapidly and gayly on over bowlders, and around fallen trees, which the flood, to which mountain torrents are constantly liable, had carried with them to the valley.

Having reached the rapids at length, they followed the winding stream in delight as it went leaping, boiling, and surging on, in miniature likeness to the grander falls above. Aliena with Dr. Leigh, watching the long moss clinging to the submerged rocks which moved and writhed like some live thing with the onward flow of the water; or gathering the spray-splashed flowers, and delicate ferns that were bending their heads to the current of air that the moving water kept in constant motion, became separated from the other couple.

The changing, shifting light ceased to play at length upon the water. The sky was becoming leaden. The mutterings of thunder loud enough to be heard above the roar of the water, at length warned Dr. Leigh of the necessity for returning.

In their own happiness they had been oblivious to their having become separated from Helen and Captain Brandon. Now, looking around to recall them from their wandering, they found that the others were no where in view. They walked on rapidly for some minutes, hoping to overtake them; the thunder growing louder, and the intervals less and less. The clouds had become dense and black, and big drops of rain began to descend.

They stopped for the time under a giant hemlock, and the rain intermitting, Dr. Leigh, leaving Aliena, climbed to the top of a great bowlder and looked around. But no glimpse of the wanderers could be seen. He returned quickly to where Aliena awaited him, and they concluded that it would be useless to continue their search, or to attempt to return now. The only course left was to find shelter for the time under the shelving rock.

The wind was increasing fearfully. They could hear it now above all other voices of nature, as it roared in its onward course, coming crashing through the pines and hemlocks upon the ledge of rock, a thousand feet above their heads, tossing and twisting them wildly, as it moved on its way. They hurried on over the rough path-way, climbing bowlders, and moving around the débris abounding here. Dr. Leigh, putting his arm around Aliena, almost carried her as they sped on before the wind, hearing it coming nearer and nearer, shrieking on down the gorge, twisting off branches from the hemlocks and pines on the ledge above them, the thunder rolling and crashing, and the lightning leaping and flashing overhead.

They reached the rock at length, in safety. Under its shelving shelter, protected from the wind and the rain that began to pour in blinding sheets, there was an intense sense of enjoyment to both, as seated here they watched the wild grandeur of the storm ; and saw the might of Him who "hurls the lightnings as a lance, and holds the winds in his fist."

The storm continued, crash after crash of near thunder and blinding lightning, the falling trees from the ledge far above them, or away up the gorge, crashing, rolling, and rumbling on down into the valley, the wind driving the rain before it in great white sheets, that broke into fine mist upon the rocks.

Tallula, swollen by the rain, into renewed and terrible force, carried with its roaring water the *débris* and bowlders, loosened in its onward course. These rumbled and crashed on through Terrora, Tempesta, and Oceana ; finding a lodgment in the valley, or bounding and bowling on with the rapids farther down the stream.

The wild passion of nature having vented itself in blinding lightning and shrieking wind, and sobbed itself to quiet, in falling tears, now as though penitent, sighed and soughed around them.

This lulling the sun burst out once more, disclosing battalions of fiery, flying dragons, in the heavens, which, as though the spirits of the storm, were scurrying before the receding wind, leaving white winged messengers of peace behind.

As Dr. Leigh and Aliena sat there in glad silence, looking up at the clouds, these seemed to dissolve into wonderful gleaming cities, gorgeous in temples, minarets, and mosques ; while the dripping, glistening earth as though not to be outdone by sunlight and cloud smiled in renewed beauty and freshness, "as a bride adorned for her husband."

Though the storm had ceased, the water pouring down the valley made it impossible for them yet to retrace their steps. And looking at the gorgeous heaven above them, and at the glad earth around them neither seemed inclined to return.

As Aliena met **Dr. Leigh's** eyes gazing with infinite love and trust into her tender, fathomless eyes, she said penitently, "**And you have** never asked me yet about the cruel past?"

" Since I found you at **Toccoa, I have had no room** in my heart for anything but the blissful present," he replied.

" But those weary years of **wretchedness and pain to** both? Do you think **I** could willingly have inflicted them?" she asked.

"That you could not love me then, is forgotten in the happiness of knowing that you do love me now. It seems such an eternity of bliss since then, that I can scarcely remember there ever was a cruel past."

" But all that dreary time, I did love you. God knows how truly, and how cruelly I have suffered," Aliena said penitently, glancing up.

" And yet you inflicted all this pain?" he said tenderly.

" Yes." said Aliena, looking appealingly into his face. " I loved you all that weary time. I have never ceased to love you since, on Lookout, I first believed you loved me. And in rejecting your love, I did violence to every emotion of my being. You could not have suffered more than I have done, or than I still suffer, when I think of the pain I inflicted, of the cruel wrong I did to you."

And Aliena went on to tell him all the sad story. Of her sorrow in her father's death, her isolated life, her imagined love for Major Baron, and of their engagement. Of her love for himself, of the pain endured in repelling his love upon Lookout mountain, and in Chattanooga, as treachery to one to whom she was plighted, shut up as he was to daily peril of his life in her defense in Vicksburg. Of Mrs. Bledsoe's wicked story, of his unspoken love, of her hopelessness for the future in her cruel distrust of mankind. Of her crucifixion of self in renewing her engagement with Major Baron in Athens. Of her suspicions as to Zara, grown out of her father's haunting presence, of the meeting Major Baron with Zara in the cemetery, his words there overheard, the shriek she had heard in the same place.

Of the longing she had felt to cast herself upon Dr. Leigh's love that evening when, during the storm, he had come to her protection, of the agony she might have saved them both if then she could have told her love.

Of her visit to Zara in prison, her knowledge of Major Baron's guilt, her loathing of him, the cruel burden of this secret, of Major Baron's passionate pleading, of her temptation then, in her shaken faith in humanity, to immolate herself to save this wicked man, as he had plead.

Of her agony when she had met Dr. Leigh that night in the Campus, and when she had torn herself from him in the library. Of his noble vindication by Colonel Harvey, the evening he had left her without a farewell word. Of the wearing, weary pain she had endured since then. Of how she had longed to see him to beg forgiveness for the cruel wrong she had done, to tell him of her love, to fall at his feet and beg forgiveness.

"And you suffered the word of a wicked woman to part us all this weary time? And you could believe that story?" said Dr. Leigh, looking at her sorrowfully yet tenderly.

"Don't reproach me," said Aliena entreatingly, raising her beautiful eyes to his, her voice trembling with emotion. "But without perfect trust I could not accept you as my heart's lord, to be held, next to God, in highest reverence and love. But think of what I have suffered, and as God knows my heart, the keenest pang has been in thought of what you endured."

"So it had to be, it seems, my precious one," said Dr.

Leigh with infinite tenderness. "And much as I loved you, longed for you, to carry you in my bosom, as I did the time when I first knew I loved you, to have you at my side, part of my very being as truly as was Eve of Adam, for whom my heart cried out when we were separated, as for my very self, my better, purer self, to whom in thought, heart and deed I could not but be forever true, yet I would not have you here now, sweet as it is, unless willingly, truly, lovingly. Time has had its bent. We have been tried, as it were, by fire. My sweet, wild bird has come to nestle at my heart. We know the ecstacy of that love which is God-ordained, which is soon to make us one," and pressing her to his heart, he imprinted a long kiss upon her trembling lips. And rising they retraced their steps toward camp, and the home to which they were now to return—to which Dr. Leigh was soon to take Aliena as his bride.

> " Which whoso list look back to former ages
> And call to count the things that then were doune
> Shall find that all the works of those wild sages,
> And brane exploits which great heroes woune,
> In love were either ended or begunne."

www.ingramcontent.com/pod-product-compliance
Lightning Source LLC
Chambersburg PA
CBHW031138120726
47905CB00006B/1729